"HAVE I ANY RIGHTS NOW?" HE EXCLAIMED.

'Jest to Earnest   *Frontispiece.*

The Works of E. P. Roe

VOLUME SEVEN

FROM JEST TO EARNEST

ILLUSTRATED

NEW YORK
P. F. COLLIER & SON

DEDICATION

THIS book is dedicated in fraternal affection to the
friend of my youth and maturer years—the REV. A.
MOSS MERWIN, who, with every avenue of earthly ambition open to him at home, and with every motive urged
upon him to remain at home, has been for years, and is
now, a faithful missionary in a foreign land.

CONTENTS

Contents

FROM JEST TO EARNEST

FROM JEST TO EARNEST

CHAPTER I

A PRACTICAL JOKE

ON a cloudy December morning a gentleman, two ladies, and a boy stepped down from the express train at a station just above the Highlands on the Hudson. A double sleigh, overflowing with luxurious robes, stood near, and a portly coachman with difficulty restrained his spirited horses while the little party arranged themselves for a winter ride. Both the ladies were young, and the gentleman's anxious and almost tender solicitude for one of them seemed hardly warranted by her blooming cheeks and sprightly movements. A close observer might soon suspect that his assiduous attentions were caused by a malady of his own rather than by indisposition on her part.

The other young lady received but scant politeness, though seemingly in greater need of it. But the words of Scripture applied to her beautiful companion, "Whosoever hath, to him shall be given, and he shall have more abundance." She had been surfeited all her life with attention, and though she would certainly have felt its absence, as she would the loss of wealth, life-long familiarity with both led her to place no special value upon them.

Therefore during the half-hour's ride her spirits rose with the rapid motion, and even the leaden sky and winter's bleakness could not prevent the shifting landscape from being a source of pleasure to her city eyes, while the

(13)

devotion of her admirer or lover was received as a matter of course.

The frosty air brought color into her companion's usually pale face, but not of an attractive kind, for the northeast wind that deepened the vermilion in the beauty's cheek could only tinge that of the other with a ghastly blue. The delicate creature shivered and sighed.

"I wish we were there."

"Really, Bel, I sometimes think your veins are filled with water instead of blood. It's not cold to-day, is it, Mr. De Forrest?"

"Well, all I can say with certainty," he replied, "is that I have been in a glow for the last two hours. I thought it was chilly before that."

"You are near to 'glory' then," cried the boy saucily, from his perch on the driver's box.

"Of course I am," said Mr. De Forrest in a low tone, and leaning toward the maiden.

"You are both nearer being silly," she replied, pettishly. "Dan, behave yourself, and speak when you are spoken to."

The boy announced his independence of sisterly control by beginning to whistle, and the young lady addressed as "Bel" remarked, "Mr. De Forrest is no judge of the weather under the circumstances. He doubtless regards the day as bright and serene. But he was evidently a correct judge up to the time he joined you, Lottie."

"He joined you as much as he did me."

"Oh, pardon me; yes, I believe I was present."

"I hope I have failed in no act of politeness, Miss Bel," said De Forrest, a little stiffly.

"I have no complaints to make. Indeed, I have fared well, considering that one is sometimes worse than a crowd."

"Nonsense!" said Lottie, petulantly; and the young man tried not to appear annoyed.

The sleigh now dashed in between rustic gate-posts composed of rough pillars of granite; and proceeding along an avenue that sometimes skirted a wooded ravine, and again wound through picturesque groupings of evergreens, they soon reached a mansion of considerable size, which bore evidence of greater age than is usual with the homes in our new world.

They had hardly crossed the threshold into the hall before they were hospitably welcomed by a widowed lady, whose hair was slightly tinged with gray, and by her eldest daughter.

The greetings were so cordial as to indicate ties of blood, and the guests were shown to their rooms, and told to prepare for an early dinner.

In brief, Mrs. Marchmont, the mistress of the mansion, had gratified her daughter's wish (as she did all her fancies) by permitting her to invite a number of young friends for the Christmas holidays. Both mother and daughter were fond of society, and it required no hospitable effort to welcome visitors at a season when a majority of their friends had fled from the dreariness of winter to city homes. Indeed, they regarded it as almost an honor that so prominent a belle as Charlotte Marsden had consented to spend a few weeks with them at a time when country life is at a large discount with the fashionable. They surmised that the presence of Mr. De Forrest, a distant relative of both Miss Marsden and themselves, would be agreeable to all concerned, and were not mistaken; and to Miss Lottie the presence of a few admirers—she would not entertain the idea that they were lovers—had become an ordinary necessity of life. Mr. De Forrest was an unusually interesting specimen of the genus—handsome, an adept in the mode and etiquette of the hour, attentive as her own shadow, and quite as subservient.

His love-making would equal his toilet in elegance. All would be delicately suggested by touch of hand or glance of eye, and yet he would keep pace with the wild and wayward beauty in as desperate a flirtation as she would permit.

Miss Lottie had left her city home with no self-sacrific-

ing purpose to become a martyr for the sake of country
relatives. She had wearied of the familiar round of met-
ropolitan gayety; but life on the Hudson during midwinter was an entire novelty. Therefore, as her little brother
had been included in the invitation, they had started on
what was emphatically a frolic to both.

Bel Parton, her companion, was another city cousin of
the Marchmonts, with whom they were in the habit of exchanging visits. She was also an intimate of Lottie's, the
two being drawn together by the mysterious affinity of
opposites.

She was indeed a very different girl from Lottie Marsden, and many would regard her as a better one. Her face
and character were of a type only too familiar to close ob-
servers of society. She was the beginning of several desir-
able things, but the pattern was in no instance finished, and
was always ravelling out on one side or the other. She had
the features of a pretty girl, but ill health and the absence
of a pleasing expression spoiled them. She had a fine education, but did not know what to do with it; considerable
talent, but no energy; too much conscience, as she had not
the resolution to obey it. Her life was passed mainly in
easy chairs, chronic dyspepsia, and feeble protest against
herself and all the world.

Lottie often half provoked but never roused her by saying: "Bel, you are the most negative creature I ever knew.
Why don't you do something or be something out and out?
Well, ''Tis an ill wind that blows nobody any good.' You
make an excellent foil for me.'

And gloriously rich and tropical did Lottie appear
against the colorless background of her friend. Bel felt
that she suffered by the comparison so frankly indicated,
but was too indolent and irresolute to change for the better
or avoid companionship with one whose positive and full-
blooded nature seemed to supplement her own meagre life.

When all appeared in the dining-room the shades and
contrasts in character became more evident. At the head

of the table sat a gentleman as yet not introduced, Mr. Dimmerly by name, a bachelor brother of Mrs. Marchmont who resided with her. He was a quaint-appearing little man, who in a greater degree than his age required seemed to belong to a former generation. His manners were too stately for his stature, and he was embarrassed by his elaborate efforts at politeness as his movements might have been by too ample garments.

He and his sister were representatives of one of the "old families" of the State, and, like their mansion, reminded one of the past. Indeed, they seemed to cherish, as a matter of pride and choice, their savor of antiquity, instinctively recognizing that their claims upon society were inherited rather than earned.

Old families do not always appear to accumulate the elements of greatness to such a degree that there is an increasing and almost irresistible impetus of force and genius. Successive generations are not necessarily born to a richer dower of mind and morals. Too often it would seem that the great qualities that in the first place launched a family on a brilliant career expend themselves, until the latest scion, like a spent arrow, drops into insignificance.

Mrs. Marchmont was regarded by society as an elegant woman, and she was, in all externals. The controlling principle of her life was precedent. What had been customary, and still obtained among the "good old families," had a flavor of divine right in it.

Alas for the Marchmont family, for the young lady of the house seemed inclined to maintain and perpetuate nothing save her own will, and had no special development in any respect, save a passion for her own way. Still she was one of those girls whom society calls a "pretty little thing," and was predestined to marry some large, good-natured man who would imagine that she would make a nice little pet, a household fairy, but who might learn to his dismay that the fairy could be a tormenting elf. She would not marry the young gentleman with whom her name was at present associated by the gossips, and who had driven over that morning to help her entertain the expected guests. Mr. Harcourt and Miss Marchmont understood each other. He was a distant relative of her mother's, and so under the disguise of kinship could be very familiar. The tie between them was composed of one part friendship and two parts flirtation. He had recently begun the practice of law in a neighboring town, and found the Marchmont residence a very agreeable place at which to spend his leisure. It was Miss Marchmont's purpose that he should form one of the gay party that would make the holiday season a prolonged frolic. He, nothing loth, accepted the invitation, and appeared in time for dinner. To many he seemed to possess a dual nature. He had a quick, keen intellect, and, during business hours, gave an absorbed attention to his profession. At other times he was equally well known as a sporting man, with tendencies somewhat fast.

Mrs. Marchmont's well-appointed dining-room was peculiarly attractive that wintry day. Finished off in some dark wood on which the ruddy hickory fire glistened warmly, it made a pleasing contrast to the cold whiteness of the snow without. A portly colored waiter in dress coat seemed the appropriate presiding genius of the place, and in his ebon hands the polished silver and crystal were doubly luminous.

And yet the family, with its lack of original force, its fading traditions of past greatness, made rather a dim and neutral tint, against which such a girl as Charlotte Marsden appeared as the glowing embodiment of the vivid and intense spirit of the present age. Her naturally energetic and mercurial nature had been cradled among the excitements of the gayest and giddiest city on the continent. A phlegmatic uncle had remarked to her, in view of inherited and developed characteristics, "Lottie, what in ordinary girls is a soul, in you is a flame of fire."

As she sat at the table, doing ample justice to the substantial viands, she did appear as warm and glowing as the coals of hard-wood, which, ripened in the sunshine, lay upon the hearth opposite.

The *bon-vivant*, Julian De Forrest, found time for many admiring glances, of which Lottie was as agreeably conscious as of the other comforts and luxuries of the hour. They were all very much upon the same level in her estimation.

But De Forrest would ask no better destiny than to bask in the light and witchery of so glorious a creature. Little did he understand himself or her, or the life before him. It would have been a woful match for both. In a certain sense he would be like the ambitious mouse that espoused the lioness. The polished and selfish idler, with a career devoted to elegant nothings, would fret and chafe such a nature as hers into almost frenzy, had she no escape from him.

There would be fewer unhappy marriages if the young, instead of following impulses and passing fancies, would ask, How will our lives accord when our present tendencies and temperaments are fully developed? It would need no prophetic eye to foresee in many cases, not supplemental and helpful differences, but only hopeless discord. Yet it is hard for a romantic youth to realize that the smiling maiden before him, with a cheek of peach-bloom and eyes full of mirth and tenderness, can become as shrewish as Xantippe herself. And many a woman becomes stubborn and acid, rather than sweet, by allowing herself to be persuaded into marrying the wrong man, and then by not having the good sense to make the best of it.

Alas! experience also proves that, of all prosaic, selfish grumblers, your over-gallant lover makes the worst. And yet, while the world stands, multitudes will no doubt eagerly seek the privilege of becoming mutual tormentors.

Lottie thought Mr. De Forrest "very nice." She liked him better than any one else she had met and flirted with since her school-days, during which period of sincerity and immaturity she had had several acute attacks of what she imagined to be the "grand passion." But as the objects were as absurd as her emotions, and the malady soon ran its course, she began to regard the whole subject as a jest, and think, with her fashionable mother, that the heart was the last organ to be consulted in the choice of a husband, as it was almost sure to lead to folly. While her heart slept, it was easy to agree with her mother's philosophy. But it would be a sad thing for Charlotte Marsden if her heart should become awakened when her will or duty was at variance with its cravings. She might act rightly, she might suffer in patience, but it would require ten times the effort that the majority of her sex would have to make.

Her mother thought that the elegant and wealthy Mr. De Forrest was the very one of all the city for her beautiful daughter, and Lottie gave a careless assent, for certainly he was "very nice." He would answer, as well as any one she had ever seen, for the inevitable adjunct of her life. He had always united agreeably the characters of cousin, playmate, and lover, and why might he not add that of husband? But for the latter relation she was in no haste. Time enough for that in the indefinite future. She loved the liberty and year-long frolic of her maiden life, though in truth she had no idea of settling down on becoming a matron. In the meantime, while she laughed at De Forrest's love-making, she did not discourage it, and the young man felt that his clear understanding with the mother was almost equal to an engagement to the daughter. He welcomed this country visit with peculiar satisfaction, feeling that it would bring matters to a crisis. He was not mistaken.

By the time they were sipping their coffee after dessert, the promise of the leaden sky of the morning was fulfilled in a snowstorm, not consisting of feathery flakes that fluttered down as if undecided where to alight, but of sharp, fine crystals that slanted steadily from the northeast. The afternoon sleigh ride must be given up, and even the children looked ruefully and hopelessly out, and then made the best of indoor amusements.

Miss Marchmont gathered her guests around the parlor fire, and fancy work and city gossip were in order. The quiet flow and ripple of small talk was suddenly interrupted by her petulant exclamation:

"Oh! I forgot to tell you a bit of unpleasant news. Mother, without consulting me, has invited a poor and poky cousin of ours to spend the holidays with us also. He is from the West, green as a gooseberry, and, what's far worse, he's studying for the ministry, and no doubt will want to preach at us all the time. I don't know when I've been more provoked, but mother said it was too late, she had invited him, and he was coming. I fear he will be a dreadful restraint, a sort of wet blanket on all our fun, for one must be polite, you know, in one's own house."

"I am under no special obligation to be polite," laughed Lottie. "Mark my words. I will shock your pious and proper cousin till he is ready to write a book on total depravity. It will be good sport till I am tired of it."

"No, Lottie, you shall not give such a false impression of yourself, even in a joke," said Bel. "I will tell him, if he can't see, that you are not a sinner above all in Galilee."

"No, my matter-of-fact cousin, you shall not tell him anything. Why should I care what he thinks? Already in fancy I see his face elongate, and his eyes dilate, in holy horror at my wickedness. If there is one thing I love to do more than another, it is to shock your eminently good and proper people."

"Why, Miss Lottie," chuckled De Forrest, "to hear you talk, one would think you were past praying for."

"No, not till I am married."

"In that sense I am always at my devotions."

"Perhaps you had better read the fable of the Frogs and King Stork."

"Thank you. I had never dared to hope that you regarded me as good enough to eat "

"No, only to peck at."

"But listen to Miss Addie's proposal. If I mistake not, there is no end of fun in it," said Mr. Harcourt.

"I've thought of something better than shocking him. These Western men are not easily shocked. They see all kinds out there. What I suggest would be a better joke, and give us all a chance to enjoy the sport. Suppose, Lottie, you assume to be the good and pious one of our party, and in this character form his acquaintance. He will soon be talking religion to you, and like enough making love and wanting you to go with him as a missionary to the Cannibal Islands."

"If you go, oh that I were king of them!" broke in De Forrest.

"You mean, you would have Lottie for dinner, I suppose," continued Miss Marchmont. "She would be served up properly as a tart."

"No," he retorted, "as *sauce piquante*. She could make a long life a highly seasoned feast."

"You evidently are an Epicurean philosopher; all your thoughts seem to run on eating," said Lottie, sharply.

"But what say you to my suggestion?" asked Addie Marchmont. "I think it would be one of the best practical jokes I ever knew. The very thought of such an incorrigible witch as you palming yourself off as a demure Puritan maiden is the climax of comical absurdity."

Even Lottie joined heartily in the general laugh at her expense, and the preposterous imposition she was asked to attempt, but said dubiously: "I fear I could not act successfully the rôle of Puritan maiden, when I have always been in reality just the opposite. And yet it would be grand sport to make the attempt, and a decided novelty. But surely your cousin cannot be so verdant but that he would soon see through our mischief and detect the fraud."

"Well," replied Addie, "Frank, as I remember him, is a singularly unsuspicious mortal. Even as a boy his head was always in the clouds. He has not seen much society save that of his mother and an old-maid sister. Moreover he is so dreadfully pious, and life with him such a solemn thing, that unless we are very bunglng he will not even imagine such frivolity, as he would call it, until the truth is forced upon him. Then there will be a scene. You will shock him then, Lottie, to your heart's content. He will probably tell you that he is dumfounded, and that he would not believe that a young woman in this Christian land could trifle with such solemn realities—that is, himself and his feelings."

"But I don't think it would be quite right," protested Bel, feebly.

Mr. Harcourt lifted his eyebrows.

"Nonsense! Suppose it is not," said Lottie, impatiently.

"But, Addie," persisted Bel, "he will be your guest."

"No, he won't. He's mother's guest, and I feel like punishing them both."

"Very well," said Lottie, lightly; "if you have no scruples, I have none. It will be capital sport, and will do him good. It would be an excellent thing for his whole theological seminary if they could have a thorough shaking up by the wicked world, which to him, in this matter, I shall represent. They would then know what they were preaching about. What do you say, Julian?"

"When did I ever disagree with you?" he replied, gallantly. "But in this case I really think we owe Miss Addie a vote of thanks for having hit upon a joke that may enliven the greater part of our visit. This embryo parson seems a sort of a scriptural character; and why should he not blindly, like Samson, make sport for us all?"

"I fear you do not understand your own scriptural allusion," sneered Bel. "Like Samson, he may also pull everything down about our ears in a most uncomfortable manner."

"I hope you won't spoil everything by tellng him or mother," said Addie, petulantly.

"Oh, no! Since you are determined upon it, I will look on and see the fun, if there is any. But, bah! He will find you all out in a day. As for Lottie palming herself off as a goodish young woman to whom any sane man would talk religion—the very thought is preposterous!''

"Don't be too confident, Miss Bel," said Lottie, put upon her mettle. "If you all will only sustain me and not awaken his suspicions with your by-play and giggling, I will deceive the ingenuous youth in a way that will surprise you as well as him. Good acting must have proper support. This is something new—out of the rut; and I am bound to make it a brilliant jest that we can laugh over all our lives. So remember, Julian, you will disconcert me at your peril."

"No fears of me. So long as your jest remains a jest, I will be the last one to spoil the sport."

With a chime of laughter that echoed to the attic of the old mansion, Lottie exclaimed, "The idea that I could ever become in earnest!"

"But the young clergyman may become dead in earnest," said Bel, who seemed the embodiment of a troublesome but weak conscience. "You know well, Mr. De Forrest, that Lottie's blandishments may be fatal to his peace."

"That is his affair," replied the confident youth, with a careless shrug.

Having arranged the details of the plot and been emphatically cautioned by Lottie they awaited their victim.

CHAPTER II

THE VICTIM

FRANK HEMSTEAD was expected on the evening train from the north, so the conspirators would not have long to wait. To pass the brief intervening time Lottie went to the piano and gave them some music like herself, brilliant, dashing, off-hand, but devoid of sentiment and feeling. Then she sprang up and began playing the maddest pranks on languid Bel, and with Addie was soon engaged in a romp with De Forrest and Harcourt, that would have amazed the most festive Puritan that ever schooled or masked a frolicsome nature under the sombre deportment required. The young men took their cue from the ladies, and elegance and propriety were driven away in shreds before the gale of their wild spirits. Poor Bel, buffeted and helpless, half-enjoying, half-frightened, protested, cried, and laughed at the tempest around her.

"I mean," said Lottie, panting after a desperate chase among the furniture, "to have one more spree, like the topers before they reform."

Though these velvety creatures with their habits of grace and elegance could romp without roughness, and glide where others would tear around, they could not keep their revel so quiet but that hurrying steps were heard. Bel warned them, and, before Mrs. Marchmont could enter, Lottie was playing a waltz, and the others appeared as if they had been dancing. The lady of precedent smiled, whereas if she had come a moment earlier she would have been horrified.

But the glow from the hearth, uncertain enough for

their innocent deeds of darkness, had now to fade before
the chandelier, and Mrs. Marchmont, somewhat surprised
at the rumpled plumage of the young ladies, and the fact
that Mr. De Forrest's necktie was awry, suggested that
they retire and prepare for supper, whereat they retreated
in literal disorder. But without the door their old frenzy
seized them, and they nearly ran over the dilatory Bel upon
the stairs. With sallies of nonsense, smothered laughter,
a breezy rustle of garments, and the rush of swift motion,
they seemed to die away in the upper halls like a summer
gust. To Mrs. Marchmont their departure had seemed
like a suppressed whirlwind.

"The young people of my day were more decorous,"
soliloquized the lady, complacently. "But then the De
Forrests have French blood in them, and what else could
you expect? It's he that sets them off."

The sound of approaching sleigh-bells hastened the
young people's toilets, and when they descended the
stairs, this time like a funeral procession, a tall figure,
with one side that had been to the windward well sifted
over with snow, was just entering the hall.

Mrs. Marchmont welcomed him with as much warmth
as she ever permitted herself to show. She was a good
and kind lady at heart, only she insisted upon covering
the natural bloom and beauty of her nature with the artificial enamel of mannerism and conventionality. During
the unwrapping process the young people stood in the
background, but Lottie watched the emergence from over-
coat and muffler of the predestined victim of her wiles with
more than ordinary curiosity.

The first thing that impressed her was his unusual height,
and the next a certain awkwardness and angularity. When
he came to be formally presented, his diffidence and lack of
ease were quite marked. Bel greeted him with a distant inclination of her head, De Forrest also vouchsafed merely
one of his slightest bows, while Harcourt stood so far away
that he was scarcely introduced at all; but Lottie went de-

murely forward and put her warm hand in his great cold one, and said, looking up shyly, "I think we are sort of cousins, are we not?"

He blushed to the roots of his hair and stammered that he hoped so.

Indeed, this exquisite vision appearing from the shadows of the hall, and claiming kinship, might have disconcerted a polished society man; and the conspirators retired into the gloom to hide their merriment.

As the stranger, in his bashful confusion, did not seem to know for the moment what to do with her hand, and was inclined to keep it, for in fact it was warming, or, rather, electrifying him, she withdrew it, exclaiming, "How cold you are! You must come with me to the fire at once."

He followed her with a rather bewildered expression, but his large gray eyes were full of gratitude for her supposed kindness, even if his unready tongue was slow in making graceful acknowledgment.

"Supper will be ready in a few moments, Frank," said his aunt, approaching them and rather wondering at Lottie's friendliness. "Perhaps you had better go at once to your room and prepare. You will find it warm," and she glanced significantly at his rumpled hair and general appearance of disorder, the natural results of a long journey.

He started abruptly, blushed as if conscious of having forgotten something, and timidly said to Lottie, "Will you excuse me?"

"Yes," she replied sweetly, "for a little while."

He again blushed deeply and for a second indulged in a shy glance of curiosity at the "cousin" who spoke so kindly. Then, as if guilty of an impropriety, he seized a huge carpet-bag as if it were a lady's reticule. But remembering that her eyes were upon him, he tried to cross the hall and mount the stairs with dignity. The great leathern bag did not conduce to this, and he succeeded in appearing awkward in the extreme, and had a vague, uncomfortable impression that such was the case.

Mrs. Marchmont having disappeared into the dining-room, the young people went off into silent convulsions of laughter, in which even Bel joined, though she said she knew it was wrong.

"He is just the one of all the world on whom to play such a joke," said Lottie, pirouetting into the parlor.

"It was capital!" chimed in De Forrest. "Lottie, you would make a star actress."

"He has an intelligent eye," continued she, a little more thoughtfully. "He may be able to see more than we think. I insist that you all be very careful. Aunt will suspect something, if he doesn't, and may put him on his guard."

Mr. Hemstead soon returned, for it was plain that his toilets were exceedingly simple. The elegance wanting in his manners was still more clearly absent from his dress. The material was good, but had evidently been put together by a country tailor, who limped a long way behind the latest mode. What was worse, his garments were scarcely ample enough for his stalwart form. Altogether he made in some externals a marked contrast to the city exquisite, who rather enjoyed standing beside him that this contrast might be seen.

To Lottie he appeared excessively comical as he stalked in and around, trying vainly to appear at ease. And yet the thought occurred to her, "If he only knew what to do with his colossal proportions—knew how to manage them—he would make an imposing-looking man." And when De Forrest posed beside him just before they went out to tea, even this thought flashed across her, "Julian seems like an elegant manikin beside a man." If De Forrest had only known it, the game of contrasts was not wholly in his favor.

But poor Mr. Hemstead came to grief on his way to the supper-room. Miss Marchmont tried to disguise her diminutive stature by a long trailing dress. Upon this he placed his by no means delicate foot, as she was sweeping out with Mr. Harcourt. There was an ominous sound of parting stitches, and an abrupt period in the young lady's graceful progress. In his eager haste to remedy his awkwardness, he bumped up against Mr. Dimmerly, who was advancing to speak to him, with a force that nearly over-threw that dapper gentleman, and rendered his greeting rather peculiar. Hemstead felt, to his intense annoyance, that the young people were at the point of exploding with merriment at his expense, and was in a state of indignation at himself and them. His aunt and Mr. Dimmerly, who soon recovered himself, were endeavoring to look serenely unconscious, with but partial success. All seemed to feel as if they were over a mine of discourteous laughter. The unfortunate object looked nervously around for the beauti-ful "cousin," and noted with a sigh of relief that she had disappeared.

"I hope she did not see my meeting with uncle," he thought. "I was always a gawk in society, and to-night seem possessed with the very genius of awkwardness. She is the only one who has shown me any real kindness, and I don't want her to think of me only as a blundering, tongue-tied fool."

He would not have been reassured had he known that Lottie, having seen all, had darted back into the parlor and was leaning against the piano, a quivering, and, for the mo-ment, a helpless subject of suppressed mirth. Mr. Dimmerly was always a rather comical object to her, and his flying arms and spectacles, as he tried to recover himself from the rude shock of his nephew's burly form, made a scene in which absurdity, which is said to be the chief cause of laughter, was pre-eminent.

But, the paroxysm passing, she followed them and took a seat opposite her victim, with a demure sweetness and re-pose of manner wellnigh fatal to the conspirators.

As Mr. Hemstead was regarded as a clergyman, though not quite through with his studies, his aunt looked to him for the saying of grace. It was a trying ordeal for the young fellow under the circumstances. He shot a quick glance at Lottie, which she returned with a look of serious expectation, then dropped her eyes and veiled a different expression under the long lashes. But he was sorely embarrassed, and stammered out he scarcely knew what. A suppressed titter from Addie Marchmont and the young men was the only response he heard, and it was not reassuring. He heartily wished himself back in Michigan, but was comforted by seeing Lottie looking gravely and reproachfully at the irreverent gigglers.

"She is a good Christian girl," he thought, "and while the others ridicule my wretched embarrassment, she sympathizes."

Hemstead was himself as open as the day and equally unsuspicious of others. He believed just what he saw, and saw only what was clearly apparent. Therefore Lottie, by tolerably fair acting, would have no difficulty in deceiving him, and she was proving herself equal to very skilful feigning. Indeed she was one who could do anything fairly that she heartily attempted.

A moment after "grace" Harcourt made a poor witticism, at which the majority laughed with an immoderateness quite disproportionate. Mrs. Marchmont and her brother joined in the mirth, though evidently vexed with themselves that they did. Even Hemstead saw that Harcourt's remark was but the transparent excuse for the inevitable laugh at his expense. Lottie looked around with an expression of mingled surprise and displeasure, which nearly convulsed those in the secret. But her aunt and uncle felt themselves justly rebuked, while wondering greatly at Lottie's unwonted virtue. But there are times when to laugh is a dreadful necessity, whatever be the consequences.

"Mr. Hemstead," said Lottie, gravely, beginning, as she supposed, with the safe topic of the weather, "in journeying east have you come to a colder or warmer climate?"

"Decidedly into a colder one," he answered, significantly.

"Indeed, that rather surprises me!"

"Well, I believe that the thermometer has marked lower

with us, but it has been said, and justly I think, that we do not feel the cold at the West as at the East."

"No matter," she said, sweetly. "At the East, as in the West, the cold is followed by thaws and spring."

He looked up quickly and gratefully, but only remarked, "It's a change we all welcome."

"Not I, for one," said Mr. Harcourt. "Give me a clear, steady cold. Thaws and spring are synonymous with the sloppy season or sentimental stage."

"I, too, think steady cold is better in the season of it," remarked Mr. Dimmerly, sententiously.

"But how about it out of season, uncle?" asked Lottie.

"Your hint, perhaps, is seasonable, Lottie," quietly remarked her aunt, though with somewhat heightened color. "I trust we shall keep the steady cold out of doors, and that *all* our guests will find only summer warmth within."

"Really, auntie, you put me in quite a melting mood."

"No need of that, Lottie, for you are the month of June all the year round," said her aunt.

"The month of April, rather," suggested Bel.

"I should say July or August," added Mr. Dimmerly, laughing.

"Would you not say November?" asked Lottie of Mr. Hemstead.

"Yes, I think so," he replied, with a blush, "for Thanksgiving comes in that month."

There was a general laugh, and Mr. Dimmerly chuckled, "Very good, you are getting even, Frank."

"I hardly understand your compliment, if it is one," said Lottie, demurely. "Is it because you are so fond of sermons or dinners that Thanksgiving glorifies the dreary month of November?"

"Neither a sermon nor a dinner is always a just cause for Thanksgiving," he replied, with a pleasant light in his gray eyes.

"Then where is the force of your allusion?" she said, with a face innocently blank.

"Well," replied he, hesitatingly, and blushing deeply, "perhaps my thought was that you might be an occasion for Thanksgiving if both sermon and dinner were wanting."

Again there was a general laugh, but his aunt said, "Frank, Frank, have you learned to flatter?"

Lottie shot a quick glance of pleased surprise at him, and was much amused at his evident confusion and flaming cheeks. To be sure his words were part of the old complimentary tune that she knew by heart, but his offering was like a flower that had upon it the morning dew. She recognized his grateful effort to repay her for supposed kindness, and saw that, though ill at ease in society, he was not a fool.

"Would it not be better to wait till in possession before keeping a Thanksgiving?" said De Forrest, satirically.

"Not necessarily," retorted Hemstead, quickly, for the remark was like the light touch of a spur. "I was grateful for the opportunity of seeing a fine picture at Cleveland, on my way here, that I never expect to own."

Lottie smiled. The victim was not helpless. But she turned, and with a spice of coquetry said, "Still I think you are right, Mr. De Forrest."

Then she noted that Mr. Hemstead's eyes were dancing with mirth at her hint to one who was evidently anxious to keep "Thanksgiving" over her any month in the year.

"I'm sure I am," remarked De Forrest. "I could never be satisfied to admire at a distance. I could not join in a prayer I once heard, 'Lord, we thank thee for this and all other worlds.'"

"Could you?" asked Lottie of Hemstead.

"Why not?"

"That is no answer."

Hemstead was growing more at ease, and when he only had to use his brains was not half so much at a loss as when he must also manage his hands and feet, and he replied laughingly: "Well, not to put too fine a point upon it, this world is quite useful to me at present. I should be sorry to have it vanish and find myself whirling in space, if I am a rather large body. But as I am soon to get through with this world, though never through with life, I may have a chance to enjoy a good many other worlds—perhaps all of them—before eternity is over, and so be grateful that they exist and are in waiting.''

"Good heavens!" exclaimed Lottie. "What a traveller you propose to be. I should be satisfied with a trip to Europe.''

"To Paris, you mean," said Bel.

"Yes," replied Mr. Hemstead, "until the trip was over."

"Then I trust she will be content with New York," insinuated De Forrest; "for Mr. Hemstead speaks as if the stars were created for his especial benefit.''

"You are enjoying some honey, Mr. De Forrest?" said Hemstead, quietly.

"Yes."

"Did the flowers grow and the bees gather for your especial benefit?''

"I admit I'm answered."

"But," said sceptical Mr. Harcourt, "when you've got through with this world how do you know but that you will drop off into space?"

"Come," said Addie, rising from the table, "I protest against a sermon before Sunday.''

They now returned to the parlor, Hemstead making the transition in safety, but with no little trepidation.

CHAPTER III

PUZZLED AND INTERESTED

ON the way to the parlor Lottie hovered near Mr. Hemstead. Unlike Micawber, she was not one to wait, but purposed that something *should* "turn up." The two other young ladies, and Harcourt and De Forrest, sat down to a game of whist. In pursuance of instructions from Lottie, De Forrest was not to be over-attentive, though it was evident that he would give more thought to her than to his game. Her demure mischief amused him vastly, and, knowing what she was, the novelty of her Puritan style had a double fascination. Making personal enjoyment the object of his life, he felicitated himself on soon possessing the beautiful and piquant creature, who, when she came to devote herself to him, would spice his days with endless variety. The thought that this high-spirited, positive, strong-minded American girl might crave better and more important work than that of an Eastern houri or a Queen Scheherezade, never occurred to him. He blundered, with many other men, in supposing that, if once married, the wayward belle would become subservient to his tastes and modes as a matter of course. In his matrimonial creed all his difficulty consisted in getting the noose finally around the fair one's neck: this accomplished, she would become a ministering captive. Many a one has had a rude awakening from this dream.

Although from Addie Marchmont's description he believed that he had little cause to fear a rival in Hemstead, still he awaited his coming with a trace of anxiety. But when the seemingly overgrown, awkward student stepped upon the scene, all his fears vanished. The fastidious Lottie, whose eye had grown so nice and critical that she could refuse the suit of many who from their wealth and position thought it impossible to sue in vain, could never look upon this Western giant in a way other than she proposed—the ridiculous subject of a practical joke. True, he had proved himself no fool in their table-talk, but mere intellectuality and moral excellence counted for little in De Forrest's estimation when not combined with wealth and external elegance. The thought that the "giant" might have a heart, and that Lottie's clever seeming might win it, and the consequent mortification and suffering, did not occasion a moment's care. Unconsciously De Forrest belonged to that lordly class which has furnished our Neros, Napoleons, and tyrants of less degree, even down to Pat who beats his wife. These, from their throne of selfishness, view the pain and troubles of others with perfect unconcern. Therefore, believing that his personal interests were not endangered by so unpromising a man as Hemstead, even Lottie did not look forward to the carrying out of the practical joke with more zest than he. If the unsuspicious victim could only be inveigled into something like love, its awkward display might become comical in the extreme. Therefore, he gave but careless heed to his game, and keen glances to Lottie's side-play. But as the other conspirators were acting in much the same manner he was able to hold his own.

Hemstead looked grave, as cards were brought out, but without remark he sat down with his aunt at a table on the opposite side of the hearth. Lottie perched on a chair a little back of them, so that while she saw their side faces they must turn somewhat to see her. When they did so she was quietly stitching at her fancy-work, but the rest of the time was telegraphing with her brilliant eyes all sorts of funny messages to the party opposite, so that they were in a state of perpetual giggle, not in keeping with whist.

Mr. Dimmerly soon bustled in, and, looking wistfully at the game in progress, was about to propose that they form one likewise at their table, for an evening without cards was to him a mild form of purgatory. But Lottie anticipated him. Giving a signal to the others and drawing down her face to portentous length, she said to Hemstead, "I fear you do not approve of cards."

"You are correct, Miss Marsden," he replied, stiffly.

As he turned away, she glanced at the card-players with a look of horror, as if they were committing sacrilege, and Harcourt had to improvise another poor joke to account for their increasing merriment.

But Mr. Dimmerly looked at his nephew in dismay and some irritation. "What under heaven can I now do, this long evening," he thought, "but gape and talk theology?"

But Lottie, in the purpose to draw out and quiz her victim, continued: "Really, Mr. Hemstead, you surprise me. Cards are the staple amusement of a quiet evening in New York. I fear I have been doing wrong all my life without knowing it."

"If you did not know you were wrong, you were not very guilty," he replied, smiling.

"Yes, but now I do know, or at least from one who will be an authority on such matters—pardon me—who is one now, I am assured that this old custom is wrong. In questions of right or wrong, I suppose a minister should guide."

"No, Miss Marsden, that is not Protestantism. Your conscience, instructed by the Bible, should guide."

"But I see no more harm in whist than in a sleigh-ride."

"Perhaps your conscience needs instruction."

"Oh, certainly, that is it! Please instruct it."

He turned quickly, but saw a face serious enough for an anxious seat in an old-time revival.

"Yes," said Mr. Dimmerly, testily. "My conscience needs instruction also. What harm is there in a quiet game of whist?"

"Well, I do not know that there is anything wrong in a 'quiet game of cards,' *per se*," commenced Hemstead, didactically.

"'Per' who?" asked Lottie, innocently.

Just then the party at the other table seemed to explode, but they made it appear as if the cause came from themselves.

"Yes, yes, nephew, speak English. You may find some reasons in Latin, but none in English, the only language of sound sense."

"Well," resumed Hemstead, somewhat confused, "I do not know that a quiet game such as you would play here would be wrong in itself. But the associations of the game are bad, and your example might be injurious."

"The associations bad!" said Lottie, lifting her eyebrows. "Cards are associated in my mind with father, mother, and quiet home evenings."

"I have chiefly seen them played by rough characters, and in questionable places," he replied quickly.

"I'm sorry you visit such places," she replied in a tone of rebuke.

Even Mr. Dimmerly and his sister laughed at this remark, as coming fom Lottie, while the others were almost convulsed. Bel managed to gasp out, as a blind, "Mr. Harcourt, if you don't behave yourself and play fair, I'll throw down my hand."

But straightforward Hemstead increased difficulties by saying, a little stiffly, "I hope, Miss Marsden, that you do not suppose that one of my calling would frequent places of improper resort."

"No, indeed," she replied quickly, "and therefore I was the more surprised when you spoke of witnessing something in 'questionable places.'"

He turned to her with a look in which perplexity and annoyance were mingled, and said hastily: "It is different with a man from a lady. A man is more out in the world, and, no matter how careful, cannot help catching glimpses of the evil substratum of society. One cannot help passing through a smoking-car occasionally, or—"

"Good heavens!" exclaimed Lottie, as if startled. "Is a smoking-car a 'questionable place'? Mr. De Forrest," she continued sharply, "did you not spend half an hour in the smoking-car coming up?"

"Yes," he replied faintly.

"You surprise me, sir," she said severely. "Mr. Hemstead declares it is a 'questionable place.' I hope hereafter you will have more regard for your reputation."

"Please do not mistake me," said Hemstead, with increasing annoyance; "I did not mean to assert any moral qualities of smoking-cars, though with their filth and fumes there would be no question in your mind about them whatever, Miss Marsden. What I meant to say was, that in such places as smoking-cars, hotel lobbies, and through the open doors of saloons, are caught glimpses of a life which we all should unite in condemning and loathing; and what I have seen has always led me to connect cards with just that kind of life. Moreover, gambling—that fearful and destructive vice—is almost inseparable from cards."

"How experiences differ!" said Lottie, reflectively. "I have had but few glimpses of the life you describe so graphically. With the bits of pasteboard that you have seen chiefly in coarse, grimy hands, I associate our cosey sitting-room at home, with its glowing grate and 'moonlight lamp,' as we call it, for father's eyes are weak. Even now," she continued, assuming the look of a rapt and beautiful sibyl, that was entrancing to Hemstead as well as De Forrest—"even now I see papa and mamma and old-fashioned Auntie Jane, and poor invalid Jennie, all gathered at home in our sacred little snuggery where father permits no visitors to come."

The look she had assumed became genuine, and her eyes suddenly moistened as the scene called up became real and present to her. With all her faults she had a warm heart, and loved her kindred sincerely.

But this touch of truth and feeling served her mischievous purpose better than she thought, for it convinced the honest-minded Hemstead that she was just what she seemed, and his sympathy went out to her at once as a well-meaning, true-hearted girl.

He was a little taken aback, however, when Lottie, ashamed of her feeling, said brusquely, "As to gambling with cards, we no more thought of it than sending to a corner grocery for a bottle of whiskey, and taking from it a drink all around between the games."

"Oh, Lottie!" laughed her aunt, "what an absurd picture you suggest! The idea of your stately mother taking a drink from a bottle of whiskey!"

"It is no more strange to me," persisted Lottie, gravely, "than Mr. Hemstead's associations. Of course I know that bad and vulgar people play cards, but they also drive horses and walk the streets, and do other things which it is perfectly proper for us to do."

"I admit, Miss Marsden, that education and custom make a great difference. I have always been taught to look upon cards with great abhorrence. What may be right for you would be wrong for me."

"No," said positive Lottie, "that will not satisfy me. A thing is either right or wrong. If you can prove to me that a quiet game of cards is wrong, I won't play any more —at least I ought not," she added hastily. "Because some vulgar and fast people gamble with them is nothing. You will take a sleigh-ride with us to-morrow, and yet loud jockeys bet and gamble over horses half the year."

Hemstead sprang up. His ungainliness disappeared, as was ever the case when he forgot himself in excitement.

"Miss Marsden," he said, "what you say sounds plausible, but years ago I saw the mangled corpse of a young suicide. He was an adept at cards, and for aught I know had learned the game as your brother might, at home. But away among strangers at the West that knowledge proved fatal. He was inveigled into playing by some gamblers, staked all his own money, then that committed to his trust. Having lost everything but life, he threw that also down the abyss. He might have been living to-day if he had known as little about cards as I do."

His manner was so earnest, the picture called up so sad and tragic, that even Lottie's red cheek paled a little, and the gigglers became quiet. She only said, "He was very weak and foolish. I can't understand such people."

"But the world is largely made up of the weak and foolish, who need safeguards rather than temptations. And history would seem to prove that even the wisest and best are at times 'weak and foolish.' I think the knowledge of card-playing can result in no harm to you, shielded as you will be, but it might to your brother. Miss Marsden," asked he, abruptly, "do you know how many professional gamblers there are in the world?"

"No."

"I do not remember the estimated number accurately, but it is very large. They often revel in wealth, but they do not make it out of each other. It is from the unwary, the 'weak and foolish' who think they can win money by playing a fair game. They are permitted to win just enough to turn their heads, and then are robbed. Remorse, despair, and suicide too often follow. Cards are the usual means employed in these great wrongs. I should be sorry to see a young brother of mine, who was soon to face the temptations of the world, go away with a knowledge that has been the ruin of so many."

This was bringing the question home to Lottie in a way that she did not expect. Her heedless, wilful, impulsive brother, the dear torment of her life, was just the one an artful knave could mislead. For a moment or two she sat silent and thoughtful. All awaited her answer save Mr. Dimmerly, who, without his whist, had dropped off into a doze, as was his wont. Then her decided character asserted itself, and she spoke sincerely for the moment.

"I do not believe in the safety of ignorance. If a young

man is weak and bad enough to gamble, he will do it with something else, if not cards. From what I hear, men bet and gamble with all uncertainties. The most innocent things are carried to vulgar and wicked excess. You can't shield one from without if lacking the will and power to say, No! I think it will be safer and wiser in the end, if a thing is right *per se*, as you say, to do it, and if wrong not to do it. To me, a game of cards is no more than a game of checkers, or a stroll in a garden."

In his eagerness to reply, Hemstead took a step forward and trod upon, not a lady's dress this time, but the tail of Mrs. Marchmont's pet dog. As may be imagined, his tread was not fairy-like, and there was a yelp that awoke the echoes. Mr. Dimmerly started out of his sleep, with a snort like the blast of a ram's horn before Jericho, and, pushing his gold spectacles to the top of his bald head, stared in bewilderment at the forms convulsed with merriment around him.

Even Hemstead joined in the laugh, though inwardly inclined to anathematize his big feet. Lottie retreated from further discussion by saying:

"I have heard that theologians were inclined to be *dog*-matic in controversy, and I fear that you are no exception, Mr. Hemstead. So, since I have had the last word, with your permission, I retire 'of the same opinion still.'."

"I submit," he rejoined, good-naturedly. "In any case my answer would have been *curtailed*."

"Ha, ha!" chimed out Lottie's laugh. "That is better than your logic."

"Frank! that you should call this dear little creature a cur!" said Mrs. Marchmont, comforting her still whining pet.

"What dis*courtesy*!" said Lottie.

"What is the matter with you all?" asked Mr. Dimmerly, rising. "From talking Latin you have got on something that I understand as well as Choctaw. Lottie, I hope you are not argued out of one of our best old English customs. I have inherited whist from a dozen generations.

So, nephew, with your leave or your frown, I must have my game."

"I cannot say, uncle, that Mr. Hemstead has argued very much, but two very painful *tales* have been presented in an im*press*ive manner. You see how moved auntie and Fido are still over one of them. But come, Mr. Hemstead, you have discharged your duty. If they play whist all night and commit suicide in the morning, your skirts are clear. Shake off the dust of your feet at them, and take a promenade in the hall with me. Cousin Julian" (with emphasis on the word cousin), "your conscience is as tough and elastic as Mr. Hemstead's is tender. You haunt smoking-cars and other questionable places; so, without serious moral harm, you can gratify uncle."

Mrs. Marchmont, who had listened with polite weariness to the latter part of the discussion, now took part in the game as quietly as she would pour tea at the head of the table. The aunt and nephew had lived in such different atmospheres that they could scarcely understand each other, and both harbored thoughts that were hardly charitable, as is usually the case in regard to those actions which have no moral qualities in themselves, and after all must be decided by each one's conscience. To Mrs. Marchmont, with her antecedents, a game of whist was one of the most innocent acts of her life.

But Hemstead was too well pleased with Lottie's arrangement to grieve deeply over what, to his conscience, was wrong, and soon forgot uncle, aunt, and cousin, and even the unlucky lap-dog, whose dismal howl had so discomfited him a moment before. Just such a luminary as Lottie Marsden had never appeared above his horizon, and her orbit seemed so eccentric that as yet he could not calculate it; but this element of uncertainty made observation all the more interesting. The wide old hall, without the embarrassment of observant eyes, was just the place to learn something more definite of one who thus far had dazzled and puzzled, while she gained his strong interest. True,

Addie and Mr. Harcourt were walking before them, but seemed so absorbed in each other as not to notice them. He felt a curious thrill when a little hand lighted, like a snow-flake, upon his arm, but soon increased its pressure with a sort of cousinly confidence. He looked inquiringly into the face turned up to him as they passed under the lamp, and thought, "In its guileless beauty it reminds me of the clear mountain lakes that I have seen in this region."

His figure was true, but not as he understood it; for Lottie's face, like the lake, would then reflect anything that happened upon the margin of her thoughts, while her heart remained hidden. He thought he saw herself, but in truth only false and vanishing images. Still, like the mirroring water, her skilful feigning could make the images seem very real. Hemstead, with his boundless faith in woman, believed all he saw, and hoped still more.

CHAPTER IV

A LITTLE PAGAN

THE joke had now taken a phase that De Forrest did not relish. While Lottie's by-play was present, and she was telegraphing to him with her brilliant eyes, it was excellent. But to sit with his back to the door leading into the hall, *vis-à-vis* to Mr. Dimmerly's puckered face, and give close attention to the game, was a trying ordeal to one who only consulted his own pleasure. And yet he feared he would offend Lottie, did he not remain at his post. She was a despotic little sovereign, and he felt that he must use all address until she was safely brought to the matrimonial altar. He comforted himself, however, with the thought that she was generous, and when he acted the rôle of martyr she usually rewarded him with a greater show of kindness, and so got through an hour with indifferent grace.

But this purgatorial hour to him was keenly enjoyed by Lottie and Hemstead, though by each for different reasons.

"I fear you think me a giddy, wayward girl," said Lottie gently.

"In frankness, I hardly know what to think," replied Hemstead.

"Frank is your name, is it not?"

"Yes."

"It seems appropriate. I hope you won't judge me too harshly."

"The danger is the other way, I fear," he said, laughing.

"Well, one of your profession ought to be charitable.

But I might naturally expect to be disapproved of by one so good and wise as you are."

"Why do you think me 'good and wise'?"

"Because you are a minister, if for no other reason."

"I am also a man."

"Yes," she said, innocently. "You are quite grown up."

He looked at her quickly; her demure face puzzled him, and he said, "I fear you think I am overgrown."

"And I fear you don't care what I think. Men of your profession are superior to the world."

"Really, I shall think you are sarcastic, if you talk in that way any more." But she looked so serious that he half believed she was in earnest.

"Are ministers like other men?" she asked, with a spice of genuine curiosity in her question. The venerable pastor of the church which she attended in New York had not seemed to belong to the same race as herself. His hair was so white, his face so bloodless, his life so saintly, and his sermons so utterly beyond her, that he appeared as dim and unearthly as one of the Christian Fathers. A young theologian on the way to that same ghostly state was an object of piquant interest. She had never had a flirtation with a man of this character, therefore there was all the zest of novelty. Had she been less fearless, she would have shrunk from it, however, with something of the superstitious dread that many have of jesting in a church, or a graveyard. But there was a trace of hardihood in her present course that just took her fancy. From lack of familiarity with the class, she had a vague impression that ministers differed widely from other men, and to bring one down out of the clouds as a fluttering captive at her feet would be a triumph indeed. A little awe mingled with her curiosity as she sought to penetrate the scholastic and saintly atmosphere in which she supposed even an embryo clergyman dwelt. She hardly knew what to say when, in reply to her question, "Are ministers like other men?" he asked, "Why not?"

"That is hardly a fair way to answer."

"You do not find me a mysterious being."

"I find you very different from other young men of my acquaintance. What to me is a matter of course is dreadful to you. Then you ministers have such strange theological ways of dividing the world up into saints and sinners, and you coolly predict such awful things for the sinners (though I confess the sinners take it quite as coolly). The whole thing seems professional rather than true."

The tone of deep sadness in which the young man next spoke caused her to look at him with a little surprise.

"I do not wonder that this mutual coolness perplexes you. If we believe the Bible, it is the strangest mystery in existence."

"You may well put that in. Do the generality of people *believe* the Bible? But as I was saying, from the very nature of your calling you come to live far away from us. Our old minister knows more about dead people than living. He knows all about the Jews and Greeks who lived eighteen centuries ago, but next to nothing of the young of his own church. My motives and temptations would be worse than Sanscrit to him—harder to understand than the unsolved problems of mathematics. What does such a man know about the life of a young lady in society? That which influences me would seem less than nothing to him."

"I think you misjudge your pastor. If you became well acquainted with him, you might find a heart overflowing with sympathy."

"I can no more get acquainted with him than if he dwelt on Mount Olympus. If I were only a doctrine, he might study me up and know something about me. But there is so much flesh and blood about me that I fear I shall always be distasteful to ministers."

"I assure you, Miss Marsden, I find you more interesting than some doctrines."

"But you are young. You are on a vacation, and can for a time descend to trifles, but you will grow like the rest. As it is, you speak very guardedly, and intimate that I would be as nothing compared with other doctrines."

"What is a doctrine, Miss Marsden?"

"Oh, bless me, I don't know exactly; a sort of abstract summing up of either our qualities or God's qualities. The only doctrine I even half understand is that of 'total depravity,' and I sometimes fear it's true."

"I think you are a great deal more interesting than the 'doctrine of total depravity,'" said Hemstead, laughing.

"Perhaps you will come to think I am synonymous with it."

"No fear. I have seen too much of you for that already."

"What redeeming features have you seen?"

He looked at her earnestly for a moment, and she sustained his gaze with an expression of such innocent sweetness that he said, a little impulsively, "All your features redeem you from that charge."

"Oh, fie!" she exclaimed, "a pun and flattery in one breath!"

"I do not mean to flatter. Although in some respects you puzzle me, I am very clear and positive as to my feeling of gratitude. While my aunt feels kindly toward me, she is formal. It seemed to me when I came out of the cold of the wintry night I found within a more chilling coldness. But when you gave me your warm hand and claimed something like kindred, I was grateful for that which does not always accompany kindred—genuine kindness. This feeling was greatly increased when instead of making my diffidence and awkwardness a theme of ridicule, you evinced a delicate sympathy, and with graceful tact suggested a better courtesy to others. Do you think then, that, after this glimpse down such a beautiful vista in your nature, I can associate you with 'total depravity'? It was plain to you, Miss Marsden, that I had seen little of society, but you acted as if that were my misfortune, not my fault. I think the impulse that leads one to try to shield or protect another who for the time may be weak or defenceless is always noble.''

If Lottie had shown a little before that she had a heart, she now became painfully aware that she had a conscience, and it gave her some severe twinges during this speech. For a moment she wished she deserved his commendation. But she was not one to do things by halves, and so, recklessly throwing aside her qualms, she said laughingly, "I don't think a gentleman of your inches at all an object of pity. You are big enough to take care of yourself.''

"And I mean to as far as I can. But we all need help at times. You know a mouse once served a lion.''

"Thank you. Now you have counterbalanced all your fine speeches and compliments. 'A mouse serving a lion!' Well, roar gently if you please.''

"I'm afraid I appear to you like another animal that once donned a lion's skin, but whose ears, alas, protruded.''

"That is rather a skilful retreat; but I imagine that you think yourself a veritable lion.''

"If you insist on my being a lion, I must refer you to ancient mythology, where one of these overrated beasts is held a crouching captive by Diana.''

"Well, that is quite a transition. First compared to a mouse, and then to the moon. I fear that if you have not visited 'questionable places,' you have permitted your mind to dwell on the 'questionable' myths of the past.

"Oh, that was in the regular order of things,'' he replied. "Before coming to the study of theology, we are put through mythology; that is, under the guidance of reverend professors we make the acquaintance of a set of imaginary beings who, had they veritably lived, and in our day, would have soon found their way to the penitentiary.''

"At the door of which the 'lion' and 'Diana' would part company, and so I should lose my gentle 'captive' and become as disconsolate as auntie would have been had you trodden on the reverse extremity of her pet.''

"Oh, pardon me, but Diana was an exception to the rest.''

"Better or worse?"

"Better, of course. She was a trifle cruel, though, was she not?"

"You have been proving me very tender-hearted."

"So every woman should be."

"I doubt whether you know much about us."

"I cannot imagine a being—not even an angel—more pure, unselfish, and true than my mother; and she is a woman."

"Miss Lottie," here broke in De Forrest, "I've played whist to the utmost limit of my conscience. You will not keep me on the rack any longer."

"Oh, no, Cousin Julian," she replied, *sotto voce*, "only on the sofa with our dear cousin Bel. "See, she sits there alone. Good-by," and she swept past, with a malicious twinkle in her eyes at his blank expression.

But Bel saw and understood the scene. With a cynical smile she went to the piano, and commenced a brilliant waltz. Under its spell Addie and Mr. Harcourt came whirling up the hall, and Lottie, who had been under restraint so long, could not resist the temptation of letting De Forrest carry her off also.

"It's only with my cousin, you know," she whispered apologetically to Hemstead.

He stood in the doorway for a few moments and watched her graceful figure with a strange and growing interest. Whether saint or sinner, this being so emphatically of flesh and blood was exceedingly fascinating. The transition from the cloister-like seclusion of his seminary life to this suburb of the gay world was almost bewildering; and Lottie Marsden was one to stir the thin blood and withered heart of the coldest anchorite. The faint perfume which she seemed to exhale, like a red rosebush in June, was a pleasing exchange for the rather musty and scholastic atmosphere in which he so long had dwelt. As she glanced by as lightly as a bird on the wing, she occasionally beamed upon him with one of her dangerous smiles. She then little thought or cared that

his honest and unoccupied heart was as ready to thaw and
blossom into love as a violet bank facing the south in spring.
He soon had a vague consciousness that he was not doing just
the prudent thing, and therefore rejoined his aunt and uncle.
Soon after he pleaded the weariness of his journey and retired. As he was about to mount the stairs Lottie whirled
by and whispered, "Don't think me past praying for."

The slang she used in jest came to him, with his tendencies and convictions, like an unconscious appeal and a divine suggestion. He was utterly unconventional, and while
readily unbending into mirthfulness, he regarded life as an
exceedingly serious thing. As the eyes of artist and poet
catch glimpses of beauty where to others are only hard lines
and plain surfaces, so strong religious temperaments are
quick to see providences, intimations, and leadings.

Hemstead went to his room with steps that deep thought
rendered slower and slower. He forgot his weariness, and
sat down before the fire to think of one known but a few
brief hours. If there are those who can coolly predict "awful things" of the faithless and godless, Hemstead was not
one of them. The young girl who thought him a good
subject for jest and ridicule, he regarded with profound
pity. Her utter unconsciousness of danger had to him
the elements of deepest pathos.

While perplexed by contradictions in her manner and
words, he concluded that she was what she seemed, a girl
of unusual force of mind, frank and kindly, and full of
noble impulses, but whose religious nature was but slightly
developed. He at that time would have been shocked and
indignant if he had known the truth. Her natural tendencies had been good. Her positive nature would never waver
weakly along the uncertain boundary of good and evil, as
was the case with Bel Parton. She was one who would be
decided and progressive in one direction or the other, but
now was clearly on the sinister side of truth and moral loveliness. Surrounding influences had been adverse. She had
yielded to them, and they had carried her further astray than

if she had been of a cautious and less forceful temperament. While therefore full of good impulses, she was also passionate and selfish. Much homage had made her imperious, exacting, and had developed no small degree of vanity. She exulted in the power and pre-eminence that beauty gave, and often exerted the former cruelly, though it is due to her to state that she did not realize the pain she caused. While her own heart slept, she could not understand the aching disquiet of others that she toyed with. That it was good sport, high-spiced excitement, and occupation for her restless, active mind, was all she considered. As she would never be neutral in her moral character, so she was one who would do much of either harm or good. Familiarity with the insincerities of fashionable life had blurred her sense of truthfulness in little things, and in matters of policy she could hide her meaning or express another as well as her veteran mother.

And yet there were great possibilities of good in her character. She had a substratum of sound common-sense; was wholesomely averse to meanness, cowardice, and temporizing; best of all, she was not shallow and weak. She could appreciate noble action, and her mind could kindle at great thoughts if presented clearly and strongly.

She could scarcely be blamed severely for being what she was, for she had only responded to the influences that had ever surrounded her, and been molded by them. Her character was rapidly forming, but not as yet fixed. Therefore her best chance of escaping a moral deformity as marked as her external beauty was the coming under an entirely different class of influences.

However earthly parents may wrong their children by neglect, or by permitting in themselves characters that react ruinously upon those sacredly intrusted to their training, the Divine Father seems to give all a chance some time in life for the achievement of the grandest of all victories, the conquest of self. Whatever abstract theories dreamers may evolve secluded from the world, those who observe closely

—who *know* humanity from infancy to age—are compelled
to admit, however reluctantly, that the inner self of every
heart is tainted and poisoned by evil. The innocence of
childhood is too much like the harmlessness of the lion's
whelps. However loftily and plausibly some may assert
the innate goodness and self-rectifying power of humanity,
as Tom Paine wrote against the Bible without reading it,
not having been able at the time to procure one in infidel
Paris, those who take the scientific course of getting the
facts first shake their heads despondingly. It is true that
parents discover diversities in their children. Some are
sweeter-tempered than others, and seem pointed horizon-
tally, if not heavenward, in their natures. Many bid fair
to stand high, measured by earthly standards. But the
approving world can know nothing of the evil thoughts
that haunt the heart.

What mother has not been almost appalled as she has
seen the face of her still infant child inflamed with rage and
the passionate desire for revenge? The chubby hand is not
always raised to caress, but too often to strike. As mind
and heart develop, darker and meaner traits unfold with
every natural grace. There is a canker-worm in the bud,
and unless it is taken out, there never can be a perfect
flower.

But Mr. and Mrs. Marsden thought of none of these
things. The mother received her estimate of life, and her
duty, from current opinion on the avenue. She complacently felicitated herself that she kept up with the changing
mode quite as well as most women of wealth and fashion, if
not better. She managed so well that she excited the admiration of some, and the envy of more; and so was content.
As for Mr. Marsden, what with his business, his newspaper,
whist, and an occasional evening at the club or some entertainment or public meeting that he could not escape, his life
was full and running over. He never had time to give a
thought to the fine theories about his children, nor to the
rather contradictory facts often reported from the nursery.

But as year after year he paid the enormous and increasing bills for nurses, *gouvernantes*, Italian music masters, and fashionable schools, he sincerely thought that few men did as much for their children as he.

Of course, a lady from whom society expected so much as from Mrs. Marsden could not give her time to her children. In the impressible period of infancy and early childhood, Lottie and her brother, and an invalid sister older than herself, had been left chiefly to the charge of servants. But Mrs. Marsden's conscience was at rest, for she paid the highest prices for her French and German nurses and governesses, and of course "had the best," she said. Thus the children lived in a semi-foreign atmosphere, and early caught a "pretty foreign accent," which their mamma delighted to exhibit in the parlor; and at the same time they became imbued with foreign morals, which they also put on exhibition disagreeably often. When through glaring faults the stylish nursery-maid was dismissed, the obliging keeper of the intelligence office around the corner had another foreign waif just imported, who at a slightly increased sum was ready to undertake the care, and he might add the corruption, of the children in the most approved style. She was at once engaged, and to this alien the children were committed almost wholly, while Mrs. Marsden would tell her afternoon visitors how fortunate she had been in obtaining a new nurse with even a "purer accent." The probabilities were that her doubtful accent was the purest thing about her. Sometimes, as the results of this tutelage grew more apparent, even Mrs. Marsden had misgivings. But then her wealthiest and most fashionable neighbors were pursuing the same course with precisely the same results; and so she must be right.

If Lottie had been born pellucid as a drop of dew, as some claim, she would not have remained so long, even in the nursery, and as she stepped out further and faster in the widening sphere of her life, surrounding influences did not improve.

Her extreme beauty and grace, and the consequent admiration and flattery, developed an unusual degree of vanity, which had strengthened with years; though now she had too much sense and refinement to display it publicly. While generous and naturally warm-hearted, the elements of gentleness and patient self-denial for the sake of others at this time could scarcely have been discovered in her character.

Indeed this beautiful girl, nurtured in a Christian land, a regular attendant upon church, was a pagan and belonged to a pagan family. Not one of her household worshipped God. Mr. and Mrs. Marsden would have been exceedingly shocked and angered if they had been told they were heathens. But at the time when Paul found among the multitudinous altars of Athens one dedicated to the "Unknown God," there were many Grecian men and women more highly cultivated than these two aristocrats of to-day. But in spite of external devoutness at church, it could easily be shown that to this girl's parents the God of the Bible was as "unknown" and unheeded as the mysterious and unnamed deity concerning whose claims the Apostle so startled the luxurious Athenians. Like the ancient Greeks, all had their favorite shrines that, to a greater or a less degree, absorbed heart and brain.

Lottie was a votaress of pleasure: the first and about the only article of her creed was to make everything and everybody minister to her enjoyment. She rarely entered on a day with a more definite purpose than to have a "good time"; and in the attainment of this end we have seen that she was by no means scrupulous.

She was as cruel a little pagan, too, as any of her remote Druidical ancestors, and at her various shrines of vanity, pleasure, and excitement, delighted in offering human sacrifices. She had become accustomed to the writhing of her victims, and soothed herself with the belief that it did not hurt them so very much after all. She considered no further than that flirtation was one of the recognized amusements of the fashionable. What the *ton* did was law and gospel to her mother; and the same to Lottie, if agreeable. If not, there was no law and no gospel for her.

She had no more scruple in making a victim of Hemstead than a Fiji Island potentate would have in ordering a breakfast according to his depraved and barbarous taste. And when even society-men had succumbed to her wiles, and in abject helplessness had permitted her to place her imperious foot upon their necks, what chance had a warm-hearted, unsophisticated fellow, with the most chivalric ideas of womanhood?

Quick-witted Lottie, on seeing Hemstead and hearing his table-talk, had modified Addie Marchmont's suggestion in her own mind. She saw that, though unsuspicious and trusting in his nature, he was too intelligent to be imposed upon by broad farce. Therefore, a religious mask would soon be known as such. Her aunt also would detect the mischievous plot against her nephew and guest, and thwart it. By appearing as a well-meaning unguided girl, who both needed and wished an adviser, she might more safely keep this modern Samson blindly making sport for her and the others, and at the same time not awaken the troublesome suspicions of her aunt and uncle. In the character of one who was full of good impulses—who erred through ignorance, and who wished to be led and helped to better things—she was nearer the truth, and could act her part more successfully.

But what could Frank Hemstead, coming from a home in which he had breathed the very atmosphere of truth and purity, know of all this? To him Lottie was the most beautiful creature he had ever seen, and in his crystal integrity he would have deemed it a foul insult to her to doubt that she was just what she seemed. To his straightforward nature, believing a woman the opposite of what she seemed was like saying to her, "Madam, you are a liar."

The world would be better if women did more to preserve this chivalric trust.

"Past praying for!" His creed taught him to pray for

all the world, and already a subtile, unrecognized impulse
of his heart led him to plead before the Divine Father for
one who seemed, in outward grace, already fitted for heavenly surroundings.

When a block of unusually perfect marble falls under
the eye of a true sculptor, he is conscious of a strong impulse to bring out the exquisite statue that is distinctly
visible to his mind. Hemstead was an enthusiast in the
highest form of art and human effort, and was developing,
as the ruling motive of his life, a passion for moulding the
more enduring material of character into moral symmetry
and loveliness. Humanity in its most forbidding guise interested him, for his heart was warm and large and overflowed with a great pity for the victims of evil. In this respect he was like his Master, who had "compassion on the
multitude." His anticipation of his life-work was as non-
professional as that of a mother who yearns over the children she cannot help loving. Lottie appeared strong and
lovely by nature. It seemed to him that the half-effaced,
yet still lingering image of God rested upon her beautiful
face more distinctly than he had ever seen it elsewhere.
The thought of that image becoming gradually blurred and
obliterated by sin—of this seemingly exquisite and budding
flower growing into a coarse, rank weed—was revolting to
his mind.

CHAPTER V

PLAIN TALK

A T last the sound of mirth and laughter ceased, and the
house became quiet.

Lottie sat warming her feet at the glowing coals
in her room, before retiring. A dreamy smile played upon
her face, coming and going with passing thoughts, even as
the firelight flickered upon it.

She was in an unusually amiable mood, for this affair
with Hemstead promised richly. If he had been an ordinary and polished society-man, the flirtation would have
been humdrum, like a score of others. But he was so delightfully fresh and honest, and yet so clever withal, that
her eyes sparkled with anticipating mirth as she saw him in
various attitudes of awkward love-making, and then dropping helplessly into the abyss of his own great, but empty
heart, on learning the vainness of his passion.

"He finds me 'more interesting than some doctrines,'
indeed! I'll put all his dry doctrines to rout in less than
a week. I'll drive text-books and professors out of his
head, and everything else (save myself) out of his heart, for
a little while. But after he gets back to Michigan, the doctrines will come creeping back into their old place, and he
will get comfortably over it like the rest. In the meanwhile, as substantial and useful results, I will have my rare
bit of sport, and he will know more about the wicked world
against which he is to preach. By and by he will marry
a pious Western giantess, whose worst dissipation is a
Sunday-school picnic, and will often petrify her soul with

horror and wonder by describing that awful little pagan, Lottie Marsden.

"And a heathen I am in very truth. Where are missionaries needed more than in Fifth Avenue? They had better not come, though; for if we would not eat them, we would freeze them."

"What are you thinking about, Lottie, that you are smiling so sweetly?" asked her room-mate, Bel Parton.

"In truth, it was a sweet thought," said Lottie, her laugh awakening sudden echoes in the still house, and sounding as oddly as a bird's song at night. "I'm glad Frank Hemstead doesn't know. If he did, I should appall instead of fascinating him."

"I think your plot against him is very wrong—wicked, indeed. He is such a sincere, good young man, that I like it less and less. *I* couldn't do such a thing."

"Still you can look on and enjoy the fun, and that is all you have to do. Poor Bel, you are always in need of an M.D.'s or a D.D.'s care. I have forsworn both."

So spoke Lottie in the arrogance of her perfect health and abounding beauty, and then (such are the seeming contradictions of character) she knelt and appeared as a white-robed saint at her devotions. But the parrot-like prayer that she hastily mumbled was of no possible value to any one. She had continued the habit from childhood, and it was mainly habit. The other motive was something like the feeling of a careless Catholic, who crosses himself, though he cannot explain what good it does him.

A moment later she might have been taken as a model of sleeping innocence.

This world is evidently sadly out of joint. We all know of the most gentle, lovely, unselfish spirits, beautiful to Heaven's eye, that are enshrined in painfully plain caskets. In the instance of Lottie Marsden, the casket was of nature's most exquisite workmanship, but it held a tarnished jewel.

It was with some misgivings that Hemstead looked forward to meeting his "cousin," on the following morning.

Would she be as radiantly beautiful, as piquant, and withal as kindly and frank as on the previous evening? Even his limited experience of the world had shown him that in the matter-of-fact and searching light of the morning many of the illusions of the night vanish. He had noted with no little surprise that ladies seemingly young and blooming had come down to breakfast looking ten years older; so he had said to himself, "She dazzled me last night. I shall see her as she is to-day."

Being an early riser, he entered the cheerful breakfast-room considerably before the others, and in a moment was entranced by the view from the windows.

The severe northeast storm had expended itself during the night, and its fine, sharp crystals had changed into snowflakes. As an angry man after many hard cutting words relents somewhat and speaks calmly if still coldly, so nature, that had been stingingly severe the evening before, was now quietly letting fall a few final hints of the harsh mood that was passing away. Even while he looked, the sun broke through a rift over the eastern mountains, and lighted up the landscape as with genial smiles. It shone, not on an ordinary and prosaic world, but rather on one that had been touched by magic during the night and transformed into the wonderland of dreams.

The trees that in the dusk of the previous night had writhed and groaned and struck their frozen branches together, gesticulating like despairing anguish, now stood serene, and decked more daintily than June would robe them. Whiter even than the pink-tinged blossoms of May was the soft wet snow that incased every twig, limb, and spray. The more he looked, the more the beauty and the wonder of the scene grew upon him. The sun was dispersing the clouds and adding the element of splendor to that of beauty. It became one of the supreme moments of his life, and in the vanishing beauty of an earthly scene he received an earnest of the perfect world beyond.

"With the exception of the broad dark river," he

thought, "this might be the Millennial morn, and nature standing decked in her spotless ascension robes, waiting in breathless expectancy."

But his musings were unexpectedly interrupted, for just at this moment Lottie Marsden put her hand lightly on his arm and said, "Cousin Frank—pardon me—Mr. Hemstead, what is the matter? You look as rapt as if you saw a vision."

He turned and seemed as startled as if he had, for standing by him and looking inquiringly into his face was a being that, with her brilliant eyes and exquisitely clear and delicate complexion, seemed as beautiful, and at the same time as frail and ready to vanish, as the snow-wreaths without.

She saw the strong admiration and almost wonder depicted on his open face, though she seemed so innocently oblivious of it, and for a moment left him under the spell, then said, "Are you so resentful at my desertion last evening that you won't speak to me?"

"Look there," he replied, and he pointed to the fairyland without.

Lottie's wonder and delight were almost equal to his own, for she had never witnessed such a scene before.

"I am so glad I came!" she said. "We see nothing like this in the city. Look at those snowy mountains. How vast and white they are!"

"And look at that little tree with its red berries gleaming against the snowy foil. They look like those ruby earrings against the whiteness of your neck."

She looked at him quickly and humorously, asking, "Where did you learn the art of complimenting?"

"I had no thought of trivial compliment in the presence of a scene like this," he answered gravely; "I was awed by the beauty I saw, and it seemed as if the Great Artist must be near. I wished to call your attention to the truth that, like all His work, the least thing is perfect. That little tree with its red berries is beautiful as well as the mountain. I now am glad too that you came, though I dreaded any one's coming before, and the necessity of returning to common-place life. But suddenly, and as silently as one of those snowflakes, you appear, and I am startled to find you in keeping with the scene, instead of an intrusion."

"And do I seem to you like a snowflake—as pure and as cold?" she asked, bending upon him her brilliant eyes.

"Not as cold, I trust, and if you were as pure you would not be human. But your beauty seemed to me as marvellous as that of the scene I had been wondering at. I am not versed in society's disguises, Miss Marsden, and can better express my thoughts than hide them. You know you are very beautiful. Why should I not say so as well as involuntarily express the fact in my face as I did a moment ago, and as every one does, I suppose, who meets you? There is nothing brought to your attention more often, and more pressed upon you. It must be so. Does not your beauty cause you much anxiety?"

"What a funny question!" laughed Lottie. "Your frankness is certainly as transparent as those snow-crystals there. I cannot say that it does. Why should it, even granting that it exists independently of your disordered imagination?"

"It exposes you to a temptation very hard to resist. Such beauty as yours should be but the reflex of character. I once saw, in an art gallery of New York, a marble face so white, pure, and sweet, that it has ever remained in my memory as an emblem of spiritual beauty. Suppose every one that came in should touch that face, and some with coarse and grimy fingers, what a smutched and tawdry look it would soon have. You cannot help the admiring glances, flattering words, and the homage that ever waits on beauty, any more than the marble face the soiling touch of any vandal hand; but you can prevent your soul from being stained and smirched with vanity and pride."

"I never had any one to talk to me in this way," said Lottie, looking demurely down. "Perhaps I should have been better if I had. I fear you think me very vain and conceited.''

"I should think it very strange if you were not somewhat vain. And yet you do not act as if you were.''

"Supposing I am vain. What difference does it make, if no one knows it?'' she asked abruptly.

"There are two who always will know it.''

"Who?''

"God and yourself. And by and by all masks must be dropped, and all the world see us as we are.''

"Do you believe that?'' she asked, a little startled at the thought.

"I know it,'' he replied, in a tone of quiet confidence that carries more conviction than loud assertion. "Moreover, your beauty involves a heavy burden of responsibility.''

"Really, Mr. Hemstead, if you keep on you will prove beauty a great misfortune, whether I possess it or not.''

"Far from it.''

"Granting for sake of argument your premise, how am I burdened with responsibility?''

"Would it not almost break your heart, if your honorable father were misappropriating money intrusted to his care?''

"Don't suggest such a thing.''

"Only for the sake of illustration. Suppose he had the qualities and position which led a great many to place their means in his hands; would that not increase his responsibility?''

"Yes, if he accepted such trusts.''

"Are there not more valuable possessions than dollars, stocks, and bonds? Every one is more or less fascinated, drawn, and won by beauty, and to the beautiful the most sacred thoughts and feelings of the heart are continually intrusted. History and biography show that beautiful women, if true, gentle, and unselfish, have great power with their own sex, and almost unbounded influence over men. Your power, therefore, is subtle, penetrating, and

reaches the inner life, the very warp and woof of character.
If a beautiful statue can ennoble and refine, a beautiful
woman can accomplish infinitely more. She can be a constant inspiration, a suggestion of the perfect life beyond
and an earnest of it. All power brings responsibility, even
that which a man achieves or buys; but surely, if one re-
ceives Heaven's most exquisite gifts, bestowed as directly
as this marvellous beauty without, and so is made pre-
eminent in power and influence, she is under a double
responsibility to use that power for good. That a woman
can take the royal gift of her own beauty, a divine heritage,
one of the most suggestive relics of Eden still left among
us, and daily sacrifice it on the poorest and meanest of
altars—her own vanity—is to me hard to understand. It is
scarcely respectable heathenism. But to use her beauty
as a lure is far worse. Do we condemn wreckers, who place
false, misleading lights upon a dangerous coast? What is
every grace of a coquette, but a false light, leading often
to more sad and hopeless wreck?"

No man had ever told Lottie more plainly that she was
beautiful, than Hemstead, and yet she disliked his compliments wofully. Her face fairly grew pale, under his words.
Had he learned of her plot? Had he read her thoughts, and
been informed of her past life? Did quiet satire and de-
nunciation lurk under this seeming frankness? She was
for the moment perplexed and troubled. Worse still, he
compelled her to see these things in a new light, and her
conscience echoed his words.

But her first impulse was to learn whether he was speaking generally, or pointedly at her; so she asked, in some
little trepidation, "Has any naughty girl tried to treat you
badly, that you speak so strongly?"

He laughed outright at this question. "No one has had
a chance," he said; "and I do not think there are many
who would take it. Moreover, I imagine that one of your
proud belles would not even condescend to flirt with a poor
awkward fellow like me. But I am not a croaking phi-

losopher, and look on the bright side of the world. It has always treated me quite as well as I deserved. I often think the world is not so bad as described, and that it would be better, if it had a chance.''

"Have you seen much of it, Mr. Hemstead?''

"I cannot say that I have. I have read and thought about it far more than I have seen. On account of my limited means and student life, my excursions have been few and far between. I have already proved to you what an awkward stranger I am to society. But in thought and fancy I have been a great rambler, and like to picture to myself all kinds of scenes, past and present, and to analyze all kinds of character.''

"I hope you won't analyze mine," she said, looking at him rather distrustfully. "I should not like to be dissected before I was dead.''

"I wish all were as able to endure analysis as yourself, Miss Marsden. In any case, you have no reason to fear a severe critic in me.''

"Why not?''

"Because you have been so lenient toward me. I have received more kindness from you, a stranger, than from my own kindred.''

"You are very grateful.''

"Shakespeare declares ingratitude a 'marble-hearted fiend.' ''

"You evidently are not 'marble-hearted.' ''

"Though possibly a fiend. Thank you.''

"I wish there were no worse to fear.''

"You need not have occasion to fear any.''

"Well, I can't say that I do very much. Perhaps it would be better for me if I did.''

"Why so?''

"Then I should be more afraid to do wrong. Miss Parton cannot do wrong with any comfort at all.''

"Well, that would be a queer religion which consisted only in being afraid of the devil and his imps.''

"What is religion? I am foolish in asking such a question, however, for I suppose it would take you a year to answer it, and they will all be down to breakfast in a few moments."

"Oh, no, I can answer it in a sentence. True religion is worshipping God in love and faith, and obeying Him."

"Is that all?" exclaimed Lottie, in unfeigned astonishment.

"That is a great deal."

"Perhaps it is. You theologians have a way of preaching awfully long and difficult sermons from simple texts. But I never got as simple an idea of religion as that from our minister."

"I fear you think I have been preaching for the last half-hour. Perhaps I can best apologize for my long homilies this morning by explaining. When an artist is in his best mood, he wishes to be at his easel. The same is true of every one who does something *con amore*. When I saw the transfigured world this morning, it was like a glimpse into heaven, and—"

"And a naughty little sinner came in just at that moment, and got the benefit of your mood," interrupted Lottie. "Well, I have listened to your sermon and understand it, and that is more than I can say of many I have heard. It certainly was pointed, and seemed pointed at me, and I have heard it said that it is proof of a good sermon for each one to go away feeling that he has been distinctly preached at. But permit me as a friend, Mr. Hemstead, to suggest that this will not answer in our day. I fear, from my little foretaste, that people will not be able to sit comfortably under your homilies, and unless you intend to preach out in the backwoods, you must modify your style."

"That is where I do intend to preach. At least upon the frontiers of our great West."

"Oh, how dismal!" she exclaimed. "And can you, a young, and I suppose an ambitious man, look forward to being buried alive, as it were, in those remote regions?"

"I assure you I do not propose to be buried alive at the West, or spiritually smothered, as you hinted, in a fashionable church at the East. I think the extreme West, where states and society are forming with such marvellous rapidity, is just the place for a young, and certainly for an ambitious man. Is it nothing to have a part in founding and shaping an empire?"

"You admit that you are ambitious, then."

"Yes."

"Is that right?"

"I think so."

"Our minister inveighs against ambition, as if it were one of the deadly sins."

"He means the ambition that is all for self. That is as wrong and contemptible as the beauty that is miserable without a looking-glass. An ardent desire to obtain my Divine Master's approval, and to be worthy of it—to be successful in serving a noble cause—cannot be wrong."

She looked at his earnest face and eyes, that seemed to glow with hidden fire, almost wistfully; and said with a tinge of sadness, "You will feel very differently, I fear, twenty years hence. Enthusiasm is a rare thing in the city, and I imagine it is soon quenched everywhere."

"So it is; it needs constant rekindling."

Just then Mrs. Marchmont and Mr. Dimmerly appeared, and soon after they all sat down to a late breakfast.

CHAPTER VI

A SLEIGH RIDE AND SOMETHING MORE

LOTTIE assumed an unusual degree of gayety during the early part of the meal, but her flow of spirits seemed unequal, and to flag toward the last. She had sudden fits of abstraction, during which her jetty eyebrows contracted into unwonted frowns.

Her practical joke did not promise so well as on the evening before. That unexpected half-hour's talk had shown some actions in a new light. She did not mind doing wicked things that had a spice of hardihood and venturesomeness in them. But to do what had been made to appear mean and dishonorable was another thing, and she was provoked enough at Hemstead for having unconsciously given that aspect to her action and character, and still more annoyed and perplexed that her conscience should so positively side with him. Thus it will be seen that her conscience was unawakened, rather than seared and deadened.

As she came to know Hemstead better, she found that he was different from what she had expected. The conventional idea of a theological student had dwelt in her mind; and she had expected to find a rather narrow and spiritually conceited man, full of the clerical mannerisms which she had often heard laughed at. But she saw that Hemstead's awkwardness would wear away, through familiarity with society, and that, when at ease, he was simple and manly in manner. She also perceived that this seclusion from the world, which was the cause of his diffidence, had been employed in training and richly storing his mind. Moreover, to one so accustomed to the insincerity of soci-

ety, his perfect frankness of speech and manner was a novelty, interesting, if not always pleasing. She read his
thoughts as she would an open page, and saw that he
esteemed her as a true, sincere girl, kind and womanly,
and that he had for her the strongest respect. She feared
that when he discovered her true self he would scorn her to
loathing. Not that she cared, except that her pride would
be hurt. But as she was more proud than vain, she feared
this honest man's verdict.

But soon her old reckless self triumphed. "Of course
what I am doing will seem awful to him," she thought.
"I knew that before I commenced. He shall not preach
me out of my fun in one half-hour. If I could make him
love me in spite of what I am, it would be the greater triumph. After all, I am only acting as all the girls in my set
do when they get a chance. It's not as bad as he makes out."

Still that was an eventful half-hour, when they looked
out upon a transfigured world together; and while she saw
nature in her rarest and purest beauty, she had also been
given a glimpse into the more beautiful world of truth,
where God dwells.

But, as the morning advanced, good impulses and better
feelings and thoughts vanished, even as the snow-wreaths
were dropping from branch and spray, leaving them as bare
as before. By the time the sleigh drove up to the door she
was as bent as ever upon victimizing the "Western giant,"
as the conspirators had named him. She was her old, decided, resolute self; all the more resolute because facing,
to her, a new hindrance—her own conscience, which Hemstead had unwittingly awakened; and it said to its uncomfortable possessor some rather severe things that day.

If Lottie were Bel Parton, she would have been in a mis-
erably undecided state. But it was her nature to carry out
what she had begun, if for no other reason than that she
had begun it, and she was not one to give up a frolic at
any one's scolding—even her own.

As she tripped down the broad stairs in a rich cloak

trimmed with fur, she reminded Hemstead of some rare tropical bird, and De Forrest indulged in many notes of admiration. Lottie received these as a matter of course, but looked at the student with genuine interest. His expression seemed to satisfy her, for she turned away to hide a smile that meant mischief.

It was quietly arranged that Hemstead should sit beside her, and he felicitated himself over their artifice as if it were rare good fortune.

Though the sun and the rising breeze had shaken off the clustering snow to a great extent, the evergreens still bent beneath their beautiful burdens, some straight cedars reminding one of vigorous age, where snowy hair and beard alone suggest the flight of years.

Though the face of nature was so white, it was not the face of death. There was a sense of movement and life which was in accord with their own spirits and rapid motion. Snow-birds fluttered and twittered in weedy thickets by the wayside, breakfasting on the seeds that fell like black specks upon the snow. The bright sunlight had lured the red squirrels from their moss-lined nests in hollow trees, and their barking was sometimes heard above the chime of the bells.

"There goes a parson crow," cried Addie Marchmont. "How black and solemn he looks against the snow!"

"Why are crows called parsons, Mr. Hemstead?" asked Lottie, as a child might.

"Indeed, I don't know. For as good a reason, I suppose, as that some girls are called witches."

She gave him a quick, keen look, and said, "I hope you mean nothing personal."

"I should never charge you with being a witch, Miss Marsden, but I might with witchery."

"A distinction without a difference," she said, seeking to lead him on.

"He means," explained De Forrest, "that you might be bewitching if you chose."

"Hush, Julian, you leave no room for the imagination," said Lottie, frowningly.

"Look at that farmyard, Miss Marsden," said Hemstead. "The occupants seem as glad that the storm is over as we are. What pictures of placid content those ruminating cows are under that sunny shed. See the pranks of that colt which the boy is trying to lead to water. I wish I were on his back, with the prairie before me."

"Indeed, are you so anxious to escape present company?"

"Now I didn't say that. But we have passed by, and I fear you did not see the pretty rural picture to which I called your attention. Were I an artist I would know where to make a sketch to-day."

"I think you will find that Miss Marsden's taste differs very widely from yours," said De Forrest; "that is, if you give us to understand that you would seek your themes in a barnyard, and set your easel upon a muck-heap. Though your pictures might not rank high they would still be very rank."

Even Lottie joined slightly in the general and not complimentary laugh at Hemstead which followed this thrust, but he, with heightened color, said, "You cannot criticise my picture, Mr. De Forrest, for it does not exist. Therefore I must conclude that your satire is directed against my choice of place and subjects."

"Yes, as with the offence of Denmark's king, they 'smell to heaven.' "

"I appeal to you, Miss Marsden, was not the scent of hay and the breath of the cattle, as we caught them passing, sweet and wholesome?"

"I cannot deny that they were."

"You have judicial fairness and shall be umpire in this question. And now, Mr. De Forrest, there is a celebrated and greatly admired picture in a certain gallery, representing a scene from the Roman Saturnalia. You do not object to that, with its classic accessories, as a work of art?"

"Not at all."

"And yet it portrays a corruption that does in truth 'offend heaven.' Your muck-heap, which did not enter my thought at all, and would not have been in my picture, could I paint one, would have been wholesome in comparison. Have I made a point, Judge Marsden?"

"I think you have."

"Finally, Mr. De Forrest, what are we to do with the fact that some of the greatest painters in the world have employed their brushes upon just such scenes as these, which perhaps offend your nose and taste more than they do heaven, and that pictures such as that farmyard would suggest adorn the best galleries of Europe?"

"What artists of note have painted barnyard scenes?" asked De Forrest, in some confusion.

"Well, there is Herring, the famous English artist, for one."

"'Herring' indeed. You are evidently telling a fish story," said De Forrest, contemptuously.

"No, he is not," said Lottie. "Herring is a famous painter, I am told, and we have some engravings of his works."

"And I have read somewhere," continued Hemstead, "that his painting of an English farmyard is the most celebrated of his works. Moreover, Judge Marsden, I must ask of you another decision as to the evidence in this case. I affirm that I did not call your attention to the farmyard itself, but to its occupants. Is not that true?"

"I cannot deny that it is."

"We all know that many eminent artists have made the painting of animals a specialty, and among them are such world-renowned names as Landseer and Rosa Bonheur. Moreover, in the numerous pictures of the Nativity we often find the homely details of the stable introduced. One of Rubens' paintings of this sacred and favorite subject, which hangs in the gallery of the Louvre, represents two oxen feeding at a rack."

"Come, Julian, hand over your sword. It won't do for you or any one to sit in judgment on such painters as Mr. Hemstead has named. You are fairly beaten. I shall admire barnyards in future, through thick and thin."

"That is hardly a fair conclusion from any testimony of mine," said Hemstead. "A barnyard may be all that Mr. De Forrest says of it, but I am sure you will always find pleasure in seeing a fine frolicsome horse or a group of patient cattle. The homely accessories may, and sometimes may not, add to the picture."

"How do you come to know so much about pictures? Theology has nothing to do with art."

"I dissent from Judge Marsden's decision now, most emphatically," replied Hemstead. "Is not true art fidelity to nature?"

"Yes, so it is claimed."

"And where does nature come from? God is the Divine Artist, and is furnishing themes for all other artists. God is the author of landscapes, mountains, rivers, of scenes like that we saw this morning, or of a fine face and a noble form, as truly as of a chapter in the Bible. He manifests Himself in these things. Now fine paintings, statuary, and music bring out the hidden meanings of nature, and therefore more clearly God's thought. Theology, or knowledge concerning our Creator, is a science to which everything can minister, and surely the appreciation of the beautiful should be learned in connection with the Author of all beauty."

"I never thought of God in that light before," said Lottie. "He has always seemed like one watching to catch me at something wrong. Our solemn old Sunday-school teacher used to say to us children just before we went home, 'Now during the week whenever you are tempted to do anything wrong, remember the text, "Thou, God, seest me."' When wasn't I tempted to do wrong? and I had for a long time the uncomfortable feeling that two great eyes were always staring at me. But this isn't sleigh-riding chit-chat," and she broke into a merry little trill from a favorite opera.

Hemstead, with his strong love of the beautiful, could not help watching her with deepening interest. The rapid motion, the music of the bells, the novel scenery of the sunlighted, glittering world around her, and, chief of all, her own abounding health and animal life, combined to quicken her excitable nature into the keenest enjoyment. From her red lips came ripples of laughter, trills from operas, sallies of fun, that kept the entire party from the thought of heaviness, and to honest-minded Hemstead were the evidences of a happy, innocent heart.

With secret exultation she saw how rapidly and unconsciously the unwary student was passing under the spell of her beauty and witchery.

One must have been cursed with a sluggish, half-dead body and a torpid soul, had he not responded to the influences under which our gay party spent the next few hours. Innumerable snow-flakes had carried down from the air every particle of impurity, and left it sweet and wholesome enough to seem the elixir of immortal youth. It was so tempered also, that it only braced and stimulated. The raw, pinching coldness of the previous day was gone. The sun, undimmed by a cloud, shone genially, and eaves facing the south were dripping, the drops falling like glittering gems.

Now and then a breeze would career down upon them, and, catching the light snow from the adjacent fence, would cast it into their faces as a mischievous school-boy might.

"Stop that!" cried Lottie to one of these sportive zephyrs. "Do you call that a gust of wind? I declare it was a viewless sprite, or a party of snow elves, playing their mad pranks upon us."

"I prefer fairies less cold and ethereal," said De Forrest, with a meaning look at the speaker.

"What do you prefer, Mr. Hemstead?" she asked. "But where we people of the world speak of fairies, sprites, and nymphs, I suppose you permit yourself to think only of angels."

"Were it so," he replied, "I should still be of the same mind as Mr. De Forrest, and be glad that you are not an angel."

"Why so?"

"You might use your wings and leave us."

"Were I one, I would not leave you after that speech. But see how far I am from it. I weigh one hundred and fifteen pounds."

"I wish you were no further off than that."

"What do you mean?"

"It's not our weight in avoirdupois that drags us down. But I am not going to preach any more to-day. Listen to the bells—how they echo from the hillside!"

"Yes, Julian, listen to Bel," said Lottie to De Forrest, who was about to speak. "I'm talking to Mr. Hemstead. See those snow-crystals on my muff. How can you account for so many odd and beautiful shapes?"

"To me all the countless forms in nature," said Hemstead, "prove an infinite mind gratifying itself. They are expressions of creative thought."

"Nonsense! God doesn't bother with such little things as these."

"We do not know what seems small or great to Him. The microscope reveals as much in one direction as the telescope in another, and the common house-fly seems in size midway in animal life."

"And do you believe that the Divine hand is employed in forming such trifles as these?"

"The Divine will is. But these trifles make the avalanche and the winter's protection for next year's harvest."

"What is that?" asked Harcourt from the front seat, where he was driving.

"Do you know," cried Lottie, "that Mr. Hemstead thinks everything we see, even to nature's smallest trifles, an 'expression of the Divine creative thought.'"

"Is that scene such an expression?" asked Harcourt, with a sneering laugh, in which the other joined.

By the road-side there was a small hovel, at the door of which a half-fed, ill-conditioned pig was squealing. When they were just opposite, a slatternly, carroty-headed woman opened the door, and raised her foot to drive the clamorous beast away. Altogether, it was as squalid and repulsive a picture as could well be imagined.

"Yes," replied Lottie, looking into his face with twinkling eyes, "was that sweet pastoral scene an expression of creative thought?"

"The woman csrtainly was not," he answered, reddening. "A thought may be greatly perverted."

"Whatever moral qualities may be asserted of her manners, costume, and character," said Harcourt, "she is not to blame for the cast of her features and the color of her hair. I scarcely know of an artist who would express any such thought, unless he wished to satirize humanity."

"You can call up before you the portrait of some beautiful woman, can you not, Mr. Harcourt?"

"Let me assist you," cried De Forrest, pulling from his inner pocket a photograph of Lottie.

"Hush, Julian. I'm sorry you do not appreciate this grave argument more; I'll take that picture from you, if you don't behave better."

"Well, I have a picture before me now, that satisfies me fully," said Mr. Harcourt, turning to Lottie with a smiling bow.

"Now, suppose that you had painted just such a likeness and finished it. Suppose I should come afterward, and, without destroying your picture utterly, should blend with those features the forbidding aspect of the woman we have just seen, would you not say that your thought was greatly perverted?"

"I should think I would."

"Well, Mother Eve was the true expression of the Divine Artist's creative thought, and the woman we saw was the perversion of it. You can trace no evil thing to the source of all good. Perfection is not the author of imperfection."

"Who does the perverting, then?" asked Lottie.

"Evil."

"I don't think it fair that one face and form should be perverted into hideousness, and another left with something of the first perfection."

"Evil is never fair, Miss Marsden."

"But is it only evil? I have heard plain children told, when resenting their ugliness, that it was wicked, for they were just as God made them."

"Can you think of a better way to make a young girl hate God than to tell her that?"

"But suppose it's true."

"I am sure it is not. Just the opposite is true. The ugly and deformed are as evil has marred them, and not as God has made them. By seeking the Divine Artist's aid more than humanity's first perfection can be regained. It is possible for even that wretched creature we saw to attain an outward loveliness exceeding that of any woman now living."

"That passes beyond the limit of my imagination," said Harcourt.

"Absurd!" muttered De Forrest.

"I fear you are not orthodox," said Bel.

"That means you do not agree with me. But please do not think that because I am a minister you must talk upon subjects that are rather grave and deep for a sleighing party."

"That's right, Cousin Frank," said Addie. "Dr. Beams will want you to preach for him next Sunday. I advise you to reserve your thunder till that occasion, when you may come out as strong as you please."

"'Chinese thunder' at best," whispered Harcourt to Addie; but all heard him.

Hemstead bit his lip and said nothing, but Lottie spoke up quickly: "No matter about the 'thunder,' Mr. Harcourt. That is only noise under any circumstances. But suppose there is the lightning of truth in what Mr. Hemstead says?"

"And suppose there is not?" he replied, with a shrug.

Hemstead gave Lottie a quick, pleased look, which Bel and De Forrest smilingly noted, and the conversation changed to lighter topics.

As they were passing through a small hamlet some miles back from the river, a bare-headed man came running out from a country store and beckoned them to stop, saying: "We're going to give our dominie a donation party to-night. Perhaps Mrs. Marchmont will do suthin' for us, or likely you'll all like to drive over and help the young folks enjoy themselves."

"Capital!" cried Lottie; "I've always wanted to attend a country donation. Do you think we can come, Addie?"

"Oh, certainly, if you wish, but I fear you won't enjoy it. You will not meet any of our 'set' there."

"I don't wish to meet them. I want to meet the other 'set' and have a frolic."

"It will be moonlight, and we will have the drive, which will be the best part of it, you will find," said Harcourt. "Yes, we will come."

"Them folks thinks that they's made of different flesh and blood from the other 'set,' as they call us, and that pretty young woman wants to come as she would go to a menagerie," muttered the man as he went back to the store. "No matter, let 'em come, they will help us make up the salary."

"Of course, Mr. Hemstead, you will enter upon this expedition with great zeal, as it will be to the advantage of one of your fraternity."

"I think, with Mr. Harcourt, that the ride will be the best part of it."

"Oh, for shame! Can it be true that two of even your trade can never agree?"

"Long ages of controversy prove that," said Harcourt.

"I think your profession has done more to keep the world in hot water than ours, Mr. Harcourt."

"We at least agree among ourselves."

"All the worse, perhaps, for the world."

"That's rather severe if you refer to the proverb, 'When rogues fall out, honest men get their dues,' " said Lottie.

"I supposed we were talking in jest; I was."

"You evidently belong to the church militant, since you strike back so hard even in jest," said Harcourt. "Very well, since you are so able to take care of yourself I shall have no compunctions in regard to your fate."

Hemstead did not understand this remark, but the others did, and significant glances were exchanged. He turned inquiringly to Lottie, feeling that in a certain sense he had an ally in her, but she seemed looking away abstractedly as if she had not heeded the remark. She was too quick to be caught easily, and the conviction grew upon him that while the others from his calling and difference in views and tastes had a natural aversion, she was inclined to be friendly. And yet she puzzled him not a little at times, as now for instance, when she turned and said, "I suppose there are a great many nice young men at your seminary."

"I never heard them called 'nice young men,' " he replied, looking at her keenly.

"Oh, I beg your pardon—good, pious, devotional young men, I mean."

"All ought to be that; do you not think so?"

"Well, yes, I think so, since they are to become ministers."

"But not otherwise?"

"I din't say that. There's a hint for you, Julian."

De Forrest's reply was a contemptuous shrug and laugh. It would be anything but agreeable to him to be thought "good, pious, and devotional"—qualities not in demand at his club, nor insisted on by Lottie, and entirely repugnant to his tastes.

"Do they all intend to be missionaries as well as yourself?" she continued.

"Oh, no; some no doubt will take city churches, and marry wealthy wives."

"Would that be wrong?"

"I am not the judge. It's a matter of taste and conscience."

"Would you not marry a lady of wealth?"

"I would marry the woman I loved; that is, if I could get her."

"Well added," said De Forrest.

"Yes, sir, I agree with you. Every man had better add that."

"Indeed they had," said Lottie, with a mischievous twinkle in her eyes.

"There is always a chance for a man who will never take 'no' for an answer," said De Forrest with a light laugh.

"Do you think so?" she said, lifting her eyebrows questioningly. "I agree with Mr. Hemstead. It's a matter of taste and conscience."

"Do you intend to be a missionary, Mr. Hemstead?" asked Bel Parton.

"I hope so," he replied, quietly.

"Yes," said Lottie; "just think of it. He is going away out to the jumping-off place at the West, where he will have the border ruffians on one side and the scalping Indians on the other. You said you would marry the woman you loved, if you could. Do you think any real nice girl would go with you to such a horrible place?"

"I'm sure I don't know. If the one I want won't venture, I can go alone."

"Do you think she'll go?" asked Lottie, so innocently that the others had no slight task in controlling their faces.

"Who will go?" said Hemstead, quickly.

"The one whom you said you wanted to."

"Now I'm sure I did not mention any one," said Hemstead, blushing and laughing.

"Well, you did not exactly speak her name."

"No, I should think not, since I don't know it myself."

"How provoking!" pouted Lottie. "I thought we were going to have a nice little romance."

"It's a pity I've nothing to tell, in view of my sympathizing audience," he replied, with a glance at the gigglers on the other seats.

"But I have been told," said Lottie, "that in emergencies committees have been appointed to select wives for missionaries, and that there are excellent women who are willing to sacrifice themselves for the sake of the cause."

An explosion of laughter followed these words, but she looked at the others in innocent surprise.

"That's a funny speech for you to make so gravely," said Hemstead. "I fear you are quizzing me. Your missionary lore certainly exceeds mine in regard to the 'committees.' But there will be no emergency in my case, and I should be sorry to have any woman, excellent or otherwise, sacrifice herself for me."

"I have certainly heard so," said Lottie, positively.

"I fear you have heard more to the prejudice of missionaries and their works than in their favor," he said somewhat gravely.

"But I am willing to hear the other side," she whispered in his ear.

"Now I protest against that," said De Forrest.

"I'll give you the privilege of whispering to Bel," said Lottie, sweetly.

"Oh, thank you," replied De Forrest, with a shrug.

"You can also help me out," she continued, as the sleigh stopped at Mrs. Marchmont's door.

As he did so he whispered in her ear, "Capital, Lottie, you are a star actress, and always my bright particular star."

"Don't be sentimental, Julian," was her only response.

At this moment Lottie's brother Dan fired a snow-ball that carried off Mr. Hemstead's hat; at which all laughed, and expected to see the young theologian assume a look of offended dignity. He disappointed them by good-naturedly springing out after his hat, and was soon romping with the boy and Mrs. Marchmont's two younger children. This was too tempting to Lottie, who joined the frolic at once.

Hemstead laughingly allowed himself to be their victim, and skilfully threw great snow-balls so as just to miss them, while they pelted him till he was white, and, as if utterly defeated, he led them a breathless chase up and down the broad path. Their cries and laughter brought half the household to the doors and windows to watch the sport.

De Forrest ventured down from the piazza with the thought that he could throw a spiteful ball or two at one he already disliked a little, as well as despised. But Hemstead immediately showed what a self-sacrificing victim he was to Lottie and the children by almost demolishing De Forrest with a huge snow-ball that stung his ear sharply, got down his neck, spoiling his collar, and necessitating such a toilet that he was late for dinner.

His plight took Lottie out of the field also, for she sank on the lower step of the piazza, her hand upon her side, helpless with laughter.

Hemstead retreated to a side door, where he shook himself after the manner of a polar bear, and escaped to his room.

CHAPTER VII

ANOTHER SPELL THAN BEAUTY'S

DE FORREST tried to laugh at his discomfiture when he appeared at the dinner-table, but he was evidently annoyed and vexed with its author.

"It was very nice of you, Mr. Hemstead," said Lottie, "to permit yourself to be pelted by us. You evidently did not think us worthy of your steel. But I fear you gave Julian a strong compliment."

"I only returned one of his."

"But he did not hit you."

"He meant to. We form our most correct judgment of people sometimes from what they intend, rather than what they do."

"Well, I thank you for my share of the sport."

"And I thank you for mine."

"What occasion have you to thank me, when I almost put your eyes out with snow?"

"You did not so blind them but that I could see a face aglow with exercise. That made a pleasing contrast to the cold white snow."

"Frank, Frank, you will make Lottie vain," said Mrs. Marchmont. "I did not know that complimenting was permitted to you."

"That is all right, sister," said Mr. Dimmerly. "That's where he shows his good blood and connection with an old family. He is gallant to the ladies. They can't get that out of him, even at a theological seminary."

Hemstead's blushing confusion increased the laugh at this speech.

"Oh, mother," exclaimed Addie, "we are all going on a frolic to-night. You know that poor, forlorn little minister at Scrub Oaks, who has six children, and gets but six hundred a year? Well, they are going to give him a donation to-night, so a dilapidated pillar of the church told us. We were invited to come, and Lottie wants to go."

"Very well, my dear, since you and our guests wish it."

"Now, auntie, that's very sweet of you to answer so," said Lottie. "I want to see the queer, awkward country people who go to such places. They amuse me vastly; don't they you, Mr. Hemstead?"

"They interest me."

"Oh, it wouldn't be proper for you to say 'amuse.'"

"Nor would it be exactly true."

"Why, Lottie," said Addie, "you know that ministers only think of people as a sad lot that must be saved."

"We'll help make a jolly lot there, to-night," said Lottie, with a swift glance at Hemstead's contracting brows. "Moreover, auntie, I want to see what a minister that lives on six hundred a year looks like. We give our pastor ten thousand."

"You need not go so far for that purpose, Miss Marsden," said Hemstead, quietly: "that is all I shall get."

"What!" she exclaimed, dropping her knife and fork.

"That, in all probability, will be my salary at first. It may be but five hundred."

"Is that all they pay you for going out among the border ruffians?"

"That is the average."

"I wouldn't go," she said indignantly.

"You may rest assured I would not, for the money."

"Frank will change his mind before spring," said his aunt; "or a year at least among the 'border ruffians,' as you call them, will cure him, and he will be glad to take a nice church at the East."

"What do you say to that, Mr. Hemstead?"

"Perhaps I would better answer by my actions," he replied.

"But I can see from the expression of your eyes and mouth a very plain answer to the contrary. Mr. Hemstead, you could be a very stubborn man if you chose."

"I hope I could be a very resolute one."

"Yes, so we explain ourselves when we will have our own way. I think Aunt Marchmont's suggestion a very good one."

"If we go to the donation we shall have to take something," said Bel.

"Oh, yes," exclaimed Addie; "I am told all sorts of queer things are brought. Let us take the oddest and most outlandish we can think of. Uncle, there is your old blue dress-coat; we will take that for the minister. Wouldn't he look comical preaching in it? And, mother, there is your funny low-necked satin dress that you wore when a young lady. I will take that for his wife."

"I understand everybody brings pies to a donation," said Harcourt. "I shall be more pious than any of them, and bring over fifty from town this afternoon. I will buy all the bake-shops out, in my zeal—enough to give the parson and all his people the dyspepsia for a month."

"If he lives on six hundred, nothing could give him the dyspepsia save his own sermons, I imagine," said De Forrest. "My young lady friends have half filled one of my bureau drawers with smoking-caps. I have one with me, and will give it to the minister."

"You vain fellow," laughed Lottie. "I never gave you one."

"Rest assured, no minister—even were he a minister to the Court of St. James—should get it, if you had."

"What will you take, Mr. Hemstead?" asked Lottie, noting his grave face.

"I shall not go."

"Why not? You spoke as if you would, this morning."

"I cannot go under the circumstances."

"Why not?" asked Addie, rather sharply.

"Could we take such gifts to a gentleman and lady, Cousin Addie?"

"Well, I suppose not," she answered, reddening.

"I see no proof that this clergyman and his wife are not in the fact that they are compelled to live on six hundred a year. Besides, I have too much respect for the calling."

"Don't you see?" said De Forrest to Addie, in a loud whisper. " 'Our craft is in danger.' "

"Your explanation is more crafty than true, Mr. De Forrest," said Hemstead, looking him straight in the eyes.

"Come," cried Lottie, "my party is not to be broken up. Mr. Hemstead, you need not look so serious or take the matter so much to heart. As you declared once before to-day, we were only 'talking in jest.' You cannot think we would willingly hurt the feelings of your brother clergyman. Surely, if you thought they were serious, it was good of you to stand up for him. We will all give money: that must be the thing the poor man needs most sorely."

"I will give twenty-five dollars if you will, Mr. Hemstead," said De Forrest, with a malicious twinkle in his eye.

"That's liberal of you, Julian. That's action in the right direction," said Lottie; and she turned to Hemstead, expecting a prompt response. But the moment she saw his face she surmised the truth and De Forrest's motive in making the offer, and what had appeared generous was now seen to be the reverse. But she determined that Julian should give the money, nevertheless. Still she did not at once interfere, but watched with no little curiosity, to see how Hemstead would extricate himself.

The young man was much embarrassed. He had an innate horror of seeming niggardly, and the course he had taken made his position more delicate. But his simplicity and truthfulness came to his aid, and he said firmly, although with a crimson face, "I am sorry I cannot accept your generous proposition, but I will give in accordance with my ability. I can give only five dollars.''

Mr. Dimmerly and Mrs. Marchmont looked annoyed, while Addie gave utterance to an audible titter. Bel laughed, and then looked as if she had done wrong.

But Lottie, with graceful tact, which was still only good acting, said: "And that, I am sure, is all that can be asked of Mr. Hemstead or of any one. But the poor man shall not lose the money, Julian, for I will supply Mr. Hemstead with what is lacking.''

"Pardon me, Miss Marsden, I cannot take it.''

"Not even for this needy minister with his six children?''

"I cannot sacrifice my self-respect for any one,'' he said. "Why cannot Mr. De Forrest give what he wishes without imposing a condition which leaves it doubtful whether he is to give at all?''

"Oh, yes, he is to give,'' said Lottie, promptly. "I take your offer, Julian. It's delightful to have such a genuine object of charity as a minister living on six hundred a year.''

This was spoken very innocently, but was in reality a keen thrust at Hemstead, who had so recently stated his prospective income at that sum. That the others understood it as such was shown by their significant glances, as they rose from the table.

Hemstead could not discover from Lottie's face whether she meant a covert allusion to himself or not.

Harcourt drove over to town, promising to be back in time. The other young people said that the long drive had made them drowsy, and retired to their rooms for a nap. Hemstead went to the parlor and tried to read, but his thoughts wandered strangely. The beautiful face of Lottie Marsden haunted him, and the puzzling contradictions of her words and manner kept rising in his mind for solution. After a prolonged revery, he came to the conclusion: "I have left nothing ambiguous about myself. If she is friendly after this she knows just who and what I am. It's plain the others think me no addition to their company, and I'm almost sorry I accepted aunt's invitation. However, I can shorten the visit if I choose;" and he turned resolutely to his book.

Instead of donning her wrapper, as did Bel, Lottie sat down before the fire, and, as was often her custom, commenced half-talking to her friend and familiar, and half-thinking aloud to herself.

"Well, he is the frankest and most transparent man I ever saw. I have been acquainted with him but a few hours, and I feel that I know him better than I do Julian, with whom I have been intimate so many years."

"He's sincerely, honestly good, too," said Bel. "I think it's too bad, Lottie, that you all treat him so. It's really wicked."

"Yes," said Lottie, meditatively. "It's a good deal more wicked than I thought it would be."

"Then you will give it up?"

"No, indeed. I haven't said that."

"How can you do it, Lottie, when you know it is wrong?"

"I knew it was wrong when I commenced. I only know now that it is a little more wrong. Why should I give up my fun on that account? I might as well die for an old black sheep as a speckled lamb."

Bel yawned at the rather peculiar and tragic ending that Lottie suggested for herself, and was soon dozing on a lounge. But either a restless spirit of mischief, or a disturbed conscience, prevented Lottie from following her example.

It would at times seem true that, when engaged in something that conscience forbids, the very opposition incites and leads to the evil. The conflict between inclination and the sense of right creates a feverish unrest, in which one cannot settle down to ordinary pursuits and duties. If principle holds the reins, and the voice of conscience is clear and authoritative, the disturbed mental and moral state will end in the firm choice of duty, and consequent peace and rest. But if, as in the case of Lottie Marsden, impulse rules in the place of principle, and conscience is merely like a half-dreaded, reproachful face, this unrest is the very hour and opportunity for temptation. Some escape from self and solitude must be found; some immediate excitement must engross the thoughts; and the very phase of evil against which conscience is vainly protesting has at the same time the most dangerous fascination.

So Lottie escaped from her own self-reproaches as a naughty child runs away from a scolding, and was soon at the parlor entrance with a noiseless tread, a grace of motion, and a motive that suggested the lithe panther stealing on its prey. The door was ajar, and a hasty glance revealed that the object of her designs was alone. Her stealthy manner changed instantly, and she sauntered into the room with quiet indifference, humming an air from Faust.

"Oh, you are here!" she exclaimed, as if suddenly becoming aware of his presence. "Why do you not take a nap like the others? I hope you are not troubled by a bad conscience."

"What suggested a bad conscience, Miss Marsden?"

"Your sleeplessness."

"I am glad it was not your own. Why are you not taking a nap? I thought you started for one."

"So I did, but found I did not want it. But you are not a Yankee that you must answer my question with another. What are you reading? Won't you read it to me?"

"I would rather not read this book to you; but I will any other that you wish."

"You must learn human nature better, Mr. Hemstead. Don't you know that you have said just enough to make me wish that book and no other? What is is about?"

"I feel sure that it will have no interest for you. It is one of the latest infidel attacks upon the Bible."

"Oh, you are afraid to have me read it."

"Yes; but not for the reasons implied in your tone."

"Don't you see that you are taking the very course to awaken my curiosity, and to make me wish to hear just that book? If you had said, 'Certainly, I'll read it to you, but you won't like it, for it's only a dry, heavy book upon a heavy subject,' I would never have looked into it, but would have asked for something else."

"That would hardly be true, Miss Marsden. Though I regard it as an evil and dangerous book, it is exceedingly clever, and well written, and it is quite popular in some circles. I suppose it has been sent up to Aunt Marchmont with other new books of note."

"I must certainly read it, since you won't read it to me. Forbid a child to do a thing, you know, and you have given the strongest motive for doing just that thing."

"You are not a child, Miss Marsden."

"What am I, then?"

"I hardly know; but you are capable of realizing one's best ideal, almost."

"Almost! thank you."

"Perhaps my language is stronger than you realize. The woman who could answer to my ideal would be nearly perfect."

"And do you think such a paragon would go out among the border ruffians with you?"

"No, nor anywhere else with me. I was speaking of my ideal."

"You do not expect to marry your ideal, then?"

"I suppose love transfigures the one we love, and that this is the only way we can ever meet our ideal in this life. But sometimes we see one who it seems might approach even the ideal of our unbiased fancy."

"It is well that you admire these exquisite creatures at a distance," she said, dryly. "I can't see why men will always be so foolish as to think pretty women are good women. But if I am not a child why may I not read that book? You intimate that it will not shake my belief."

"I do not think it would—at least I hope it would not."

"You are not sure."

"I'm sure it will not shake the Bible. Every age has teemed with infidel books. Yet God's Word stands to-day as strong and serene as that mountain yonder, to which the setting sun has given a crown of light."

"Your figure is pretty, but unfortunate. The sun is indeed 'setting,' and soon the mountain will lose its crown of light and vanish in darkness."

"But does it vanish," he asked quickly, "in the transient darkness, like a cloud tipped with light? Such a cloud is a fit emblem of this brilliant book, and of multitudes like it that have preceded, but which, like lurid vapors, have vanished from men's thought and memory. Even with my immature mind I can detect that this clever work is but an airy castle, soon to fall. What infidel book has ever gained or kept a lasting hold upon the popular heart? Let the darkness swallow up the mountain there. If we go where it is at midnight, we shall find it intact, and just as firm as when the sun is shining upon it. The searching light of every day, from year to year and age to age, will find it there just the same. The long night of moral darkness which culminated in the fifteenth century, though it hid the Bible, did not destroy it. Luther at last found and brought it out into the broad light of general study and criticism. For generations it has been assailed on every side, but it stands in the calm, unchanging strength that yonder mountain would maintain, were it surrounded by children shooting against it with arrows. Believe me, I do not fear for the Bible. If all the light of human knowledge were turned upon it in one burning focus, its intrinsic truth would only be revealed more clearly; and if superstition, as in the past, or infidelity, as was the case in France, creates temporary darkness, the moment that, in the light of returning reason, men look for the Bible, they find it like a great solemn mountain, that

cannot be moved while the world lasts, just where God
has placed it.''

"Mr. Hemstead, don't you know that young gentlemen
o not talk to young ladies as you do to me?"

"You know very well that I am not a society-man."

"Oh, I'm not complaining. I rather like to be talked to
as if I had some brains, and was not a doll. If you are so
sure about the Bible, why do you fear to have me read arguments against it?"

"I am not so sure about you. If I should listen to a
plausible story against you, without knowing you or giving
you a fair hearing, I might come to be prejudiced—to believe you very unworthy—when the reverse would be true.
So the minds of many, from reading books of this nature,
and not giving the Bible a fair hearing, become poisoned
and prejudiced.''

"Then why do you read it?"

"For the same reason that would influence a physician
to study a disease—not that he may catch it, but that he
may understand and know how to treat it. This book is
a mental and moral disease, and I do not wish you to run
the risk of catching it, though I do not think it would
prove fatal if you did. Your own heart and experience
would probably correct the error of your head. Such
books as these won't answer in times of illness or deep
trouble. We turn from them as instinctively and certainly as we do from noise, glare, and gayety."

The mountain without was now in the shadow. The
early twilight of the December evening had darkened the
wintry landscape; but the ruddy glow of the hickory fire
revealed how beautiful Lottie's face could be, when composed into womanly truth and thoughtfulness.

"I have never had a serious sorrow or illness, and I
wonder what I should do if I had?" she queried musingly,
as these sombre events, which sooner or later must come
into every life, rose up before her.

"I know well what you will do when they come, as come

they will to us all," said Hemstead, gently. "As surely as
you would cling to a strong arm were you sinking in deep
waters, just so surely you will turn to the Bible, and to
Him who said, 'Let not your heart be troubled, neither let
it be afraid.'"

The truth, if given a hearing, is ever powerful—the
truths of our own sad experience—the answering and
remedial truth of God.   Unexpectedly and unintentionally
on her part, both these phases of truth had gained the ear
of Lottie Marsden.   The sorrowful and suffering days of the
future threw back their shadows upon her, and her heart
sank at their prospect; and with the certainty of intuition
she recognized the answering truth, and felt that she would
indeed be glad to cling to One who had the right and power
to utter such tender, reassuring words as Hemstead had
quoted.

Of all spells, that of truth is the strongest.   Under it
the impulsive girl buried her face in her hands and, with
a quick sob, cried, "Oh, that I were better!"

Then, springing up, she gave Hemstead a strange, earnest look through her tears, as if she would read his soul.
But she saw only honest sympathy.

He was about to speak again, but she abruptly left the
room.

CHAPTER VIII

FINDING ONE'S LEVEL

LOTTIE met De Forrest on the stairs, and he was about to apologize for his long sleep, but she rushed by him like a summer gust. A moment later she burst into her room and startled indolent Bel out of her last luxurious doze by dropping into a chair by the fire and indulging in what girls call a "good cry."

"What is the matter?" asked Bel, anxiously.

Lottie's tears were the only answer.

"What has happened?" cried Bel, rising hastily. "Let me call auntie or Julian."

"If you call either you are no friend of mine," said Lottie, springing to the door, locking it, and taking the key.

"Why, Lottie, I don't understand—"

"There is no need that you should. Nothing is the matter—only I'm blue—I've been thinking of awful things. I was in one of my moods this afternoon, now I'm in one of my tenses."

"Unusually intense, I should think. I have not seen you so moved since Tom Wellesly threatened to blow out his brains for you."

"He hadn't any to blow out," snapped Lottie, "or he wouldn't have thought of doing it for such a girl as I am."

"Well," sighed Bel, who at times was one of Job's comforters, "I've heard he has never been the same since."

"I hope he has been wiser, then. How can men be such stupid owls as to fall in love with me! Can't they see I'm a wicked little heathen?"

"That is just the kind men like," sneered Bel, misanthropically. "You expect to captivate (and of course you will) this sincere and saintly young minister. He already thinks that you are by far the best of our party, and has some of the first symptoms that your victims usually manifest."

Lottie sprang up, dashed away her tears, and commenced restlessly pacing the room.

"Bother on the men," she exclaimed. "Why will they be so silly! The world's a perfect jumble, and we are all lunatics and fools, crying for what is not good for us, and turning our backs upon what is. I'm disgusted with everybody, and myself in particular. Now if this overgrown student makes a fool of himself, like the others, I shall lose faith in mankind, and I know there is nothing to hope from womankind."

"I should think you were having a mood and a tense at the same time this evening," said Bel, looking with some surprise at her friend. "What has stirred you up so? Have you and Julian had a quarrel?"

"We shall have plenty more, I foresee," said Lottie, seizing on the suggestion to hide the truth. Bel smiled satirically. All these harsh words were but the harmless lightnings of a summer gust that was passing away.

"It's only a lovers' tiff," she thought, "and now the billing and cooing are to come."

"Oh, well," said Bel, soothingly, "you and Julian will soon make up, and then you and all the world will change for the better."

"We have made up," said Lottie faintly, finding, like many another sinner in this line, that the first fib requires the second to cover it up.

"Well, well; get over your mood quickly, for the supper-bell will ring in a moment, and you are not ready to come down."

What emergency of life can obliterate from the mind of a pretty woman the necessity of a toilet? To Bel, Lottie seemed to come to her senses at once as she sped to her bureau and commenced brushing her rumpled hair. But the languid maiden was quite startled as Lottie wheeled suddenly upon her, declaring, while she brandished the hairbrush in the most tragic and impresive manner, "If that Hemstead makes a fool of himself he may, but he shall do it with his eyes open; I will not deceive him any more."

Thus conscience, that had been skirmishing all day, appeared to gain one point of advantage, and Lottie, having made this virtuous resolve, gained in mental serenity, while the mirror that reflected her fair face helped to bring back her complacency.

"Bel,"said Lottie, as they were leaving their room, "not a whisper of all this to any one, as you value my friendship."

But before they reached the supper-room her resolution failed, as is often the case when one acts from impulse rather than principle. She found that she could not so lightly throw away Hemstead's good opinion. She had been admired, loved, and flattered to her heart's content, but the respect, esteem, and trust of a sincere, true man formed a new offering, and it was so attractive that she could not bring herself to turn from it at once. Then her strong pride cast its weight into the scale, and she thought: "He talks to me and treats me as if I were a woman of heart and mind, and I'm going down to show him I'm a wicked fool. I shall not do it, at least not now. Little fear but that the disagreeable truth will come out soon enough."

"But it is wrong to deceive him," whispered conscience.

"Suppose it is," answered the wayward will, "I am all wrong myself and always have been."

"You promised to show him your real self," still urged conscience.

"Well, I will, some other time."

With conscience thwarted and unsatisfied, serenity vanished again, and instead of being reckless and trivial at the table, as she intended, she was rather silent, and a trifle sullen, as one often is even when vexed with one's self.

Hemstead was expecting a subdued and thoughtful

young lady to appear, whose pensive manner would indicate a nature softened and receptive. While her bearing
was not what he anticipated, it was somewhat akin, and
showed, he thought, that the truth was not without effect.

De Forrest was still more puzzled; but soon concluded
that Lottie was provoked that he had slept so long instead
of devoting himself to her. True, she had just come from
the parlor, where he found Hemstead standing by the window, looking out into the gloom, but she had found him,
no doubt, so heavy and stupid that she had rushed to her
room in a fit of vexation. This theory was entirely recon-
cilable with his vanity, and therefore conclusive; and he
tried to make amends by excessive gallantry, which only
annoyed Lottie. This he ascribed to her resentment for his
neglect, and only redoubled his unwelcome attentions.

While Hemstead's heart was in a tumult of joy and
thankfulness that so early in his acquaintance, and so unexpectedly, he had been able to speak to her as he wished
and with such seeming effectiveness, he had the good taste
and tact to indicate by no words or sign that anything unusual had occurred between them. He sought to draw the
others, and even De Forrest, into general conversation, so
that Lottie might be left more to herself.

With a mingled smile and frown, she recognized his purpose, and with a reckless laugh in her own soul, thought,
"He imagines I am near conversion, when I never felt so
wicked before in my life."

But catching a glimpse of Bel's surprised face, and seeing that her abstraction was noted by the others, she speedily rallied, and assumed the manner that she had maintained
throughout the day.

"It is so delightful to see his large gray eyes turn toward
me wistfully and trustingly, that I cannot undeceive him
yet;" and so conscience was dismissed, as history records
has been often the case with some honest old counsellor in
a foolish and reckless court.

The prospective sleigh-ride and donation party were the

prominent themes, and they hastened through the meal that they might start early.

Upon this occasion De Forrest managed to get the seat by Lottie, in his eagerness to make amends, and Hemstead sat opposite with Bel. As far as he could gather in the uncertain moonlight, Hemstead thought that De Forrest's attentions were not particularly welcome, and, though he scarcely knew why, was glad. He would probably explain by saying that De Forrest was not worthy of her.

Lottie's periods of depression never lasted long, and again the frosty air and quick motion set her blood tingling with life. In order to escape De Forrest's whispered sentimentalities, she began to sing. Her naturally good voice had been somewhat injured by straining at difficult music, under superficial instruction, instead of thorough training for it, but within a moderate compass, and in simple music, was sweet and strong.

De Forrest was enthusiastic in his praise of selections that were beyond her abilities. Though most of the airs were unfamiliar to Hemstead, he was satisfied that they were incorrect, and certain that the music was not over good. Therefore he was silent. This piqued Lottie, for one of her purposes in the choice of what she sang was to impress him, from the barbarous West, with the idea of her superior culture. At last she said, "I fear you do not like operatic and classical music very much, Mr. Hemstead?"

"We do not often hear such music very perfectly rendered in our part of the West. There are airs from the opera that are very pretty;" and he suggested one that was simple.

The truth began to dawn on the quick-witted girl, but De Forrest said, patronizingly, "It requires a cultivated taste to appreciate such music as you were singing, Miss Lottie."

"It is not with the music probably, but my rendering of it, that Mr. Hemstead finds fault."

"Two of the airs were new to me, and the other I have heard but seldom," said Hemstead, evasively.

"How about that one?" asked De Forrest.

"Well, in sincerity then, I think Miss Marsden does herself injustice by attempting music that would tax the powers of a prima donna."

"The boor!" whispered De Forrest to Lottie.

After a moment she said firmly, "Mr. Hemstead has only said plainly what you thought, Julian."

"Oh, Miss Lottie—" he began to protest.

"I'm not a fool," she continued, "so please don't waste your breath. You have heard all the star singers, and know how ridiculously far beneath them I fall, when I try to sing their music. I think you might have told me. It would have been truer kindness than your hollow applause. Why our teachers make us the laughing-stock of society, by keeping us upon these absurd attempts at music beyond us, to the exclusion of everything else, is something that I can't understand. My ear is not over nice, but I have always had a suspicion that I was executing, in the sense of murder, the difficult *arias* that the old weazen-faced Italian professor kept me at till brother Dan said, in truth, that I was turning into a screech-owl. But no one, save he and Mr. Hemstead, has been honest enough to tell me the truth. Thus, on many occasions, I have taxed the politeness of people to the utmost, no doubt, and been the cause of innumerable complimentary fibs, like those you have just been guilty of, Julian. Perhaps, Mr. Hemstead, you think a style of music like this more suited to my powers;" and she struck into a well-known plantation song.

"No," said he, laughing, "I think you do yourself still greater injustice."

"You probably think I cannot sing at all."

"On the contrary, I think you have an unusually good voice. I wish you would sing that air that you were humming when you came into the parlor this afternoon. I liked that, and imagine it is suited to your voice."

"What was it? Oh, I remember. An air from Faust, that Marguerite sings at her spinning-wheel. I think I can give that pretty decently."

She sang it sweetly, with taste and some power. Hemstead's appreciation was hearty, and she knew it was sincere.

"Now that you have done me such good service," she said laughing, "and shown that mediocrity is my musical position, let us have some old-fashioned ballads, and all sing them together in sleigh-riding style."

"Pardon me, Miss Marsden, I assign you to mediocrity in nothing."

"Oh, no, not you; my own abilities place me there. But come, each one sing;" and she commenced a ballad, well known to the others, but not to him.

It sounded very well indeed, only Harcourt's bass was much too light for the other voices.

"Why don't you sing?" asked Lottie of Hemstead.

"I do not know the air or words."

"Shall we try Old Hundred?" asked De Forrest. "Ahem! The long metre doxology.

"'Praise God from whom all blessings flow.'"

Addie and Harcourt joined in laughingly. Bel began with them, but stopped when she saw that Lottie did not sing.

"Do you believe that 'all blessings flow' from God?" asked Hemstead of De Forrest.

"I suppose so, according to Old Hundred," he said lightly.

"You don't 'suppose so' at all, Julian. You know it, as we all do, however we may act," said Lottie, with emphasis.

"With such a belief, I would at least treat Him with respect," said Hemstead, quietly. "I should be sorry to be under deep and continued obligations to One toward whom I failed in ordinary courtesy."

"I knew it was wrong," muttered Bel, "but—"

"I have no such belief," said Harcourt, "so your sharp homily does not apply to me."

"Where do your blessings come from?" asked Hemstead.

"Well, those I don't get out of my clients, from where this snow does—the laws and forces of nature."

"Your faith is like the snow, I think—very cold."

"If it's cold in winter, it's warm in summer," retorted he, flippantly; and Addie giggled approvingly, for the reason that it sounded flippant and smart.

They had now reached the hamlet of Scrub Oaks, in the centre of which was a small house that seemed bursting with light and noise. Whenever the door opened it appeared to fly open from a pressure within.

De Forrest acted as escort to the ladies, while Hemstead accompanied Harcourt in his effort to find a sheltered place for the horses. This pleased the young lawyer, and he said, good-naturedly, "Don't think, Mr. Hemstead, that I do not respect your honest convictions, and I meant no slur upon them. You take things too seriously."

"I suppose we all ought to make more allowance for what is said in mere sport and repartee," said Hemstead. "But what to you is law and force is to me a personal Friend. You know that there are some names—like those of mother and wife—that are too sacred for jest."

"Thus people misjudge and misunderstand each other, simply because they see things from different points of view," replied Harcourt. "De Forrest provokes me, however. He has no doubts worthy of the name, for he reads nothing save the sporting news and fashionable literature of the day, and yet he likes to give the impression that he is in with us, who read *books* and think."

"If you will only read fairly, Mr. Harcourt, I have no fears but that in time you will think rightly. An honest jury must hear both sides and have no prejudices."

The young men now sought the rest of the party, who had squeezed their way into the little parsonage. It was so replete with life and bustle that it appeared like a social bombshell, with effervescing human nature as an explosive material, and might burst into fragments at any moment.

CHAPTER IX

"THE OTHER SET"

THE minister and his wife were scarcely host and hostess on this occasion, as a self-appointed committee of ladies had taken upon themselves the duty; but, like all corporations, this committee had no soul and a very indefinite body. No one knew just who they were, or where to find them, and some of the members, in the bewilderment of unaccustomed official position and honors, seemed to have lost themselves, and bustled aimlessly all over the house. The more staid and practical sisters of the committee were down in the kitchen, breathlessly setting tables which were almost as speedily cleared by people whose appetites were as keen as the winter night without.

"I do declare," ejaculated Mrs. Gubling, as one devastating tableful rose lingeringly from the repast, and another flock began to gather in hungry expectancy at the door—"I do declare, I'm near beat out. Is this a starvin' community? At this rate they'll eat up all there is in the house, and the minister and his wife and babies into the bargain."

"Well," said Mrs. Rhamm, conveying the last bit of corned beef, which had been reluctantly left upon the plate as "manners," to a rather capacious mouth, "if they would eat up some of the babies it wouldn't be so bad. I don't see why poor ministers will have so many babies."

"The Lord takes care of 'em. We don't," suggested Mrs. Gubling.

"We all do our part, I s'pose. The worst of it is that it makes it oncomfortable for a church to give a small salary."

"I wish our church was more uncomfortable then. It's a shame we give Mr. Dlimm only six hundred. But come, if we don't git another table set they'll eat us up."

"I'd like to see 'em," said Mrs. Rhamm, with a disdainful sniff.

"Well, you be a bit old and tough," chuckled Mrs. Gubling.

With the solace of this sally, which seemed true, if not true wit, these hard-featured mothers in Israel set about their tasks with the deftness that long experience gives.

At the time De Forrest conveyed the ladies into the hall, the upstairs members of the committee were buzzing around somewhere else, for there was no one to receive them. They were gradually hustled or carried into the parlor or main room, and here Hemstead and Harcourt found them in characteristic conditions. Addie's and De Forrest's elegant noses were decidedly *retrousses;* Bel appeared both disgusted and frightened; while Lottie's face wore an expression of intense and amused curiosity. She was seeing "the other set" to her heart's content, and all was as new and strange as if she had visited another land.

Harcourt joined Addie, and they began to whisper satirical criticisms on the remarks and manners of those around. Hemstead's interest mainly centred in watching Lottie, and in noting the effect of her contact with plain and uncultured people. He was glad he did not see the repulsion of a little mind and a narrow nature, as was the case with most of the others. Though it was evident that she had no sympathy with them, or for them, there was intelligent interest and wide-awake curiosity. While the others were incasing themselves in exclusive pride, she was eager to investigate and get *en rapport* with this new phase of humanity. But trammelled by her city ideas, she felt that she could not speak to any one without the formality of an introduction. But the ice was broken for her unexpectedly. Feeling her dress pulled, she turned and found a very stout old lady sitting near her, who asked in a loud whisper, "Been down to supper yet?"

"No," said Lottie, "I don't wish any."

"I do, but I'm afeard I won't get none. You see I'm big and clumsy anyway, and now I'm so lame with the rheumatiz that I kin hardly move."

"It's too bad," said Lottie, pathetically, but with a swift comical glance at the others.

"Yes, it's kinder orful to be so helpless," said the old woman, with a complacent sigh, delighted at having a sympathetic auditor. "I'm dreadfully afeard I won't git no supper. I'm like the withered man at the pool of Bethesdy. Whenever they are ready for another batch 'while I'm a-comin' another steppeth down before me.'"

"Well, you're not very much withered, that's one comfort to be thankful for," said Lottie.

"I'd like to be thankful for my supper, if I could only git a chance," persisted the old woman.

"You shall have a chance. When is the pool troubled? When shall we put you in?"

"There! now is the time," said her new acquaintance, dropping her affected and pious tone, and speaking with sharp eagerness. "See, one batch is comin' up, and 'nother is going down."

"Mr. Hemstead, will you assist me in escorting this old lady to the supper-table?"

Hemstead's face was aglow with approval, and he instantly complied, while the others, understanding Lottie better, were convulsed with laughter.

It was no easy thing for them unitedly to manage the hobbling mountain of flesh. When they came to the steep, narrow stairway, matters were still more serious.

"You shall go first," whispered Lottie to Hemstead, "for if she should fall on me, good-by, Lottie Marsden."

Hemstead patiently, carefuly, and with the utmost deference, assisted the helpless creature down the stairs.

"You're as polite to her as if she were a duchess," said Lottie, in a low tone.

"She is more than a duchess. She is a woman," he replied.

Lottie gave him a quick, pleased look, but said, "Such old-fashioned chivalry is out of date, Mr. Hemstead."

"He's right, miss," said the old woman, sharply. "I'm not Dutch."

Lottie dropped behind to hide her merriment at this speech, and Hemstead appeared, with his charge clinging to his arm, at the kitchen door, which her ample form nearly filled.

"My sakes alive! Auntie Lammer, how did you get down here?" said Mrs. Gubling. "We hain't ready for you yet."

"No matter," said Mrs. Lammer, "I thank the marcies I've got down safe, and I'm goin' to stay till I git my supper."

"Can I help you?" asked Lottie, glancing curiously around the room.

They looked with even more curiosity at her; and a strange contrast she made, in her rich and tasteful costume and rare beauty, with those plain, middle-aged, hard-working women, and the small, dingy room.

For a moment they stared at her without reply, then gave each other a few suggestive nudges; and Mrs. Rhamm was about to speak rather slightingly, when good-natured Mrs. Gubling said: "You are very kind, miss, but you don't look cut out for our work. Besides, my dear, it's an orful dangerous place down here. I'm afraid we'll git eat up ourselves before the evening is over. I'm sure you would be, if you stayed. I wouldn't mind taking a bite myself;" and the good woman and her assistants laughed heartily over this standing joke of the evening, while Auntie Lammer, seeing that Mrs. Gubling was the leading spirit of the supper-room, quivered in all her vast proportions with politic and propitious mirth.

All this was inexpressibly funny to Lottie, who had the keenest sense of the absurd, and with a sign to Hemstead she drew him away, saying, "This exceeds any play I ever saw. I didn't know people who were not acting could be so queer and comical."

"Well, Miss Lottie," he said, as they ascended the stairs, "I admit that humanity everywhere often has its ridiculous side, but I have been laughed at too much myself to enjoy laughing at others."

"And why should you be laughed at so much?"

"I suppose it is the fate of overgrown, awkward boys, who have a tendency to blurt out the truth on all occasions."

"Such a tendency as that will always make you trouble. I assure you."

"It hasn't with you, yet."

"Our acquaintance has been very brief."

"And yet I seem to know you so well! I would not have believed it possible in one short day."

"I think you are mistaken. But you have ceased to be a stranger to me. I have remarked before to-day, that I knew you better than some I have seen from childhood."

"I am happy to say that I wish to conceal nothing."

"Few can say that."

"Oh, I don't mean that I am better than other people, only that it's best to appear just what we are. People should be like coin, worth their face—"

"I was in search of you," interrupted De Forrest, as they stood talking a moment near the head of the stairs in the hall. "We did not know but that the sylph you escorted away had made a supper of Hemstead, with you as a relish. Have you seen enough of this bear-garden yet?"

"No, indeed," said Lottie; "I'm just beginning to enjoy myself."

From openly staring at and criticising the party from Mrs. Marchmont's, the young people began to grow aggressive, and, from class prejudices, were inclined to be hostile. There were whispered consultations and finally one habitué of the store and tavern thought he could cover himself with glory by a trick, and at the same time secure a kiss from Lottie, the prettiest. The conspiracy was soon formed. A kissing game in one of the upper room was suspended for a moment, and one of the tall girls accompanied him down as if they were a delegation, and on the principle that in designs against a woman a female confederate is always helpful in disarming suspicion.

He approached Lottie with the best manners he could assume, and said, "We are having some games upstairs. Perhaps you would like to join us. We'd like to have you."

"Do come," added the tall girl; "they are real nice."

"Certainly," said Lottie, who was now ready for another adventure. "Come; let us all go."

"The others needn't come unless they want to," said the young man; for he didn't relish the lawyer's presence, whom he knew by reputation, nor the searching look of the tall stranger whom he did not know.

"Mr. Hemstead, you and Julian come," said Lottie, and as they ascended the stairs she studied this new specimen of Scrub Oaks, who was a loafer of the village as De Forrest was an idler of the town. They both belonged to the same genus, though the latter would have resented such a statement as the foulest insult.

The manners and the smart finery of her new acquaintance amused Lottie very much. When they reached the room, they found it full of whispering, giggling young people.

The tall girl, as instructed, said, "Now let us form a ring with our hands on this rope."

This having been done, she said, "Now, Mr. Shabb, you must go inside first"; and then, with a nudge to Lottie, she explained, "He'll try to hit our hands with his, and if he hits your hands you will have to go inside the ring."

What else he would do, she left to be disclosed by action. Then he of the flaming necktie and bulging cheek took his place with a twinkling eye that meant mischief. De Forrest and Hemstead declined to play, but the latter slipped forward and stood near Lottie. He was not sure, but dimly remembered seeing this game before, when it was not played so innocently as the tall girl had described.

The young rustic made extravagant but purposely vain efforts to strike the hands of others, and Lottie watched the scene with laughing curiosity. Suddenly he wheeled round and struck her hands sharply; and to her horrified surprise it seemed but a second later that his repulsive face was almost against her own. But something came between, and, starting back, she saw the baffled youth imprint a fervent kiss on the back of Hemstead's hand.

There was a loud laugh at him from those who had expected to laugh with him. He swaggered up to Hemstead, and said threateningly, "What do you mean?"

"What do *you* mean?" asked Lottie, confronting him with blazing eyes. "It is well this gentleman interposed. If you had succeeded in your insult I should have had you punished in a way that you would not soon forget."

"It's only part of the game," muttered he, abashed by her manner.

"Part of the game?"

"Yes," giggled the tall girl, faintly; "it's a kissing game."

"Did you know it was such?" asked Lottie, indignantly, of De Forrest and Hemstead.

"Indeed I did not," said De Forrest; "and if you say so I'll give this fellow the flogging, anyway."

"Come right out, and do it now," was the pert response.

"All I can say is, Miss Marsden," explained Hemstead, "that I suspected something wrong, and took means to prevent it. How these nice-looking girls can allow this fellow to kiss them is more than I can understand."

"No lady would," said Lottie, as she swept disdainfully

out; and under the withering influence of these remarks
kissing games languished the rest of the evening; only young
children, and a few of the coarser-natured ones, participating.
But soon the absurdity of the whole scene overcame Lottie,
and she laughed till the tears stood in her eyes.

As they were slowly descending the stairs a faded little
woman said, "I'm glad to see you enjoying yourself, Miss
Marchmont. It was very kind of you and your party to
come so far."

"I am not Miss Marchmont," said Lottie, "though I
came with her."

"Well, as the minister's wife, I would like her and all
her party to know of our grateful appreciation."

"You thank us beyond our deserts. But are you the
minister's wife? I am glad to make your acquaintance;"
and she held out her hand, which Mrs. Dlimm seemed glad
to take.

At this moment there came the cry of an infant from one
of the upper rooms.

"Oh, there goes my baby," said Mrs. Dlimm; "I thought
I heard it before"; and she was about to hasten on.

"May I not go with you and see the baby?" asked
Lottie.

What mother ever refused such a request? In a moment Lottie was in the one small room in which, on this
portentous occasion, the three younger children were hud-
dled, the others being old enough to take part in what, to
them, was the greatest excitement of their lives, thus far.

Lottie looked curiously around, with the quick appre-
ciative eye by which ladies seem to gather accurately at a
glance the effect of a costume and the style and character
of an apartment and its occupants. But she politely, and
from a certain innate interest, gave such attention to the
baby as to win the mother's heart. It was but an ordinary
baby, although the fattest and sturdiest member of a rather
pinched household; but Lottie wonderingly saw that to the
faded mother it was a cherub just from heaven.

Lottie could not understand it. A perfumed baby, in lace and muslin, might be a nice pet if the nurse were always within call; but the sole care of this chubby-cheeked Moloch, that would sacrifice its mother as unconsciously and complacently as the plant absorbs moisture, seemed almost as prosaic and dreadful as being devoured alive.

"Does no one help you take care of that child?" asked she.

"Well, my husband and the elder children help some."

"Haven't you a nurse for all these children?"

"No, indeed. It's as much as we can do to clothe and feed them."

"Don't you keep any servants at all?"

"Yes, we have a girl in the kitchen, but she's almost as much bother as she is worth."

"How do you get along?"

"I hardly know—somewhat as the birds do out of doors."

"Are you happy?"

"I've hardly time to think. I think I am, though—happy as most people. Some days bright, some days cloudy, and now and then a storm. That's the way it is with all, I imagine. We all have our crosses, you know, but by and by all will come right."

"I should be cross enough with all your crosses."

"They might make you patient. The crossest people I know are those who shun all crosses."

"Now I think of it, I'm inclined to believe that's true," said Lottie, reflectively. Then she whispered, as she walked softly to the mother's side, "Baby is going to sleep, isn't it?"

With different expressions they both peered into the full-moon face, two features of which, the eyes, were becoming obliterated by the white, drooping lids. Lottie looked as if she were examining a zoölogical specimen. Mrs. Dlimm gazed with a smile of deep content and tenderness.

The undisturbed rest of the child upon her bosom was

a type of her own mind at that moment. She was nature's child, God's child, and the babe was hers.

To the true and simple children of nature, who, without thought of self or the public eye, are quietly doing their duty in their own little niches, these moments of peace with strange thrills of joy are constantly coming. If this worn mother could look down upon the child, and her plain, pale face grow beautiful with spiritual light, how must the God who inspires all love—who is the source of tenderness—have regarded her?

The expression of this woman's face puzzled Lottie beyond measure. It was so incongruous, irreconcilable with the burdens, the weary cares, and ceaseless toil and anxiety of her lot. It was so out of keeping with the noisy throng and confused bustle that filled the house, and it dimly suggested to the proud belle a condition of mind before undreamt of in her philosophy.

Some new and curious thoughts stole into her heart as she watched the mother slowly rocking backward and forward, uttering a low, crooning lullaby—the gentlest sound that ever falls on mortal ears. For some reason there came into her soul a sudden loathing of her own selfishness and callousness.

After the child had been laid in the cradle, she asked, "What did you mean when yor said, 'It will all come right some day'?"

"Well, I suppose I meant that God's little children often get sorely perplexed with their cares and troubles in this world, but when we get home and sit down to rest and think it all over, it will then seem right."

"Home?"

"Yes, *home* in our Heavenly Father's house. That's the only real home we have. We only 'stop,' as the Irish say, here and there for a little while in this world."

"And do you think of heaven as a pleasant home and rest after what seems to me your very hard life?"

"Certainly. How do you think of it?"

"Well, to tell the truth, I have not thought much about it."

Before Mrs. Dlimm could reply, there came anything but a heavenly interruption. It was as if Moses and Aaron were within the cool and shadowy tabernacle, feasting on spiritual manna, and there came a delegation from the Hebrew camp, clamoring for the "leeks and onions of Egypt."

Though the congregation often said, "It's a pity Mrs. Dlimm is such a meek and quiet little woman," and though the self-appointed committee of ladies was so large, and the minister himself was downstairs, yet when the first real emergency of the evening arose, the upstairs members of the committee were helpless, and the best thing Mrs. Gubling, the leading spirit downstairs, could do, was to "slick up," as she said, and "go tell the parson's wife." But seeing Mr. Dlimm on the way, she beckoned him aside with a portentous nod. He, poor man, heard her tidings with dismay. He had fallen into the habit of taking all his difficulties either to the Lord or to his wife, and in this case he felt that both must come to his aid.

With Mrs. Gubling he at once hastened to the nursery, and entered rather abruptly.

Mrs. Dlimm raised her finger impressively, then pointed to the cradle.

"But, my dear—" began her husband, rather impatiently.

"Hush," said the wife, in a low tone; "whatever's the matter don't wake the baby, for then I can't do anything."

"Mrs. Dlimm," said Mrs. Gubling, "they've eat up about everything there is downstairs, 'cept me, and there's three tables yet. It's such a fine night, and the sleighing's so good, that lots more have come than we expected. I don't know how much money they brought, but they hain't brought provisions enough."

"What shall we do?" asked Mr. Dlimm, nervously.

"If it takes the last penny we have in the world," said his wife, with grave dignity, "no one shall leave our house hungry. You must step over to the store, Mr. Dlimm, and buy enough to satisfy every one."

"I feel just as you do, my dear," he said, with the air of one who sees duty clearly, though it is far from being agreeable. "Just give me our poor little hoard from your bureau drawer, and I'll go at once."

Lottie witnessed the scene with mingled amusement and indignation, and then, her face aglow with a sudden purpose, sped away also.

CHAPTER X

HUMAN NATURE

THE dismal tidings from the lower regions, that the larder had been stripped and that scarcely even a pie remained, soon became an open secret, about which every one was whispering and commenting. The supperless wore a defrauded and injured air. The eyes of many who had not left so important a duty to the uncertainties of the future, but, like Auntie Lammer, had availed themselves of the first opportunity, now twinkled shrewdly and complacently. They had the comfortable consciousness of taking care of themselves. But the greater number were honestly indignant and ashamed that such a thing should have happened. This feeling of mortification was increased when the committee reported but a small sum of money handed in as yet. The majority were provoked at others, and a few at themselves, for having brought so little. As the situation became clearer, all began to act characteristically, some preparing to slink away and escape a disagreeable state of things, and others putting their heads together in the wish to remedy matters. Some giggled, and others looked solemn. Some tried to appear resigned, as if it were a dispensation of Providence, and others snarled about "them mean Joneses and Rhamms."

Lottie hastily summoned her party together, and told them of the dire emergency, as Mrs. Gubling had stated it.

"Now," said she, "if you gentlemen have got any wit worth the name, you must hit on some way of helping the parson out of his scrape, for I have taken a great interest in

him, or rather his wife. She is the queerest little woman
I ever saw. I shouldn't wonder if she were an angel in
disguise.''

"As you are undisguised," whispered De Forrest.

"Oh, be still, Julian. That compliment is as delicate as
Auntie Lammer's appetite. But see, some of these mean
'locusts of Egypt,' after eating their minister out of house
and home, are preparing to go. We must get a collection
before a soul leaves the house. Julian, you lock the back
door, and, Mr. Hemstead, you stand by the front door; and
now, Mr. Harcourt, you are a lawyer, and know how to talk
sharply to people: you give these cormorants to understand
what we expect them to do before they leave.''

Hemstead obeyed with alacrity; for the effort to help the
overburdened pastor of Scrub Oaks meet the rigors of winter
seemed about to end in disastrous failure. He had noticed,
with satisfaction, that many of the people shared his regret,
and wished to do something, but through lack of leadership
the gathering was about to break up, each one blaming some
one else, and all secretly mortified at the result.

Harcourt thought a moment, and then, stepping to a
position where he could be seen through open doors and
heard from the upper story, clapped his hands loudly to
secure silence and draw attention to himself.

"Do you know where your pastor has gone?" he asked.
"He is out now buying provisions with his own money to
feed a crowd who came here under the false pretence of
giving a donation, but, in truth, seemingly to eat him out
of house and home.''

Flushes of shame and anger flashed into nearly every
face at these stinging words, but Harcourt continued remorselessly: "You know who I am, and I thought I knew
something about you. I had heard that the people back
in the country were large-handed, large-hearted, and liberal,
but we must be mistaken. I think this the quintessence of
meanness, and if you break up to-night without a big collection I will publish you throughout the land. I want

you to understand that your minister has nothing to do with what I say. I speak on my own responsibility."

"Capital!" whispered Lottie. "That was red-hot shot, and they deserved it. If that don't drain their pockets, nothing will."

But she was not a little surprised and disgusted, when a stalwart young farmer stepped out, and with a face aflamed with anger, said in harsh emphasis: "I was sorry and ashamed to have this affair end as it promised to, and was going to come down handsomely myself, and try to get some others to, but since that sprig of the law has tried to bully and whip us into doing something, I won't give one cent. I want you to understand, Tom Harcourt, that whatever may be true of the people back in the country, you, nor no other man, can drive us with a horsewhip."

The young man's words seemed to meet with general approval, and there were many confirmatory nods and responses. They were eager to find some one to blame, and upon whom they could vent their vexation; and this aristocratic young lawyer, whose words had cut like knives, was like a spark in powder. Many could go away and half persuade themselves that if it had not been for him they might have done something handsome, and even the best-disposed present were indignant. It seemed that the party would break up, before the minister returned, in a general tumult.

The young farmer stalked to the front door, and said threateningly to Hemstead, "Open that door."

"No, don't you do it," whispered Lottie.

He threw the door open wide.

"Oh, for shame!" she said aloud; "I did not think that of you, Mr. Hemstead."

Without heeding her he confronted the young farmer and asked, "Do you believe in fair play?"

"Yes, and fair words, too."

"All right, sir. I listened quietly and politely to you. Will you now listen to me? I have not spoken yet."

"Oh, certainly," said the young farmer, squaring himself and folding his arms on his ample chest. "Let every dog have his day."

Hemstead then raised his powerful voice, so that it could be heard all through the house, and yet he spoke quietly and calmly.

"The gentleman who last addressed you now in the spirit of fair play offers to listen to me. I ask all present, with the same spirit of candor and politeness, to hear me for a few moments. But the door is open wide, and if there are any who don't believe in fair play and a fair hearing all around, they are at liberty to depart at once."

No one moved. And the young farmer said, with the sternness of his square face greatly relaxing, "You may shut the door, sir. We will all listen when spoken to in that style. But we don't want to be driven like cattle." Then, yielding further to the influence of Hemstead's courtesy, he stepped forward and shut the door himself.

"Thank you, sir," said Hemstead, heartily, and then continued: "I am a stranger among you, and am here to-night very unexpectedly. My home is in the West, and, like yourselves, I belong to that class who, when they give, give not from their abundance, but out of their poverty. There has been a mistake here to-night. I think I understand you better than my friend Mr. Harcourt. From the pleasantness of the evening more are present than you looked for. There are many young people here who I suspect have come from a distance, unexpectedly, for the sake of a ride and frolic, and were not as well prepared as if their households had known of it before. Long drives and the cold night have caused keen appetites. When the result became known a few moments ago, I saw that many felt that it was too bad, and that something ought to be done, and no one was more decided in the expression of this feeling than the gentleman who last spoke. All that was needed then, and all that is needed now, is to consider the matter a moment and then act unitedly. I ask you as Christian men and women, as humane, kind-hearted people, to dismiss from your minds all considerations save one—your pastor's need. I understand that he has six little children. A long, cold winter is before him and his. He is dependent upon you for the comforts of life. In return, he is serving the deepest and most sacred needs of your natures, and in his poverty is leading you to a faith that will enrich you forever. It is not charity that is asked. A church is a family, and you are only providing for your own. How could any of you be comfortable this winter if you knew your minister was pinched and lacking? The Bible says that the laborer is worthy of his hire. You have only to follow the impulse of your consciences, your own better natures, and I have no fears. A few moments ago your pastor had a painful surprise. You can have a very agreeable one awaiting him by the time he returns. You can make his heart glad for months to come, and so make your own glad. Though I am a stranger, as I said, and a poor man, yet I am willing to give double what I proposed at first, and if some one will take up a collection will hand in ten dollars."

"Give me your hand on that," said the young farmer, heartily; "and there's ten dollars more to deep it company. When a man talks like that, I am with him, shoulder to shoulder. Will some one bring me the dominie's hat?"
One was soon forthcoming.

"And now," said the young man, stepping up to Lottie, "you seem to take a sight of interest in this matter, miss. I think you can look five dollars out of most of the young chaps here. I'll go around with you, and see that each one comes down as he or she ought. If anybody ain't got what they'd like to give, I'll lend it to 'em, and collect it, too," he added, raising his strong, hearty voice.

Thus through Hemstead's words and action the aspect of the skies changed, and where a desolating storm had threatened there came a refreshing shower. What he had said commended itself to so many that the mean and crotchety found it politic to fall in with the prevailing spirit.

Amid approving nods, whispered consultations, and the hauling out of all sorts of queer receptacles for money, the graceful city belle and the blunt, broad-shouldered farmer started on an expedition that, to the six little Dlimms, would be more important than one for the discovery of the North Pole.

"No coppers now!" shouted the young man.

Lottie, fairly bubbling over with fun and enjoyment, was all graciousness, and with smiles long remembered by some of the rustic youth, certainly did beguile them into generosity at which they wondered ever after.

The result was marvellous, and the crown of the old hat was becoming a crown of joy indeed to the impoverished owner, who now had the promise of some royal good times.

That fast-filling hat meant nourishing beef occasionally, a few books for the minister's famishing mind, a new dress or two for the wife, and a warm suit for the children all round.

No one was permitted to escape, and in justice it could now be said that few wished to, for all began to enjoy the luxury of doing a good and generous deed.

When they had been to nearly all, Lottie said to her now beaming companion, "Go and get Mrs. Dlimm, and seat her in the large rocking-chair in the parlor."

The poor little woman, having witnessed all the earlier scenes from the stairs with strong and varying feelings, had, during the last few moments, seen Lottie pass with such a profusion of greenbacks in her husband's hat that in a bewildering sense of joy and gratitude she had fled to the little nursery sanctuary, and when found by some of the ladies was crying over the baby in the odd contradictoriness of feminine action. She was hardly given time to wipe her eyes before she was escorted on the arm of the now gallant farmer, to the chair of state in the parlor.

Then Lottie advanced to make a little speech, but could think of nothing but the old school-day formula; and so the stately introduction ended abruptly but most effectively, as follows:

"As a token of our esteem and kindly feeling, and as an expression of—of—I—we hereby present you with—with the reward of merit;" and she emptied the hat in the lady's lap.

Instead of graceful acknowledgment, and a neatly worded speech in reply, Mrs. Dlimm burst into tears, and springing up threw her arms around Lottie's neck and kissed her, while the greenbacks were scattered round their feet like an emerald shower. Indeed the grateful little woman, in her impulse, had stepped forward and upon the money.

The city belle, to her great surprise and vexation, found that some spring of her own nature had been touched, and that her eyes also were overflowing. As she looked around deprecatingly, and half-ashamed, she saw that there was a prospect of a general shower, and that many of the women were sniffling audibly, and the brusque young farmer stood near, looking as if he could more easily hold a span of runaway horses than he could hold in himself.

At this moment Hemstead stepped forward, and said: "My friends, we can learn a lesson from this scene, for it is true to our best nature, and very suggestive. Your pastor's wife standing there upon your gift that she may kiss the giver (for in this instance Miss Marsden but represents you and your feeling and action) is a beautiful proof that we value more and are more blessed by the spirit of kindness which prompts the gift than by the gift itself. See, she puts her foot on the gift, but takes the giver to her heart. The needs of the heart—the soul—are ever greater than those of the body, therefore she acknowledges your kindness first, because with that you have supplied her chief need. She does not undervalue your gift, but values your kindness more. Hereafter, as you supply the temporal need of your pastor, as I believe you ever will, let all be provided with the same honest kindness and sympathy. Let us also all learn, from this lady's action, to think of the Divine Giver of all good before his best earthly gifts."

Mrs. Dlimm had recovered herself sufficiently by this

time to turn to the people around her and say, with a
gentle dignity that would scarcely have been expected
from her: "The gentleman has truly interpreted to you
my very heart. I do value the kindness more even than
the money which we needed so sorely. Our Christian
work among you will be more full of hope and faith because of this scene, and therefore more successful."

Then, as from a sudden impulse, she turned and spoke
to Hemstead with quaint earnestness: "You are a stranger,
sir, but I perceive from your noble courtesy and bearing—
your power to appreciate and bring out the best there is in
us—that you belong to the royal family of the Great King.
Your Master will reward you."

Poor Hemstead, who thus far had forgotten himself in
his thought for others, was now suddenly and painfully
made conscious of his own existence, and at once became
the most helpless and awkward of mortals, as he found all
eyes turned toward him. He was trying to escape from the
room without stepping on two or three people—to Lottie's
infinite amusement, though the tears stood in her eyes as
she laughed—when Mrs. Gubling, ignorant of all that had
happened, appeared from the kitchen, and created a diversion in his favor.

The good woman looked as if pickles had been the only
part of the donation supper in which she had indulged, and
in a tone of ancient vinegar, said, "Them as hasn't eaten
had better come and take what they can git now."

A roar of laughter greeted this rather forbidding invitation. But, before any one could reply, Mr. Dlimm, red and
breathless from his exertions, also entered, and with a faint
smile and with the best courtesy he could master under the
trying circumstances, added: "I am sorry any of our friends
should have been kept waiting for supper. If they will now
be so kind as to step down, we will do the best we can for
them."

The good man was as puzzled by a louder explosion of
mirth as Mrs. Gubling had been. The stout farmer whis-

pered something to Lottie, and then, with an extravagant flourish, offered his arm to Mrs. Gubling.

"Go 'long with you," she said, giving him a push; but he took her along with him, while Lottie brought the parson to where his wife stood surrounded by greenbacks like fallen leaves, which in the hurry of events had not been picked up. The good man stared at his wife with her tearful eyes, and Mrs. Gubling stared at the money, and the people laughed and clapped their hands as only hearty country people can. Lottie caught the contagion, and laughed with them till she was ashamed of herself, while the rest of her party, except Hemstead, laughed at them and the "whole absurd thing," as they styled it, though Harcourt had a few better thoughts of his own.

Mrs. Rhamm's lank figure and curious face now appeared from the kitchen in the desire to solve the mystery of the strange sounds she heard, and the unheard-of delay in coming to supper. Lottie's coadjutor at once pounced upon her, and escorted, or rather dragged her to where she could see the money. She stared a moment, and then, being nearsighted, got down on her knees, that she might look more closely.

"She is going to pray to it," cried the farmer; and the simple people, aware of Mrs. Rhamm's devotion to this ancient god, laughed as if Sydney Smith had launched his wittiest sally.

"Mrs. Gubling," contiued the young man, "if you are not chairman of the committee, you ought to be, for you are the best man of the lot."

"I'd have you know I'm no man at all. It's no compliment to tell a woman she's like a man," interrupted Mrs. Gubling, sharply.

"Well, you've been a ministering angel to us all, this evening; you can't deny that; and I now move that you and the dominie be appointed a committee to count this money and report."

It was carried by acclamation.

"Now, while the iron is hot, I'm going to strike again. I move that we raise the dominie's salary to a thousand a year. We all know, who know anything, that he can't support his family decently on six hundred."

In the enthusiasm of the hour this was carried also by those who at the same time were wondering at themselves and how it all came about. Strong popular movements are generally surprises, but the springs of united and generous action are ever within reach, if one by skill or accident can touch them. Even perverted human nature is capable of sweet and noble harmonies, if rightly played upon.

CHAPTER XI

A POSSIBLE TRAGEDY

WHILE the money was being counted, Lottie led Mrs. Dlimm into the hall, and introduced her to Hemstead, saying, "This is the magician whose wand has transformed us all."

"You are the wand then," he said, laughing.

"What is the wand without the magician?" she asked, shyly watching the effect of her speech.

His quick flush bespoke the sensitive nature that it was becoming her delight to play upon, but he said: "According to legends, magic power was exerted in two ways—by a magician, as you suggested, and by ordinary mortals who happened to find a wand or spell or some potent secret by which they and any one could perform marvels. Now I assure you that I am the most ordinary of mortals, and without my wand I could not conjure at all."

Lottie gave him a look at this point which heightened his color, but he continued: "Miss Marsden, in her generosity, shall not give to me the credit for events which I trust will add a little sunlight to your life this winter, Mrs. Dlimm. It is to be shared chiefly by herself and that manly young fellow there, who is a member of your church, I suppose. It was Miss Marsden who brought us the tidings of the evil out of which this good has come. She not only took up the collection with such a grace that no one could resist, but she suggested the collection in the first place."

"What do you know about my irresistible grace? You haven't given me anything."

"You will place me in an awkward dilemma if you ask anything, for I have given you all the money I have with me," he said, laughing.

"Perhaps he would give himself," said simple, innocent Mrs. Dlimm, who, from Lottie's coquetry and the expression of Hemstead's eyes, imagined that an understanding or an engagement existed between them.

Lottie laughed, till the tears came, at Hemstead's blushing confusion, but said after a moment, "That would be a graceless request from me."

"I don't think you would have to ask twice," whispered Mrs. Dlimm.

"Did you ever hear of the man who was given a white elephant?" asked Lottie, in her ear.

"No, what about him?" said Mrs. Dlimm, simply.

Lottie laughed again, and putting her arm around the little lady said, aloud:

"Mrs. Dlimm, you and your baby could go right back to the Garden of Eden, and I rather think Mr. Hemstead could be your escort."

"I trust we are all going to a far better place," she replied, quickly.

"I fear I'm going the other way," said Lottie, shaking her head. But she was surprised at the expression of honest trouble and sympathy that came out upon the face of the pastor's wife.

"Miss Marsden does herself injustice," said Hemstead, quickly. "You have seen her action. All that I have seen of her accords with that."

"But you have not known me two days yet altogether," said Lottie.

"No matter. The last time I was in a picture gallery, I spent most of the time before one painting. I did not require weeks to learn its character."

"I shall judge you by your action, Miss Marsden," said Mrs. Dlimm, gratefully. "My creed forbids me to think ill of any one, and my heart forbids me to think ill of you.

Those tears I saw in your eyes a short time since became you better than any diamonds you will ever wear. They were nature's ornaments, and proved that you were still nature's child—that you had not in your city life grown proud, and cold, and false. It is a rare and precious thing to see outward beauty but the reflex of a more lovely spirit. Keep that spirit, my dear, and you will never lose your beauty even though you grow old and faded as I am. I wish I could see you again, for your full, sunny life has done me more good than I can tell you."

Again, Lottie's warm heart and impulsive nature betrayed her, and, before she thought, she exclaimed in sincerity: "I wish I deserved what you say, and I might be better if I saw more of such people as you and Mr. Hemstead. If he will drive me over to-morrow, I will come and see you. I think he will, for I haven't told you that he is a minister, and would, no doubt, like to talk to your husband."

"I might have known it," said the little woman, stepping forward and shaking Hemstead's hand most cordially. "I congratulate you, sir. You have chosen a princely calling—a royal one, rather—and can tread directly in the steps of the Son of God. I predict for you success—the success a true minister craves. You have the promise within you of winning many from evil."

"Believe me," said he, earnestly, "I would rather have that power than be a king."

"You may well say that, sir," she replied, with a dignity of which Lottie did not think her capable. "Any common man may have kingly power, and the meanest have cursed the world with it. But the power to win men from evil is godlike, and only the godlike have it."

Lottie looked curiously at the object of her practical jest. The words of the pastor's wife seemed to have drawn his thoughts away from the speaker and herself, and fixed them on his future work and its results. It is in such moments of abstration—of self-forgetfulness, when one's mind is dwelling on life's purposes and aims—that the spirit shines through the face, as through a transparency, and the true character is seen. Lottie saw Hemstead's face grow so noble and manly, so free from every trace of the meanness of egotism and selfishness, that in the depths of her soul she respected him as she had never any man before. Instinctively she placed Julian De Forrest, the rich and elegant idler, beside this earnest man, self-consecrated to the highest effort, and for the first time her soul revolted from her cousin with something like disgust.

What she had imagined became real at that moment, and De Forrest appeared, looking bored and uneasy.

"I have found you at last," he said. "We became so wedged in the parlor that there was no getting out, but now they have completed the laborious task of counting a sum that a bank clerk would run over in two minutes, and it is to be announced with a final flourish of trumpets. Then the stingy clodhoppers that you have inveigled into doing something that they will repent of with groanings that cannot be uttered to-morrow will go home resolving to pinch and save till they make good what they have given." He then added carelessly to Mrs. Dlimm, not waiting for an introduction, "I am surprised that you and your husband are willing to stay among such a people."

Before she could answer, he said to Lottie, "Are you ready to go home? Harcourt and Addie say we ought to start at once."

Lottie was provoked at his rudeness, and furtively watched Mrs. Dlimm's face, to see what impression he made upon her. Indeed her face was a study for a moment as she measured De Forrest's proportions with a slow, sweeping glance, which he thought one of admiration. But, instead of turning contemptuously or resentfully away, her face was pitiful.

They were now summoned to hear the result, but Lottie found opportunity to whisper to Mrs. Dlimm, "What do you think of him?"

"I don't know what to think. It is painfully evident that he is not a man."

Mrs. Dlimm's verdict had a weight with Lottie that she would hardly have believed possible a few hours before. There was a quaint simplicity and sincerity about her, an unworldliness, that gave her words something of the authority of the other world.

The abstraction that had been on Hemstead's face passed to Lottie's, and she heard with inattentive ear the young farmer say with hearty emphasis, "We present you, as an expression of our goodwill, with two hundred and fifty dollars."

She heard, but still did not heed the pastor's grateful reply. De Forrest whispered to her often, but her brow only contracted at his interruption to her busy thought. Suddenly she noted Hemstead's eye resting on her with a questioning expression. Then with a seeming effort she came out of her revery, and tried to be her old self again.

When Mr. Dlimm ceased, the farmer called out heartily: "Good for you, dominie. Now I call for a vote of thanks to the stranger who showed us a way out of our scrape. I understand that his name is the Rev. Mr. Hemstead. Also a vote of thanks to such a young lady as the city doesn't often send us, who, if she will permit a country compliment, is like the rose, good enough for a king, yet sweet to all. I call on both for a speech."

Lottie, blushing and laughing, declared that she was one who believed "that a woman should keep silence in meeting," and requested Hemstead to answer for both.

"Miss Marsden does not need words," said Hemstead. "She has a better kind of eloquence, and speaks to us through good and kindly deeds. My part in the happy results of this evening is slight. It is comparatively easy to suggest good and generous action, but it is harder to perform. It is one thing to preach, and quite another to practise. You have had the hard part—the practicing—and yet have done it as if it were not hard, as duty seldom is when performed in the right spirit; and therefore deserve the greater credit. If what you have done from generous impulse to-night you will henceforth do from steady principle, you will all have cause to remember this evening gratefully. That 'it is more blessed to give than receive' is true, not only because the Bible declares it, but because human experience proves it."

Loud applause followed these words, and then the farmer said, "Now, Mr. Harcourt, you are welcome to publish all you have seen at Scrub Oaks to-night."

At this Harcourt stepped forward and said: "Although not called on for a speech, I shall make a short one. I have learned a thing or two this evening. When I make a blunder I am not ashamed to acknowledge it. Mr. Hemstead and I both wished to bring about the same thing, only I went about it the wrong way, and he the right. What I then said as a threat, I now say as a promise. I shall write for our country paper a report of this meeting, and it will be greatly to your credit. I take back my former harsh words. I congratulate you on your action, and commend you for it."

"Give me your hand on that," cried the farmer. "Three cheers for Tom Harcourt. If you are ever up for office, sir, you may count on the vote of Scrub Oaks."

Thus, with cheery laughter and mutual good feeling, the eventful donation party broke up, leaving a happier family in the little parsonage than had ever dwelt there before.

In a few moments the party from Mrs. Marchmont's were on the road, though it proved difficult to hold the chilled and spirited horses long enough for them to get seated. De Forrest again took his place by Lottie, but she determined to make the conversation general.

"I've had a splendid time," she exclaimed, "and am very much obliged to you, Addie and Mr. Harcourt, for bringing me."

"I'm glad you enjoyed yourself," said Addie, "and hope

that you have now had enough of the 'other set,' as you call them. I don't see how you can endure them."

"Nor I either," said Bel, "although I suppose we ought to mingle with them occasionally. But I am tired to death."

"I was disgusted with them from first to last," said De Forrest—"the uncouth, ill-bred crew. I couldn't endure to see you, Miss Lottie, going around with that clodhopper of a farmer, and, worst of all, how could you touch that great mountain of flesh they called Auntie Lammer?"

"Many men of many minds," trilled out Lottie; but she thought of Hemstead's treatment of the poor old creature in contrast.

"Whoa there, steady now," cried Harcourt to the horses; and Hemstead, though sitting with his back to him, noted that he was too much engrossed with their management to speak often, even to Addie who sat beside him.

"Mr. Hemstead said that Auntie Lammer was more than a duchess," added Lottie, laughing.

"True, she's a monster. But what did Mr. Hemstead call her?"

"He said she was a 'woman,' and was as polite as if paying homage to universal womanhood."

"I think," said De Forrest, satirically, "that Mr. Hemstead might have found a better, if not a larger type of 'universal womanhood' to whom he could have paid his homage. I was not aware that he regarded bulk as the most admirable quality in woman. Well, he does not take a narrow view of the sex. His ideal is large."

"Come, Mr. De Forrest," said Hemstead, "your wit is as heavy as Mrs. Lammer herself, and she nearly broke my back going down stairs."

"Oh, pardon me. It was your back that suffered. I thought it was your heart. How came you to be so excessively polite then?"

"I think Miss Marsden is indulging in a bit of fun at my expense. Of course a gentleman ought to be polite to any and every woman, because she is such. Would it

be knightly or manly to bow to a duchess, and treat some
poor obscure woman as if she were scarcely human?
Chivalry," continued he, laughing, "devoted itself to
woman in distress, and if ever a woman's soul was burdened, Aunt Lammer's must be. But how do you account
for this, Mr. De Forrest? It was Miss Marsden that took
pity on the poor creature and summoned me to her aid.
She was more polite and helpful than I."

"I have just said to her that I do not understand how
she can do such things save in the spirit of mischief," he
replied, discontentedly. "It really pained me all the evening to see you in contact with such people," he added tenderly, aside to Lottie.

"Well, I can understand it," said Hemstead, emphatically.

"I suppose Mr. Hemstead believes in the brotherhood,
and therefore the sisterhood of the race. I was, in his estimation, taking care of one of my little sisters;" and Lottie's
laugh trilled out upon the still night.

"Whoa now, steady, steady, I tell you," cried Harcourt;
and all noted that at Lottie's shrill laugh the horses sprang
into a momentary gallop.

After a moment Hemstead replied, "You are nearer right
than you think. In weakness, helplessness, and childish ignorance, she was a little sister."

"Well, so be it. I have had enough of Mrs. Lammer
and undeserved praise. Now all join in the chorus.

"Three fishers—" and she sang the well-known song,
and was delighted when Hemstead, for the first time, let
out his rich, musical bass.

But before they had sung through the first stanza, Harcourt turned and said, "You must be still, or I can't manage the horses."

In fact, they were going at a tremendous pace, and Hemstead noted that Harcourt was nervous and excited. But
no one apprehended any danger.

"How cold and distant the stars seem on a winter evening!" said Lottie, after a moment's silence. "It always depresses me to come out into the night after an evening of gayety and nonsense. There is a calm majesty about the heavens which makes my frivolity seem contemptible. The sky to-night reminds me of a serene, cold face looking at me in silent scorn. How fearfully far off those stars are; and yet you teach, do you not, Mr. Hemstead, that heaven is beyond them?"

"But that Limbo," added De Forrest, with a satirical laugh, "is right at hand in the centre of the earth."

"The real heaven, Miss Marsden," said Hemstead, gently, "is where there are happy, trusting hearts. Where the locality is I do not know. As to that nether world, if you know its location you know more than I do, Mr. De Forrest. I don't propose to have anything to do with it. Prisons may be a painful necessity, but we don't fear them or propose to go to them. On the same principle we need not trouble ourselves about God's prison house."

At this moment from an adjacent farmhouse, a large dog came bounding out with clamorous barking. The excited horses were ready at the slightest provocation to run, and now broke into a furious gallop. Harcourt sawed on the bits and shouted to them in vain. He was slight in build, and not very strong. Moreover, he had grown nervous and chilled and had lost his own self-control, and of course could not restrain the powerful creatures that were fast passing from mere excitement into the wild terror which is akin to a panic among men when once they give way before danger.

"Good God!" exclaimed Harcourt, after a moment; "I can't hold them, and we are near the top of a long hill with two sharp turnings on the side of a steep bank, and there's a bridge at the bottom. Whoa! curse you, whoa!"

But they tore on the more recklessly. Bel and Addie began to scream, and this increased the fright of the horses. Hemstead looked searchingly for a moment at Lottie, and saw with a thrill that her white face was turned to him and not to De Forrest.

"Is there danger?" she asked, in a low tone.

"Good God!" exclaimed Harcourt again, "I can't hold them."

Hemstead rose instantly, and turning with care in the swaying sleigh braced himself by planting one foot on the middle of the seat. He then said quietly, "Will you give me the reins, Mr. Harcourt? I am well braced and quite strong. Perhaps I can manage them."

Harcourt relinquished the reins instantly.

"Hush!" Hemstead said sternly to Addie and Bel, and they became quiet—the weaker minds submitting to the roused and master mind.

Fortunately the trouble had occurred where there was a straight and level road, and a little of this still remained. The question with Hemstead was whether he could get control of the rushing steeds before they reached the hill.

CHAPTER XII

MISS MARSDEN ASKS SOMBRE QUESTIONS

LOTTIE MARSDEN, although greatly alarmed by their critical situation, was naturally too courageous to give way utterly to fear, and not so terrified but that she could note all Hemstead did; and for some reason she believed he would be equal to the emergency. His confidence, moreover, communicated itself to her. She saw that he did not jerk or saw on the reins at first, but, bracing his large powerful frame, drew steadily back, and that the horses yielded somewhat to his masterful grasp.

"Pull," cried Harcourt, excitedly; "you can hold them."

"Yes, jerk their cursed heads off," shouted De Forrest, in a way that proved his self-control was nearly gone.

"Hush, I tell you!" said Hemstead, in a low tone. "I might break the lines if I exerted my whole strength. Then where should we be? I don't wish to put any more strain upon them than I must. See, they are giving in more and more."

"But the hill is near," said Harcourt.

"You must let me manage in my own way," said Hemstead. "Not another sound from any one."

Then in a firm tone, strong but quiet like his grasp upon the reins, he spoke to the horses. In three minutes more he had them prancing with many a nervous start, but completely under his control, down the first descent of the hill.

"Will you take the reins again?" he said to Harcourt.

"No, hang it all. You are a better horseman than I am."

"Not at all, Mr. Harcourt. I am heavier and stronger than you probably, and so braced that I had a great advantage. You had no purchase on them, and were chilled by long driving."

"Where did you learn to manage horses?" asked Lottie.

"On our Western farm. We had plenty of them. A horse is almost human: you must be very firm and very kind."

"Is that the way to treat the 'human'?" said Lottie, her bold and somewhat reckless spirit having so far recovered itself as to enable her to laugh.

"Yes, for a man, if he attempts to manage at all; but I suppose the majority of us are managed, if we would only acknowledge it. What chance has a man with a coaxing, clever woman?"

"Look there," said Harcourt, as they were turning the first sharp angle in the road to which he had referred. "Where should we have been if we had gone round this point at our speed when I held the reins?"

The steep embankment, with grim rocks protruding from the snow and with gnarled trunks of trees, was anything but inviting.

"Come, De Forrest," continued Harcourt, "brush up your mathematics. At what angle, and with what degree of force, should we have swooped down there on a tangent, when the horses rounded this curve?"

"O-o-h!" exclaimed Lottie, looking shudderingly down the steep bank, at the bottom of which brawled a swift stream among ice-capped rocks. "It's just the place for a tragedy. We were talking about heaven and the other place when the horses started, were we not? Perhaps we were nearer one or the other of them than we supposed."

"Oh, hush, Lottie!" cried Bel, still sobbing and trembling; "I wish we had remained at home."

"I echo that wish most decidedly," muttered De Forrest. "The whole evening has been like a nightmare."

"I am sorry my expedition has been a source of wretchedness to every one," said Lottie, coldly.

"Not every one, I'm sure," said Hemstead. "Certainly not to me. Besides, your expedition has made a pastor and a whole parish happy, and I also dimly foresee a seat in Congress for Harcourt as a result."

"Very dimly indeed," laughed Harcourt. "Still, now that our necks are safe, thanks to Mr. Hemstead, I'm glad I went. Human nature lies on the surface out at Scrub Oaks, and one can learn much about it in a little while. Come, little coz, cheer up," he said to Addie, drawing her closer to him. "See, we are down the hill and across the bridge. No danger of the horses running up the long hill before us, and by the time they reach the top they will be glad to go the rest of the way quietly."

"You had better take the reins again, Mr. Harcourt," said Hemstead.

"Oh, Mr. Hemstead, please drive," cried the ladies, in chorus.

"No," said he; "Mr. Harcourt is as good a driver as I am. It was only a question of strength before."

"The majority is against me," laughed Harcourt. "I won't drive any more to-night. You take my place."

"Well, if you all wish it; but there's no need."

"Let me come over, too, and sit between you and Bel," said Addie eagerly.

"No, she can sit with Julian," said Lottie, "and I will go to Mr. Hemstead. He shall not be left alone."

"Oh, Miss Lottie! please forgive me," pleaded De Forrest; "It mean what I said a moment since."

"Well, I'll forgive you, but shall punish you a little. Stop the horses again, Mr. Hemstead; that is, if you don't object to my company."

The horses stopped very suddenly.

"Please don't leave me," said De Forrest.

"It's only carrying out the mischief we plotted, you know," she whispered.

"Well, I submit on that ground only," he replied dis-contentedly, and with a shade of doubt in his mind. It seemed very strange, even to him, that Lottie could coolly continue to victimize one who had just rendered them so great a service. But the truth was, that she, in her desire to escape from him, had said what she thought would be apt to quiet his objections without much regard for the truth. She hardly recognized her own motive for wishing to sit by Hemstead, beyond that she was grateful, and found him far more interesting than the egotistical lover, who to-day, for some reason, had proved himself very wearisome.

Hemstead heard nothing of this, and was much pleased when Lottie stepped lightly over and took her place socially at his side.

"It's very kind of you," he said.

"I didn't come out of kindness," she replied, in a low tone for his ear alone.

"Why then?"

"Because I wanted to."

"I like that reason better still."

"And with good reason. Will you take me again over this awful road to see Mrs. Dlimm?"

"With great pleasure."

"But it's such a long drive! You will get cold driving."

"Oh, no! not if you will talk to me so pleasantly."

"I won't promise how I'll talk. In fact I never know what I'll do when with you. You made me act very silly this afternoon."

"Is a flower silly when it blooms?"

"What do you mean?"

"You wished you were better."

"Oh, I see; but suppose I would like to remain—for a while at least—a wicked, little undeveloped bud?"

"You can't. The bud must either bloom or wither."

"Oh, how dismal! Were you afraid, Mr. Hemstead, when the horses were running? I was."

"I was anxious. It certainly was a critical moment with that hill before us."

"How queer that we should have been talking of the future state just then! Suppose that, instead of sitting here cosily by you, I were lying on those rocks over there, or floating in that icy stream bleeding and dead?"

He turned and gave her a surprised look, and she saw the momentary glitter of a tear in his eye.

"Please do not call up such images," he said.

She was in a strangely excited and reckless mood, and did not understand herself. Forces that she would be long in comprehending were at work in her mind.

Partly for the sake of the effect upon him, and partly as the outgrowth of her strange mood, she continued, in a low tone which the others could not hear: "If that had happened, where should I have been now? Just think of it—my body lying over there in this wild gorge, and I, myself, going away alone this wintry night. Where should I have gone? Where should I be now?"

"In paradise, I trust," he replied, bending upon her a searching look. Either his imagination or her thoughts gave her face a strange expression as seen in the uncertain moonlight. It suggested the awed and trembling curiosity with which she might have gone forward to meet the dread realities of the unknown world. A great pity—an intense desire to shield and rescue her—filled his soul.

"Miss Marsden," he said, in a tone that thrilled her in connection with the image called up, "your own words seem to portray you standing on the brink of a fathomless abyss into which you are looking with fear and dread."

"You understand me perfectly," she said. "That is just where I stand; but it is like looking out into one of those Egyptian nights that swallow up everything, and there is nothing but a great blank of darkness."

"It must be so," said Hemstead, sighing deeply "Only

the clear eyes of faith can see across the gulf.   But you are a brave girl to stand and look into the gulf."

"Why should I not look into it?" she asked, in a reckless tone.   "I've been brought face to face with it to-night, and perhaps shall soon be again. *It's always there.* If I had to go over Niagara, I should want to go with my eyes open."

"But if you were in the rapids above the falls, would you not permit a strong hand to lift you out? Why should you look down into the gulf? Why not look up to heaven? That is *'always there'* just as truly."

"Do you feel sure that you would have gone to heaven if you had been killed to-night?"

"Yes, perfectly sure."

"You are very good."

"No; but God is."

"A good God ought to prevent such awful things."

"He did, in this case."

"No; you prevented it."

"Suppose the horses had started to run at the top of the hill instead of where it was level; suppose a line had broken; suppose the horses had taken the bits in their teeth—I could not hold two such powerful animals.   Do you not see that many things might have happened so that no human hand could do anything, and that it would be easy for an all-powerful Being to so arrange and shape events that we should either escape or suffer, as He chose, in spite of all that we could do.   I am glad to think that I can never be independent of Him."

"If it was God's will that they should stop, what was the use of your doing anything?"

"It is ever God's will that we should do our best in all emergencies.   He will help only those who try to help themselves.   He calls us his children, not his machines. The point I wish to make is, that when we do our best, which is always required of us, we are still dependent upon Him."

"I never had it made so plain before. The fact is, Mr. Hemstead, I don't know much about God, and I don't half understand myself. This day seems like an age. I have had so many strange experiences since I stood with you in the breakfast-room this morning—and have been near, perhaps, still stranger experiences, for which I feel little prepared—that I am excited and bewildered. I fear you think very poorly of me."

"You do often puzzle me very greatly, Miss Marsden," he replied. "But I think you are prone to do yourself injustice. Still that is far better than hypocritical seeming. Whatever your fault is, you proved to me last night, and most conclusively again this evening, that you have a kind, generous heart. More than all, you have shown yourself capable of the noblest things."

Lottie made no reply, but sat silent for some time; and, having reached the level once more, Hemstead gave his attention to the horses, till satisfied that they recognized their master and would give no further trouble.

"Won't you sing again?" he asked.

"Yes, if you will sing with me."

"I would rather listen, but will accept your condition when I can."

She would only sing what he knew, and noted in pleased surprise that his musical culture was by no means trifling.

"How could you take time from your grave theological studies for such a comparatively trifling thing as music?" she asked.

"Some practical knowledge of music is no trifling matter with me," he replied. "In view of my prospective field of work, next to learning to preach, learning to sing is the most important. I shall have to start the hymns, as a general thing, and often sing them alone."

"How can you look forward to such a life?"

"I can look forward in grateful gladness. I only wish I were more worthy of my work."

"Did I not know your sincerity I should say that was affectation."

"Who was it that preached to the 'common people,' and in the obscure little towns of Palestine eighteen centuries ago? Am I better than my Master?"

"You are far better than I am. No one has ever talked to me as you have. I might have been different if they had."

"Miss Marsden," said Hemstead, earnestly, as they were driving up the avenue to the Marchmont residence, "when you stood beside me this morning I pointed you to a world without, whose strange and marvellous beauty excited your wonder and delight. You seem to me on the border of a more beautiful world—the spiritual world of love and faith in God. If I could only show you that, I should esteem it the greatest joy of my life."

"That is a world I do not understand; nor am I worthy to enter it," she said in sudden bitterness, "and I fear I never shall be; and yet I thank you all the same."

A few moments later they were sitting round the parlor fire, recounting the experiences of the evening.

Before entering the house Lottie had said, "Let us say nothing about runaway horses to aunt and uncle, or they may veto future drives."

To Hemstead's surprise Lottie seemed in one of her gayest moods, and he was reluctantly compelled to think her sketch of the people at the donation a little satirical and unfeeling. But while she was portraying Hemstead as the hero of the occasion, she had the tact to make no reference to Harcourt. But he generously stated the whole case, adding, with a light laugh, that he had learned once for all that coaxing and wheedling were better than driving.

"Appealing to their better natures, you mean," said Hemstead.

"Yes, that is the way you would put it."

"I think it's the true way."

"Perhaps it is. Human nature has its good side if one can only find it, but I'm satisfied that it won't drive well."

"I think work among such people the most hopeless and discouraging thing in the world," said Mrs. Marchmont, yawning.

"It doesn't seem to me so, aunt," said Hemstead. "On the contrary, are not people situated as they are peculiarly open to good influences? Next to gospel truth, I think the influence of refined, cultivated families could do more for the people at Scrub Oaks than anything else. If they did not alienate the plain people by exclusiveness and pride, they would soon tone them up and refine away uncouthness and unconscious vulgarity in manners. Let me give you a practical instance of this that occurred to-night. I asked a pretty young girl why she and the little group around her had giving up the kissing games, and she replied that 'Miss Marsden had said that no lady played such games, and she wouldn't any more.' Young people are quick and imitative, and I noticed that they watched Miss Marsden as if she were a revelation to them, and many, no doubt, obtained ideas of lady-like bearing and manner that were entirely new to them, but which they will instinctively adopt. I think she would be surprised if she could foresee how decided and lasting an influence this brief visit of one evening will have on many that were present."

"But refined people of standing cannot meet with such a class socially," replied his aunt, with emphasis. "Such a mixing up would soon bring about social anarchy. Lottie is a little peculiar, and went there as a stranger upon a frolic."

"Now, auntie, that designation 'peculiar' is a very doubtful compliment."

"I didn't mean it for one, my dear, though I meant no reproach in it. You get too many compliments as it is. Frank, like all young, inexperienced people, has many impractical ideas, that time will cure. Young enthusiasts of every age are going to turn the world upside down, but I note that it goes on very much the same."

"I think evil has turned the world upside down," said

Hemstead. "The wrong side is up now, and it is our duty to turn the right side back again. We can't carry exclusiveness beyond this brief life. Why, then, make it so rigid here? The One who was chief of all was the friend of all."

"Oh, well," said Mrs. Marchmont, in some confusion, "we can't expect to be like Him. Then what is appropriate in one place and age is not in another."

"No, indeed, Mr. Hemstead," said Lottie, with twinkling eyes. "I'd have you to understand that the religion appropriate to our place and age is one that pleases us."

"I didn't say that, Lottie," said Mrs. Marchmont, with some irritation.

"Very true, auntie, but I did! and, as far as I can judge, it's true in New York, whatever may be the case in the country. But come, we've had supper, and have kept you and uncle up too late already. Kiss your saucy niece good-night; perhaps I'll be better one of these days."

"If kissing will make you better, come here to me," said Mr. Dimmerly. "I wouldn't mind doing a little missionary work of that kind."

"No, indeed," laughed Harcourt; "we'll all turn missionaries on those terms."

"Yes," said De Forrest, "I'll promise to be a devoted missionary all my life."

"There, I said that you would have a religion you liked," retorted Lottie, pirouetting to the dining-room door. "But I'm too far gone for any such mild remedies. There's Bel, she's trying to be good. You may all kiss her;" and, with a look at Hemstead he did not understand, she vanished.

CHAPTER XIII

A LOVER QUENCHED

BEL followed her friend to their room, full of irritable reproaches. But Lottie puzzled her again, as she had done before that day. Gayety vanished from the face as light from a clouded landscape, and with an expression that was even scowling and sullen she sat brooding before the fire, heeding Bel's complaining words no more than she would the patter of rain against the window.

Then Bel changed the tune; retaining the same minor key, however.

"I suppose now that you will give up your shameful plot against Mr. Hemstead, as a matter of course."

"I don't know what I'll do," snapped Lottie.

"Don't know what you'll do! Why, he about the same as saved our lives this evening."

"He saved his own at the same time."

"Well," said Bel, exasperatingly, "I wish Mr. Hemstead and all who heard the fine speeches about your 'kind, generous heart' could hear you now."

"I wish they could," said Lottie, recklessly. "They couldn't have a worse opinion of me than I have of myself."

"But what do you intend to do about Mr. Hemstead?"

"I don't intend to do anything about him. I half wish I had never seen him."

"That you can trifle with him after what has happened to-night is something that I did not think, even of you, Lottie Marsden."

"I haven't said I was going to 'trifle with him.' He's a

man you can't trifle with. The best thing I can do is to let him alone.''

"That is just what I think."

"Very well then, go to sleep and be quiet."

"How long are you going to sit 'mooning' there?"

"Till morning, if I wish. Don't bother me."

"After coming so near having your neck broken, you ought to be in a better frame of mind."

"So had you. Neither breaking my neck nor coming near it will convert me."

"Well, I hope you will get through your moods and tenses to-day. You have had more than I ever remember within so short a time."

With this comforting statement Bel left her friend to herself, who sat staring into the fire in the most discontented manner.

"'Capable of the noblest things,' indeed," she thought. "I would like to know who is capable of meaner things. And now what do you intend to do, Lottie Marsden? Going on with your foolish, childish jest, after the fun has all faded out of it? If you do, you will make a fool of yourself instead of him. He is not the man you thought he was, at all. He is your superior in every respect, save merely in the ease which comes from living in public instead of seclusion, and in all his diffidence there has been nothing so rude and ill-bred as Julian's treatment of Mrs. Dlimm. Julian indeed! He's but a well-dressed little manikin beside this large-minded man;" and she scowled more darkly than ever at the fire.

"But what shall I do? I can't be such a Christian as Bel is. I would rather not be one at all. What's more, I cannot bring my mind to decide to be such a Christian as Mr. Hemstead is. I should have to change completely, and give up my old self-pleasing and wayward life, and that seems like giving up life itself. Religion is a bitter medicine that I must take some time or other. But the idea of sobering down at my time of life!"

"But you may not live to see age. Think what a risk you ran to-night," urged conscience.

"Well, I must take my chances. A plague on that Hemstead! I can't be with him ten minutes but he makes me uncomfortable in doing wrong. All was going smoothly till he came, and life was one long frolic. Now he has got my conscience all stirred up so that between them both I shall have little comfort. I won't go with him to Mrs. Dlimm's to-morrow. He will talk religion to me all the time, and I, like a big baby, shall cry, and he will think I am on the eve of conversion, and perhaps will offer to take me out among the border ruffians as an inducement. If I want to live my old life, and have a good time, the less I see of Frank Hemstead the better, for, somehow or other, when I am with him I can't help seeing that he is right, and feeling mean in my wrong. I will just carry out my old resolution, and act as badly as I can. He will then see what I am, and let me alone."

Having formed this resolution, Lottie slept as sweetly as innocence itself.

To Hemstead, with his quiet and regular habits, the day had been long and exciting, and he was exceedingly weary; and yet thoughts of the brilliant and beautiful girl, who bewildered and fascinated him, awaking his sympathy at the same time, kept him sleepless till late. Every scene in which they had been together was lived over in all its minutiæ, and his conclusions were favorable. As he had said to her, she seemed "capable of the noblest things."

"She never has had a chance," he thought. "She never has given truth a fair hearing, probably having had slight opportunity to do so. From the little I have seen and heard, it seems to me that the rich and fashionable are as neglected—indeed it would appear more difficult to bring before them the simple and searching gospel of Christ, than before the very poor."

Hemstead determined that he would be faithful, and would bring the truth to her attention in every possible

way, feeling that if during this holiday visit he could win
such a trophy for the cause to which he had devoted himself,
it would be an event that would shed a cheering light down
to the very end of his life.

It was a rather significant fact, which did not occur to
him, however, that his zeal and interest were almost entirely
concentrated on Lottie. His cousin Addie, and indeed all
the others, seemed equally in need.

It must be confessed that some sinners are much more
interesting than others, and Hemstead had never met one
half so interesting as Lottie.

And yet his interest in her was natural. He had not
reached that lofty plane from which he could look down
with equal sympathy for all. Do any reach it, in this
world?

Lottie had seemed kind to him when others had been
cold and slightly scornful. He had come to see clearly that
she was not a Christian, and that she was not by any means
faultless through the graces of nature. But she had given
ample proof that she had a heart which could be touched,
and a mind capable of appreciating and being aroused by
the truth. That her kindness to him was only hollow acting he never dreamed, and it was well for her that he did
not suspect her falseness, for with all her beauty he would
have revolted from her at once. He could forgive anything
sooner than the meanness of deception. If he discovered
the practical joke, it would be a sorry jest for Lottie, for
she would have lost a friend who appeared able to help her;
and he, in his honest indignation, would have given her a
portrait of herself that would have humiliated her proud
spirit in a way that could never be forgotten.

But with the unquenchable hope of youth in his heart,
and his boundless faith in God, he expected that, at no distant day, Lottie's remarkable beauty would be the index of
a truer spiritual loveliness.

But, as is often the case, the morning dispelled the
dreams of the night, to a degree that quite perplexed and

disheartened him. Lottie's greeting in the breakfast-room was not very cordial, and she seemed to treat him with cool indifference throughout the whole meal. There was nothing that the others would note, but something that he missed himself. Occasionally, she would make a remark that would cause him to turn toward her with a look of pained surprise, which both vexed and amused her; but he gave no expression to his feelings, save that he became grave and silent.

After breakfast Lottie said nothing to him about their visit to Mrs. Dlimm, from which he expected so much. Having waited some time in the parlor, he approached her timidly as she was passing through the hall, and said, "When would you like to start upon our proposed visit?"

"Oh, I forgot to say to you, Mr. Hemstead," she replied rather carelessly, "that I've changed my mind. It's a very long drive, and, after all, Mrs. Dlimm is such an utter stranger to me that I scarcely care to go."

But, under her indifferent seeming, she was watching keenly to see how he would take this rebuff. He flushed deeply, but to her surprise only bowed acquiescence, and turned to the parlor. She expected that he would remonstrate, and endeavor to persuade her to carry out her agreement. She was accustomed to pleading and coaxing on the part of young men, to whom, however, she granted her favors according to her moods and wishes. While she saw that he was deeply hurt and disappointed, his slightly cold and silent bow was a different expression of his feeling from what she desired. She wanted to take the ride, and might have been persuaded into going, in spite of her purpose to keep aloof, and she was vexed with him that he did not urge her as De Forrest would have done.

Therefore the spoiled and capricious beauty went up to her room more "out of sorts" than ever, and sulkily resolved that she would not appear till dinner.

In the meantime Hemstead went to his aunt and informed her that he would take the morning train for New York, and would not return till the following evening.

"Very well, Frank," she replied; "act your pleasure. Come and go as you like."

The good lady was entertaining her nephew more from a sense of duty than anything else. From their difference in tastes he added little to her enjoyment, and was sometimes a scource of discomfort; and so would not be missed.

Lottie had a desperately long and dismal time of it. Either the book she tried to read was stupid, or there was something wrong with her. At last she impatiently sent it flying across the room and went to the window. The beautiful winter morning exasperated her still more.

"Suppose he had talked religion to me," she thought, "he at at least makes it interesting, and anything would have been better than moping here. What a fool I was, not to go! What a fool I am, anyway! He is the only one I ever did act toward as a woman might and ought—even in jest. He is the only one that ever made me wish I were a true woman, instead of a vain flirt; and the best thing my wisdom could devise, after I found out his beneficent power, was to give him a slap in the face, and shut myself up with a stupid novel. 'Capable of noble things!' I imagine he has changed his mind this morning.

"Well, what if he has? A plague upon him! I wish he had never come, or I had stayed in New York. I foresee that I am going to have an awfully stupid·time here in the country."

Thus she irritably chafed through the long hours. She would not go downstairs as she wished to, because she had resolved that she would not. But she half purposed to try and bring about the visit to Mrs. Dlimm in the afternoon, if possible, and would now go willingly, if asked.

At the first welcome sound of the dinner-bell she sped downstairs, and glanced into the parlor, hoping that he might be there, and that in some way she might still bring about the ride. But she found only De Forrest yawning

over a newspaper, and had to endure his sentimental reproaches that she had absented herself so long from him.

"Come to dinner," was her only and rather prosaic
response.

But De Forrest went cheerfully, for dinner was something that he could enjoy under any circumstances.

To Lottie's disappointment, Mr. Dimmerly mumbled
grace, and still Hemstead did not appear. For some reason
she did not like to ask where he was, and was provoked at
herself because of her hesitancy. The others, who knew of
his departure, supposed she was aware of it also. At last
her curiosity gained the mastery, and she asked her aunt
with an indifference, not so well assumed but that her color
heightened a little, "Where is Mr. Hemstead?"

"He went down to the city," replied Mrs. Marchmont,
carelessly.

The impulsive girl's face showed her disappointment
and vexation, but she saw that quick-eyed Bel was watching her. She wished her friend back in New York; and,
with partial success, sought to appear as usual.

"Oh, dear!" she thought; "what shall I do with myself
this afternoon? I can't endure Julian's mooning. I wish
Mr. Harcourt was here, so we could get up some excitement."

Without excitement Lottie was as dull and wretched as
all victims of stimulants, left to their own resources.

But the fates were against her. Harcourt would not be
back till evening, and she did not know when Hemstead
would return. Addie and Bel vanished after dinner, and
De Forrest offered to read to her. She assented, having no
better prospect.

She ensconced herself luxuriously under an afghan upon
the sofa, while the persistent lover, feeling that this would
be his favored opportunity, determined to lay close siege to
her heart, and win a definite promise, if possible. For this
purpose he chose a romantic poem, which, at a certain
point, had a very tender and love-infused character. Here

he purposed to throw down the book in a melodramatic manner, and pass from the abstract to reality, and from the third person to the first. He was more familiar with stage effects than anything else, and had planned a pretty little scene. As Lottie reclined upon the sofa, he could very nicely and comfortably kneel, take her hand, and gracefully explain the condition of his heart; and she was certainly in a comfortable position to hear.

A man less vain than De Forrest would not have gathered much encouragement from Lottie's face, for it had a very weary and bored expression as he commenced the rather stilted and very sentimental introduction to the "gush" that was to follow.

She divined his purpose as she saw him summoning to his aid all his rather limited elocutionary powers, and noted how he gave to every line that verged toward love the tenderest accent.

But the satirical side-gleam from her eyes, as she watched him, was anything but responsive or conducive to sentiment; and finally, as she became satisfied of his object, the smile that flitted across her face would have quenched the most impetuous declaration as effectually as a mill-pond might quench a meteor.

But Julian, oblivious of all this, was growing pathetic and emotional; and if she escaped the scene at all, she must act promptly.

She did so, for in five minutes, to all appearance, she was asleep.

At first, when he glanced up to emphasize a peculiarly touching line, he thought she had closed her eyes to hide her feelings; but at last, when he reached the particular and soul-melting climax that was to prepare the way for his own long-desired crisis, having given the final lines in a tone that he thought would move a marble heart, he laid the book down to prepare for action, and the dreadful truth dawned upon him. She was asleep!

What could he do? To awaken her, and then go forward, would not answer. People were generally cross when disturbed in their sleep; and he knew Lottie was no exception. He was deeply mortified and disappointed.

He got up and stalked tragically and frowningly to the hearth-rug, and stared at the apparently peaceful sleeper, and then flung himself out of the room, very much as he was accustomed to when a spoiled and petulant boy.

After he was gone, Lottie quivered with laughter for a few moments; then stole away to her room, where she blotted out the weary hour with sleep unfeigned, until aroused by the supper-bell.

CHAPTER XIV

LOTTIE A MYSTERIOUS PROBLEM

AFTER a brief toilet, Lottie came down to tea looking like an innocent little lamb that any wolf could beguile and devour. She smiled on De Forrest so sweetly that the cloud began to pass from his brow at once.

"Why should I be angry with her?" he thought; "she did not understand what I was aiming at, and probably supposed that I meant to read her asleep, and yet I should have thought that the tones of my voice— Well, well, Lottie has been a little spoiled by too much devotion. She has become accustomed to it, and takes it as a matter of course. When we are married, the devotion must be on the other side of the house."

"I thought Mr. Hemstead would be back this evening?" she said to her aunt.

"No, not till to-morrow evening. You seem to miss Frank very much."

Then Lottie was provoked to find herself blushing like a school-girl, but she said, laughingly, "How penetrating you are, auntie. I do miss him, in a way you cannot understand."

But the others understood the remark as referring to her regret that he had escaped from her wiles as the victim of their proposed jest, and Bel shot a reproachful glance at her. She could not know that Lottie had said this to throw dust into their eyes, and to account for her sudden blush, which she could not account for to herself.

Before supper was over, Harcourt came in with great news, which threw Addie into a state of feverish excitement, and greatly interested all the others.

"Mrs. Byram, her son, and two daughters, have come up for a few days to take a peep at the country in winter, and enjoy some sleigh-riding. I met Hal Byram, and drove in with him. Their large house is open from top to bottom, and full of servants, and to-morrow evening they are going to give a grand party. There are invitations for you all. They expect most of their guests from New York, however."

Even languid Bel brightened at the prospect of so much gayety; and thoughts of Hemstead and qualms of conscience vanished for the time from Lottie's mind. The evening soon passed, with cards and conjectures as to who would be there, and the day following, with the bustle of preparation.

"I don't believe Frank will go to such a party," said Addie, as the three girls and De Forrest were together in the afternoon.

"Let us make him go by all means," said Lottie. "He needn't know what kind of a party it is, and it will be such fun to watch him. I should not be surprised if he and Mrs. Byram mutually shocked each other. We can say merely that we have all been invited out to a little company, and that it would be rude in him not to accompany us."

Mrs. Marchmont was asked not to say anything to undeceive Hemstead.

"It will do him good to see a little of the world," said Lottie; and the lady thought so too.

The others were under the impression that Lottie still purposed carrying out her practical joke against Hemstead. At the time when he had saved them from so much danger the evening before, they felt that their plot ought to be abandoned, and, as it was, they had mainly lost their relish for it. Hemstead had not proved so good a subject for a practical joke as they had expected. But they felt that if Lottie chose to carry it on, that was her affair, and if there were any fun in prospect, they would be on hand to enjoy it. The emotions and virtuous impulses inspired by their moment of peril had faded almost utterly away, as is usually the case with this style of repentance. Even Bel was growing indifferent to Lottie's course. Harcourt, who with all his faults had good and generous traits, was absent on business, and had partially forgotten the design against Hemstead, and supposed that anything definite had been given up on account of the service rendered to them all.

Lottie was drifting. She did not know what would be her action. The child of impulse, the slave of inclination, with no higher aim than to enjoy the passing hour, she could not keep a good resolve, if through some twinges of conscience she made one. She had proposed to avoid Hemstead, for, while he interested, he also disquieted her and filled her with self-dissatisfaction.

And yet for this very reason he was fascinating. Other men admired and flattered her, bowing to her in unvarying and indiscriminating homage. Hemstead not only admired but respected her for the good qualities that she had simulated, and with equal sincerity recognized faults and failures. She had been admired all her life, but respect from a true, good man was a new offering, and, even though obtained by fraud, was as delightful as it was novel. She still wished to stand well in his estimation, though why she hardly knew. She was now greatly vexed with herself that she had refused to visit Mrs. Dlimm. She was most anxious that he should return, in order that she might discover whether he had become disgusted with her; for, in the knowledge of her own wrong action, she unconsciously gave him credit for knowing more about her than he did.

She had no definite purpose for the future. Instead of coolly carrying out a deliberate plot, she was merely permitting herself to be carried along by a subtle undercurrent of interest and inclination, which she did not understand, or trouble herself to analyze. She had felt a passing interest in gentlemen before, which had proved but passing. This was no doubt a similar case, with some peculiar and piquant elements added. A few weeks in New York after her visit was over, and he would fade from memory, and pass below the horizon like other stars that had dazzled for a time.

The honest old counsellor, conscience, recklessly snubbed and dismissed, had retired, with a few plain words, for the time, from the unequal contest.

She met Hemstead at the door on his return, and held out her hand, saying cordially, "I'm ever so glad to see you. It seems an age since you left us."

His face flushed deeply with pleasure at her words and manner. Expecting an indifferent reception, he had purposed to be dignified and reserved himself. And yet her manner on the morning of his departure had pained him deeply, and disappointed him. It had not fulfilled the promise of the previous day, and he had again been sorely perplexed. But his conclusion was partly correct.

"She is resisting the truth. She sees what changes in her gay life are involved by its acceptance; and therefore shuns coming under its influence."

What a strange power God has bestowed upon us! There is some one that we long to influence and change for the better. That one may know our wish and purpose, recognize our efforts, but quietly baffle us by an independent will that we can no more coerce and control than by our breath soften into spring warmth a wintry morning. We can look pleadingly into some dear one's eyes, clasp his hands and appeal with even tearful earnestness, and yet he may remain unmoved, or be but transiently affected. Though by touch or caress, by convincing arguments and loving entreaty, we may be unable to shake the obdurate will, we can gently master it through the intervention of another. The throne of God seems a long way round to reach the friend at our side—for the mother to reach her child in her arms—but it usually proves the quickest and most effectual way. Where before were only resistance and indifference, there come, in answer to prayer, strange relentings, mysterious longings, receptivity, and sometimes, in a way that is astonishing, full acceptance of the truth.

"The wind bloweth where it listeth," were the words of

the all-powerful One, of the beautiful emblem of His own mysterious and transforming presence.

Again He said, "How much more shall your Heavenly Father give the Holy Spirit to them that ask him."

Here is a power, a force, an agency, that the materialist cannot calculate, weigh, or measure, or laugh scornfully out of existence.

As upon a sultry night a breeze comes rustling through the leaves from unknown realms of space, and cools our throbbing temples, so the soul is often stirred and moved by impulses heavenward that are to their subjects as mysterious as unexpected.

To a certain extent, God gives to the prayerful control of Himself, as it were, and becomes their willing agent; and when all mysteries shall be solved, and the record of all lives be truthfully revealed, it will probably be seen that not those who astonished the world with their own powers, but those who quietly, through prayer, used God's power, were the ones who made the world move forward.

While Hemstead would never be a Mystic or a Quietest in his faith, he still recognized most clearly that human effort would go but little way in awakening spiritual life, unless seconded by the Divine power. Therefore in his strong and growing wish that he might bring the beautiful girl, who seemed like a revelation to him, into sympathy with the truth that he believed and loved, he had based no hope on what he alone could do or say.

But her manner on the previous morning had chilled him, and he had half purposed to be a little distant and indifferent also.

It did not occur to him that he was growing sensitive in regard to her treatment of himself, as well as of the truth.

He readily assented to Lottie's request that he should accept Mrs. Byram's invitation, and found a strange pleasure in her graciousness and vivacity at the supper-table.

His simple toilet was soon made, and he sought the parlor and a book to pass the time while waiting for the others.

Lottie was a veteran at the dressing-table, and by dint of exacting much help from Bel, and resting content with nature's bountiful gifts—that needed but little enhancing from art —she, too, was ready considerably in advance of the others, and, in the full *un*dress which society permits, thought to dazzle the plain Western student, as a preliminary to other conquests during the evening.

And he was both dazzled and startled as she suddenly stood before him under the chandelier in all the wealth of her radiant beauty.

Her hair was arranged in a style peculiarly her own, and powdered. A necklace of pearls sustained a diamond cross that was ablaze with light upon her white bosom. Her arms were bare, and her dress cut as low as fashion would sanction. In momentary triumph she saw his eye kindle into almost wondering admiration; and yet it was but momentary, for almost instantly his face began to darken with disapproval.

She at once surmised the cause; and at first it amused her very much, as she regarded it as an evidence of his delightful ignorance of society and ministerial prudishness.

"I gather from your face, Mr. Hemstead, that I am not dressed to suit your fastidious taste."

"I think you are incurring a great risk in so exposing yourself this cold night, Miss Marsden."

"That is not all your thought, Mr. Hemstead."

"You are right," he said gravely, and with heightened color.

"But it's the style; and fashion, you know, is a despot with us ladies."

"And, like all despots, very unreasonable; and wrong at times, I perceive."

"When you have seen more of society, Mr. Hemstead," she said, a little patronizingly, "you will modify your views. Ideas imported in the 'Mayflower' are scarcely in vogue now."

He was a little nettled by her tone, and said with a tinge

of dignity, "My ideas on this subject were not imported in the 'Mayflower.' They are older than the world, and will survive the world."

Lottie became provoked, for she was not one to take criticism of her personal appearance kindly, and then it was vexatious that the one whom she chiefly expected to dazzle should at once begin to find fault; and she said with some irritation, "And what are your long-lived ideas."

"I fear they would not have much weight with you were I able to express them plainly. I can only suggest them, but in such a way that you can understand me in a sentence. I should not like a sister of mine to appear in company as you are dressed."

Lottie flushed deeply and resentfully, but said, in a frigid tone, "I think we had better change the subject. I consider myself a better judge of these matters than you are."

He quietly bowed and resumed his book. She shot an angry glance at him and left the room.

This was a new experience to her—the very reverse of what she had anticipated. This was a harsh and discordant break in the honeyed strains of flattery to which she had always been accustomed, and it nettled her greatly. Moreover, the criticism she received had a delicate point, and touched her to the very quick; and to her it seemed unjust and uncalled for. What undoubtedly is wrong in itself, and what to Hemstead, unfamiliar with society and its arbitrary customs, seemed strangely indelicate, was to her but a prevailing mode among the ultra-fashionable, in which class it was her ambition to shine.

"The great, verdant boor!" she said in her anger, as she paced restlessly up and down the hall. "What a fool I am to care what he thinks, with his backwoods ideas! Nor shall I any more. He shall learn to-night that I belong to a different world."

De Forrest joined her soon and somewhat reassured her by his profuse compliments. Not that she valued them as coming from him, but she felt that he as a society man was giving the verdict of society in distinction from Hemstead's outlandish ideas. She had learned from her mother—indeed it was the faith of her childhood, earliest taught and thoroughly accepted—that the dictum of their wealthy circle was final authority, from which there was no appeal.

Hemstead suffered in her estimation. She tried to think of him as uncouth, ill-bred, and so ignorant of fashionable life—which to her was the only life worth naming—that she could dismiss him from her mind from that time forth. And in her resentment she thought she could and would. She was very gracious to De Forrest, and he in consequence was in superb spirits.

As they gathered in the parlor, before starting, De Forrest looked Hemstead over critically, and then turned to Lottie and raised his eyebrows significantly. The answering smile was in harmony with the exquisite's implied satire. Lottie gave the student another quick look and saw that he had observed their meaning glances, and that in consequence his lip had curled slightly; and she flushed again, partly with anger and vexation.

"Why should his adverse opinion so nettle me? He is nobody," she thought, as she turned coldly away.

Though Hemstead's manner was quiet and distant, he was conscious of a strange and unaccountable disappointment and sadness. It was as if a beautiful picture were becoming blurred before his eyes. It was more than that—more than he understood. He had a sense of personal loss.

He saw and sincerely regretted his cousin Addie's faults; but when Lottie failed in any respect in fulfilling the fair promise of their first acquaintance, there was something more than regret.

At first he thought he would remain at home, and not expose himself to their criticism and possible ridicule; but a moment later determined to go and, if possible, thoroughly solve the mystery of Lottie Marsden's character; for she was more of a mystery now than ever.

CHAPTER XV

HEMSTEAD SEES "OUR SET"

THEY soon reached Mrs. Byram's elegant country house, which gleamed afar, ablaze with light. The obsequious footman threw open the door, and they entered a tropical atmosphere laden with the perfumes of exotics. Already the music was striking up for the chief feature of the evening. Bel reluctantly accepted of Hemstead's escort, as she had no other resource.

"He will be so awkward!" she had said to Lottie, in irritable protest.

And at first she was quite right, for Hemstead found himself anything but at home in the fashionable revel. Bel, in her efforts to get him into the presence of the lady of the house, that they might pay their respects, reminded one of a little steam yacht trying to manage a ship of the line.

Not only were Lottie and De Forrest smiling at the scene, but also other elegant people, among whom Hemstead towered in proportions too vast and ill-managed to escape notice; and to Addie her cousin's lack of ease and grace was worse than a crime.

Bel soon found some city acquaintances, and she and her escort parted with mutual relief. Hemstead drifted into the hall, where he would be out of the way of the dancers, but through the open doors could watch the scene.

And this he did with a curious and observant eye. The party he came with expected him to be either dazzled and quite carried away by the scenes of the evening, or else shocked and very solemn over their dissipation. But he was rather inclined to be philosophical, and to study this new phase of life. He would see the *crême de la crême*, who only would be present, as he was given to understand. He would discover if they were made of different clay from the people of Scrub Oaks. He would breathe the social atmosphere which to Addie, to his aunt, and even to Lottie, he was compelled to fear was as the breath of life. These were the side issues; but his chief purpose was to study Lottie herself. He would discover if she were in truth as good a girl—as full of promise—as he had been led to believe at first.

Of course he was a predestined "wall-flower" upon such an occasion. Addie had said to Mrs. Byram, in a tone hard to describe but at once understood, "A cousin from the West, who is studying for the ministry"; and Hemstead was immediately classed in the lady's mind among those poor relations who must be tolerated for the sake of their connections.

He was a stranger to all, save those he came with, and they soon completely ignored and forgot him, except Lottie, by whom he was watched, but so furtively that she seemed as neglectful as the rest.

It was one of the fashions of the hour—a phase of etiquette as ill-bred as the poorest social slang—not to introduce strangers. Mrs. Byram and her daughters were nothing if not fashionable, and in this case the mode served their inclination, and beyond a few formal words they willingly left their awkward guest to his own resources.

He could not understand how true courtesy permitted a hostess to neglect any of her guests, least of all those who from diffidence or any cause seemed most in need of attention. Still, in the present instance, he was glad to be left alone.

The scenes around him had more than the interest of novelty, and there was much that he enjoyed keenly. The music was good, and his quick ear kept as perfect time to

it as did Lottie's feet. He thought the square dances were
beautiful and perfectly unobjectionable—a vast improvement on many of the rude and often stupid games that he
had seen at the few companies he had attended, and Lottie
appeared the embodiment of grace, as she glided through
them.

But when a *blasé*-looking fellow, in whose eye lurked all
evil passions and appetites, whirled her away in a waltz, he
again felt, with indignation, that here was another instance
in which fashion—custom—insolently trampled on divine
law and womanly modesty. He had seen enough of the
world to know that Lottie, with all her faults, was too good
to touch the fellow whose embrace she permitted. Could
she—could the others—be ignorant of his character, when
it was indelibly stamped upon his face?

But Hemstead soon noticed that this man's attentions
were everywhere received with marked pleasure, and that
Mrs. Byram and her daughters made much of him as a
favored guest. In anger he saw how sweetly Lottie smiled
upon him as they were passing near. She caught his dark
look, and, interpreting it to mean something like jealousy,
became more gracious toward her *roué*-looking attendant,
with the purpose of piquing Hemstead.

A little later Bel came into the hall, leaning upon the
arm of a gentleman. Having requested her escort to get
her a glass of water she was left alone a few moments.
Hemstead immediately joined her and asked, "Who is that
blase-looking man upon whose arm Miss Marsden is leaning?"

"And upon whom she is also smiling so enchantingly?
He is the beau of the occasion, and she is the belle."

"Do you know anything about him? I hope his face
and manner do him injustice."

"I fear they do not. I imagine he is even worse than
he looks."

"How, then, can he be such a favorite?"

She gave him a quick, comical look, which intimated,
"You are from the back country," but said, "I fear you

will think less of society when I tell you the reasons. I admit that it is very wrong; but so it is. He has three great attractions: he is brilliant; he is fast; he is immensely rich—therefore society is at his feet."

"Oh, no; not society, but a certain clique who weigh things in false balances," said Hemstead, quickly. "How strange it is that people are ever mistaking their small circle for the world!"

Bel gave him a look of some surprise, and thought, "I half believe he is looking down upon us with better right than we upon him."

After a moment Hemstead added, "That man there is more than fast. I should imagine that Harcourt was a little fast, and yet he has good and noble traits. I could trust him. But treachery is stamped upon that fellow's face, and the leer of a devil gleams from his eye. He is not only fast, he is bad. Does Miss Marsden know his character?"

"She knows what we all do. There are hard stories about him, and, as you say, he does not look saintly; but however wrong it may be, Mr. Hemstead, it is still a fact that society will wink at almost everything when a man is as rich and well connected as he, that is, as long as a man sins in certain conventional ways and keeps his name out of the papers."

Here her escort joined her, and they passed on; and Hemstead stood lowering at the man, the pitch of whose character began to stain the beautiful girl who, knowing him somewhat, could willingly and encouragingly remain at his side.

True, he had seen abundant proof that she had a heart, good impulses, and was capable of noble things, as he had told her; but was she not also giving him equal proof that the world inthralled her heart, and that senseless and soulless fashion, rather than the will of God, or the instincts of a pure womanly nature, controlled her will?

He had no small vanity in which to wrap himself while

he nursed a spiteful resentment at slights to himself. It was a tendency of his nature, and a necessity of his calling, that he should forget himself for the sake of others. Lottie awoke his sympathy, and he pitied while he blamed.

But he desponded as to the future, and feared that she would never fulfil her first beautiful promise. He realized, with a vague sense of pain, how far apart they were, and in what different worlds they dwelt. At one time it had seemed as if they might become friends, and be in accord on the chief questions of life. But now that she was smiling so approvingly upon a man whose very face proclaimed him villain, he saw a separation wider and more inexorable than Hindoo caste—that of character.

And yet with his intense love of beauty it seemed like sacrilege—the profanation of a beautiful temple—that such a girl as Charlotte Marsden should permit the associations of that evening. It was true that he could find no greater fault with her in respect to dress, manners, and attendants, than with many others—not as much as with his own cousin. But for some reason that did not occur to him it was peculiarly a source of regret that Lottie should so fall short of what he believed true and right.

His thoughts gave expression to his face, as in momentary abstraction he paced up and down the hall. Suddenly a voice that had grown strangely familiar in the brief time he had heard it said at his side, "Why, Mr. Hemstead, you look as if at a funeral. What are you thinking of?"

Following an impulse of his open nature, he looked directly into Lottie's face, and replied, "You."

She blushed slightly, but said with a laugh, "That is frank," but added, meaningly, "I am surprised you cannot find anything better to think about."

"I think Mr. Hemstead shows excellent judgment," said Mr. Brently, the young man whose face had seemed the index of all evil. "Where could he find anything better to think about?"

"Mr. Hemstead's compliments and yours are very different affairs. He means all he says. Mr. Hemstead, permit me to introduce to you Mr. Brently of New York. I wish you could induce him to be a missionary."

The young rake laughed so heartily at this idea that he did not notice that Hemstead's acknowledgment was frigidly slight; but Lottie did.

"How absurdly jealous!" she thought; yet it pleased her that he was.

"I shall never be good enough to eat, and so cannot be persuaded to visit the Cannibal Islands in the rôle of missionary." Brently was too pleased with his own poor wit, and too indifferent to Hemstead, to note that the student did not even look at him.

"I expect that you will lecture me well for all my folly and wickedness to-morrow," said Lottie, with a laugh.

"You are mistaken, Miss Marsden," Hemstead answered coldly. "I have neither the right nor the wish to 'lecture' you;" and he turned away, while she passed on with an unquiet, uncomfortable feeling, quite unlike her usual careless disregard of the opinions of others.

At that moment a gentleman and lady brushed past them on their way to the drawing-room, and he heard Lottie whisper, "There are Mr. and Miss Martell after all. I feared they were not coming."

A moment later he saw a tall and beautiful girl enter the parlors upon the arm of a gentleman who was evidently her father. Mrs. Byram received them with the utmost deference, and was profuse in her expressions of pleasure that they had not failed to be present. Having explained their detention, they moved on through the rooms, receiving the cordial greetings of many who knew them, and much attention from all. They were evidently people of distinction, and from the first Hemstead had been favorably impressed with their appearance and bearing.

From the gentleman's erect and vigorous form it would seem that his hair was prematurely gray. His face indicated intellect and high-breeding, while the deep-set and thoughtful eyes, and the firm lines around his mouth, suggested a man of decided opinions.

The daughter was quite as beautiful as Lottie, only her style was entirely different. She was tall and willowy in form, while Lottie was of medium height. Miss Martell was very fair, and her large blue eyes seemed a trifle cold and expressionless as they rested on surrounding faces and scenes. One would hardly suppose that her pulse was quickened by the gayety and excitement, and it might even be suspected that she was not in sympathy with either the people or their spirit.

And yet all this would only be apparent to a close observer, for to the majority she was the embodiment of grace and courtesy, and as the Lanciers were called soon after her arrival, she permitted Harcourt to lead her out as his partner. They took their stations near the door where Hemstead was standing at the moment. Lottie and Mr. Brently stood at the head of the parlor; and Hemstead thought he had never seen two women more unlike, and yet so beautiful.

While he in his isolation and abstraction was observing them and others in much the same spirit with which he was accustomed to haunt art galleries, Harcourt, seeing him so near, unexpectedly introduced him to Miss Martell, saying good-naturedly: "You have one topic of mutual interest to talk about, and a rather odd one for a clergyman and a young lady, and that is—horses. Miss Martell is one of the best horsewomen of this region, and you, Mr. Hemstead, managed a span that were beyond me—saved my neck at the same time, in all probability."

The young lady at first was simply polite, and greeted him as she naturally would a stranger casually introduced. But from something either in Harcourt's words, or in Hemstead's appearance as she gave him closer scrutiny, her eye kindled into interest, and she was about to speak to him, when the music called her into the graceful maze of the dance. Hemstead was as much surprised as if a portrait on the wall had stepped down and made his acquaintance, and in his embarrassment and confusion was glad that the lady was summoned away, and he given time to recover himself.

Lottie had noted the introduction, and from her distance it had seemed that Miss Martell had treated him slightingly, and that she had not spoken, but had merely recognized him by a slight inclination; so, acting upon one of her generous impulses, the moment the first form was over and there was a brief respite, she went to where he stood near Miss Martell, and said kindly, but a little patronizingly, "I'm sorry you do not dance, Mr. Hemstead. You must be having a stupid time."

He recognized her kindly spirit, and said, with a smile, "A quiet time, but not a stupid one. As you can understand, this scene is a quite novel one to me—a glimpse into a new and different world."

"And one that you do not approve of, I fear."

"It has its lights and shadows."

Lottie now turned to speak to Miss Martell, and evil-eyed Brently, her partner, had also been standing near, waiting till Harcourt should cease to occupy her attention so closely.

The young lady was polite, but not cordial, to Lottie; she did not vouchsafe a glance to Brently. But he was not easily abashed.

"Miss Martell," he said suavely, "will you honor me for the next waltz?"

"You must excuse me, sir," she said coldly.

"Well then, some time during the evening, at your own pleasure," he urged.

"You must excuse me, sir," she repeated still more frigidly, scarcely glancing at him.

"What do you mean?" he asked insolently, at the same time flushing deeply.

She gave him a cold, quiet look of surprise, and, turning her back upon him, resumed conversation with Harcourt.

Lottie was a little indignant and perplexed at this scene; but noted, with a feeling of disgust, that her partner's face, in his anger, had the look of a demon.

But her own reception had been too cool to be agreeable, and this, with the supposed slight to Hemstead, caused Miss Martell to seem to her, for the time, the embodiment of capricious pride.

Harcourt said, "Brently does not seem to be in your good graces, Miss Martell; and that is strange, for he is the lion of the evening."

"I can well imagine that he belongs to the cat species," she replied. "I have no personal grievance against Mr. Brently, but I do not consider him a gentleman. My father knows that he is not one, and that is enough for me."

Harcourt flushed with both pleasure and shame; and as the next form just then required that he should take his companion's hand, he did so with a cordial pressure, as he said, "Men would be better—I should be better—if all young ladies showed your spirit, Miss Martell."

At the next pause in the dance she said, in a low tone, "Come, let us have no 'ifs.' Be better anyway."

She detected the dejection which he tried to mask with a light laugh, as he replied, "I often wish I were, but the world, the flesh, and devil are too much for me."

"Yes, and always will be for *you*. Who can fight such enemies alone? Besides, you are reading and thinking in the wrong direction. You are going out into the desert."

"Well, it's kind of you to care," he said, with a look that deepened the faint color of her cheeks.

"I am not inhuman," she replied quietly. "Is it a little thing that a mind should go astray?"

He looked at her earnestly, but made no reply.

Soon after, Lottie saw with surprise, during one of the intervals between the forms, that Miss Martell turned and spoke freely and cordially to Hemstead. Her surprise became something akin to annoyance, as, at the close, she took his arm and began to walk up and down the wide hall, evidently becoming deeply interested in his conversation. She soon shook off moody Brently, who could think of nothing but the slight he had received, and, taking De Forrest's arm, also commenced promenading in the hall. She noted, with satisfaction, that Hemstead was not so occupied with his new and fascinating acquaintance as to be oblivious of her presence.

Soon after Mr. Martell joined his daughter, and was introduced to Hemstead; and they went out to supper together.

Lottie managed that she and De Forrest should find seats near them in a roomy angle, where, being out of the crush, Mr. Martell and his little party could season Mrs. Byram's sumptuous viands with Attic salt. And the flavor of their wit and thought was so attractive that they soon had a group of the most intelligent and cultivated of the company around them, and Lottie saw that Hemstead, who had been neglected by his own party, was becoming appreciated by the best people present. Miss Martell, with the tact of a perfect lady, had the power of putting him at his ease and drawing him out. Hemstead's mind was no stagnant, muddy pool, but a living fountain, and his thought sparkled as it flowed readily on the congenial topics that Mr. and Miss Martell introduced. The freshness and originality of his views seemed to interest them and others greatly; but what pleased him most was that Lottie, who sat near, was neglecting her supper and De Forrest's compliments in her attention to the conversation. Her face showed a quick, discriminating mind, and as the discussion grew a little warm on a topic of general interest, he saw from her eager and intelligent face that she had an opinion, and he had the tact to ask her for it just at the right moment. Though a little embarrassed at his unexpected question, she expressed her thought so briefly and brightly that the others were pleased, and she was at once taken into the circle of their talk, which of course became more animated and spicy with her piquant words and manner added. It was evident that she was enjoying this employment of her brain more than she had that of her feet. The lower pleasure paled before the higher; and she was grateful to Hemstead for having drawn her within the charmed circle.

De Forrest did not grieve over Lottie's absorption, as it gave him more time for the supper-table and champagne; and to the latter he and a good many others were so devoted that they were hardly their poor selves the rest of the evening. In Brently's case it was most marked after the ladies had retired. He began to talk quite loudly and boisterously of his slight, and at one time was about to seek Miss Martell, and demand an explanation, but was prevailed upon by his friends to be quiet.

CHAPTER XVI

HOW WOMAN MAKES OR MARS

IN the changes that occurred alter leaving the supper-room, Miss Martell took Harcourt's arm and said in a low tone, "I was glad to see that you did not take any wine."

"And I am glad you cared to see. But how could I, after your gentle hint? I know my weakness. If I had indulged in one glass I might have taken too many, as I am sorry has been the case in more instances than one to-night."

"You admit, then, that it is a weakness?" she said gently, fixing her eyes, that were no longer cold and expressionless, upon him.

"In truth, I must admit that I have many weaknesses, Miss Martell."

"You certainly possess one element of strength, in that you recognize them. Knowledge of danger is often the best means of safety. But how is it that you are so ready to acknowledge weakness of any kind? I thought that men scoffed at the idea that they could be weak or in danger from any temptation."

"If they do, they either do not know themselves, or they are not honest. I do know myself, to my sorrow, and it would seem like sacrilege to me not to be truthful and sincere with you. And yet it is when I am with you that I most despise myself."

"How, then, can you endure my presence?" she asked, with a shy, half-mischievous glance.

He flushed slightly, and tried to disguise a deeper meaning with a slight laugh, as he said, "If I were shut out of Eden, I should often be tempted to look over the hedge."

She did not reply at once, nor lift her eyes to his, but the color deepened upon her cheeks; and if he had seen the expression of her averted face, his might have appeared more hopeful.

After a moment she turned and said, with a smile, "I think the fact that you would like to look over the hedge a very promising sign. It proves that you regret our lost Eden purity, and would like to possess it again. If you will only let your wishes develop into right action, instead of looking wistfully over the hedge, you may be welcomed within the gate of the better Paradise."

He looked at her searchingly, but she again turned away her face, and would not meet his eyes. After a moment, he said, "I do not think you used the pronoun 'our,' correctly. There is nothing akin between my moral state and yours."

"Yes, there is," she replied earnestly. "If you struggle as hard to do right as I do, you are trying very hard indeed."

With a quick glance of surprise he said, "It has ever seemed to me that you were developing as naturally and inevitably as a moss-rose."

"Nonsense!" she answered, a little abruptly. "I am as human as you are. I have doubtless had advantages over you in being more sheltered and less tempted. But in a world like ours, and with natures like ours, every one must struggle hard who would live a good life. Even then we need Divine help."

They had now passed into a large conservatory, where they supposed they were alone. He took her hand and said, with a manly sincerity that made his face almost as noble as hers was beautiful: "Miss Martell, you are holier than I am. You are as much above me as heaven is above the earth. And yet, because you have not said to me, 'Stand aside, for I am holier than thou'; because you have made a claim, which I can scarcely understand, of kindred weakness—of like need of effort to do right—you have given me a little hope that possibly at some distant day I may find a way out of my doubts and weaknesses. I should like to be a true and believing man.''

"Please do not think that I have it in my heart to say 'Stand aside' to any one. Such a spirit is most unchristian, and in me would be most unwarranted. Do not think I meant that when I repulsed Mr. Brently. He has forfeited every right to the title of gentleman. I believe he is utterly bad, and he shows no wish to be otherwise; and I was disgusted by the flattering attentions he received from those with whom he had no right to associate at all. When will society get beyond its vulgar worship of wealth! But, Mr. Harcourt, please don't talk about a 'possible way out of your doubts and weaknesses at some distant day.' You paid me the highest compliment in your power, when you refrained from wine at supper to-night. I am going to ask a personal favor. Won't you let it alone altogether? Mr. Harcourt,'' she added, her eyes filling with tears, "I cannot bear to think of a nature like yours becoming a slave to such an appetite, and it does seem to master those who are naturally the noblest.''

He turned away to hide his own feeling, while she, with clasped hands, stood looking at him, as his good angel might. When he turned to her, he spoke calmly, and almost humbly: "I will not protest too much, Miss Martell. I will make no loud and absolute promises, but it seems to me, while I stand here in your presence, I could not do a mean or ignoble thing again. But in that degree that I revere you, I distrust myself. But I pledge you my honor, that I will try to do what you ask, and more.''

"You give me just the kind of promise I like best,'' she said, giving him her hand with a happy smile. "But I cannot tell you how much I wish you could seek God's help, as simply, as believingly, as I do.''

"Ah, there is the trouble,'' he replied, in deep dejection. "My mind is tossed upon a sea of doubt and uncertainty." Then, as from a sudden impulse, he said, "But I could worship you. You are the most beautiful woman here to-night, but instead of making your beauty the slave of contemptible vanity, and employing it, like Miss Marsden and others, merely to win flattery and attention, you turn from all, and forget yourself and your own pleasure, that you may keep a man that is hardly worth saving from going to the devil. If I go, after your kindness to-night, it will be because I ought."

Here her father called her from the door. The character of the entertainment was becoming such that he was anxious to get away. As they left the conservatory, she said in a low, hasty tone, "I am not so unselfish as you think; for it would make me very unhappy if you did not become what you are capable of being."

"Since you care personally what becomes of me, you have given me a double incentive," he answered eagerly, as they passed out.

As they disappeared, Lottie Marsden stepped out from behind a large lemon-tree, with an expression upon her face quite as acid as she unripe fruit that had helped to conceal her. How she came to witness the scene described requires some explanation. As they left the supper-room, she shook De Forrest off for a time, and when Miss Martell parted from Hemstead, she joined him. After the attention he had received, she was not in as patronizing a mood as before.

"Are you willing to take a short promenade with such a guy as I am, Mr. Hemstead?" she asked.

"Yes, if you are willing to link yourself with so much awkwardness."

"I wish I had your grace of mind, Mr. Hemstead."

"You have no occasion to find fault with nature's gifts to you."

"I fear you think I should find much fault with myself, if not with nature. But I can hardly find fault with you after your kindly tact in the supper-rom. I wanted to join your breezy, sprightly chat, and you gave me a chance so nicely.''

"Because I wished you to join it. It was not a deed of charity, and you well repaid me. Indeed, I saw so much thought in your face, that I wanted more of the same kind.''

"I think you see more than we give you credit for,'' she said, looking doubtfully at him.

" 'We'? who are 'we'? Yes, I am seeing a good deal here to-night. As you went to see the 'other set' a few evenings ago, I also am seeing some new phases of character.''

"And some new phases in one that you had a pretty good opinion of that night. I imagine you no longer consider me 'capable of the noblest things.' ''

"I have not changed my mind on that point at all, but—'' and here he hesitated.

"But you are discovering that I am also capable of just the reverse.''

He flushed, but said gravely, "You put my thought too strongly, Miss Marsden. It would be nearer the truth, if you care for my opinion at all, to say that I do not understand you.''

She also flushed, but said a little coldly, "I am not surprised; I scarcely understand myself.''

"I find you full of puzzling contradictions,'' he added.

"Since I cannot contradict you, I will seek some fallible creatures like myself;'' and she vanished, leaving him as uncomfortable and puzzled as ever he had been in his life.

She had scarcely entered the parlor before both De Forrest and Brently sought her hand for a waltz. The latter had disgusted her before, and now he was too tipsy for even the willing blindness of girls like Addie Marchmont, so she escaped with De Forrest, but soon found that his step was out of tune with the music, or her own mind so preoccupied that their feet made discord with the notes. Therefore she led her subservient attendant into the conservatory, and got rid of him for a time by the following ruse.

"I dropped something in the supper-room. Please find it, and look till you do."

De Forrest's ideas were too confused for him to ask what she had lost; and once in the supper-room again, the champagne was so inviting that he, with Brently and others, finished another bottle.

With thoughts dwelling on Hemstead's words, she strolled to the further end of the walk, and around into another aisle, wishing to be alone for a few moments. It was then that Harcourt and Miss Martell entered, and before she was aware she heard the uncomplimentary reference to herself, and understood the significance of the unexpected scene.

"That is what Mr. Hemstead thinks me capable of," she thought, with tingling cheeks—"making my 'beauty the slave of contemptible vanity,' and employing it merely to win flattery and attention for myself. You put it very plainly, Mr. Harcourt. I know what is your opinion of me certainly. I wish I cared as little what Mr. Hemstead thinks; and why I should care any more I'm sure I don't know. Yes, I do, too. He's a true, good man, and is the first one that ever treated me as if I were a true, good woman. But now I have made it clear to him, as well as to Harcourt and Miss Martell, what I really am. I knew what Brently was as well as the rest, and yet I smiled upon him because the others did. By this time both of my most ardent admirers are tipsy. What is their admiration worth?"

As she entered the parlors she saw at a glance what would be the character of the remaining hours. The sensuous spirit of wine would inspire the gayety and intensify the natural excitement of the occasion. Heretofore she could join in a fashionable revel with the keenest zest, but she could not to-night. Unconsciously Miss Martell had given her a stinging rebuke. She had been shown how a beautiful woman might employ the power of her fascinations to lure men into purer and nobler life, as Hemstead had suggested the morning after his arrival. As she remembered that she had used her beauty only to lure men to her feet, that she might enjoy a momentary triumph, soon to be forgotten in other conquests, she was already more than dissatisfied with herself—an unusual experience with Lottie Marsden.

She refused half a dozen invitations to dance, and was about ascending to the dressing-room, when Harcourt met her in the hall and said, ''I think I had better send De Forrest home. Hemstead will go with him.''

"What is the matter with Julian?"

"Well, they say he mistook a decanter of brandy for wine. At any rate he is under the table, 'looking for something of yours,' he says; though what he does not say or does not know. What's more, we can't get him up, for he says you told him not to leave the dining-room till he found it. I fear we shall have to use force, unless you can manage him.''

Then with a burning flush of shame she remembered how, in her wish to be alone, she had sent him into temptation, instead of trying to shield and protect, as had Miss Martell in the case of Harcourt, whose abstemiousness had excited the surprise of more than one. But without a word she went directly to the supper-room; and there witnessed a scene that she never forgot.

The elegant De Forrest was crawling about the floor, uttering her name continually in connection with the most maudlin sentiment, and averring with many oaths that he would never rise till he had found what she had lost.

Brently, almost equally drunk, sat near, convulsed with laughter, saying with silly iteration, "He's looking for Miss Marsden's heart.''

Mrs. Byram and her son stood helplessly by, their manner showing that their wish to be polite was almost mastered by their disgust. Hemstead, who was trying to get De Forrest up, had just given a stern rebuke to one of the giggling waiters as Lottie entered.

It did not take her over a moment to comprehend all. While her face was crimson, she acted decidedly and with a certain dignity. Going directly to De Forrest she said, "Julian, I have found what I lost. Get up and come with me."

His habitual deference to her wishes and words served him now. Her tone and manner were quiet but very firm and positive, and he at once sought to obey. Hemstead and Harcourt helped him to his feet.

"I am going home, Julian, and wish you to go with me," she continued in the same tone.

"Certainly (hic) my dear (hic) I'll do anything (hic) in the world (hic) or anywhere else for you."

A look of intense disgust flitted across her face, but she turned, and said emphatically to the others: "I am more to blame for this than he. I sent him here some time since, when I knew, or ought to have known, that he should have been kept away from temptation. May I trespass so far upon your kindness as to ask all present to remain silent in regard to this scene."

"I know little of etiquette," said Hemstead, "but surely any one would fail utterly in true courtesy, did they not accede to that request."

"Thank you, Mr. Hemstead," said Lottie, with a look he did not soon forget. "Will you order the sleigh to the door? Mr. Harcourt, will you get Mr. De Forrest's hat and coat?"

The door leading into the parlor had been closed and locked as soon as the trouble commenced, and thus the guests were ignorant of the disgraceful scene.

"Julian, I wish you to sit quietly here till I return," said Lottie, in the most decided manner.

He had sense enough left to know that something was wrong, and that his safest course was to yield to her. So, muttering, maudlin, and dishevelled, he sat almost helplessly in the chair where he was placed, with not a trace of his former elegance left.

Lottie looked at him a second, with a strange expression, then, taking Mrs. Byram aside, asked:

"Will you be so kind as to have the doors of the parlors leading into the hall closed, as if accidentally, when we pass out?" Adding, "I think if Mr. Byram can get Mr. Brently to his room now, it would also be well."

Mrs. Byram commenced many professions of regret, but Lottie merely said, "I cannot think about it now. I can only act," and she hastened away to prepare for the drive home.

A moment later De Forrest was steadied through the hall and helped into the sleigh.

"Shall I sit by him?" asked Harcourt.

"No," said Lottie, in the same decided voice. "I will take care of him. I was the cause of his trouble, and will not leave him till he is safely home. You will greatly oblige me if you will remain with Addie and Bel, and disarm their suspicion and that of others. Mr. Hemstead will accompany me, and we will send the sleigh back immediately."

"Miss Marsden," said Harcourt, "you are a noble-hearted girl. I will do whatever you wish."

"Thank you for what you have done. That is all."

"The horses are restless; I will sit with the coachman," said Hemstead, surmising that Lottie would desire all the seclusion possible under the circumstances. He was not mistaken, for as Harcourt retired she said in a low tone, "You are right. I should be glad to escape now even from your eyes, that are friendly, I trust."

"Yes," he replied, with an emphasis that did her good —"most friendly;" and they drove away through the cold white moonlight and colder and whiter snow; and to Lottie, with her burdened conscience and heavy heart, the calm night seemed more than ever like a face regarding her with cold and silent scorn.

CHAPTER XVII

MIDNIGHT VIGILS

THERE were indeed four strangely assorted characters in that sleigh as they were carried beyond the sounds of music and gayety, which, to Hemstead and Lottie Marsden at least, were little less than mockery. There was the stolid coachman, who, whatever were his thoughts, had been trained to appear oblivious of everything save his duty, and to be but an animate part of the "establishment." He was much like the horses he drove, living his narrow, material life in the passing hour, knowing little and caring less about the past or the future.

Hemstead, in contrast, had a mind as ethereal as faith could make it, and a fancy enriched by wide reading. Heretofore he had lived chiefly in the past and future, his studies making him at home in the one, and his hopes leading him forward into the other. But now a silent form near him had a strange power to concentrate his thoughts on the present. The man who had speculated and reasoned about sinners in the abstract, and who had classified and divided them up into well-defined shades and degrees, was now sorely puzzled over two of them, who, in a certain sense, were under his charge. What was also odd, his deepest sympathy and desire to help did not appear drawn toward the greater sinner. Indeed, for the tipsy youth he had hardly a sentiment other than contempt. Broad, impartial rules of action and feeling seemed perfectly correct in the seminary. He forgot that he was not carrying them out. It did not occur to him that he was like a physician who stepped by the sicker patient to a better and more promising one. In justice it must be said that he would have put himself to any personal inconvenience, and have made any effort in his power, were the question brought to an issue, in order to work a transformation in De Forrest's character. But for some reason it was so perfectly natural to take an absorbing interest in Lottie's moral state that he never asked himself why he had not a similar solicitude for Addie or Bel Parton.

Rigid and impartial rules are very well till fallible men come to apply them to their most fallible fellow-creatures.

Only God can mercifully apply a perfect law to imperfect humanity, and if He had a "beloved disciple," might not Hemstead have a favorite sinner?

And an oddly related couple were those two young people whom all supposed destined for a union, that in the judgment of friends would be most fitting, but that in truth would be unnatural and productive of wretchedness. Though Hemstead's mind dwelt unwaveringly upon them, he never once looked back during the drive. He would have seen a strange sight if he had—a beautiful woman, with a face looking almost spirit-like in the pale moonlight, with her arm, for the first time, around a man whom she was beginning in the depths of her soul almost to loathe. No embrace of affection was that, but a mechanical act prompted by a stern and remorseful sense of duty. She shrank from the man whose swaying form she steadied. It was settled that night in her own soul, as if by a decree of fate, that she would never marry Julian De Forrest. And yet it was one of the good traits in her character, that, while she drew back in shuddering aversion from any close personal relation to him, she at the same time had generous, regretful pity, and, if she could be kind to him at a distance, would be a very faithful friend.

But why did her eyes turn so often and so wistfully up to the tall great-coated form before her? She did not know. She did not even ask herself.

Are we ever guided by reason, will, deliberate choice? Are there not often strong half-recognized instincts that sway us more profoundly, even as the plant unconsciously turns its leaves and blossoms toward the sun, and sends its roots groping unerringly to the moisture?

So absorbed was she in looking at the square, burly form before her, that the sleigh suddenly stopped at Mrs. Marchmont's door, and Hemstead looked around and caught her eye. What was more, he saw her apparently loving embrace of De Forrest. He was not versed in the conditions of intoxication, nor did he realize that De Forrest was so far gone as to make the act necessary. But he could see her blush, even in the moonlight.

Without a word he assisted her out, but had some difficulty with De Forrest, who, from the fumes of liquor and the cold air, had grown very drowsy. But Hemstead's grasp was so strong and masterful, that while he roused, he also steadied and supported him up the steps. Lottie said to the coachman, "Mr. De Forrest is not well, so we came home earlier. You may now return for the others."

The man heard her with a stolid face that might have been mahogany, but when by himself it relaxed into a grim smile as he chuckled, "I've seen people have such spells afore; but if you was my darter, miss, I'd make you give that chap the mitten, 'cause sich bad spells is wonderful apt to grow on a feller."

Mrs. Marchmont and Mr. Dimmerly had retired, and the rather dull servant who admitted them was too sleepy to note anything. Lottie promptly dismissed her, and told her she would wait for the others.

Hemstead saw De Forrest to his room. He had become so stupid that he did mechanically what was urged, and the student soon left him sleeping heavily.

But Hemstead's heart was strangely burdened. He had come to the conclusion that under all Lottie's coquetry and cousinly freedom with De Forrest she had hidden a real attachment, and that perhaps an engagement, or at least an understanding, existed between them. He did not think at the time why this relation should so depress him. He would probably have explained it by his natural regret that such a girl should be mismated to such a man. But it might well have been doubted whether his heart would have become suddenly like lead, had he discovered that his own cousin was engaged, even to Brently, however sincere might have been his regret. But he descended to the parlor with the unselfish purpose and wish to bring her mind again under the spell of truth, if possible, hoping that the events of the evening would suggest the need of a better philosophy than she had learned in the past.

But he would have no little difficulty in maintaining his disinterestedness and general missionary spirit in the interview that awaited him.

For a young man but a few years past his majority, with an impressible nature and a warm heart, to watch through the witching hour of midnight with a maiden like Lottie Marsden, and all the time have no other thought than her moral improvement, is perhaps asking too much of human nature. With the very best intentions and with the absolute conviction, as he supposed, that the young lady could only be a subject for his missionary zeal, unconsciously the beautiful picture she made with the firelight flickering upon her face, and the snowy opera-cloak thrown around her, stole into his heart that was large and empty, waiting for an occupant.

"I have drawn a chair close up to the fire," she said, "for you must be cold after riding on that high seat with the coachman."

"I am not cold, but I thank you all the same."

"You have been kinder to me than I deserved, Mr. Hemstead."

Truly Lottie's gratitude would be a dangerous thing to any man, as she expressed it then; and the disinterested student was conscious of a strange thrill at heart. But he said, with a flush of pleasure: "I do not know that I have.

At any rate friends should not keep a debit and credit account with each other.''

"And can you still feel friendly to me after this evening?''

"Do I look savagely hostile?'' he asked smilingly.

"I feared you would despise me. I certainly despise myself.''

"From the fact that you so evidently blame yourself I am less disposed to blame.''

"But you rightly think me most worthy of blame.''

"Do you honestly care what I think, Miss Marsden? My opinions have been formed in what must seem a plain and homely world to you, quite devoid of the elegance and fashion to which you have been accustomed.''

"I begin to think it is a better world than mine, and tonight I am sick of elegance and fashion. Yes, I honestly do care now what you do think. I have been flattered and lied to all my life, and you are the first man who ever told me the unvarnished truth.''

He rose and paced thoughtfully up and down the room; then looked dubiously at her. She was so exquisitely beautiful, and seemed in such a kindly mood, that he was greatly tempted to temporize and say smooth things, lest he should offend and drive her away. But conscience whispered, "Now is your opportunity to speak the 'unvarnished truth,' whatever be the consequences''; and conscience with Hemstead was an imperative martinet. She waited in curious and quiet expectancy. This sincere and unconventional man was delightfully odd and interesting to her. She saw the power and fascination of her beauty upon him, and at the same time perceived that in his crystal integrity he would give her his honest thought. She interpreted his hesitancy, and said, "You fear that I shall be offended?''

"Yes.''

"I promise you to listen patiently—yes, gratefully—to the severest things you can say.''

"I may test your promise severely. I am a plain and

awkward man. Will you permit a plain and homely illustration of my thought?"

"I'm in a mood for plain words to-night. They will be
in keeping with the former events of the evening, which
were plain enough."

"Well, then, were it possible that I could be the fortunate possessor of a statue by Phidias, I would not use it as
a hat-stand. If I possessed a painting by Rubens, I would
not turn it into a fire-screen."

He hesitated, as he saw the hot blood mount to her
face; but she said quietly, "Go on. I think I understand
you."

He continued in a tone that was as gentle as his words
seemed harsh. "Believe me, I am speaking in kindness,
and only because you are brave enough to give me leave.
As Phidias might embody beauty itself in marble, so God
has bestowed it on you. When I was looking upon that
marvellous scene—that transfigured world—the morning
after my arrival, you appeared and seemed a part of it.
Do you remember what I said then? I have reluctantly
thought to-night that you could wear your coronet of beauty,
not only as a benignant queen, but as a petty tyrant—that
you could put it to ignoble uses, and make it a slave to
self. It seemed at times that you only sought to lead men
to bow in admiration to you, instead of inspiring them to
stand erect in true manhood, with their faces heavenward.
A woman endowed as you are can always do with a man
one of two things: either fascinate him with her own personality, so that his thought is only of her; or else through
her beauty and words and manner, that are in keeping,
suggest the diviner loveliness of a noble life and character.
I am satisfied that one could not be in Miss Martell's society
without being better, or wishing to be better. You might
have the same influence, and to a greater degree, because
you naturally have more force and quicker sympathies.
There is more magnetism in your nature, and you could
understand and help, if you chose, a wider range of char-

acter than she. I doubt very much whether Miss Martell could make herself much at home among the plain country folk that you quite carried by storm the other evening. God has given you the power and beauty. Will you let me ask, in the spirit of kindness, not criticism, Are you using these gifts for Him, or for yourself?"

Lottie's eyes were moist, but her brow was contracted into a thoughtful frown, as she sat lowering at the fire. After a few moments' silence, she said, in a tone of bitterness:

"As I feel and see things to-night, I should say, for neither God nor myself, but solely and expressly for the sake of the Evil One. What good, what happiness, do all the compliments, all the attention I ever received, secure to me to-night? I thought I was using all for my own benefit. That was my only purpose and aim, but every flattering thing that I can remember is only a burden to think of now. I am the worse for my beauty, as you regard it. I cannot think of any one that I have made better; but many that I have made worse. I seem to have been receiving all my life, and yet to-night I feel as if I had nothing but a burden upon my heart."

Hemstead's words were not reassuring. Indeed, Lottie thought them a trifle harsh, though spoken so kindly.

"You cannot feel otherwise, Miss Marsden. You have been seeking to keep and use for yourself what God meant you should use for Him. You feel very much as you would, did you take a large sum of money, left in your hands as a sacred trust, and go on a pleasure trip with it. He has intrusted to you the richest and rarest gifts, and every day that you have misappropriated them is a burden upon your conscience. You will feel the same after a long life of adulation, in which every whim has been gratified. Believe me, Miss Marsden, it is a very sad thing to come to the end of one's life with no other possession than a burdened conscience and a heavy, guilty heart. I long to save you from such a fate. That would be a wretchedly poor result of a lifetime for one endowed as you are."

"Your words are very severe, Mr. Hemstead," she said in a low tone, burying her face in her hands.

"Faithful are the wounds of a friend," he replied.

"I never thought I could permit any one to speak to me as you have done, nor would I endure it from you, did I not recognize something like sympathy in the voice with which you speak such cutting words. But I fear they are true, after all. A burdened conscience and a guilty heart seem all there is of me to-night."

He was about to reverse the picture, and portray in strong and hopeful terms what she might be, and what she could accomplish, when the sleigh-bells announced the return of the rest of the party. She sprang up and said hastily: "I do not wish to meet them to-night, and so will retire at once. As physician of the 'mind deceased' you clearly believe in what is termed the 'heroic treatment.' Your scalpel is sharp, and you cut deeply. But as proof that I have kept my word, and am not offended, I give you my hand."

He took it in both of his, but did not speak. She looked up at him through the tears that still lingered, and was touched to see that his eyes were as moist as hers. Giving his hand a cordial pressure, she said as she left him: "You cannot look at me in harsh criticism through tears of sympathy. Your face is kinder than your words. I am glad you do not despise me."

Hemstead admitted Harcourt and the young ladies into the shadowy hall, and then bade them good-night. He, too, was in no mood for Addie's gossip or Bel's satire. They had also found Harcourt strangely silent and preoccupied.

The evident influence of Miss Martell over Harcourt, and their intimate relations require some explanation. He was an orphan, and his father had been a friend of Mr. Martell. During the last illness of the elder Mr. Harcourt, he had asked his friend to take some interest in his son, and, when possible, to give him friendly counsel. To a man like Mr. Martell, such a request was like a sacred obligation; and he had sought to do more than was asked. He wrote the young man almost fatherly letters, and often invited him to his house. Thus it came about that the influence of Mr. Martell and his daughter did more to restrain the wayward tendencies of young Harcourt than all other things combined; and it must be confessed that the little blue-eyed girl had more influence than the wise old father. She seemed to take almost a sisterly interest in him, and occasionally wrote such a sweet little letter than he would reform his college life for a week thereafter. But he seemed to have a dash of wild blood that would break out only too often into indiscretions, the rumors of which filled his kind friend Mr. Martell with anxiety. But Alice, his daughter, ever insisted that he would "come out all right."

"Tom has a good heart, father," she would say; and so, with woman's faith, she hoped where her father feared.

If Harcourt could have been continually under their influence he would undoubtedly have developed into a far better man. But, between absence at college and the law-school and some travel during vacations, he saw less and less of them. Alice also was kept very steadily at school, and during the last two years of her studies they had missed each other in vacations, and seldom met.

But something more than maidenly modesty and pride made Alice shy and reserved when with Harcourt. She would think more about him, but talk less to him than to others when in company. She was a peculiarly sensitive, diffident girl, and instinctively shrank from the man who had for her the strongest interest.

On the completion of her studies her father had taken her abroad, and they had spent two or three years in travel. The extraordinary graces of her person were but the reflex of her richly cultivated mind. Even abroad she had many admirers; but with tact, firmness, and inimitable grace, she ever sought to prevent false hopes, and so had fewer offers than an ordinary coquette. But many who soon learned that they could never establish a dearer relation became strong friends, and also better men; for Alice Martell seemed to have the power of evoking all the good there was in a man, and of putting him under a kind of sacred obligation to be true and manly, as the result of her acquaintance. However deep and lasting regret may have been, no man ever left her presence in harsh and bitter contempt for the very name of woman, as too often had been the case with Lottie Marsden. Those who knew her least said she was cold, and those who knew her true, womanly heart best wondered at her continued indifference to every suit. And sometimes she wondered at herself— how it was that all the attention she received scarcely ever quickened her pulse.

But when after long absence she returned and met the friend and playmate of her childhood—the wayward youth to whom she was accustomed to give sisterly counsel—her pulse was so strangely accelerated, and the blood so quick to mount to her face at his every word and look, that she began to understand herself somewhat.

They had but recently returned to their residence on the banks of the Hudson; and Harcourt was made a welcome visitor.

Having completed his professional studies, the young man had succeeded largely to the practice of his deceased father, and was doing well in a business point of view. He had inherited enough property to secure a good start in life, but not enough to rob him of the wholesome stimulus which comes from the need of self-exertion. He had an acute, active mind. Abundance of intellect and fire flashed from his dark eyes, and we have seen that he was not without good and generous traits. But in his spiritual life he had become materialistic and sceptical. His associates were brilliant, but fast men; and for him also the wine-cup was gaining dangerous fascination.

Mr. Martell, in the spirit of the most friendly interest, soon learned these facts after his return, and also the gossip, which brought a sudden paleness to his daughter's cheek, that he was engaged, or virtually engaged, to Addie Marchmont.

While Alice therefore was kind, she seemed to avoid him; and he found it almost impossible to be alone with her. She had always dwelt in his mind, more as a cherished ideal, a revered saint, than as an ordinary flesh-and-blood girl with whom he was fit to associate, and for a time after her return her manner increased this impression. He explained the recognized fact that she shunned his society by thinking that she knew his evil tendencies, and that to her believing and Christian spirit his faithless and irregular life was utterly uncongenial. For a short time he had tried to ignore her opinion and society in reckless indifference; but the loveliness of her person and character daily grew more fascinating, and his evil habits lost in power as she gained. For some little time before Mrs. Byram's company, he had been earnestly wishing that he could become worthy of at least her esteem and old friendly regard, not daring to hope for anything more. It never occurred to him that gossip had coupled his name with his cousin Addie, and that this fact influenced Miss Martell's manner as well as his tendencies toward dissipation. He laid it all to the latter cause, and was beginning to feel that he could live the life of an ascetic, if this lovely saint would only permit his devotion.

And Alice, so sensitive where he was concerned, thought she saw a change in him for the better, and in the spirit of womanly self-sacrifice was resolving to see more of him than was prudent for her peace of mind, if by so doing she could regain her old power to advise and restrain.

With gladness she recognized her influence over him at Mrs. Byram's company, and, as we have seen, made the most of it. But, with surprise and some strange thrills at heart, she noted that he and Addie Marchmont did not act as an engaged couple naturally would; and observed, with disgust, that Miss Marchmont seemed more pleased with Brently's attentions than Lottie Marsden had been.

That a man of Harcourt's force and mind should be captivated by such a girl as Miss Marchmont, had been a mystery; and she thought, when seeing them together in Mrs. Byram's parlors, "They take it more coolly than any people I ever saw."

Addie appeared engrossed with the attentions of others, and Harcourt not in the least jealous or annoyed. In brief, they acted like cousins, and not in the least like lovers.

But in the sensitive delicacy of her character she would not permit her mind to dwell on the problem of their relations, and bent all her thoughts upon her effort to win Harcourt to a better life.

And she had moved him that evening more deeply than she could know. Neither she, nor any finite power, could plant righteous principle within his soul and transform his character; but she had created, for the time at least, an utter distaste for all low and sensual pleasures, and an honest and absorbing wish to become a true, good man. He felt that he could not, in her society, and breathing the pure atmosphere of her life, be his old self.

Never did a man return from a fashionable revel in a more serious and thoughtful mood, and equally with Lottie and Hemstead he was glad to escape, from the trifling chat and gossip of Addie and Bel Parton, to the solitude of his own room.

CHAPTER XVIII

THE "day after the ball" has its proverbial character,
and Saturday was so long and dismal to several of
the revellers that it occurred to them that their
pleasure had been purchased rather dearly. It seemed an
odd coincidence, that those who had been bent on securing
all the pleasure possible, with no other thought, suffered
the most. Bel and Addie could scarcely endure their own
company, they were so weary and stupid; and they yawned
through the day, irritable and dishevelled, for it was too
stormy for callers.

De Forrest did not appear until dinner, and then came
down moody and taciturn. The young ladies had heard
of his illness the evening before, with significant glances.
Mrs. Marchmont partly surmised the truth, but politely
ignored the matter, treating it only as a sudden indisposition; and so the affair was passed over, as such matters
usually are in fashionable life until they reach a stage too
pronounced for polite blindness.

De Forrest but dimly recollected the events of the preceding evening. He was quite certain, however, that he
had been drunk, and had made a fool of himself.

Though his conscience was not over tender upon this
subject, and though such occurrences were not so exceedingly rare in fashionable life as to be very shocking, he still
had the training and instinct of a gentleman, to a sufficient
degree to feel deep mortification.

If he had become tipsy among those of his own sex, or
while off on a fishing excursion, he would have regarded it

as a light matter; but, even in his eyes, intoxication at an evening company, and before the girl in whose estimation he most wished to stand well, was a very serious matter. He could not remember much after going a second time to the supper-room in compliance with Lottie's request, but had a vague impression that she and Hemstead had brought him home. He was left in torturing uncertainty how far he had disgraced himself, because it was a subject concerning which he could not bring himself to make inquiries. That those he met at the dinner-table treated him with their usual quiet politeness proved nothing. Human faces mask more thoughts than are expressed. Hemstead's grave silence was somewhat significant; but De Forrest cared so little for his opinion that he scarcely heeded the student's manner.

Lottie Marsden was the one he most wished, and yet most dreaded to see. But Lottie did not appear.

Whether it was true, as she believed, or not, that she was the more guilty, she certainly was the greater sufferer, and that Saturday became the longest and dreariest period of pain that she had ever experienced. She awoke in the morning with a nervous headache, which grew so severe that she declined to leave her room during the day. Bel, Addie, and her aunt all offered to do anything in their power; but she only asked to be left alone. She was so unstrung that even words of kindness and solicitude jarred like discord.

It was torture to think, and yet her brain was unnaturally active. Everything presented itself in the most painfully bare and accurate manner. The glamour faded out of her gay young life, and she saw only the hard lines of fact. Hemstead's words repeated themselves over and over again, and in their light she questioned the past closely. It was not in keeping with her positive nature and strong mind to do things by halves. With fixed and steady scrutiny she reviewed the motives of her life, and estimated the results. They were so unsatisfactory as to startle her. Although the spent years had been filled with continuous and varied activity, what had she accomplished for herself or any one else? Were not all her past days like water spilled on barren sands, producing nothing?

As she had before intimated, she had been receiving homage, flattery, and even love, all her life, and yet now her heart had no treasures to which she could turn in solid satisfaction, nor could memory recall efforts like that she saw Miss Martell making in behalf of Harcourt. The adulation received was now empty breath and forgotten words, and nothing substantial or comforting remained.

But, if memory could recall little good accomplished, it placed in long and dark array many scenes that she would gladly have forgotten.

What can be worse—what need we fear more—than to be left alone forever with a guilty and accusing conscience, and no respite, no solace? What perdition need a man shrink from more than to go away from his earthly life, to be alone with memory—a pale and silent spectre—who will turn the pages of his daily record, and point to what was, and what might have been?

A shallow-minded girl would have been incapable of this searching self-analysis. A weak, irresolute girl like Bel Parton would have taken a sedative, and escaped a miserable day in sleep. But, with all her faults, Lottie abounded in practical common-sense; and Hemstead's words and her own experience suggested that she might be doing herself a very great wrong. She felt that it was no light matter to make one's whole life a blunder, and to invest all one's years and energies in what paid no better interest than she had received that day. Her physical pain and mental distress acted and reacted upon each other, until at last, wearied out, she sobbed herself to sleep.

Both De Forrest and Hemstead were greatly in hopes that she would be at the supper-table, but they did not see her that day. The former, with his aching head and heavy heart, learned, if never before, that the "way of transgressor is hard.'' But, though the latter could not be regarded as a transgressor, his way was hard also that long day; and he whom Lottie, in the memory of his severe words, regarded somewhat as her stern accuser, would have been more than ready to take all her pains and woes upon himself, could he have relieved her.

He now bitterly condemned himself for having been too harsh in the wholesome truth he had brought home to the flattered girl. It was rather severe treatment; still she was vigorous, and would be all the better for it. But now her faithful physician, as he heard how ill and suffering she was, almost wished that he had but faintly suggested the truth in homœopathic doses.

At the same time he supposed that her indisposition was caused more by her shame and grief at the conduct of De Forrest than by anything he had said. The impression that she was attached or engaged to De Forrest was becoming almost a conviction.

Though Lottie had never, by a word, bound herself to her cousin, yet her aunt and all the household regarded her as virtually engaged to him, and expected that the marriage would eventually occur. With Hemstead, they regarded her illness and seclusion as the result of her mortification at his behavior, and, underneath their politic politeness, were very indignant at his folly. But they expected that the trouble would soon blow over, as a matter of course. The mantle of charity for young men as rich and well-connected as De Forrest is very large. And then this slip could be regarded somewhat in the light of an accident; for when it became evident that Bel understood the nature of De Forrest's ''spell,'' as the coachman called it, Lottie had taken pains to insist that it was an accident for which she was chiefly to blame; and had also said as much to Mrs. Marchmont. Thus they all concluded that her relations with De Forrest would not be disturbed.

Harcourt was the happiest of the party; but it must be confessed that, clearer than any law points, he saw still among blooming exotics a being far more rare and beautiful, who stood before him the whole day with clasped hands and entreating eyes, whose only request was, "be a true man." Under the inspiration of her words and manner he began to hope that he might eventually grant her request.

As far as Lottie's intruding image would permit, Hemstead concentrated all his energies on the great sermon, the elaborate effort of many months, that he expected to preach on the morrow. He hoped that Lottie, and indeed all, would be there, for it seemed that if they would only give him their thoughtful attention he would prove beyond a shadow of a doubt that they were in God's hands, and that it would be worse than folly not to submit to His shaping and molding discipline.

At last Sunday morning came. It was a cold, chilly, leaden day, and even a glance from the windows gave one a shivering sense of discomfort.

The gloom of nature seemed to shadow the faces of some of the party as they gathered at a late breakfast; and of none was this more true than of Lottie Marsden, as, pale and languid, she took her wonted place. Her greeting of De Forrest was most kindly, and he seemed greatly reassured, and brightened up instantly. But Lottie's face did not lose its deep dejection.

To the others she appeared to take very little notice of Hemstead; but he thought that he observed her eyes furtively seeking his face, with a questioning expression. Once he answered her glance with such a frank, sunny smile that her own face lighted up. As they were passing into the parlor he said, in a low tone, "I wished a hundred times yesterday that I could bear your headache for you."

"That is more kind than just. It is right that I should get my deserts," she replied, shaking her head.

"Heaven save us from our deserts," he answered quickly.

Before she could speak again, De Forrest was by her side and said, "Let me wheel the lounge up to the fire, and I will read anything you wish this morning."

"Oh, no; I'm going to church."

"Miss Lottie, I beg of you do not go. You are not able."

"Yes, I am; the air will do me good. It's the Sunday before Christmas, Julian, and we both ought to be at church."

"Oh, certainly, I'll go if you wish it."

"I hope your sermon will do me good, Mr. Hemstead. I'm wofully blue," she said, as she left the room to prepare for church.

"I think it will," he replied; "for I have prepared it with a great deal of care."

The building was a small but pretty Gothic structure, and its sacred quiet did seem to Lottie somewhat like a refuge. With an interest such as she had never felt in the elegant city temple, she waited for the service to begin, honestly hoping that there might be something that would comfort and reassure.

But Hemstead went through the preliminary services with but indifferent grace and effect. He was embarrassed and awkward, as is usually the case with those who have seldom faced an audience, and who are naturally very diffident. But as he entered upon his sermon his self-consciousness began to pass away, and he spoke with increasing power and effect.

He took as his text words from the eleventh chapter of St. John, wherein Jesus declares to his disciples, in regard to the death of Lazarus, "I am glad, for your sakes, that I was not there, to the intent ye may believe."

The importance of faith—believing—as the source of Christian life, and the ground of man's acceptance with God, was his subject, from which he wandered somewhat —a course often observed in the ministerial tyro.

He presented his views strongly, however; but they were partial and unripe, giving but one side of the truth, and therefore calculated to do injury rather than good. He did not—he could not—overestimate the importance of faith, but he unwittingly misrepresented God, in his efforts to inspire this faith, and the Christian life resulting; and he undervalued our earthly state and its interests.

He sketched in strong outlines the experience of the little family at Bethany, portraying with vivid realism the suffering of the man whom Jesus loved; the anxiety of the sisters when Lazarus became ill; this anxiety passing into fear, dread, sickening certainty, and despair; the anguish of bereavement, the loneliness and heart-breaking sorrow of four days; and that most agonzied wrench of the heart when the beloved form is left alone to corrupt in the dark and silent sepulchre.

Having presented this picture in such true and sombre colors that the gloom was reflected from the faces of all his hearers, they being reminded that this would be their lot ere long, he passed suddenly from the painful scenes of Bethany to Bethabara, beyond Jordan, where was sojourning the mysterious Prophet of Nazareth, who had so often proved His power to heal every disease. He enlarged upon the fact that Jesus, seeing all the suffering at Bethany, which He could change by a word into gladness, did not interfere, but decreed that the terrible ordeal should be endured to the bitter end.

From this he reasoned that the transient sorrows of the household at Bethany were of little moment, and that God, in the advancement of His own glory and the accomplishment of His great plans, would never turn aside because His human children in their short-sighted weakness would stay His heavy hand if they could. He knew all that was occurring at Bethany, but calmly permitted it to take place, and in this case it was the same as if He had willed it.

He then proceeded to show that the Divine purpose had not only a wide and general sweep, embracing the race, and extending through all time, but that there was a minute providence encompassing each life. If there were any good in us, God would bring it out, nor would He spare us in the effort. The preacher, unfortunately and unconsciously to himself, gave the impression that God acted on the principle that He could accomplish far more with the rod of affliction than with anything else, and that when He fully set about the task of winning a soul from sin, His first step was to stretch it upon the rack of some kind of suffering. He also intensified this painful impression by giving the idea that God thought little of the processes, which might be so painful to us, but fixed His eye only on the result. If people became sullen, rebellious, or reckless under His discipline, they were like misshappen clay, that the potter must cast aside. The crude ore must go into the furnace, and if there were good metal in it the fact would appear.

"Sooner or later," he said, "God will put every soul into the crucible of affliction. Sooner or later we shall all be passing through scenes like that of the family at Bethany. We may not hope to escape. God means we shall not. As Christ firmly, while seeing all, left events at Bethany to their designed course, so He will as surely and steadily carry out the discipline which He, as the unerring physician of the soul, sees that each one of us requires. Does the refiner hesitate to put the crude ore into the crucible? Does the sculptor shrink from chiselling the shapeless block into beauty? Does not the surgeon, with nerves of steel and pulse unquickened, cut near the very vitals of his agonized patient? He sees that it is necessary, in order to save from greater evil, and therefore he is as remorseless as fate. If to cure some transient, physical infirmity, man is justified in inflicting—nay, more, is compelled to inflict—so much suffering upon his fellow-creatures, how much more is God justified in His severest moral discipline, which has as its object our eternal health. Though we shrink from the sorrow, though we writhe under the pain, though our hearts break a thousand times, He will not waver in His calm, steadfast purpose. He sees eternity; the present is as nothing to Him. He will break our grasp from all earthly idols, even though He tear our bleeding hearts asunder. If we are trusting in aught save Him, that upon which we are leaning will be snatched away, even though we fall at first

into the depths of despairing sorrow. What He makes us
suffer now is not to be considered, in view of His purpose to
wean us from this world and prepare us for the next. Christ,
as we learn from our text, is as inflexible as fate, and does
not hesitate to secure the needful faith by remaining away,
even though the message of the sisters was an entreaty in
itself. Nay, more, he distinctly declares to his disciples, ' I
am glad, for your sakes, that I was not there, to the intent
ye may believe. '

"In conclusion, we assert that we ought to rise above our
human weakness and co-work with God. Instead of clinging so to the present, we ought to think of the eternal future,
and welcome the harshest discipline which prepares us for
that future. We should mortify ourselves, trample our
earthly natures under our feet. To that degree that we can
bring ourselves to think less of earth, we shall think more
of heaven. Our business, our earthly hopes and plans, our
dearest ties, may be fatal snares to our souls. The husband
may make an idol of his wife, the mother of her child. God
jealously watches; we should watch more jealously. The
sisters may have been loving their brother and trusting to his
protection more than in Christ. We should hold all earthly
possessions in fear and trembling, as something not our own,
but only committed for a brief time to our trust. We should
remember that the one great object of this life is to secure
that faith which leads to preparation for the life to come.
The harsher our experiences are here, the better, if they
more surely wean us from earth and all earthly things, and
make eternity the habitation of our thoughts. We see how
stern and resolute God is in His great purpose to stamp out
unbelief from the world. Jesus would not save the family
at Bethany that He loved—the family that freely gave hospitality and love in return when nearly all the world was
hostile. Do not think, then, that He will spare us. Let us
therefore not spare ourselves, but with remorseless hands
smite down every earthly object that hides from our view
the wide ocean of eternity. As the wise men from the East

travelled steadily across arid wastes with eyes fixed only on the strange bright luminary that was guiding them to Bethlehem, so we should regard this world as a desert across which we must hasten to the presence of our God.''

As Hemstead forgot himself, and became absorbed in his theme, he spoke with impressiveness and power; and everywhere throughout the audience was seen that thoughtful contraction of the brow and fixed gaze which betoken deep attention. But upon the faces of nearly all was the expression of one listening to something painful. This was especially true of Miss Martell and her father, while Harcourt's face grew cold and satirical. Lottie looked pale and sullen, and De Forrest was evidently disgusted. Mr. Dimmerly fidgeted in his seat, and even complacent Mrs. Marchmont seemed a little ruffled and disturbed, while her daughter Addie was in a state of irritable protest against both preacher and sermon. Poor Bel was merely frightened and conscience-stricken— her usual condition after every sermon to which she listened.

As, during the brief remnant of the service, Hemstead dropped into consciousness of the world around him, he felt at first, rather than saw, the chill he had caused, instead of a glow answering to his own feelings. As he looked more closely, he imagined he detected a gloomy and forbidding expression on the faces turned toward him. The Gospel— the message of good news that he had brought—appeared to shadow the audience like a passing cloud.

After dismission, the people aroused themselves as from an oppressive dream. The few greetings and congratulations that he received as he passed down the aisle seemed formal and constrained, and, he thought, a little insincere. He was still more puzzled as he overheard Miss Martell say to Harcourt at the door, "I am sorry you heard that sermon.''

"I am, too," he replied, "for it seemed true.''

"It's only half-truth," she said earnestly.

"The Lord deliver me, then; this half is more than I can stand.''

Lottie scarcely spoke during the drive home, and Hemstead noted, with pain, that her face had a hard, defiant look. It occurred to him that he had not seen any who appeared to have enjoyed the service.

There were long pauses at the dinner-table, and after one of the longest, Mr. Dimmerly abruptly remarked, in his sententious manner: "Well, nephew, I suppose you gave us a powerful sermon this morning. It has made us all deucedly uncomfortable, anyhow. But I've no doubt the old rule holds good, the worse the medicine is to take the more certain to cure."

Lottie's response to this remark was a ringing laugh, in which the others, in the inevitable reaction from the morbid gloom, joined with a heartiness that was most annoying to the young clergyman.

"You must excuse me, Mr. Hemstead," said she, after a moment, "I have had the blues all day, and have reached that point where I must either laugh or cry, and prefer the former at the dinner-table."

Hemstead stiffly bowed as his only response. He was too chagrined, puzzled, and disappointed to venture upon a reply, and after this one lurid gleam of unnatural mirth the murky gloom of the day seemed to settle down more heavily than before.

After dinner De Forrest tried to secure Lottie's society for the afternoon. The refusal was kind, not careless, as had been often the case. Indeed, her whole manner toward him might be characterized as a grave, remorseful kindness, such as we might show toward a child or an inferior that we had wronged somewhat.

De Forrest, finding that Lottie would persist in going to her room, went to his also, and took a long, comfortable nap.

Bel wanted to talk about the sermon, but as Lottie would not talk about anything, she, too, soon forgot her spiritual anxieties in sleep.

But Lottie sat and stared at her fire, and Hemstead, deserted by all, stared at the fire in the parlor; and both were sorely troubled and perplexed.

CHAPTER XIX

THE PREACHER TAUGHT BY THE PAGAN

WE have said that Lottie Marsden was a pagan. That is not necessarily a reproach. Socrates was a pagan. But Lottie, in the main, was a very ordinary pagan, not better than the average. Her only superiority over other idolaters, and many nominal Christians, it might be added, was her practical common-sense. The more she thought, the more unsatisfactory Hemstead's sermon grew, and the more sure she became that there was a wrong somewhere: in him, or her, or in religion itself.

Her whole nature revolted at the idea of God given that morning.

In her vivid fancy, she saw an unrelenting, unimpassioned, and yet all-powerful Being, from whom there was no escape, calmly subjecting one human life after another to the severest crucial tests. If one could endure them, all might be well. If, in the composition of one's character, there existed good metal, it would come out of the furnace fine gold perhaps; but if, as she feared might be true of herself, there was only dross, then the fiery trials awaiting would be as useless as cruel.

"Why couldn't an all-powerful God find a pleasanter and surer way of making us good?" she asked in bitterness. "I know there is something wrong in what Mr. Hemstead preached this morning. He is different from his own doctrines, and to my mind a great deal better. He was severe upon me, but not calmly and stonily severe. He looked as if he felt for me deeply, and would, even at cost to himself, give me aid if I tried to do right. If he had shown me my faults in the calm, cold distance of immeasurable superiority which he ascribed to God, I would not have listened to a word. But his voice was gentleness itself, and it evidently pained him to give me pain; but when he came to show our relations to God, I seemed to come into the presence of stony-hearted, stony-faced fate. If this is the real God that ministers preach about, little wonder that they have such a hard time of it in persuading us to love Him. Little wonder that people forget Him as long as they can. But Mr. Hemstead seems to want us to think of these awful things nearly all the time; and what's worse, to begin torturing and mortifying ourselves, even before God is ready to commence. No, I thank you. No such religion for me. If I must go into the fiery furnace, I won't go till I must."

She sprang up, and restlessly paced the room. "He's a very cheerful apostle of such a gloomy gospel," she thought. "Gospel! I thought 'gospel' meant 'good news.' I never heard worse than he told us this morning. If what he preached is true religion, he's a very inconsistent professor of it, and I would like to tell him so.

"What's more, I will if I can find him;" and acting upon the impulse she left the room.

The "miserable sinners," as the prayer-book has it, whom Hemstead had in fact made quite miserable for a time, grew more comfortable after dinner; and by three o'clock, so far from employing hair-cloth and scourgings, or even the mildest form of a crusade against the weaknesses of the flesh, were all dozing and digesting in the most luxurious manner. Lottie was the only "sinner" who remained "miserable"; but she was not more "out of sorts" than the one who, *ex officio*, as the world is prone to believe, ought to have been calm and serene upon his theological height above the clouds.

As she entered the parlor with her velvet-like tread, she

paused a moment to observe the Boanerges of the morning. As he sat alone before the fire, with his elbows upon his knees and his face buried in his hands, he looked more like a weak mortal than a "son of thunder." He did not look a bit like one who, with face as firm and inflexible as God's purpose, was anxious to step into the fiery furnace before it was ready.

She drew a few steps nearer, and stood over him with a curious expression on her face, which could so well mask or reveal her thought as she chose. She had come downstairs in a state of irritable and defiant protest against his doctrines, and with no little vexation at him for being their mouthpiece. If she had found him calmly pacing the floor, pondering on human frailty and folly, or if he had been reading judicially a semi-sceptical work, that he might demolish the irreverent author, she would have made an onslaught whose vigor, if not logic, would have greatly disturbed his equanimity and theological poise. But when she saw his attitude of deep dejection, and when twice he sighed long and heavily, her woman's nature was disarmed, and she began to think that his doctrines were as hard upon him as upon the rest. Instinctively she took his part against God, whose formative hand appeared too heavy for them both.

Therefore, instead of the hard, bitter words that she intended to speak, she said, with a little quaver in her voice, "Mr. Hemstead, I almost believe that you feel as bad as I do."

When he looked up she was sure he felt worse. But he seemed to try to forget his own trouble as he said kindly, "I'm sorry you feel bad."

"Well," said Lottie, sitting down on the opposite side of the hearth, while the fire, on which Hemstead had thrown some damp green wood, smoked dismally between them, "I do think you are a little sorry."

"Can I help you in any way? I wish you knew how gladly I would do so."

"Yes, I believe that, too. You don't look a bit as if you would like to throw me into a fiery furnace, and see if I would come out a lump of gold or a good-for-nothing cinder."

His only reply was a look of perplexed inquiry, but his gray eyes were so kind, and yet withal so full of dejection, that she again thought, "He is dreadfully inconsistent with his doctrines"; and she said, with a trace of archness in her tone, "I think you look as if you needed a little help and comfort yourself."

He turned away his face, but after a moment said, "You never spoke truer words, Miss Marsden."

Then Lottie, who before had felt in such need of cheer herself, forgot this need in her wish to help the great desponding man before her, whose mingled weakness and strength surprised her more and more. In a tone that would have softened flint she said, "I wish I were good enough to help you."

Then he perpexed her by saying, with sudden energy, "And I wish you were bad enough."

"What do you mean by that?"

"Pardon me," he said hastily. "My words were figurative, and exaggerated by deep feeling. I meant that I wished you, or some one, could be human and charitable enough to understand me, and help me to triumph over my weakness without condemning too severely."

"Well," said Lottie, with a little sigh of satisfaction, "I think I'm bad enough. I'm very human, anyway, and I think I'm in a mood to be charitable to-day; for, if my conscience tells me the truth, I'm awfully in need of charity myself."

He looked up quickly and hopefully as he said, "Then my sermon did *you* some good after all."

"Not a bit of it. I can have plenty of charity for you, but not a particle for your sermon—no more than I would for a thumb-screw of the Inquisition."

This unmeasured condemnation of the pet child of his brain—a part of himself as it were—of which he had been so proud, cut to the quick, and he flushed deeply and almost resentfully at first. But he made no reply, and sat lowering at the smoky hearth while he sank into a lower depth of despondency. Preaching was his chosen life-work, and yet this was the verdict against his first great sermon.

Lottie looked hopelessly at him, not knowing what to say or do next, and regretting that she had spoken so hastily and harshly.

At last he sighed: "I don't understand it. I had spent months over that sermon. I fear I have mistaken my calling."

"Well," said Lottie, rather brusquely, "I wouldn't feel so forlorn and miserable over that. I don't think it's much of a calling anyway."

"Oh, Miss Marsden!" he ejaculated, in a shocked tone.

"I'm sincere in what I say," she continued earnestly. "Please don't misunderstand me. As far as I am a judge I think your sermon was well written, and it certainly was delivered effectively; for, though none of us liked it, we couldn't help listening. But its strongest effect was to make me wish I was an infidel and, like Mr. Harcourt, did not believe in anything. I honestly think that it will be a very poor calling to go out among the poor people on the frontier and preach such a gospel as you gave us this morning. In the name of pity, haven't they enough to contend with now? In addition to the scalping Indians, the border ruffians, the grasshoppers, and grinding poverty, are you going to give them a religion in which the furnace of affliction and the crucible of trial flame as the centre? Poor creatures! I suppose they are in hard and hot places most of the time, but don't make them think that God puts them there, and that there is no chance to get out till He is through with them. I can tell you beforehand, that people are not going to get into the fiery furnace and commence having a miserable time of it before they must. Let us be as comfortable as we can, while we can. If you feel that you have mistaken your calling—and I hope you have— I'm sure that father, at my request, will find you a better one in New York."

Poor Hemstead was as satisfied as Luther had been that this was a temptation of the devil; but before him was no such apparition as that against which the great reformer could hurl his ink-horn without leaving a spot.

With the lurid flash of Lucifer as he fell from heaven, the thought passed through his disquieted mind, "And in New York I might win the hand and heart of this beautiful girl." But every quality of his soul frowned so darkly on this thought, which held out Lottie Marsden as a bribe, that it soon skulked away. His mind reverted to the main difficulty, and he said, "Surely, Miss Marsden, I did not preach such a religion as you suggest."

"You surely did, Mr. Hemstead, as I could soon prove to you. I am glad you are so inconsistent a professor of your religion."

"Am I an inconsistent professor?" he asked sadly.

"Indeed you are," she replied; and both mischief and kindness lurked in her eyes. "You don't live up to your doctrines at all."

"Little wonder, then," he exclaimed, in bitter self-condemnation, "that all turn from my teaching."

She looked at him with a curious smile, as she thought, "What a child he is! He is but wax in my hands. If he should marry a cold-hearted, selfish woman, with a spice of petty, teasing malice in her nature, she could sit down quietly at his hearth and torture to death this overgrown man, with whole libraries in his brain. I could wring his soul now, by making him think that he had lived so unworthily that we could not listen to his most unworthy sermon."

She led him out of his strong self-condemnation into equal perplexity, by saying, "Unlike most of the world, you are so much better than your creed as to be utterly inconsistent."

He came and sat down near her, with such an appealing, helpless look that she laughed outright.

"Please don't laugh at me," he said, with the glimmer of a smile, "because this to me is a more serious matter than you or any one can understand."

"I don't laugh unfeelingly, I assure you," she said earnestly. "I never was more sincere in my life than I was this afternoon, but I am one of those ridiculous mortals who cannot take things coolly, and, as I said at dinner, there are times when I must either laugh or cry. I never passed a more miserable day in my life than yesterday. You, terrible magician, whom I have scarcely known for a week, have awakened in my heart a giant; and yesterday and to-day he has been shaking my soul with his mutterings and threatenings. I could always manage my conscience before, and snub it into quietness when it became unruly. But, as I said, from a whining child it has suddenly grown into a threatening giant, more harsh even than you the other evening. I went to church this morning, hoping to find some comfort, some remedy; but, bad as is the disease, the remedy seems far worse. I came downstairs this afternoon in no amiable mood with you or your theology, but was disarmed by seeing you in as bad a plight as myself. I fear your medicine will kill both doctor and patient. During the past week you have been a strong, genial man, with a human, genuine enjoyment of our every-day life. If you were a little blue and puritanical, it was in a common-sense way that I could understand, and your criticism of myself I think in the main was just. Anyway, you made me wish I was a better girl, and I was thinking how to begin; then came this awful Sunday, and your awful sermon, which made me both fear and hate God, and want to keep away from Him as far and as long as I can."

"Your words perplex and sadden me beyond measure," said Hemstead. "You belong to the very class that I had hoped to benefit—those who admit that they are without faith, but who are not so averse to the truth but that they may be won by it. And yet you say that the whole force of my sermon is to make you wish that you could be an infidel. I cannot understand it. If I have mistaken my calling I could not make you or any one comprehend the depth of my sorrow, or the bitterness of my disappointment. In the calling of the ministry it has ever seemed to me that I could work a century with enthusiasm. But in any other work I should be but a drudge, for my heart would not be in it. You know how young men often feel about these things. One has a natural bent for the law, another for medicine, and another for business or science. I had fondly hoped that I was a predestined minister, and this hope has strengthened with years and become inwrought with every fibre of my soul. I was willing to commence in a very humble way, and anywhere that God would set me to work; but if the effect of my preaching is to drive people away from Him, the sooner I give it all up the better.''

"How different our tastes and plans for life are!" said Lottie, musingly. "It appears strange that you should have set your heart so strongly on what is so dismal to me. And yet such is the evident depth of your regret that I do feel for you very much.''

Hemstead rose and took a few abrupt turns up and down the room. Lottie watched him with increasing interest. He had shown her his weakness, and she perceived that he would also show his strength. After a moment he leaned on the mantel before her, and said in quiet, decisive tones:

"Miss Marsden, I have given you the right to speak to me very plainly. I honestly wish light on this subject, and intend to settle this question at the earliest moment possible. God knows I do not wish to thrust myself unbidden into the sacred office. If I am not worthy of the calling, then the sooner I find it out the better, and so try to content myself with some humbler work. Not only from what you have said, but from the remarks and aspect of others, I am satisfied that my effort this morning was worse than a failure. You have a mind of unusual vigor, and a good faculty in expressing your thought. Won't you give me a keen, truthful analysis of the whole service? It is to the world I am to preach; and I wish to know just how what I say strikes the world. I know that Christian doctrines have ever been unpalatable, but if there is something in my presentation of them that is going to make them tenfold more so, then I will be dumb. I would rather hide in a desert that drive one soul from God, as you intimated. You were brave enough to let me speak to you almost harshly, I fear; now see if I have not equal courage. Say the very worst things that you believe true, and you may help me very much toward coming to the most important decision of my life."

"Oh, dear!" said Lottie. "I'm not fit to counsel a downy chicken. I wish you didn't take this matter so to heart. You look as if I might be your executioner."

"You can be my faithful surgeon and do some wholesome cutting."

"Well," said Lottie, dismally. "I'd rather give you ether or laughing-gas first."

"That is more kind than wise," he replied, smiling; "in moral and mental surgery the patient should have all his faculties."

"There!" she exclaimed with animation, "we are illustrating by contrast my chief complaint against your preaching. When you told me my faults you did so gently, and appeared pained in giving me pain; and now I am honestly sorry to say words that I know will hurt you. And I know my words will hurt and discourage you; for if the trouble were in you it might be remedied, but it is in what you teach, and of course you teach what you believe, and won't say smooth things, as I fear other ministers do sometimes. You represented God calm and unchangeable as fate, as unrelenting and unimpassioned. In this spirit you portrayed Him taking up one life after another and putting it into the furnace of affliction, to see what He can make of it. You illustrated His manner of doing this by the sculptor with his cold, unfeeling marble, by the refiner with crude ore, and by the surgeon, and you forgot to say that the last stupefies his patients before cutting. You gave me the impression that as soon as God set about making us better we should find ourselves in trouble, and that, like certain schoolmasters of the old régime, He had faith in nothing save the rod. You know the natural feeling of children toward such pedagogues. How can we help feeling in the same way toward God? Then you presented God as full of inflexible purposes, but the oftener you told us that we could not help ourselves, and that there was no use in resisting, the more I felt like resisting. The idea of cutting and carving character out of quivering human hearts as if they were marble! The idea of putting one, like a lump of ore, into a crucible, and then coolly sitting by to see what becomes of it! I'm not a lump of ore, and if I need harsh treatment I want it done sympathetically, feelingly, or I shall become a Tartar instead of a saint. The tears in your eyes the other night, Mr. Hemstead, did me more good than all your wise words.''

Hemstead looked as if a light were dawning upon him.

''You spoke of this life,'' continued Lottie, ''as if it were nothing, and as if God didn't care—indeed approved of our having a hard time here, that we might be more sure of a good time hereafter. You spoke of God as jealously watching, lest we should love earthly friends more than Him, and said that He was bound to be first, if He had to snatch away everything that we loved most. Therefore, even the mother must keep chilling her natural love for her child, or else God will make the innocent little thing suffer and die, just to give the mother a lesson. You said that we should hold all earthly possessions in fear and trembling, and that the harsher our experiences were, here, the better, if they only wean us from earth. If this is true, we had better have no possessions and form no ties. The monks and nuns are right. Let us shut ourselves up, and wear hair-cloth instead of merino, and catch our death of cold by moping around bare-foot at all unseasonable hours. All you said may be good religion, but it's mighty poor sense, and very unnatural."

Hemstead shaded his burning face with his hands.

"There, I knew I should hurt you. No doubt I seem very irreverent, but you have no idea how I am restraining myself for your sake. I'm just that provoked and indignant— Well, well, what's the use? As you said, we can't help ourselves, and into the fiery furnace Lottie Marsden will go before long; only there will be nothing left of me but a little cinder. Why couldn't the Being you call all-wise and all-powerful, devise some nicer way, one more in accordance with the nature He has given us? Suppose heaven is a grander place than this world, that is no good reason for hating the world. This earth is our present home, and it looks sensible that we should make the most of it, and enjoy ourselves in it. Suppose my father should say, 'Lottie, I want you to hate and despise your present home, because in five years I'm going to give you a palace; and if you can only fall downstairs once or twice, and have a fit of illness so as to get weaned from it, I shall be glad.'

"How strangely and monstrously unnatural all that kind of talk is when you come to put it into plain English!" proceeded Lottie after a moment, tapping the floor impatiently with her foot. "If you must preach such doctrines as you did this morning, I am sorry for you; and, if they are true, I am sorry for the world, myself included. The trouble is not in you. I am sure you can make almost an orator in time, if you can get a theme that won't give men the shivers, and set their teeth on edge. I never understood religion and never liked it; and now that I do begin to understand it, I like it less than ever."

Hemstead sat down in his chair—indeed he sank into it, and the face he turned toward her was white and full of pain.

"Miss Marsden," he said slowly, "I fear I have given

you, and all who heard me, a very false impression of God and Christianity; and yet I thought I was speaking the truth.''

''Oh, I knew you were honest. There isn't a dishonest fibre in your nature; but I wish you were all wrong. Oh, how delighted I should be if you were a heretic without knowing it, and we could find out a religion that wouldn't make one's blood run cold to think of it!''

''But my religion does me good, Miss Marsden. It cheers, sustains, and strengthens me.''

''Now you see how inconsistent you are. You preach one thing, and feel and act another.''

''I begin to see how I was misled in my sermon, and why what I said was so repugnant to you; and yet my mind is confused. It still appears to me that I developed the thought of the text. Christ said, 'I am glad I was not there, to the intent ye may believe.' These words would seem to show that He regarded our transient pains as of very secondary importance compared with the accomplishment of His great purposes. Why did He not go to Bethany at once, if it were not so?''

''Well, it's an awful text, or you give it an awful interpretation. Let me take the thought out of the realm of theology or religion, and bring it down to practical life. Suppose you go to New York to-morrow and remain a few days, and to-morrow night the house burns up, and I with it. Would your first thought be, 'I am glad I was not there to put out the fire or to rescue that naughty girl, Lottie Marsden, because her sudden death, for which she was all unprepared, will be a warning to many, and result in great good'? I may be wrong, Mr. Hemstead, but I think you would get pretty well scorched before you would permit even such a guy as I am to become a warning to other naughty girls.''

''I can't imagine myself leaving *you* in danger,'' said Hemstead, with a look that brought the blood into Lottie's face.

"I thought you would feel so," she continued heartily. "You can preach awfully against sinners, but when you come to put your doctrines in practice, you say as you did to me, 'I wish I could bear all for you.' Heaven knows I'm selfish enough, but I can at least understand and appreciate generous and kindly sympathy, and could be won by it. But this cool and inflexible elaboration of character, where only the end is considered, and all our timid shrinking and human weakness are ignored—this austere asceticism which despises the present world and life—is to me unnatural and monstrous. I confess I never read the Bible very much, and have not listened when it was read. I have half forgotten the story of Lazarus. You left off where Lazarus was in his grave, and Christ was glad He was not there to prevent his death. But that was not all the story. I think, if I remember rightly, Christ raised him to life. Come, get a Bible, and let us read the whole story, and see if we cannot find something that will not make the word 'gospel' a mockery."

"Won't you read it?" asked Hemstead, humbly, handing her the Bible.

"Yes, if you wish me to, though it seems very funny that I should be reading the Bible to you."

"I begin to have a hope that you will teach me more than I ever learned from it before," he replied earnestly.

As in sweet, unaffected, girlish tones she read the ancient story of human suffering and sorrow, the scenes passed in seeming reality before the student. He was intensely excited, though so quiet. When one with a strong mind recognizes that he is approaching a crisis in life, there is an awe that calms and controls. Lottie, with her intense vitality, could arouse even a sluggish nature. But to earnest Hemstead, with his vivid fancy and large faith, this beautiful but erratic creature reading the neglected Bible, to find for him a sweeter and sunnier gospel than he had preached, seemed a special providence that presaged more than he had dared to conjecture; and he listened as one who expected a new revelation.

Indeed his darkness was losing its opaqueness. Rays of light were quivering through it. Her plain and bitter words of protest against his sermon had already shown him, in a measure, that he had exaggerated, in his first crude sermonizing, one truth, and left out the balancing and correcting truth. Familiar with all the story of Lazarus, his mind travelled beyond the reader, and with mingled joy and self-condemnation he already began to see how he had misrepresented the God of Love. With intense eagerness he watched and waited to see the effect of the complete story on Lottie's mind.

When she came to the words, "Jesus said unto her, *I* am the resurrection and the life: he that believeth in me, though he were dead yet shall he live: and whosoever liveth and believeth in me shall never die"—she stopped and said, "This is very remarkable language. What does it mean?"

"Read on; read to the end," he urged.

She caught his eager expectancy, and read, with an absorbing interest, the truth that now seemed stranger than any fiction.

When she reached the words, "He groaned in spirit, and was troubled," she raised her eyes in a quick glance of inquiry.

"Read on," said Hemstead, in breathless interest.

A moment later, the shortest verse in the Bible was upon her lips. Then she ceased reading aloud, and the student saw her eyes hastily, as if she were unable to endure the momentary delay of pronunciation, scanning the story to its end.

"Mr. Hemstead," she asked excitedly, "why did Jesus weep and groan, when in a few moments Lazarus would be alive, and the scene of mourning be changed to one of joy?"

With tears in his eyes, he replied, "There is One guiding you—guiding us both—who can answer that question better than I."

"We believe that Jesus Christ is God, do we not?" she half mused, half questioned, her brows contracting with intense thought.

"Yes," he said reverently.

"Why, Mr. Hemstead, don't you see—don't you see? This Being who is so keenly sympathetic, so tenderly alive to a scene of sorrow, that He weeps and groans, though knowing that joy is coming in a moment, is not the calm, passionless, inflexible God you chilled our hearts with this morning. Why, this is the very extravagance of tender-heartedness. This is a gentleness that I can scarcely understand. What mother, even, would first weep with her children over a sorrow that she was about to remove with a word! And yet this all-powerful Jesus, who can raise the dead to life, seems to cry just because the others do—just as if He couldn't help it—just as dear, good Auntie Jane's eyes moisten when she hears of any one in trouble. Mr. Hemstead, there is surely a mistake somewhere. How do you reconcile this Christ with the one you presented this morning?"

"I don't, and cannot."

"And yet He *did* say to His disciples, 'I am glad I was not there,'" continued Lottie, in deep perplexity.

Hemstead paced the room excitedly a few minutes, and then exclaimed, "It's growing as clear and beautiful as the light."

"It seems to me flat contradiction," said Lottie, dejectedly. "There are the words, 'I am glad I was not there'; and there is the fact that He let Lazarus die; and there also are the facts of His weeping and raising Lazarus: and, now I think of it, He performed many miracles equally kind, and helped and encouraged all sorts of people."

"Certainly He did," cried Hemstead. "Blind idiot that I was in developing a crude theological idea of my own, instead of simply presenting the God of the Bible! I can never thank you enough, Miss Marsden, for your strong good sense that has dissipated my fog-bank of words. I think I see the way into light. You have placed a clew in my hands which I trust will lead, not only me, but others into peace. I fear I did present to you a calm, unimpassioned, inflexible Being this morning—a God of purposes and decrees and remorseless will; and I have felt before that this was the God of theology and religious philosophy, rather than the God of the Bible. Your words have shown me that I gave you a crude and one-sided view. Thoughts are thronging so upon my mind that I am confused, but it comes to me with almost the force of an inspiration that Christ's tears of sympathy form the key to the whole Bible.''

"Well," said Lottie, in a low tone, "I can see how they might become the key to my heart. Come, Mr. Hemstead, I have been a heathen up to this time; and I hope you have been a heretic. If you can explain the Bible in accordance with Christ's tears, as He wept, when the kindest man living would have smiled, in view of the change so soon to occur—then preach by all means. That is the kind of gospel we want. If I could believe that God felt with, and for, his creatures as tenderly as that, it seems to me that I could go to Him as naturally as I ever went to Auntie Jane in my troubles."

Hemstead was pacing the room, as was his custom when excited. His face was aglow with earnest, elevating thoughts. His ungainliness had utterly vanished; and Lottie acknowledged that she had never seen a nobler-looking man. She felt that perhaps they were both on the threshold of a larger and richer life than they had ever known before. She saw dimly, as through a mist, that which her heart longed to believe—the truth that God does care about His earthly children—that He was not to her a mere shaping force or power, but a tender, gentle-hearted helper. Therefore she waited eagerly, and hopefully for Hemstead to speak.

But he felt that the glad tumult in his mind rendered him unfit to be her guide just then, and therefore said: "Miss Marsden, I want to think calmly and carefully over what you have said. I want to take this briefest of all texts, 'Jesus wept,' as a lamp in my hand, and with it explore the rest of the Bible. Already it seems that it may be like carrying a light into a treasure vault, and that where before was darkness, gems and riches now will glitter."

"And I, who have had the good fortune to strike the light for you, am in the meantime to sit outside of the 'treasure vault,' and perhaps neither see nor get any of the 'gems.' I don't agree at all to your gloating alone over what may be discovered."

"And can you think I would wish to 'gloat alone'?" said Hemstead, reddening. "It will be my chief joy to bring back all I find to you."

"I'm not that kind of a girl," said Lottie, with a little emphatic gesture. "If I wanted something from the top of a mountain, I would not send a man for it, but would go with him after it. This helpless waiting, or languid looking on, while men do everything for us, is as absurd in one direction as the Indian custom of making the squaw do all the hard work in another. I don't see why we can't take this genial little lamp of a text, and do some exploring together. I will hold the lamp, and you do the looking. Here is the Bible, and there is your seat beside this dismal, smoking fire. I fear you have treated it as you did us this morning—put on green wood."

"I think you are right in both cases," he said, his telltale color again suddenly rising.

"No matter, it was good wood in both cases, as you will see when it becomes ripe and dry."

"It will never do for me to become dry as a preacher, Miss Marsden."

"Yes, it will in my sense, for then you will kindle more easily, and therefore kindle others. But come, I am holding the lamp, '*Jesus wept.*' Everything you can find in the Bible that will confirm the hope of God's sympathy—that He cares for us as we are, with all our faults and weaknesses—will be most welcome."

Lottie was so positive and determined, and her manner so irresistible, that Hemstead had no thought, save that of compliance. She had that piquant imperiousness to which men are willing slaves when it is manifested graciously, and by a pretty woman. He was like a ship caught in a gale, and there was nothing to do but scud before it. At the same time, it seemed that she was driving him swiftly toward the haven and rest of a better and broader faith.

Therefore he sat down by the dismal, smoky hearth, but turned expectantly to her face, which, in contrast, was all aflame with hope and interest.

"The impression grows upon me," he said, "that you are being guided, and therefore you shall guide me."

"I want to settle the question," she replied, "whether I can love and trust God; or whether, as I feared this morning, I must dread and almost hate Him. It seems to me that the only thing religion does for Cousin Bel is to make her uncomfortable. If what you told us, and what she experiences, is true religion, then I shall ignore it and forget all about it as long as I can—till God commences with me, and puts me by way of trial into the fiery furnace of affliction. I fear only a cinder would be the result. But if the natural explanation of these two words, 'Jesus wept,' is true, then God is kinder, gentler, and more sympathetic than any human friend. Prove to me that the One who, out of pure tender-heartedness, cried just because others around Him were crying, though even about to remove the cause of their sorrow, is the God of the Bible, and I will thank you, with lasting and unmeasured gratitude. Then your teaching will be a gospel—good news in very truth. You say the Old and New Testaments both make one Bible, do you not?"

"Yes."

"Well, it is the Old Testament that I most dread. It is so full of wars and bloodshed, and strange, stern rites. And then the old prophets say such awful things! Still, I admit that it's all very vague and dim in my mind. Can you find anything in the Old Testament that corresponds with the words 'Jesus wept'?''

The student rapidly turned the leaves of the large Bible upon his lap, and read:

"Like as a father pitieth his children, so the Lord pitieth them that fear Him.

"For He knoweth our frame: He remembereth that we are dust."

"That fits like light to the eye," exclaimed Lottie, with exultation. "What becomes of your sermon, Mr. Hemstead, in view of such texts? Truth is not contradictory."

"You shall see in a moment, Miss Marsden, what becomes of my sermon," and he hastily left the room.

While Lottie was wondering at his action, he returned and threw the manuscript on the hearth. But while the green wood had been smoking so dismally, it had also dried and kindled; and Hemstead's heavy sermon, so far from quenching the rising flame, seemed just the encouragement needed to develop a cheerful blaze, in the midst of which 'it perished, like a narrow, sour, but sincere, well-meaning old martyr of former days.

In committing this unripe fruit of his brain—his heart had dictated but little of it—to the flames, Hemstead would have felt, a few hours earlier, as a Hindoo mother might when casting her child to the crocodiles of the Ganges. Now with exultation he saw it shrivel, as its teachings had shrivelled within his own mind a little before.

"Like as a father pitieth his children," was a better gospel than "like as a sculptor chisels his marble," or "like as a surgeon cuts remorselessly with pulse unquickened, though the patient writhes."

Preacher and pagan stood together by the hearth, and saw perish the Gospel of Fear—of gloomy asceticism—which for so many centuries, in dim, damp cloisters and stony cells has chilled the heart and quenched the spirit.

And yet, to-day, in the broad light of Bible lands, and in the midst of the wholesome and suggestive duties of family life, do not many, under false teachings like that of Hemstead's sermon, find spiritual paths as dark and painful as those of ascetics who made self-mortification the business of life? Christ spake truly when He said, "Men love darkness rather than light." We fill the service of the Author of Light with gloom. The hermit thought he could best serve God in the chill and dimness of a cave; and the anchorite's cave has been the type of our shadowy, vault-like churches, and of the worshippers' experience ever since.

God is too wise and good to teach a religion utterly repugnant and contradictory to the nature He has given us. A child's hand may lead a multitude; a giant's strength can drive but few.

Christ's tears had fallen on the ice in Lottie's heart, and melted it away. It was now tender, receptive, ready for the seeds of truth. Hemstead's sermon had only hardened it.

Like the Hebrew mothers with their little children, she had pushed her way through frowning doctrines and stately attributes that appeared to encompass God, as did the rebuking disciples of old their gentle Master; and there seemed One before her who, like Jesus, was ready to take her in His arms and lavish upon her tenderness without limit.

The glow of the burning sermon lighted up the faces of the Preacher and one who could no longer be called a Pagan, for she stood before the altar of "the unknown God," and was strongly inclined to place her heart upon it. She believed, though as yet she did not trust. She understood but little of Bible truth, yet it was no longer a repellent darkness, but rather a luminous haze against which Jesus stood distinctly, tearful from sympathy.

As the obnoxious sermon sank into ashes, Hemstead turned and took Lottie's hand with a pressure that made it ache for hours after, and said: "Now you have seen what has become of my sermon and many of my old beliefs. The furnace of God's discipline shall no longer, as you have said,

flame as the lurid centre of my Gospel; but Jesus Christ, as
you have discovered Him, the embodiment of love and sympathy, shall be its centre."

With a smile upon her lips, but with tears in her eyes,
Lottie replied, "And such a gospel would win even the border ruffians. Yes," she added, hesitatingly, "I half believe
it might win even such a little pagan as Lottie Marsden."

Just then a broad ray of light glinted into the room, and
illuminated Lottie's face into such marvellous beauty that
Hemstead was spellbound. He was too intent on watching
her to be aware that the ray rested on him also; but she exclaimed: "Oh, Mr. Hemstead! you don't know how your
face is lighted up by the setting sun. If I believed in
omens, I should know that your successful work will be
out on the frontier—in the West, whence comes, after this
dreary day, such a beautiful light, which suggests, I hope,
the fame and glory you are to win there."

"This light from the West falls equally upon you," he
said impulsively.

There was a sudden crimson in her face, deeper than that
caused by the setting sun.

She gave him a quick, shy glance, to gather his meaning,
but said, "Omens are only half-truths, I have heard."

Under a vague but strong impulse he had spoken foolishly, he thought; and suggested that, in seeking to change
her character, his motive in part might be a presumptuous
hope of his own. Therefore a deeper flush crimsoned his
face; but he said quietly: "I believe that, in our day,
omens are will-o'-the-wisps of the imagination. What need
is there of such fitful lights, when the sun of God's truth is
shining in this Bible? Shall we explore further?"

Again they sat down and sought to reconcile the apparently conflicting truths of God's mercy and justice—of His
severity and unutterable tenderness. Proofs of both were
found upon the page of inspiration "as thick as leaves in
Vallombrosa." It was clearly evident that God would
make no terms with sin, whatever He might do for the

sinner. But the Divine man, as He stands between justice
and the erring, appeared to solve the problem. And if
God's discipline was at times severe, and Christ was glad
when faith-inspiring sorrow came, it was also seen that He
could *weep* with the weak human children who cried under
the rod, though heaven might result from the transient pain.

CHAPTER XX

THE DAWNING LIGHT

SOME little time before the supper-bell rang, De Forrest sauntered in, and witnessed a scene that both surprised and puzzled him. And yet a lover would scarcely have found, in the quiet and pretty picture that the parlor and its occupants made, any ground for jealousy. Hemstead was at the centre-table, under the now-lighted chandelier, reading aloud from the Bible. Lottie sat by the hearth, the firelight playing upon an unusually grave and thoughtful face.

"Well," he exclaimed, "you look for all the world like an old married couple keeping Sunday together."

Of course Hemstead flushed. But why should Lottie's color grow richer than the ruddy firelight warranted? She knew she was blushing, and the fact puzzled her, for it was a new experience to find the blood flying into her face, and her heart in a sudden flutter.

She was also excessively annoyed at De Forrest's intrusion, for such it seemed, though he had an equal right to the parlor with herself. We usually judge unjustly, in proportion as we feel strongly.

But the habit of her old, insincere life swayed her, and she said lightly, "If, instead of dozing away the whole afternoon, you would follow Mr. Hemstead's example and read the Bible, you would be the better for it."

"I would have read to you all the afternoon, if you had given me a chance, and even from the Bible if you had asked for it," De Forrest replied, with an injured air.

"Well, you see Mr. Hemstead is a predestined missionary, and he no doubt thought, and correctly too, that he would never find a truer object of missionary effort than myself; so I have obtained a better knowledge of the Bible this afternoon than ever before."

They were now joined by others, and the conversation became general. Soon after they went out to supper.

The depression of the sermon appeared to have passed from the rest, as well as from Lottie and Hemstead, though for different reasons. The latter had gone out of themselves toward God, and had found Him the source of light and cheer. The others had forgotten Him, and still remained in the dim, chill grottoes of their unbelief, illumining their darkness by such artificial and earth-lighted tapers as the occasion offered. Mrs. Marchmont's apartments were cosey and elegant, the supper was inviting, the ruddy wood-fire and easy chairs suggested luxurious comfort; and why should they not be comfortable, and quietly forget their dismal thoughts about God, and the self-denial of the Cross? The current of ordinary and worldly life, which Hemstead's sincere but mistaken words had rudely interrupted, now began to flow on as quietly and smoothly as before.

But with Lottie it was very different, and the tides of her life seemed seeking new channels.

Bel, and to a certain extent the others, noted peculiarities in her manner and that of Hemstead. Her moodiness was gone, but in its place was not her old levity. When Moses came down from the presence of God, his face shone so that he was compelled to veil its brightness; and it has ever seemed true that nearness to God and His truth gives spiritual light and attractiveness to the plainest features.

Lottie was more than beautiful that evening. She was radiant. Like a sunrise in June, two forms of pure, ennobling love were dawning in her heart; and the first, faint, unrecognized emotions illumined her face strangely at times. Her manner was unusually gentle, and while responding to the general conversation she had many moments of abstraction, and was evidently carrying on a chain of thought very different from that appearing upon the surface of their table-talk. But all remembered that Lottie abounded in moods, and she was what the commonplace call "an odd girl."

But why Hemstead, after his gloom and chagrin at dinner, should now be beaming, was not so clear. Bel thought, "The poor moth! Lottie has been dazzling him with her dangerous smiles. It's a shame."

After supper Harcourt appeared, and sacred music was in order. Even De Forrest and Addie joined in this with considerable zest. It was the proper and about the only thing that could be done on a Sabbath evening. The most irreligious feel better for the occasional indulgence of a little religious sentimentality. When the æsthetic element is supreme, and thorny self-denial absent, devotion is quite attractive to average humanity. Moreover, the dwarfed spiritual nature of the most materialistic often craves its natural sustenance; and Sabbath evening at times suggests to the worldly that which alone can satisfy. The "Sun of Righteousness" sheds a pale, reflected ray upon them; but this is better than utter darkness, and may lure forward where the Divine smile will beam fully upon them. Do not let us undervalue Sunday evening sentiment and sacred music, even though occurring where there was a dance yesterday, and where there will be a revel to-morrow. There must always be a first support on which the grovelling vine can begin to climb heavenward.

Though sentiment, like pale moonlight, causes no ripe and wholesome growth, it is better than darkness, and is proof that the vivifying light is shining somewhere.

In the case of Hemstead, however, the words of praise and prayer composing the hymns sung were the intelligent utterances of a believing heart to the natural object of its faith and devotion.

Lottie was not much given to sentiment, even in religion, and the sacred words, a week before, would have come from her lips only, while she thought of other things; but now she was surprised to find how her heart was stirred by them, and how, from being empty phrases, they were becoming full of beautiful meaning.

That was a memorable Sabbath evening to her. It seemed as if within her old, earth-born, material life, a subtile spiritual one had been kindled, which illumined and glorified everything.

She felt as if endowed with a new sense, by means of which she was becoming dimly conscious of a new and different world. She was more than happy: she was thrilling with strange and mysterious joy, and was elated beyond measure, as if Christian principle and heaven were already won; as many a pilgrim is happier before the quickly coming fall into the "Slough of Despond" than ever again until within the gates of the Celestial City.

Lottie's flame-like spirit was not prone to take anything coolly; and now that her soul was kindled by fire from heaven, and in addition her whole nature awakened by the as yet unrecognized, but strongest of earthly forces—the natural love of her heart for the one to whom only had been given the power to inspire it, little wonder that her but half-suppressed excitement was surprising both to herself and others—little wonder that she was more radiant than ever she had been upon the gayest and most brilliant occasions.

There was nothing unnatural in her experience. She had looked upon the face of Him who is the light and life of the world. Let her enjoy the brief ecstasy. Never chill the soul that is thrilling with the first strong pulses of spiritual life by discouraging doubts. Remind such, if you will, that now, as with the disciples of old, the moments on the Mount of Transfiguration are few, and the days of work and self-denial on the lowly plain many. But do not fail to close your homily with the assurance that the work and self-denial are of earth, while the illumined mount is the type of an eternal heaven.

The evening was passing. While devotion burned more

brightly, sentiment was flickering out. The others were growing weary. Hemstead had the tact to see this, and he also wished to be alone that he might think over the bewildering experiences of the day. Therefore he suggested that they close with Ray Palmer's beautiful hymn, that from the first moment of faith, until faith's fruition, is the appropriate language of those who accept of God's remedy for evil.

> "My faith looks up to Thee,
> Thou Lamb of Calvary,
> Saviour divine.
> Now hear me while I pray,
> Take all my guilt away,
> Oh, let me from this day
> Be wholly Thine."

He hoped that with Lottie it might crown the teachings of the day, and fix her thoughts on the true source of help.

This hope found a richer fulfilment than he expected, for to her awakened spirit the lines seemed inspired to express her deepest need. As the last words trembled from her lips the rush of feeling was too strong for repression, and she impetuously left the room.

CHAPTER XXI

MISUNDERSTOOD

LOTTIE was conscious of a strange lightness of heart when she awoke on the morrow. It seemed as if her life had been unexpectedly enriched. She could not understand it, nor did she seek to, being contented with the fact that she was happy. She had always been seeking her own enjoyment, and now she was happier than ever before. She was not a philosopher who must analyze everything. She widely differed from some prudent people who must take an emotion to pieces, and resolve it into its original elements, and thus be sure that it is properly caused and wholesome before enjoying it. Many seem to partake of life's pleasures as did the members of the royal family of their feasts, in the days of the ancient Roman empire, when it was feared that poison lurked in every dish.

We have seen, however, that Lottie was not morbidly conscientious. She had gathered honey everywhere, and often in spite of conscience' protest. But now, for a rarity, conscience appeared with, and not against her. She was satisfied with the fact that she felt better than ever before; and the majority of even somewhat experienced Christians ask, as their ground of confidence, not "What is truth?" "What has God promised?"—but, "How do I *feel* to-day?" Little wonder, then, if inexperienced Lottie, with everything to learn, was content with being happy.

She had always looked upon religion as a painful necessity at some remote and desperate emergency of the future; but, after the hours spent with Hemstead, it seemed a source of joy beyond all the pleasures of her highly favored life. She was like one who had been living in the glare of artificial light, brilliant enough, it is true, but who had suddenly come out into the natural sunshine, and found it warmer, sweeter—in brief, just what she craved and needed.

The distrust of these exalted and emotional states is general, and often well-founded, especially when experienced by such mercurial temperaments as that of Lottie Marsden. And when it is remembered that her ideas of true religion were of the vaguest kind, the conservative will think, "Whatever may take place in a book, the morning dew would be the type of all this feeling in real life."

And this would be true—alas, it is true of multitudes— had she been stirred by merely human causes, as sympathetic excitement, or appeals to her feelings or fears. But, as we have said before, she had looked upon the face of the Son of God. Circumstances, and the story of Lazarus, had concentrated her mind on Jesus Christ, as in that old and touching record He stands before the world in one of His most winning attitudes. She did not understand how she connected with Him the hope and happiness she felt. She was no doubt like many who, eighteen centuries ago, knew little of Christ, but in the midst of their pain and anguish suddenly felt His healing touch, and exulted with great joy, forgetting that only one disease had been cured, or one trouble banished, and that they still remained in a world where pain and trouble threatened to the very end. But here was the ground of hope for those whom Jesus touched, as well as for Lottie: in curing *one* evil, He had proved His power and willingness to remove *every* evil, and when pain of body and the suffering of guilt again oppressed, the true source of help was known, and so Christ eventually became their Good Physician, intrusted with the entire care of their spiritual health.

No doubt at the time of Christ many a heart was stirred and borne heavenward, on the wings of strong emotion, by the eloquence of some gifted rabbi, by a gorgeous ceremonial in the Temple, or by the chantings of the multitudinous priests. But the emotions passed away, as they do now; and men and women relapsed into their old, material, selfish lives. They may have looked back with regret upon the ecstasy that once thrilled them, and wished that it could always have been maintained; but they found this impossible. So, now, the emotion goes, and the combinations that once produced it never return, or fail to inspire it again. Looking to themselves and their own feelings—to inadequate means of help—such persons are of course disappointed; and so gradually grow hard and legal, or apathetic and unbelieving. When in trouble, when the natural springs of life begin to fail, there seems no real and practical help.

If human experience proves anything it is that every life needs the personal and practical help—the direct touch and word—of One who is Divinely powerful and Divinely patient.

Many days of folly—of sin, sorrow, and deep despondency—are before Lottie still; but she has seen her God weeping from sympathy with weak humanity, and a moment later rescuing from the hopeless extremity of death and corruption. Here is not some vague thing like a half-forgotten emotion or an exalted religious experience in which to trust, but One who, instead of being a vanished, half-forgotten sensation, a philosophy, or even a sound creed and a logical doctrine, is a living personal and powerful Friend, who can put forth His hand and sustain, as He did the timid Apostle who was sinking in the threatening waves.

The temple of Lottie's faith was yet to be built; but she had been so fortunate as to commence with the true "cornerstone."

During the morning hours she was the object of considerable and perplexed thought on the part of several of the household. There was in her face the sweet spiritual radiance of the evening before, and the same gentleness and considerateness of manner marked her action. Mrs. Marchmont and her daughter said, "It is one of Lottie's moods."

Bel surmised that she was a little sentimental over Hemstead, and was indignant that she should herself indulge, and awake in the student, feelings that doubtless, on Lottie's part, would end with the visit. As for De Forrest, he was thoroughly puzzled. The idea that Hemstead could be anything to her was perfectly preposterous; and as for religion, that was a decorous thing of form and ceremonial pertaining to Sunday, and this was Monday. And yet, from some cause, Lottie seemed different from her old self.

He could not complain, however, for she had never been kinder to him; and if her eyes did seek Hemstead's face rather often, she could see nothing there which for a moment could compare with his own handsome features. He also concluded that it was a "mood"; but liked the new and gentle Lottie quite as well as the piquant, and often rather brusque, girl of other days.

But to Hemstead, as with chatting and reading they whiled away the morning hours around the parlor fire, Lottie was the bright particular star. Her face, now transfigured in its spiritual light, captivated his beauty-loving soul; while her words and manner suggested the hope that she, with himself, had found her way into the Holy of Holies. If this could ever be true, he felt that he could go to his work in the Western wilds, content and grateful, and that a long and toilsome life would be illumined by this dear memory. He, too, like Lottie, was on the Mount; but both would soon have to come down to the plain where the "multitude" was, and some of them "lunatic"; and when in the plain they would be very much like the multitude.

After dinner, in compliance with an invitation from Dr. Beams, they all went over to the church, to aid in decorating it with evergreens. They found Miss Martell and several other ladies at work; also a sprinkling of gentlemen and a few young men who were on the border line between boys and beaux, and who were frequently passing from one character to the other.

Miss Martell greeted Hemstead more cordially than she

did any of the others in the party from Mrs. Marchmont's; and seemed slightly surprised at Lottie's gentle and hearty salutation.

De Forrest remained closely at the latter's side, but Hemstead noted with deep and secret satisfaction that there was in her grave kindness nothing responsive to his constant and lover-like attention. Her brow often contracted, as if his sentiment annoyed her, and she treated him as one who, for some reason, must be borne patiently.

"She is probably engaged, but is ceasing to love him," he thought. "She never could have respected him, and now he has forfeited whatever affection she may have had. Still she feels that she is chained to him, and must endure the life-long martyrdom of an ill-mated marriage;" and his heart overflowed with a great pity.

It did not occur to him that he was a miracle of disinterestedness when Lottie was concerned; and that her troubles moved him more than the woes of all the world besides. Like many another life-voyager, with hand upon the helm, he thought he was directing his course, when in fact a strong and subtile current was sweeping him he knew not whither.

He and Lottie did not have much to say to each other, but their eyes often met, and at times, in his frank impulsiveness, he looked at her so earnestly and sympathetically that she turned away to hide her heightened color. She was becoming conscious, with a secret wonder, that he, as no man ever before, had the power to cause her blood to ebb and flow in the most unaccountable manner.

A short time after their arrival he wandered over to the side of the chapel where Miss Martell was working, and she seemingly fascinated him. They apparently became so absorbed in each other's words as to think of no one else, and Lottie grew pale and quiet, feeling, in the meantime, an unreasonable resentment toward Miss Martell. If Lottie has received a little grace, she is, and ever will be, the natural possessor of abundance of human nature. Is this pale and silent girl the one whose cheeks, a little before, were aflame, and every nerve tingling with the most unwonted sensations, and for no better reason apparently than that Hemstead had seen her tugging at a fibrous spray of hemlock, and had severed it with his knife? That was all the others had seen; but there was a great deal more, for in the act their hands had touched, and both had seemed in a positive state in the power to give, and in the negative in readiness to receive, a subtile influence, compared with which electricity is a slow and material agent. And he had lifted his large gray eyes to hers full of—he did not realize what, nor did she—but the cause was there, and the effect followed.

But now, with secret uneasiness, Lottie notes that he seems oblivious of her in his eager talk with Miss Martell.

Soon after joining the latter, Hemstead had said, in his straightforward manner, "You intimated to Mr. Harcourt yesterday that you were 'sorry he heard my sermon.'"

With a little embarrassment she replied, "I do not think that Mr. Harcourt was in the right condition of mind to be benefited by your line of thought."

"Do you think that any one could be benefited by it?"

She was a little puzzled. Was he, like some young clergymen she had known, eager for a few crumbs of praise for his first crude efforts? She was not one to give any faint and hollow commendation, and yet she did not wish to hurt his feelings. But her reply had a tinge of satire in it, for she had no patience with the weakness of vanity.

"I will hardly venture an opinion. You, who have given so much time and thought to these subjects, ought to be a better judge than I."

He felt, rather than saw, the delicate barb, and flushed slightly as he replied, "I admit that perhaps I ought to be, but whether I am or not, is quite another question. I am sure that your views upon the subjects treated yesterday are far truer than mine were. The wretched, heretical sermon that I inflicted upon you has already justly suffered an *auto da fé*. Before the day was over I saw that instead of preach-

ing the gospel I had been elaborating, from a partial premise, a crude view of my own. I shall no longer preach,
that is, if I preach at all, as if human nature were the raw
material which God intended to work up without any regard
to the process, or how much refuse there was, or what became
of it. Is not Christ weeping from sympathy at the grave of
Lazarus a true manifestation of God's feeling toward us?"

"Mr. Hemstead," Miss Martell exclaimed, "I cannot tell
you how glad I am to know your change of views. Most
emphatically I say yes to your question. God is seeking to
develop my character; only He is more patient and gentle
than my good, kind father. But why do you say, 'If I
preach at all'?"

His head bowed in honest humility, as he replied, in a
low tone, "I often doubt whether I am worthy—whether
I am called."

She now saw that she had misjudged him, and was eager
to reassure and confirm his purpose for life; and the con-
verse that followed had grown so absorbing as to cause
Hemstead to forget for the time one, who by some right,
divine or otherwise, had suddenly taken possession of his
thoughts with a despotism as sweet as absolute.

But while Miss Martell was speaking most earnestly to
Hemstead, she saw some one enter the chapel door. Her
color came and went. The sentence upon her lips faltered
to a lame conclusion, and though she became deeply absorbed in the process of twining the fragrant cedar with
the shiny laurel, she did not work as deftly as before.
Looking round to see the cause, Hemstead caught one of
Lottie's reproachful glances, and was soon at her side with
a sense of almost guilty neglect.

Addie Marchmont found work of any kind, even preparation for the Christmas festival, stupid and tiresome; therefore she welcomed the diversion of Harcourt's coming with
double zest; and with extravagant exclamations of delight
summoned him to her side. Miss Martell stood at some
distance, and had turned her back toward them. Harcourt

did not see her at first, but the quest of his restless eyes indicated his hope that she was there. In the meantime he laughed and jested with Addie in something of his old-time style.

Lottie Marsden, like many of her young American sisters, could be decidedly pronounced at times; but a certain amount of grace and good taste characterized her manner. Addie had never been taught restraint of any kind, and to her a church was just the place for a little wild nonsense, and all present were compelled to feel that both her words and manner went beyond the limits of good taste, to say the least. To Harcourt, in his present state of mind, they were so annoying as to be almost offensive, and, thinking that Miss Martell was not presnt, he was about to leave the church in order to escape.

But Miss Martell, with her back toward them, had no means of knowing that Harcourt was not encouraging Addie, and that her freedom with him was not warranted by their relations.

"I have an engagement," said Harcourt, abruptly; and he was about to hasten away, when between intervening groups his eye caught a glimpse of a figure rising for a moment out of one of the high-backed pews, and suggesting to him the object of his thoughts. As he stepped over to speak to Lottie, his eye lingered in that direction. Instead of going directly out, he strolled to the further end of the audience room, speaking and bowing to one and another, but not permitting his eyes to wander long from the bent figure of a lady who sat with her back toward him, apparently wholly absorbed in wreathing evergreens,

She felt that he was coming toward her—she heard his voice, and soon knew that his eyes were scanning her downcast face—but she would not look up till he spoke.

"Won't you deign me even a glance, Miss Martell?" he asked.

The color deepened somewhat in her cheeks, but she looked him full in the face, and said quietly, "Why use the word 'deign,' Mr. Harcourt?"

"I suppose because my conscience suggests that from you I deserve glances of dis-*dain*."

"Such 'glances' are not becoming from any one, and certainly not from me. Besides," she added, a little bitterly, at the thought of such a brainless, frivolous girl as Addie Marchmont enchaining a man like Harcourt, "people do not get their deserts in this world."

"You certainly will not."

"How is that?" she asked quickly, not taking his meaning.

"The world is not rich enough to give it you."

Her brow contracted into a sudden frown, and she said, a trifle coldly, "I do not enjoy that style of compliment, Mr. Harcourt."

"Is there any that you do enjoy?"

Her head bent over her work; her thoughts were swift and many, and in the quiet moment that Harcourt waited for an answer to his commonplace question, she fought and won a battle which, if never known on earth, would never be forgotten in heaven. She mastered self and selfishness, in the very citadel of their strength. Fierce though brief was the struggle that took place beneath that gentle, calm exterior, for the human heart is ever the same—wilful, passionate. With many it is often like the wild storm that *will* spend itself to the end, no matter how much of wreck and ruin is wrought. With such as Miss Martell, it is like the storm which, at its height, heard the words of the Divine Master, "Peace, be still."

"Let him marry Addie Marchmont if he will," she concluded. "I will be kind and gentle to him all the same, and, cost me what it may, I will still see him, and seek to make him a true, good man."

So with woman's tact she turned his question, which savored only of sentimental gallantry, to good account, and said quietly, "You know the only 'style of compliment' that I like, and you enriched me with it at Mrs. Byram's company—the promise you made me."

Harcourt sighed involuntarily. She seemed too angelic —too far above and beyond him. As with a ministering spirit from heaven, her only thought was to win him from evil. Her face was pale from the hidden conflict which had cost her more dearly than he would ever know. Her eyes beamed upon him with a gentle, yet sweet, strange, spiritual light. She scarcely appeared flesh and blood. But he was very human, and his heart craved from her human love and earthly solace. Though now, as at other times, this seemed as presumptuous to him as if some devotee had sacrilegiously fallen in love with his fair patron saint, still he felt a sudden and strong irritation that they should be so far apart.

She misunderstood his sigh, and added, "Am I a hard task-mistress?"

He shook his head, but there was dejection in his tone as he replied, "There have been many forms of idolatry in the world, but I have thought that those who worshipped the stars must have become a little discouraged at times—they are so far off."

Her face had the pained expression of one misunderstood, but who cannot well explain. She said only, "Idolatry is ever profitless." She meant to hint, he thought, that his worship of her certainly would be.

He was chilled at heart. His quick, impetuous spirit prompted him toward recklessness. She saw that he was about to leave abruptly. As she played to win him, not for herself, but heaven, she saw that she had made a mistaken move, though she could not understand his manner. In her maidenly pride and delicacy, she would have let him go if she had thought only of herself; but, conscious of her other motive, she could seek to detain him, and asked, "What did you mean, Mr. Harcourt, by your fanciful allusion to star-worship?"

"I meant," he replied bitterly, "that to ordinary flesh and blood, kneeling in the cold before a distant star, be it ever so bright, is rather chilling and discouraging. The

Greeks were shrewder. They had goddesses with warm, helping hands, and with a little sympathetic, human imperfection.''

It hurt her cruelly that he so misjudged her; and in her confusion, she again said that which he interpreted wrongly.

"It is folly, then, to worship anything so cold and distant." She was about to add plainly, "I am neither a star nor a goddess, but a sincere, human friend—human as yourself." She was about to make some delicate allusion to the time when he often sought her sisterly advice. But he, in the blindness of strong feeling, saw in her words only rebuke for the presumption of his love, and he harshly interrupted her.

"No doubt it is; but let me remind you of a fact often true in missionary experience. After the poor devils have been bereft of the objects of their fond and credulous worship, by proof that their deities are indifferent, they cease to have any faith at all;" and with a cold and rather formal bow he left her side and also left the church.

Miss Martell's head bent lower than ever over her work, and it was a long time before she lifted it or spoke to any one. But the others were occupied with themselves, and no one had noted this little side scene save Addie, who pouted that Harcourt had remained, but not at her side, after his expressed intention of leaving. No one surmised that two who had been present were sorely hurt. When we receive our slight cuts and bruises through life, there are usually outcry and abundant sympathy. But when we receive our deep wounds, that leave scars, often only God knows; and it is best so, for He can heal, but the world can only probe.

CHAPTER XXII

"YOU MUST WAIT AND SEE"

"HOW can you leave Miss Martell?" asked Lottie, as Hemstead approached propitiatingly with a large armful of the choicest evergreens.

"Well, I can," he replied with a smile.

"As yet, but the next time you will stay longer, and the next longer still."

"That depends. I would not remain at her side, nor at any one's, if I thought they were tiring of me a little."

"Oh, she got tired of you."

"Well, yes; a little, I think. She suddenly seemed to lose her interest in the conversation. Still she was very good to talk to me as long and as kindly as she did. She is a very superior woman. It has never been my good fortune to meet just such a lady before."

"Make the most of your rare 'good fortune.'"

"I have."

"And now that she is tired of you, you come back to me as a *dernier ressort*."

"Coming back to you, is like coming back home, for you have given me the only home-like feeling that I have had during my visit."

The language of coquetry was to Lottie like her mother-tongue, and she fell into it as naturally as she breathed. Only now, instead of suggesting the false hope that he had been missed and she had cared, it expressed her true feeling, for she did care.

De Forrest now returned from a momentary absence, and had it not been for his garrulity the little group would have been a rather silent one. Both young men sought to supply Lottie with the sprays of green that she was twining. She took the evergreens chiefly from De Forrest's hands, but gave her thoughts and eyes to Hemstead. He, with man's usual penetration, thought De Forrest the favored one, and was inclined to reverse his half-formed opinion that she was destined to pathetic martyrdom, because bound by an engagement to a man whom she could not love.

"He can't think much of me," thought Lottie, with a sigh, "or he couldn't speak so frankly." She, too, was losing her wonted quick discernment.

Only lynx-eyed Bel Parton partially surmised the truth, and suspected that Lottie was developing a genuine, though of course a passing interest, in the student whom at first she had purposed to beguile in mere reckless sport.

During the remainder of the afternoon and evening, De Forrest was Lottie's shadow, and she could escape him, and be with Hemstead, only by remaining with all the others. She was longing for another of their suggestive talks, when, without the restraint of the curious and un-sympathetic, they could continue the theme that De Forrest had interrupted on Sunday afternoon.

She was thinking how to bring this about, when the old plan of visiting Mrs. Dlimm occurred to her, and she adopted it at once.

Getting a moment aside with Hemstead, by being down to breakfast a little before the others, she said, "After my naughty behavior in regard to our visit to Mrs. Dlimm, will you still take me there?"

"I wish you would give me a chance," he answered eagerly.

"Well, I will, at ten this morning. But please say nothing about it. Drive to the door in the cutter, and I will be ready. If the matter is discussed, there may be half a dozen other projects started."

Hemstead ate but an indifferent breakfast, and there was also a faint glow of expectant excitement in Lottie's face.

Hemstead promptly sought his aunt, and asked if he might have a horse and the single sleigh.

"I hope another time will answer," said Mrs. Marchmont, carelessly. "Addie wishes the horses this morning, but I believe proposes taking you all out."

But Hemstead was not to be baffled, and acted with more energy than prudence perhaps. Lottie from her window saw him posting with long strides toward the village, and exultingly surmised his object. At ten he drove up to the door with a neat little turnout from the livery stable; and she tripped down and took a seat at his side, and they were off before the rest of the household realized their purpose.

They all looked at each other questioningly, as a few moments later they gathered in the parlor for a general sleigh-ride.

Mr. Dimmerly, who had quietly watched proceedings, broke out into his cackling laugh, as he chuckled, "He shows his blood. A dozen seminaries could not quench him utterly."

Mrs. Marchmont frowned. She rigidly applied the rules of propriety to all save her own children, and she justly thought that both Hemstead and Lottie had failed in courtesy to her and her guests, by stealing away, as it were, without any explanations. But people of one idea often fail in more than mere matters of courtesy; and Hemstead and Lottie were emphatically becoming people of one idea. And they both had misgivings and a sense of wrong-doing as they drove away without a word of explanation.

Mrs. Marchmont was still more puzzled when Addie exclaimed petulantly, "I thought the agreement was that Lottie should carry out the joke when and where we could all enjoy it."

The lady was led to suspect that there was something on foot that might need her investigation, and she quietly resolved to use her eyes and ears judiciously. She well knew that her proud and fashionable sister, Lottie's mother, would hold her to strict account if Lottie did anything foolish.

Bel merely shrugged her shoulders cynically. She had a certain kind of loyalty to her friend, and said all her harsh things to Lottie herself, and not behind her back.

De Forrest had no other resource than to believe that Lottie was carrying out the practical joke; but a sorry jest he found it that morning, during which he scarcely spoke to any one.

They drove over to town for Harcourt, but he greatly provoked Addie by pleading that his business would not permit absence. During the rest of the drive they all might have formed part of a funeral procession.

But the snow-crystals did not sparkle in the sunlight more brightly than Lottie's eyes, as she turned to her companion, and said, "I am so delighted that we are safely off on our drive."

"Oh, it's the 'drive' you are thinking of. That is better than I hoped. I thought we were visiting Mrs. Dlimm."

"So we are, and I want to see her too," said Lottie, with a sudden blush.

"Well, I'm glad you don't dread the long, intervening miles, with no better company than mine."

"It's a good chance to learn patient endurance," she replied, with a look delightfully arch. "So please drive slower."

The horse instantly came to a walk.

"That is the other extreme," she continued. "You always go to extremes, as, for instance, your quixotic purpose to go out among the border ruffians."

"Honestly, Miss Marsden," said Hemstead, his laughing face suddenly becoming grave, "you do not now think, in your heart, my purpose to be a home missionary 'quixotic'?"

"I don't know much about my heart, Mr. Hemstead, except that it has always been very perverse. But I now wish I had a better one. You have disturbed the equanimity with which I could do wrong most wofully. I even feel a little guilty for leaving them all this morning, with no explanations."

"It was hardly right, now I think of it," said Hemstead, reflectively.

"Have you just thought of it? How preoccupied you have been! What *have* you been thinking about? Yes, it was wrong; but as it is the first wicked thing I have caught you in I am quite comforted. I have been hoping all along that you would do something just a little bit encouragingly wicked."

"How little you understand me! My wickedness and consequent twinges of conscience have been my chief sources of trouble thus far."

"Oh, well, your conscience is like Auntie Jane. A speck of dust gives her the fidgets where other people would not see any dust at all. If your conscience had to deal with my sins there would not be ashes and hair-cloth enough for you."

"What good can ashes, hair-cloth, or any kind of self-punishment, or even self-condemnation, do us?"

"Well, we ought to be sorry, at least."

"Certainly, but there must be more than that. Many a wrong-doer has been sincerely sorry, but has been punished all the same. I cannot tell you, Miss Marsden, how much good you did me on Sunday afternoon. My mind had been dwelling on the attributes of God—upon doctrines as if they were things by themselves and complete in themselves. I almost fear that I should have become, as I fear some are, the disciple of a religious system, instead of a simple and loyal follower of Christ. But you fixed my eyes on a living personality, who has the right to say, 'I forgive you,' and I am forgiven; who has right to say, 'I will save you,' and I am saved. If He is the Divine Son of God, as He claims to be, has He not the right?"

"Yes. He must be able to do just what is pleasing to Him," said Lottie.

"Then look upon Him as you saw Him at the grave of Lazarus—the very embodiment of sympathy. Suppose that in sincere regret for all the wrong you have ever done, and with the honest wish to be better, you go to such a being and cry, 'Forgive.' Can you doubt His natural, inevitable course toward you? If pardoning love and mercy should encircle you at once, would it not be in perfect keeping with His tears of sympathy?''

"And is that all I have to do to get rid of the old, dark record against me? Oh, how black it looked last Saturday!''

"That is all. What more can you do? Who was it that said, 'Be of good cheer, thy sins be forgiven thee'?''

"Mr. Hemstead,'' said Lottie, in a low tone, "I have felt very strangely—differently from any time before in all my life—since last Sunday afternoon. I seemed to look upon Christ as if He were before me, and I saw the tears in His eyes, as I saw them in yours the evening you said such plain things to me, and I have felt a peculiar lightness of heart ever since. That hymn we sang on Sunday evening expressed so exactly what I felt that I was overpowered. It appeared written for me alone. Do you think that I can be a Christian?''

Hemstead's eyes glistened, and his heart bounded at the thought; but he felt that he was in a grave and responsible position, and after a moment's thought answered wisely: "I can base no safe and positive answer on your feeling. I have already learned, from my own experience and that of others, that religious feeling is something that comes and goes, and cannot be depended upon. The test question is, How will you treat this Jesus whom you have seen, and who has proved Himself both worthy to win and keep your trust? A little strong feeling and sentiment in regard to Him can-not do you much good. What practical relation do you in-tend to hold toward Him? No doubt many that saw Him weep, and then raise Lazarus after he had been four days dead, were profoundly moved, but the majority went on in their old ways all the same. You abound in strong common-sense, and must see that more that even sincere, deep feel-ing is necessary. What do you propose to *do?* Are you

willing to take up your cross and before His faithful
follower?"

"That involves a great deal," said Lottie, with a long
breath.

"It does indeed," he replied earnestly. "I would give
my life to make you a Christian, and yet I would not seek
to win you for Him by false pretences, or hide any part of
the rugged path of self-denial. Count well the cost. But,
believe me, Miss Marsden," he added, in a tone that
brought a sudden paleness to her cheek, "not following
Him involves far more that is sad and terrible."

Tears stood in Lottie's eyes. She was silent a few moments, and was evidently thinking deeply. The young
clergyman was desperately in earnest, and fairly trembled
in the eagerness of his expectation. He hoped that Lottie
would come to a solemn and half-heroic and formal decision. But he was both puzzled and disappointed by the
sudden and brusque manner with which she turned upon
him as she said: "Where is the heavy cross that I must
take up? Show it to me, and I will think about it. Where
is the rugged path? This one that leads to Mrs. Dlimm is
very pleasant. I don't see anything very awful in being
a Christian nowadays. Of course I shall have to give up
all my old nonsense and flirt— Well, I suppose I might
as well say it out. But there are no Inquisitions, with
thumbscrews and racks, any longer. Come, Mr. Hemstead,
you are a Christian. What heavy cross are you bearing?
I hope you are not in the rugged path of self-denial this
morning, while taking me to Mrs. Dlimm's. I don't know
any one who appears to enjoy the good things of life more
than you. I don't know what answer to give to your solemn
and far-reaching questions. I haven't much confidence in
what Lottie Marsden will do. All I know is that I feel as
I imagine one of those children did whom Jesus took in his
arms and blessed."

"But suppose," urged her anxious spiritual guide, who
felt that she was giving a reason for her faith that would

hardly satisfy the grave elders of the church—"suppose that at some future time He should impose a heavy cross, or ask of you painful self-denial, would you shrink?"

She turned her dewy eyes upon him with a look of mingled archness and earnestness that he never forgot, and said significantly, "I do not remember the New Testament story very perfectly, but when the last, dark days came, women stood by their Lord as faithfully as the men—didn't they?"

Hemstead bowed his head in sudden humility, and said: "You are right. It was not woman who betrayed, nor did woman desert or deny Him. Still I treasure the suggestion of your answer beyond all words."

The tears stood thick in Lottie's eyes, and she was provoked that they did. Her strong feelings were quick to find expression, and Hemstead seemed to have the power, as no one else ever had, to evoke them. But she had a morbid dislike of showing emotion or anything verging toward sentiment; therefore she would persist in giving a light and playful turn to his sombre earnestness.

"I did not mean," she said, "to be so hard upon the men, nor to secure so rich a tribute to my sex. I imagine we all stand in need of charity alike. Only do not expect too much of me. I dare not promise anything. You must wait and see."

"Though you promise so little, you inspire me with more confidence than many whom I have heard make great professions;" and the light of a great joy and a great hope shone in his eyes.

"You look very happy, Mr. Hemstead," said Lottie, gratefully. "Would you be very glad to have me become a Christian?"

He looked at her so earnestly that the rich blood mounted to her very brow. After a moment, he replied, in a low, trembling tone: "I scarcely dare trust myself to answer your question, and yet I do not exaggerate when I assure you that if I could feel that you were a Christian before I go away, it seems as if I could never see a dark day again. Oh, Miss Marsden, how I have hoped and prayed that you might become one!''

Her head bowed low in guilty shame. She compared her purpose toward him with his toward her. Before she thought, the words slipped out, "And for all my wrong to you, you seek to give me heaven in return."

He looked at her inquiringly, not understanding her remark; but after a moment, said, "It would be heaven to me on earth, even in my lonely work in the West, if I could remember that, as a result of our brief acquaintance, you had become a Christian."

"Well," she said emphatically, "our acquaintance does promise to end differently from what I expected; and it is because you are different. You are not the kind of a man that I expected you would be."

"But I understood you from the first," remarked Hemstead, complacently. "My first impression when you gave me your warm hand, and the only true welcome I received, has been borne out. Though at times you have puzzled me, still, the proof you gave—on the evening of my arrival —of a true, generous, and womanly nature, has been confirmed again and again. It has seemed to me that your faults were due largely to circumstances, but that your good qualities were native."

Again Lottie turned away her burning cheeks in deep embarrassment. Should she tell him all? She felt she could not. To lose his good opinion and friendship now seemed terrible. But conscience demanded that she should be perfectly frank and sincere with him, and her fears whispered, "He may learn it from the others, and that would be far worse than if I told him myself."

But her moral strength was not yet equal to the test. The old, prevailing influences of her life again swayed her, and she guided the conversation from the topic as a pilot would shun a dangerous rock.

"I will tell him all about it at some future time," she

thought; "but not yet when the knowledge might drive him away in anger."

She seized upon one of his words, which, when spoken, had jarred unpleasantly upon her feeling.

"Why do you speak of our acquaintance as brief? Are we to be strangers again after this short visit is over?"

"I most positively assure you that you can never be a stranger to me again," he said eagerly. "But in a few days you will go to New York, and I thousands of miles in another direction. If I should tell you how you will dwell in my thoughts like an inspiration, I fear you would think me sentimental. But in your absorbing city life I fear that I shall soon become as a stranger to you."

"Well," said Lottie, averting her face, "I don't think I'll promise you anything this time either. You must wait and see. But is that dreadful frontier life of yours a foregone conclusion?"

"Yes," he said, with quiet emphasis.

"There are plenty of heathen in New York, Mr. Hemstead. You found one of them in me, and see how much good you have done; at least, I hope you have."

"There are also plenty of Christians in New York to take care of them. I commend some of the heathen to you."

"I fear that they will remain heathen for all that I can do."

"No, indeed, Miss Marsden. Please never think that. No one has a right to say, 'I can do nothing,' and you least of all. Apart from your other gifts, you abound in personal magnetism, and almost instantly gain control of those around you."

"How mistaken you are! I have no control over you."

"More than you think, perhaps," he said, flushing deeply.

It was his heart that spoke then, and not his will, instructed by deliberate reason.

She too blushed, but said laughingly, "What are words?

Let me test my power. Take a church in New York, instead of a thousand miles out of the world."

"You are not in earnest," he said, a little sadly. "You would not seek to dissuade me from what I regard as a sacred duty?"

"But is it 'a sacred duty'? There are plenty of others —less cultivated, less capable of doing good—in the refined and critical East."

"That is not he way a soldier reasons. Some one must go to the front of the battle. And what excuse can such a vigorous young fellow as I am have for hanging back?"

As he turned his glowing face upon her she caught his enthusiasm, and said impulsively, "And in the front of the battle I would be, if I were a man, as I often wish I were."

"The line of God's battle with evil is very long, Miss Marsden. I think you can find the front in New York as truly as I in the West. In this fight woman can often do as much as man. Won't you try?"

"I shall not promise you anything," she said. "You must wait and see."

They were now before the parsonage in the hamlet of Scrub Oaks. The sound of the bells brought Mrs. Dlimm's faded face to the window, and on recognizing them she clapped her hands for joy, as one of her own children might have done; and a moment later was smiling upon the little porch, the very embodiment of welcome.

CHAPTER XXIII

A RATIONALIST OF THE OLD SCHOOL

"I KNEW you would come," said Mrs. Dlimm, taking both of Lottie's hands with utter absence of formality. "Husband said I needn't look for you any more, but I felt it in my bones—no, my heart—that you would come. When I feel a thing is going to take place it always does. So you are here. I am very glad to see your—Mr. Hemstead—too. This is splendid." And Mrs. Dlimm exultantly ushered Lottie into the room that, when last seen, was crowded with such a motley assembly. Hemstead meanwhile drove the horse to an adjacent shed.

"But he isn't my Mr. Hemstead," said Lottie, laughing.

"Well, it seems as if he were related, or belonged to you in some way. When I think of one, I can't help thinking of the other."

"Oh, dear!" exclaimed Lottie, still laughing, blushing, and affecting comic alarm; "being joined together by a minister's wife is almost as bad as by the minister himself."

"Almost as good, you mean. You would have my congratulation rather than sympathy if you secured such a prince among men."

"How little you know about him, Mrs. Dlimm! He is going to be a poor, forlorn home missionary; and your husband's increased salary will be royal compared with his."

"He will never be forlorn; and how long will he be poor?"

"All his life possibly."

"That's not very long. What will come after? What kind of a master is he serving?"

"Do you know," said Lottie, lowering her tone, and giving her chair a little confidential hitch toward the simple-hearted lady with whom formality and circumlocution were impossible, "that I am beginning to think about these things a great deal?"

"I don't wonder, my dear," said Mrs. Dlimm, with a little sigh of satisfaction. "No one could help thinking about him who saw his manly courtesy and tact the evening you were here."

"Oh, no," said Lottie, blushing still more deeply; "I did not mean that. Please understand me. Mr. Hemstead is only a chance acquaintance that I have met while visiting my aunt, Mrs. Marchmont. I mean that when I was here last I was a very naughty girl, but I have since been thinking how I could be a better one. Indeed, I should like to be a Christian, as you are."

In a moment the little lady was all tender solicitude. She was one who believed in conversion; and, to her, being converted was the greatest event of life.

But just then Hemstead entered, and she had enough natural, womanly interest—not curiosity—to note the unconscious welcome of Lottie's eyes, and the quick color come and go in her face, as if a fire were burning in her heart and throwing its flickering light upon her fair features.

"Chance acquaintance, indeed!" she thought. "Why, here is this city-bred girl blushing as I once did about Mr. Dlimm. Whether she knows it or not, her blushes must tell the same story as mine."

But though Mrs. Dlimm was so unconventional, she had tact, and turned the conversation to the subject of the donation party.

"See here," she exclaimed exultantly, tugging a bulky commentary; "this is one of the results of your coming the other evening. Mr. Dlimm has been wanting this book a long time, and now he pores over it so much that I am getting jealous."

"The opinions expressed in such a ponderous volume ought to have great weight, surely," said Hemstead, smiling.

"And do you know," she continued, in an aside to Lottie, "that each of the children has had a new warm winter suit? and, wonderful to tell, I have bought myself a dress right from the store, instead of making over something sent me by brother Abel's wife from New York."

Lottie's eyes moistened, and she said in half soliloquy, "I didn't know it was so nice and easy to make others happy."

"Ah! depend upon it, you are learning lots of things," said Mrs. Dlimm, significantly. "When God begins to teach, then we *do* learn, and something worth knowing, too."

"I thought that God's lessons were very hard and painful," said Lottie to Hemstead, with a spice of mischief in her manner.

"Mrs. Dlimm is a better authority than I was," he replied. "Do you know," he continued, addressing their hostess, "that Miss Marsden has done more to teach me how to preach than all my years at the seminary?"

"Surely," exclaimed Mrs. Dlimm, "that's a rather strong statement. I can understand how Miss Marsden can do a great deal for one. We have had very nice experience in that direction; but just how she should teach you more than all the grave professors and learned text-books is not clear at once."

"Well, she has," he maintained stoutly. "I doubt whether your husband gets as much light upon the Bible from that huge commentary there as Miss Marsden gave me in one afternoon."

Mrs. Dlimm turned her eyes inquiringly toward Lottie, who said, laughingly, "It would seem, last week, that I was a heathen and Mr. Hemstead a heretic."

"And what are you now?"

"Oh, he's all right now."

"And not you?"

"I fear I shall always be a little crooked; but I hope I am not exactly a heathen any longer."

"Miss Marsden was a heathen, as Nathanael was a shrewd and dishonest Jew," said Hemstead.

"What kind of a Jew was Nathanael?" asked Lottie, innocently.

"Christ said, when he first saw him," replied Mrs. Dlimm, smiling, "'Behold an Israelite indeed, in whom is no guile.'"

Then both were puzzled at Lottie's sudden and painful flush, but they ascribed it to her modesty; and Hemstead, to give her time to recover herself, gave a brief sketch of his sermon, and how, in the afternoon, while reading, at Lottie's suggestion, the complete story of Lazarus, they both had seen the unspeakable sympathy of Christ for those He sought to save.

"Oh, dear!" thought Lottie, "when shall I escape the consequences of my foolish jest? 'Without guile,' indeed!"

Mr. Dlimm now appeared, and he and Hemstead were soon discussing the rendering of an obscure passage, upon which the big commentary gave the conflicting opinions of a dozen learned doctors. Mrs. Dlimm carried Lottie off to her sanctum, the nursery—the fruitful source of questions and mysteries the learned doctors would find still more difficult to solve.

"And you are contented with this narrow round of life?" asked Lottie, curiously, as Mrs. Dlimm finished the narration of what seemed to her very tame experience.

"Narrow!" said Mrs. Dlimm, reproachfully; "my life and work are not narrow. I have six little immortals to train. A million years hence they will either bless or reproach me. What consideration in fashionable life is equal to that? Besides, my husband is engaged in the same kind of work that brought the Son of God from heaven to earth. It is my privilege to help him. Scrub Oaks is as much of a place as many of the villages in which

He preached, and I am grateful that I can take part in so royal a calling."

"Mrs. Dlimm," said Lottie, with sudden animation, "I shouldn't wonder if you and your husband were very great people in heaven."

"Oh!" cried the little lady, laughing. "We never think of that. Why should we? But I know there will be a nook there for us, and the thought makes me very happy."

"And you really and truly have been happy in all your toil and privations?"

"Yes," said Mrs. Dlimm, with a strange, far-away look coming into her large blue eyes; "when everything on earth has been darkest I have been most happy, and this has confirmed my faith. Little children are sources of great joy, but they also cause much pain and anxiety. Yet when I have been suffering most—when the wardrobe has been scanty and the larder almost bare—God has taken me to His heart as I clasp this child here, and comforted by assuring me, 'Never fear, my child, I will take care of you and yours.' See how He keeps His word. He sent you here, with your bright, sunny face. He sent Mr. Hemstead here; and between you both we shall make a long stage of our homeward journey most pleasantly."

"I never heard any one talk like you before," said Lottie, musingly. "You seem to believe all the Bible says, as if it were actually right before you."

"Believe! Why not? The idea of God not keeping His word!"

"And is faith just the certainty that God will keep His word?"

"That is just faith; and though this great world—for little bits of which people lose their souls—shall pass away, God's word shall stand until His least promise is fulfilled."

"That is not our creed on Fifth Avenue," said Lottie sadly. "The world first, God last. But you sometimes, surely, wish that Mr. Dlimm was rich, and that you could have for him and the children and yourself all that heart could wish?''

"I used to feel so occasionally, but I have got past that now. God loves my husband and children better than I do, and He will provide what is best for us all. I simply try to rest in His arms as this child does in mine.''

"How strange it all is!" said Lottie, thoughtfully.

"Why strange? Your earthly father provides for you the best he can; and if our Heavenly Father provides for us in the same way, surely will not His be the better provision? What an absurd, unnatural thing it is to suppose there is anything better than what God will give His own dear children. Are not both earth and heaven His? and He has promised the best of both to us.''

"I can scarcely realize it all yet," said Lottie, with tears in her eyes. "I suppose it is because you are so natural and true that you seem so odd to me, who have been brought up among those that I fear look at things in false lights.''

"I think I understand you, my dear," said Mrs. Dlimm, hopefully. "A child's penny toy will hide a great mountain if held too near the eyes. It is thus the eyes of the worldly are blinded by trifles till I fear some will never see God or heaven. But He is teaching you better. As long as you follow His gentle leadings, and the pure impulses of your own heart, all will be well. But as soon as you begin to take counsel of the world and its self-seeking spirit, you will find yourself in trouble. If we wish to prosper and be happy in God's world, we must do His will. This is good, sound common-sense, which the experience of every age has borne out. It often seems hard at first, my dear, as you will find out. The scourging was very hard to bear; but Paul and Silas, singing in prison, with their feet made fast in the stocks, were better off than their jailer, who was about to kill himself, and the magistrates, who, no doubt, were in mortal fear because of the earthquake. We, too, can sing, whatever happens, as long as God and conscience are upon our side.''

It will thus be seen that Mrs. Dlimm was a rationalist as well as a believer, though not of the new school.

For some reason, her philosophy was peculiarly accepta-ble to Lottie, and, though scarcely conscious why, the ex-hortation to follow the impulses of her own heart seemed especially natural and right; but her fashionable mother would have been alarmed indeed, if she had known that her beautiful daughter was becoming the disciple of Mrs. Dlimm.

Though their call was by no means a short one, it passed all too quickly. The memory of it would never fade from Lottie's mind; and it became another link in the chain by which God was seeking to bind her to a better future than her friends could dream of in their earthly ambition.

"I am very glad I made this visit," Lottie said, as they were hastening home lest they should be late to dinner. "It was very kind of you to take me so far."

He turned and lifted his eyebrows comically.

"What do you mean by that?" she asked.

"To hear you, one would think that I had been a martyr for your sake, while, in truth, I never enjoyed myself more."

"Yes," said she; "but you welcome afflictions and trials of your patience."

"Would that I might be ever thus afflicted!" he ex-claimed impulsively. Then, suddenly becoming conscious of the natural suggestion of his words, he blushed deeply; but not more so than Lottie, who turned away her face to hide her flaming cheeks. He, misinterpreting the act, thought that she meant a hint that such remarks were not agreeable, and was thinking how to remedy what he now regarded as a very foolish speech, when she, with woman's tact, led the conversation to unembarrassing topics, and be-fore they were aware the horse stopped at Mrs. Marchmont's door.

Lottie disarmed both suspicion and censure to a consid-erable extent by saying, "I had promised Mrs. Dlimm to come and see her again, and wished to keep my word. I knew no one would care to go there save Mr. Hemstead, so I took him to see the parson while I visited the parson's wife. I enjoyed my call very much, too; and as Mr. Hemstead and Mr. Dlimm had a great argument over a knotty theological point, I suppose he feels somewhat repaid also."

This put matters in quite another light. That one should go to see a parson's wife, and the other to discuss theology with the parson, was very different from stealing off for an indefinite ride with the purpose of being alone together. De Forrest was quite comforted, and was even inclined to regard Lottie as rather considerate in not asking him to accompany her when visiting such undesirable people as the Dlimms. Though why she should wish to visit them herself was a mystery. But then, he thought, "Lottie is odd and full of queer moods and whims. Let her indulge them now, because, as my wife, they will scarcely be the thing." He was still more comforted by noting that she did not have a great deal to say to Hemstead—indeed, that she rather avoided him.

"She has had enough, and too much, of his heavy stupid company," he thought, "and finds that even the carrying out of the practical joke is too hard work. If I can only get another good opportunity, I won't wait till she goes to sleep before bringing the question to an issue."

But Lottie gave him no opportunity, and, while kind and gentle toward him, adroitly managed that they should never be alone.

And Hemstead also, who had found their private *tête-à-têtes* so delightful and productive of good results, was equally unable to be alone with her. Not that Lottie was averse, but because she saw that lynx-eyed Bel was watching her; and again for the hundredth time she wished her cynical friend back in the city.

Lottie's manner and apparent reserve were so marked at one time that Hemstead began to grow troubled, though why he scarcely knew. There was no cause, save the pe-

culiar sensitiveness of one whose sunshine is beginning to
come, not from the skies, but from the changing features
of a fellow-mortal.

Lottie quickly saw his shadowed face, and surmised the
cause. Soon after, when his eyes were questioningly seeking hers, she gave him such a sunny, genial smile as to
assure him that, whatever might be the cause of her somewhat distant manner, it did not result from any estrange-
ment from him.

Heretofore, when Lottie had liked a gentleman, she had
been frank in showing that preference within the limits of
lady-like bearing. But, for some reason, she began to grow
excessively shy in manifesting any interest in Hemstead that
the others could note. The reason with which she satisfied
herself explained her feeling but partially.

"They will think I am still trying to carry out my
wicked, foolish joke."

But she did long for another unrestrained talk with him,
and watched keenly to secure it without exciting remark.
De Forrest did all he could to prevent this, however, and
Bel unconsciously became his ally. With woman's quick
perception, she saw that Lottie was indulging in something
more than a "mood," and felt that it was a duty she owed
to her friend to prevent mischief.

Thus Monday and Tuesday passed away, Lottie being
too circumspect to give Bel sufficient cause for speaking
plainly.

Dan and Mr. Dimmerly were the only ones of the household who regarded the change in Lottie with unmixed satisfaction. Not giving a thought to the cause, they were
pleased with the gentleness and attention which resulted.

"Lottie," said her brother Dan, as she kissed him good-
night, after telling a marvellously good story, "what has
come over you? You make me think of Auntie Jane."

"I must be growing good indeed if I remind any one of
Auntie Jane," thought Lottie, exultantly.

CHAPTER XXIV

THE TERROR OF A GREAT FEAR

LONG before Harcourt reached his law office, he was satisfied that he had blundered foolishly, and done Miss Martell great injustice. Her right to refuse his unwelcome love was perfect, and her manner of doing so, as he understood her, had been most delicate, even in his estimation. At the same time she had never given him the slightest ground for his implied aspersion that in her pure, Christian life she shone down upon him with the cold distance of a "star."

He recalled her words and bearing in Mrs. Bryam's conservatory, and the degree in which his unreasonable passion had blinded him grew more apparent.

"Why should I expect her to love me?" he asked himself in bitterness. "It is a hundred-fold more than I deserve, or had a right to hope, that she should put out her hand to save me."

He was on the point of returning twenty times, and asking her pardon for his folly, but that bane of our life—that hindrance to more good and happiness than perhaps any other one cause—pride, deterred, and Monday evening passed, an unhappy one to the object of his thoughts as well as to himself.

On Tuesday pride was vanquished, and as soon as his business permitted he repaired to the Martell mansion, eager to ask forgiveness. To his deep disappointment, he learned that Mr. Martell and his daughter had driven up to town, crossed on the ferryboat, and were paying some visits on the other side of the river.

He now purposed to call again as soon as they returned, but was unexpectedly detained until quite late in the evening. He approached the familiar place that now enshrined, to him, the jewel of the world, in both a humble and an heroic mood. He would not presume again, but in silence live worthily of his love for one so lovely. He would be more than content—yes, grateful—if she would deign to help him climb toward her moral height.

As he stood on the piazza, after ringing the door-bell, he was in greater trepidation than when he had made his first plea in court, and was so intent in trying to frame his thoughts into appropriate language that he did not note for the moment that no one answered. Again he rang, but there was no response. There were lights in the house, and he knocked upon the door quite loudly. A housemaid soon after appeared, with a scared and anxious face.

"Is Miss Martell at home?" he asked, a sudden boding of evil chilling his heart.

"Indade an' she is not. Would to God she was!"

"What do you mean?"

"Faix, an' I'm sure I'm glad ye's come, Misther Harcourt. The coachman is down at the shore, and he'll tell ye all."

Harcourt dashed through the snow and shrubbery, over rocks and down steeps that gave him one or two severe falls, that he might, the nearest way, reach Mr. Martell's boathouse. Here he found the coachman peering out upon the dark waters, and occasionally uttering a hoarse, feeble shout, which could scarcely be heard above the surf that beat with increasing heaviness upon the icy beach.

The man seemed nearly exhausted with cold and anxiety, and was overjoyed at seeing Harcourt; but he told the young man a story which filled him with deepest alarm. It was to this effect:

Mr. and Miss Martell had been delayed in leaving a friend's house on the opposite side of the river until it was too late to reach the boat on which it was their intention to cross. They had been prevailed upon by their hospitable host to send their sleigh up to a later boat, while they remained for an early supper, and then should cross in a boat rowed by an experienced oarsman, who was a tenant on the gentleman's place.

"It was quite a bit after dark when I got back, but Mr. Martell and the young lady hadn't come over yet. I first thought they was goin' to stay all night, and that I should go arter them in the mornin'; but the woman as sews says how she was sittin' at one of the upper winders, and how she sees, just afore night, a light push out from t'other side and come straight across for a long while, and then turn and go down stream. I'm afeard they've caught in the ice."

"But what became of the light?" asked Harcourt, half desperate with fear and anxiety.

"Well, the woman as sews says it went down and down as long as she could see."

A faint scream from the house now arrested their attention, and hastening up the bank they heard the servants crying from the upper windows of the mansion, "There it comes! there it comes again!"

Harcourt rushed to the second story of the house. A door leading into an apartment facing the river was open, and without a thought he entered and threw open the blinds. Away to the south, where the river enters the Highlands, he saw a faint light, evidently that of the lantern carried in the boat. Familiar with the river, the whole state of things flashed upon him. In the last of the ebb tide their boat had become entangled in the ice, but had been carried down no very great distance. Now that the tide had turned, it was coming back, with the mass of ice in which it had become wedged.

And could that faint glimmer indicate the presence of the one who never before had been so dear? Could Miss Martell, the child of luxury, so beautiful and yet so frail and delicate, be out in the darkness and cold of this winter night, perishing perhaps, with the lights of this her elegant home full in view?

Then, for the first time, he recognized that the room he was in must be Miss Martell's sleeping apartment. Though the light was low and soft, it revealed an exquisite casket, in keeping with the jewel it had once held, but might no more enshrine. On every side were the evidences of a refined but Christian taste, and also a certain dainty beauty that seemed a part of the maiden herself, she having given to the room something of her own individuality.

It would be hard to describe Harcourt's sensation as a hasty glance revealed the character of the place. He felt somewhat as a devout Greek might, had he stumbled into the sacred grotto of his most revered goddess.

But this thought was uppermost in his mind—"Here is where she should be; yonder—terrible thought—is where she is. What can I do?"

Again he dashed back to the shore, calling the coachman to follow him. When the man reached the water's edge, he found that Harcourt had broken open the boat-house, and was endeavoring to get out the boat.

"Ye'll gain nothing there, wid that big boat," said the coachman. "The master has been away so long that it's all out o' order. The water can get in it as soon as yer'self. The young lady's little scollop—the one as is called Naughty Tillus—is sent away for the winter."

"Stop your cursed croaking," cried Harcourt, excitedly, "and help me out with this boat. If I can't save her, I can at least drown with her."

"Divil a lift will I give ye. It will do the master and young lady no good, and I'll not have your drownding on my conscience."

Harcourt soon found that he could not manage the large boat alone, and the matches he struck to guide him revealed that the man had spoken truly, and that the craft was in no condition for the service he proposed.

"Great God!" he cried, "is there no way to save her?"

He sprang upon the boat-house, and there, away to the south, was the dim light coming steadily up the stream. The moon had not yet risen; the sky was overcast with wildly flying clouds; the wind was rising, and would drive and grind the ice more fiercely. It was just the night for a tragedy, and he felt that if he saw that light disappear, as a sign that the boat had been crushed and its occupants swallowed up by the wintry tide, the saddest tragedy of the world would have taken place.

He groaned and clenched his hands in his impotent anguish.

"Oh, God!" he cried, "what can I do to save her."

He clasped his throbbing temples, and cried to think. It soon occurred to him that Mrs. Marchmont's boat might be in better condition. Hemstead was strong and brave, and would assuredly join him in the effort to rescue them. Without a word he rushed up the bank, sprang into his cutter, gave his spirited horse a cut from the whip, which caused him at once to spring into a mad gallop, and so vanished from the eyes of the bewildered and terrified servants, who were left alone to their increasing fears.

"Save *her*—save *her*," muttered the coachman, as, stiff and numb with cold, he followed Harcourt more slowly to the house. "It's kind o' queer how he forgits about the old man."

CHAPTER XXV

A TRUE KNIGHT

A S the dusk deepened into night upon this memorable evening, Hemstead stood at the parlor window, and looked out so long and intently that Lottie joined him at last, and asked, "What can you see without, and in the darkness, so much more attractive than anything within?"

"Do you see that faint light out there upon the river?"

"Yes."

"Well, I've been watching it for some time, and it troubles me. I noticed this afternoon that there was ice coming down with the tide. Is it possible that some one, in crossing with a small boat, has been caught in the ice and carried downward?"

"Why should you think that? Nothing is more common than lights upon the river at night."

"Yes, but not of late. Since the last severe cold I have noticed that the river was almost deserted, and the papers state that it is freezing north of us. But it is the peculiarity in the movement of the light that perplexes me. When I saw it first, it appeared as if coming across the river. Suddenly, when quite over toward this side, it seemed to stop a moment, then turn directly down the stream."

"Uncle," cried Lottie, "you know all about the river. How do you account for what Mr. Hemstead has seen?" and she explained.

"Lights are very deceptive at night, especially upon the

water," said Mr. Dimmerly, sententiously. "It's probably a hardy water-rat of a boatman dropping down with the tide to a point opposite to where he wishes to land."

"Yes, that is it, Mr. Hemstead, so dismiss your fears. Your brow is as clouded as that murky sky there."

"That comparison is quite oriental in its extravagance," he said, his anxious face relaxing into a sudden smile. "But then you are a bit tropical yourself."

"Well, you can't complain if I remind you of the tropics this dreary winter night; so I'll bear out your fanciful conceit. Your face, a moment since, was like a burst of sunshine."

"Your figure now is incorrect as well as extravagant; for, whatever light my face has, it is but the reflection of your kindness."

"I hope you do not mean to suggest that you have any tendency toward 'mooning'?"

"'Mooning' is the indulgence of sickly sentiment, is it not—a diluted moonlight kind of feeling?"

"Very well defined. Does experience give you such accuracy?" said Lottie, laughingly.

"I can honestly say no; and most surely not in your case."

"I'm glad to hear it," said Lottie. "I should be sorry to think that cold, diluted moonlight was the type of any of my friends' regard."

"You may rest assured," he replied impulsively, "there is nothing 'cold or diluted' in my regard for you—"

"There is the supper-bell," interrupted Lottie, hastily.

"What are you looking at?" asked De Forrest, uneasily noting the fact of their standing together within the shadowy curtains. He had just descended from the toilet which, with him, was a necessity before each meal.

"Mr. Hemstead has seen a light upon the river, and bodes from it some vague danger to some vague, indefinite people. Come, Mr. Hemstead, come away, or before we know it you will be off on the quixotic attempt to rescue what uncle calls a 'hardy water-rat,' that all the water of the river could not drown."

"Oh, I see," sneered De Forrest; "Mr. Hemstead wishes to get cheaply, standing here within and in good company, the credit of being willing to attempt a perilous rescue."

"You are jumping at conclusions very rapidly, Julian, and not very charitable ones either," said Lottie, reproachfully.

"Come, Mr. De Forrest," said Hemstead, quietly, "we will test this question of cheapness. I will go with you to investigate that light."

"Nonsense!" replied the exquisite. "As Miss Marsden suggested, Don Quixote may be your model knight, but he is not mine."

"Now I didn't suggest any such thing," said Lottie, decidedly vexed.

"Come, young people, tea is waiting," called Mrs. Marchmont.

"Well, I did," said De Forrest to Lottie, aside; "and what's more, I believe it's true," and he placed her reluctant hand upon his arm, and drew her to the supper-room.

But Hemstead lingered a moment, to watch the light, with increasing uneasiness. In his silent abstraction at the table it was evident to Lottie that his mind was dwelling upon the problem of the mysterious glimmer far out upon the river. Before the meal was over, he abruptly excused himself, but soon returned as if relieved, and said, "It is no more to be seen."

"I told you how it was," said Mr. Dimmerly. "The man floated down as far as he wished, and now has pulled ashore."

The explanation fully satisfied the rest, and sounded plausible to Hemstead; and the evening promised to pass quietly and uneventfully away. Mrs. Marchmont's parlor was a picture of cosey elegance. Bel, and Addie with her mother and uncle, made a game of whist at one table; while Hemstead in subdued tones read the latest magazine at another. De Forrest was half-dozing in his chair, for the article was rather beyond him; and while Lottie's fair face was very thoughtful, it might be questioned whether the thought was suggested by the reader or by what he read. But the article was finished, and for the relief of change Hemstead paced the room a few moments, and then half-aimlessly went to the window and looked out toward the river. His abrupt exclamation startled them all.

"There is the light again!"

A moment later he stood, bare-headed, upon the piazza, straining his eyes out into the darkness.

"I feel impressed that there is something wrong—that some one is in danger," he said to Lottie, who had followed him.

"You will take cold standing here without your hat," she said.

"So will you. Where is your hat, that you should talk prudence to me?"

But the others were more thoughtful of themselves, and were well protected as they now also came out upon the piazza.

"Well, it is a little queer," said Mr. Dimmerly.

"I suppose one ought to go and see what it means," said Bel, hesitatingly. "But then there are those better able to go than any one from here."

"Hush!" said Hemstead.

Far and faint there seemed to come a cry for help across the darkness.

"That is enough," he cried; "some one is in distress and danger. Come, Mr. De Forrest. The case has lost all its quixotic elements, and you may now emulate the Chevalier Bayard himself."

"Oh, please don't go, gentlemen!" cried Lottie. "See, the night is very dark; the wind is rising; the water must be very rough. You may just throw away your own lives in the vain attempt to save utter strangers."

"Miss Marsden is right," said De Forrest, as if greatly

relieved. "The attempt is perfectly foolhardy, and I am not a fool. If some one is in a boat that is fast in the ice, he has only a few more miles to drift before coming opposite a large town, where there are many better able to help than we are."

"Hush!" cried Hemstead; "do you hear that?"

Faint and far away, as a response to De Forrest's words, came again more clearly the cry for help.

"That is enough," again said Hemstead, excitedly; and he started for his hat.

Lottie laid her hand upon his arm, and said with seeming earnestness, "Surely, Mr. Hemstead, you will not be guilty of the folly of going alone upon such a desperate attempt as this?"

"I surely will; and you surprise me greatly that you seek to detain me," he said, almost sternly.

"But you alone can do nothing."

"As I am a man I will try. Where can I get the key of the boat-house?"

"If the young gentleman will go, I will go with him," said a voice from the darkness beyond the piazza, which they recognized as that of Mrs. Marchmont's coachman. "I've been to sea in my day, and am not afraid of a little water, salt or fresh."

"Good for you, my fine fellow. I'll be with you at once," cried Hemstead.

"I've got the key of the boat-house, a lantern, and an axe to cut the ice, so you have only to put on your coat and hat."

"There," said Hemstead to Lottie; "a way is provided already. How could you wish to keep me back?" and without waiting for an answer he hastily seized his hat and coat from the hall rack.

But before he could spring down the piazza steps she again stopped him a moment, as she said, in a low, husky tone: "I did not wish to detain, but to test you. I wish you to go. I am proud of you, though my heart trembles

at your peril. But you shall not go till you are protected
and equipped. See, your hands are bare; they will become
numb, and so useless. Where are your gloves? The wind
will carry your hat away. Here, you shall be my knight
upon this occasion, and, if you will, may wear my colors;"
and she snatched the ribbon from her hair, and tied his hat
firmly down.

In a low, thrilling tone, meant only for her, he said:
"Now you are the Lottie of my ideal; now you are yourself
again, and your words have given me tenfold my former
courage and strength. Good-by;" and ere she was aware,
he had seized her hand and pressed a kiss upon it, in true
old knightly style.

"God bring you back safely," she said, with a quick sob.

Heaven heard the prayer. He did not, for he was off
with a bound; and the darkness swallowed him up as he
followed the stout-hearted ex-sailor.

Lottie stood where he left her, unconscious that the wintry wind was blowing her unconfined hair wildly about.

"Miss Lottie," said De Forrest, approaching her humbly.
She raised her hand deprecatingly.

"Really, Miss Lottie," he persisted, "I would have gone
if you had wished me to."

"Hark!" she said, in a low tone. "Can you hear them?"

Lynx-eyed Bel, standing unnoticed in the shadow, had
witnessed and comprehended the scene more fully than the
others, and speedily brought Lottie to her senses by whispering in her ear: "Come, don't make a goose of yourself.
If Mr. Hemstead is your 'knight,' he has not gone to fight
a dragon, but to row a boat, and rescue a fisherman in all
probability. Your hair is down and blowing about your
eyes, and you look like a guy generally."

Even Lottie, in her highly-wrought state, was not proof
against such bald prose as this; and she turned and hastened
to her room.

Bel followed, proposing now, at last, to open Lottie's
eyes to her folly. Her first words of wisdom were, as Lot-

tie, with wet eyes, stood binding up her hair, "What a fool you are beginning to make of yourself over this Western student!"

"Hush!" said Lottie, imperiously.

"There it is again. You haven't been yourself since he came. If your mother knew what was going on—"

"Bel," said Lottie, in a tone that quite startled that nervous young lady, "do you value my friendship at all?"

"Certainly; and that is why I wish to prevent you from drifting into trouble: and it's not right for you to get him into—"

Lottie's warning gesture was so emphatic that Bel paused.

"Has it ever occurred to you," Lottie continued, in a tone that Bel had never heard her use before, "that I am not a child, and that you are not my natural guardian? Not another word, please, about Mr. Hemstead, or we are strangers;" and she quietly finished her toilet and left the room.

She had hardly reached the lower hall before there was a furious ring at the door. Before it could be opened Mr. Harcourt burst in, and called, "Where is Mr. Hemstead?"

At the first sound of his voice Addie rushed out and clung to his arm, crying hysterically, "What *is* the matter?"

He drew back, with an impatience akin to disgust, and repeated his question: "Where is Mr. Hemstead? Why don't some one speak?"

"Mr. Harcourt," said Mrs. Marchmont, in offended dignity, "I think you might, at least, have answered Addie's question and told us what the trouble is."

"Trouble enough, God knows. Mr. and Miss Martell have been caught in the ice, out in an open boat, for hours. Do you see that light there? Good heavens! there is another light shooting out toward it—"

"Yes," cried Lottie, in a sudden ecstasy of delight; "there goes my brave, true knight to the rescue, and he will save them, too; see how he gains upon them. That is Mr. Hemstead's voice. I know it well. He is shouting encouragement to them. Hear the feeble answering cry."

"That's a woman's voice," Harcourt cried, after listening a moment as if his life depended on what he heard. "Thank God, she has not perished with cold;" and he dashed away toward the river bank.

Addie and her mother looked at each other. They, too, like the coachman, had been struck with Mr. Harcourt's choice of pronouns.

But the prudent lady did not forget herself or her duty a moment. She made them all come in from the bleak piazza, and had the light turned down in the parlor, so that they could see through the window just as well—a more comfortable point of observation.

But De Forrest quite ostentatiously muffled himself up to his eyes, that he might go down and "help."

Approaching timidly, he said to Lottie as she stood at the window, "Can you not take another knight into your service this evening?"

"Oh, yes, Julian," she replied good-naturedly; "a regiment in so good a cause as this. Hasten to the shore. You may be of some possible help;" and, with a gesture of dismission, she turned again to her watch.

De Forrest slowly departed, feeling that this was a very different farewell from that bestowed on Hemstead, of which he had caught an aggravating glimpse.

While the others were eagerly talking and surmising, and the servants bustling about, preparing for those who would soon be brought in, chilled and wet with spray, Lottie stood at her post motionless, oblivious of all around, and as intent upon Hemstead's light as if she were to be rescued instead of Miss Martell.

CHAPTER XXVI

ON A CRUMBLING ICE-FLOE

THE plan suggested by their host, of sending their sleigh home by the ferry, while they crossed in a boat, just suited Miss Martell, and she proposed having a good vigorous pull at the oars herself. She had always been fond of out-of-door sports, a taste which her father had judiciously encouraged; and thus had saved her, no doubt, from the life of an invalid, for she had inherited the delicacy of a feeble mother, who years before, in spite of all that wealth could do to prevent it, had passed away.

Just at this time Miss Martell was waging that pathetic war with her own heart which so many women must fight out in silence; and she welcomed eagerly any distraction of thought—anything that would so weary the body that the mind could rest. She dreaded the long, monotonous ride home, and so warmly seconded the new plan that her father yielded, though somewhat against his judgment.

Through the little delays of a hospitality more cordial than kind, they were kept until the early December twilight was deepening into dusk. But the oarsman lighted his lantern, and was confident that he could put them across most speedily. The boat was staunch and well built, and they started with scarcely a misgiving, Miss Martell taking an oar with much zest. Their friends waved them off with numberless good wishes, and then from their windows watched till the boat seemed quite across, before drawing the curtains and concluding that all was well.

At first they did not meet much ice, and everything

promised a safe and speedy passage; but, when they were well past the middle of the river, two dark masses were seen just before them. There appeared to be a wide opening between them, through which they could see the water ripple.

"I think we can shoot through," said the oarsman, standing up a moment; "perhaps it will be the safest course, for we don't know what's above."

"Very well," said Mr. Martell, "I will steer you as well as I can. Pull strongly till we are again in clear water."

Miss Martell bent her supple form to the oar, and her strokes counted as well as those of the strong, practiced man; and the boat sped, all too quickly, into what afterward seemed the very jaws of destruction.

The opening narrowed instead of widening. The ice above, for some reason, appeared to gain on that below.

In growing alarm, Mr. Martell saw that they were becoming shut in, and pointed out the fact to the oarsman.

"Shall we turn around?" he asked, excitedly.

The man stood up again, and instantly decided.

"No, we have not time; the tide is running very swiftly. The ice would close on us before we could get around. Our best chance is to push through. I can see water beyond." They bent to their oars again with the energy which danger inspires.

But there was not time. The opening closed too rapidly. Suddenly the bow struck the upper cake, and, being well out of the water, ran up on the ice, causing the boat to take in water at the stern. For a second it seemed that they would be overturned and drowned at once.

But just at this moment the upper cake struck the lower ice, and the boat, being well up on the first cake, was not crushed between the two masses, as would have been the case had the ice closed against its sides while they were deep in the water. For a moment they were saved, while the upper and lower floes crunched and ground together under the keel, lifting the light craft still further above the tide and throwing it over on one side. Without a second's pause, the now consolidated field of ice swept downward, carrying with it the wedged and stranded skiff.

The lantern gleamed on the pale faces of those who realized that they had just passed through a moment of supreme peril and perhaps had before them as great if not equally imminent dangers.

The oarsman hastily examined the boat, and found that it had been injured, though to what extent he could not tell. Water was oozing in slowly from some point near the keel, but they were too high out of the water to know whether more dangerous leaks had been made. They tried to break their way out, but found that the two cakes had become so joined together as to form a solid mass, upon which they could make no impression.

They called aloud for help, and Miss Martell's plaintive cry was blended again and again with the hoarse, strong shoutings of the men. But the river was wide; the tide swept them out toward its centre, and then nearer the less peopled eastern shore. The evening was cold and bleak; few were out, and these so intent upon reaching warm firesides that they never thought of scanning the dark waste of the river; and so, to all the cries for aid there was no response, save the gurgling water, that sounded so cold as to chill their hearts, and the crunching of the ice as the rushing tide carried them downward, and away from the gleaming lights of their own loved home—downward and past the lights from Mrs. Marchmont's mansion, where, even in her peril, poor Alice Martell could picture Harcourt at Addie's side, and she forgotten. As the imagined scene rose vividly before her, the wild thought passed through her mind: "Since it must be so, perhaps I can find more rest beneath these waters than in my home yonder. It may be for the best, after all, and God designs mercy in what at first seemed so terrible."

As people saw Miss Martell's quiet and rather distant bearing in society, as many admired her chiselled and faultlessly refined features, they little imagined that, as within snowy mountains are volcanic fires, so within her breast was kindling as passionate a love as ever illumined a woman's life with happiness, or consumed it with a smouldering flame.

But death is stern and uncompromising, and snatches away all disguises—even those which hide us from ourselves. In bitterness of heart the poor girl learned, while darker than the night the shadow of death hovered over her, how intense was her love for one who she believed loved another. If but a hand's breadth away, beneath the rushing tide, there was a remedy for the pain at her heart, why need she fear?

"My child," said a tremulous voice.

Then, with a natural and remorseful rush of love for one who had been as tender toward her as a mother since that mother commended her to his care, she put her arms around him and whispered, "I am not afraid, father. Mother and heaven may be nearer than we think."

"Thank God, my child—thank God you are not afraid. I was trembling for you—not myself. You are young, and I trusted that there was a happy life before you. But the home where mother is promises me far more than the one yonder, whose lights are growing so faint."

"I am not afraid, dear father. I am content, if it's God's will, to go to that better home and be with you and mother."

"God bless you, my child; and blessed be the God of mercy who has given you so true a faith. It would be terrible to me beyond words if now you were full of hopeless dread."

But the poor oarsman had no such faith—only the memory of his dependent wife and children, and his material life, which never before had seemed so sweet and precious. He kept shouting for aid until exhausted, and then despairingly sat down to await the result.

Mr. Martell, in the true Christian spirit, sought to impart

to his humble companion in peril some of his own confidence in God's mercy and goodness; but in vain. An intelligent, sustaining faith cannot be snatched like a life-preserver in the moment of danger; and the man appeared scarcely to heed what was said.

Downward and past the twinkling lights of many comfortable homes the remorseless tide still swept them, until the huge outlines of the two mountains at the portal of the Highlands loomed out of the darkness.

"If we get down among the mountains, we might as well give up," said the oarsman, sullenly. "We might as well be cast away at sea as down in that wild gorge; though for that matter it seems, to-night, as if one's neighbors wouldn't step out of doors to keep a body from drowning. Why no one has heard us is more than I can understand, unless it is accordin' to the old sayin', 'None's so deaf as them as won't hear.'"

But there was nothing strange in the fact that they had been unnoted. The north wind blew their voices down the river. There was a noisy surf upon the shore, and those who chanced to see the light supposed it to come from some craft hastening to its winter quarters near the city. So fate seemed against them, and they drifted down and down until the black shadow of "Storm King" swallowed them up.

But now they became conscious that their motion was growing less steady and rapid. A little later, and the floe apparently paused in its downward progress, and there was only some slight movement caused by the increasing gale.

Then came what seemed interminable hours of weary waiting under the sombre shadow of "Cro' Nest" mountain. The strange and almost irresistible drowsiness that severe cold induces began to creep over Miss Martell, but her father pleaded with her to fight against it; and, more for his sake than her own, she tried. They took turns in endeavoring to break the ice around them with the boat-hook. The exercise kept their blood in circulation, but was of little avail in other respects. The ice was too heavy and solid for their feeble strokes.

At last the tide turned, and the dreary, monotonous waiting in their hopeless position was exchanged for an upward movement that would soon bring them above the mountains again, where, from the thickly peopled shores, there would be a better chance of being seen and rescued.

There was no certainty that they would be missed, and therefore sought for, as the coachman, not finding them on his return, might conclude that they had been prevailed upon to remain all night with the friend they were visiting.

But any exchange from the black, rayless shadows that surrounded them would be a relief; and it was with a faint feeling of hopefulness that they recognized their movement northward, which slowly increased in speed as the tide gained mastery of the slight natural current of the river.

The strengthening northern gale had thrown up quite a "sea," and the experienced oarsman soon saw that the ice-field by which they were surrounded was breaking up under the influence of the waves. This might at last bring relief, or increase their danger. If the ice should all break up around them and leave their boat tight and sound, they could row ashore. If the boat had been or should become so injured as to leak badly, it might fill with water before they could reach land. Thus, in any case, the trying nature of their peculiar position was aggravated by a terrible uncertainty and suspense.

As they emerged from the Highlands into the broad waters of Newburgh Bay, their worst fears seemed about to be realized. Here, for many miles, the north wind had an unrestrained sweep, and the waves grew larger and more violent. Under their increasing force the ice-floe crumbled around them rapidly, until at last little was left save the mass of double thickness caused by the union of the two large cakes between which the boat had been caught. This, at last, began to give under the weight of the boat, and let it more deeply into the water. Then, to their dismay, they saw that the seams of the boat had been so wrenched apart that the water came in rapidly.

They tried to keep it down by baling. The frosty gale tossed Mr. Martell's white hair, while with his hat he worked, in pathetic earnestness, for the sake of his daughter; but in spite of all that he and the oarsman could do, the water gained on them, wetting their feet and creeping up their legs with the icy chill of death.

Every moment or two the man would pause in his work and send forth a cry of such terrible power and earnestness that it would seem some one must hear.

Again Alice Martell saw the distant lights of her own home, but she turned from them to those that gleamed from the nearer residence of Mrs. Marchmont. Was *he* there, safe and happy, looking love into the eyes of Addie Marchmont, while every moment she sank lower into the cold river? The thought sent a deeper chill to her heart than the icy tide from which she could no longer keep her feet.

"God and man is agin us," said the oarsman, savagely. "What is the use of trying any longer! The sooner it's over the better;" and he was about to give up in despair. Alice, with equal hopelessness of any earthly aid, was about to turn her eyes from the faint rays which, barbed with the thoughts suggested above, pierced her heart like arrows, when the throwing open of the hall-door by Hemstead let out such a broad streaming radiance as attracted her notice. By calling the attention of the others to it, she inspired in them a faint hope.

But when, soon after, the door was closed, and the lights had their usual appearance, the flicker of hope sank down into a deeper darkness.

Alice turned to her father, and in close embrace and with a oneness of spirit and hope that needed not outward expression, they silently lifted their thoughts from the dark earth to the bright heaven whose portals they soon expected to enter.

Just then a voice from earth recalled them to earthly

hope and the prospect of human help. It was Hemstead's
shout of encouragement from the shore. Then they saw the
glimmer of a lantern moving hither and thither; a moment
later it became stationary, then shot out toward them.

With cries of joy they recognized that they had been
seen, and that an attempt to rescue them was being made.

In the apathy of their despair the water had gained
dangerously; but with the energy of hope, that is ever
greater than that of fear or despair, they set to work anew.
Again the wintry winds tossed Mr. Martell's white hair, as
for want of something better he baled with his hat, and
Alice's little numb hands were lifted every moment as if
in pathetic appeal, as she dipped them in the ice-cold water
at her feet, and threw out a tiny cupful, which the gale
carried away in spray.

"Come quick. We can't keep afloat much longer,"
cried the oarsman.

"Ay, ay," shouted the ex-sailor in a voice as hoarse as
the winds in the cordage of his old ship.

"Courage!" cried Hemstead; and his tones, in contrast,
rang out like a bugle, inspiring hope in the chilled hearts of
those who, a little before, had despaired, and also sending
an almost equal thrill of delight to the heart of Lottie Marsden, as, with the half-frenzied Harcourt, she stood in Mrs.
Marchmont's open door.

The sailor-coachman was a good oarsman, and Hemstead
pulled fairly. Both were very strong, and they drove the
boat through the short, chopping waves, rather than over
them, caring not how much water was shipped.

A little later came the shout, "Quick, quick! The ice is
giving under us, and the boat sinking."

"Oh! come!—save my father!" cried Alice Martell, in a
tone that might have moved the very ice around her to pity.

"My child, my child!" came the agonized voice of the
father. "Never think of me, if you can save her."

Hemstead's nature was anthracite, and now glowed at
white heat in his grand excitement. He was no longer

a man, but a giant, and would have ruined everything, snapped his oars, dragged the oar-pins from their sockets, thus rendering his massive strength utterly useless, had not the cool, wary ex-sailor taken command of the little craft, and insisted on seamanship. Under his skilful direction the student was like a powerful engine, with a steady, measured stroke, and the boat fairly flew, until their oars struck floating ice, and then they had to slacken up, for to strike a mass of ice at their speed would be to sink at once.

"Steady now," cried the ex-sailor. "You pull; I will stand and steer."

Their boat was roughly grazed several times, but glided through without serious injury.

"Now or never!" cried the oarsman; "we're sinking."

Alice hid her face on her father's breast. Life had grown strangely sweet during the brief time since, at Hemstead's voice, hope had revived; and it seemed a bitter thing to perish almost within the grasp of rescuing hands.

"Oh! come!" groaned the father. "Great God! this is hard."

With a despairing cry she heard the water rush and gurgle around her, and closed her eyes, not expecting to open them again in this world. But strong hands grasped and lifted her drenched, helpless form tenderly into the boat.

With mingled hope and fear she looked up, and by the lantern's light recognized Frank Hemstead.

"My father," she gasped.

"Safe, my darling, thank God," said Mr. Martell, taking her into his arms; "and they have pulled our stout oarsman in, too. So we are all safe."

"Well, I hope so," said the ex-sailor, with a little depressive dubiousness. "We shipped a sight o' water comin' out. There's a deal of ice runnin', and so chopped up one can skerce see it. I must be skipper and all, mind, if we are to come safe out. Here, Mr. Hemstead, you bale; and you, too, messmate, if yer hain't shipped too much water yerself. I'll sit well up toward the bow, where I can see and pull around the ice. Besides, with this cargo, we've got to cross the waves kind o' easy and keerful, or they'll swamp us.''

Thus in this instance the ex-sailor appeared a special providence, and gradually took them out of the ice-strewn tide in the centre of the river to smoother, clearer water nearer the shore. Soon after, drenched and half-frozen, they reached Mrs. Marchmont's boat-house.

Miss Martell's powers of endurance were nearly exhausted; and when the lantern, held aloft, revealed Harcourt's pale face—when she knew that it was his arms that received her in her helplessness, and she heard him murmur, ''I now believe there's a merciful God, and thank Him''—in the strong reaction of feeling she became unconscious.

CHAPTER XXVII

THE MEETING AND GREETING

MR. MARTELL'S garments were frozen upon him, and he was so stiff and numb with cold that with difficulty he made his way up the bank with the support of De Forrest and the gallant coachman, who had suddenly blossomed out into a hero. Harcourt and Hemstead formed with their hands what is termed a "chair," and bore the apparently lifeless form of Miss Martell swiftly toward Mrs. Marchmont's residence. The poor oarsman was so glad to be on solid ground once more that he was able to hobble along at a good pace by himself.

The wind again played mad pranks with Lottie's hair as she at last stood impatiently on the piazza, and then dashed off through the snow to meet them.

"Oh, thank God, *you* are safely back. But Miss Martell —she is not—she is not—"

"Don't suggest such a thing," groaned Harcourt. "Of course she has only fainted."

Hemstead could not speak, even to Lottie. With white face and set teeth he sought to keep up to the end. The effort he was now putting forth was less that of muscle than sheer force of will. As with Miss Martell, he, too, was reacting from the tremendous strain that the last hour had brought. He trembled with almost mortal weakness as he slowly mounted the piazza steps. He staggered under his share of their burden as he crossed the hall. Lottie, puzzled by his silence, now saw his deathly pallor with alarm, and instinctively stood at his side.

"You had better take Miss Martell directly to her room," said Mrs. Marchmont.

"In here, quick," gasped Hemstead. He tottered to the nearest sofa, and, a second later, lay unconscious at Miss Martell's feet.

At this moment Alice again became conscious. Hemstead's condition did more to revive her than all restoratives; for, woman-like, she thought of him more than herself. She sat up and exclaimed faintly: "Oh, can't something be done for him? Quick. It looks as if he had given his life for us;" and she looked around, not far enough to see the expression of Harcourt's face as he welcomed her back to consciousness, but only to see Addie clinging to his arm, repeatedly asking to be assured that *he* was not hurt.

"Thank heaven you are safe," he bent down and whispered.

"Don't think of me. Look at Mr. Hemstead."

Again he misunderstood her, and with bitterness thought, "After all my anguish on her account, she gives me not even a thought, and her first words are, 'Don't think of me';" and he felt that fate had been very cruel in sending Hemstead to her rescue instead of himself.

Mrs. Marchmont now appeared upon the confused scene, and proved that she was equal to the occasion. It was a sad pity that she had not imparted to her daughter a little of her own capability. She bade De Forrest, and the still stout and hearty ex-sailor, carry Hemstead at once to his room, while she and one of the maids assisted Miss Martell to hers. No opportunity whatever was given for any romantic and affecting scenes.

Lottie had stood for a second in dismay, after seeing her "true knight" sink on the floor, and then, like a sensible girl, instead of going off into hysterics, went like a flash to her aunt's wine-closet for brandy. But before she could find it Mrs. Marchmont had caused both the rescued and the rescuer to be conveyed to the privacy of their own

rooms, where they could at once receive the prosaic treatment that their condition required.

The room which a moment before had presented a scene
which she would never forget was empty, Harcourt having
gone for a physician.

She met Mr. Dimmerly on the stairs, who took the brandy
from her, saying: "That's sensible. We'll rub him down
with it, inside and out, and he'll be all right in the morning. Now you see how blood tells. Making a parson of
him can't change the fact of his coming from an old family.
He has been as brave to-night as the Dimmerlys were a
thousand years ago."

But Lottie was not a bit interested in the millennial
Dimmerlys, and, putting her arms around her uncle's neck
in a way that surprised that ancient fossil, she coaxed:

"Won't you promise me, uncle, that as soon as he is safe
you will come out and let me know?"

"Safe! He's safe now. Who ever heard of even a half-
blooded Dimmerly dying from a mere faint? Old age is
the only disease that runs in our family, my dear. But
I will let you know as soon as he is comfortably asleep. I
am going to make my proper parson nephew almost drunk,
for once in his life; and you needn't expect to see him much
before ten o'clock to-morrow."

Lottie, finding her services were not needed in Miss
Martell's room, went down to the kitchen, where she found
the half-frozen oarsman—now rigged out in the dress-coat
and white vest of the colored waiter—and the brave coachman who had put his old sea-craft to such good use. They
were being royally cared for by the cook and the laundress.
The poor fellow who out in the boat had thought that the
hearts of even his neighbors were as cold and hard as the ice
that was destroying them had now forgotten his misan-
thropy, and was making a supper that, considering the
hour, would threaten to an ordinary mortal more peril
than that from which he had escaped. She drew from him
—and especially from the coachman—the narrative of their

thrilling experience, and every moment Hemstead grew more heroic in her eyes.

"Bless you, miss," said the bluff ex-sailor, his tongue a little loosened by the whiskey he had taken as an antidote for the cold and wet, "there's stuff enough in him to make a hundred such as t'other young gentleman as wouldn't go. Sudden spells, like that he had t'other night, is all he'll ever be 'stinguished for, I'm a-thinking. But I ax your pardon, miss."

"I can forgive you anything to-night, my brave fellow," said Lottie, blushing. "Though you have given Mr. Hemstead so much credit, he will give you more to-morrow. Take this and get something to remember this evening by;" and she slipped a twenty-dollar banknote into his hand.

"Now bless your sweet eyes!" exclaimed the man, ducking and bobbing with bewildering rapidity; "it's your kindness that'll make me remember the evening to my dying day."

"How could you speak so of Mr. De Forrest, when the young leddy is engaged to him?" said the cook, reproachfully, after Lottie had gone.

"No matter," said the ex-sailor, stoutly. "I've had it on my conscience to give her a warnin'. I hadn't the heart to see such a trim little craft run into shallow water, and hoist no signal. If she was my darter, she'd have to mitten that lubber if he was wuth a million."

As Lottie passed through the hall with silent tread, she saw that De Forrest was in the parlor, and to escape him continued on up to her room, musing as she went: "What a strange blending of weakness and strength Mr. Hemstead is! Well, I should like that. I should like a man to be as strong as Samson generally, but often so weak that he would have to lean on me."

Whom did Lottie mean by that indefinite word "man"? It did not occur to her that there was a very definite image in her mind of one who was pale and exhausted, and whom it would now be a dear privilege to nurse back into strength and vigor.

She met her uncle and the physician in the upper hall, and the latter said: "Mr. and Miss Martell are doing as well as could be expected, when we consider the fearful ordeal they have passed through. As far as I can foresee, a few days' rest and quiet will quite restore them."

"And Mr.—Mr. Hemstead?" faltered Lottie, the color mounting into her face, that anxiety had made unwontedly pale.

"The brave fellow who rescued them? Now he is the right kind of a dominie—not all white choker and starch. No fear about him, Miss Marsden. He's made of good stuff, well put together. A night's rest and a warm break-fast, and he will be himself again;" and the old doctor bustled away.

"What delightful prose!" thought Lottie, and she tripped lightly to her room and kissed the sullen and offended Bel good-night; and, very grateful and at peace with all the world, soon fell asleep.

But she had a disagreeable dream. Again she saw Hem-stead at Miss Martell's feet; but now, instead of being pale and unconscious, his face was flushed and eager, and he was pleading for that which the king cannot buy. She awoke sobbing, called herself a "little fool," and went to sleep again.

But in the morning the dream lingered in her mind in a vague, uncomfortable way.

She was early down to breakfast, for she was eager to speak to Hemstead, and tell him how she appreciated his heroism. But either his exhaustion was greater than the physician had believed, or his uncle's sedatives were very powerful, for he did not appear.

There was nothing better for her than to endure De For-rest's explanations why he had not gone, and his assurances that if he had "only known, etc."; to which she gave an impatient hearing, quite unlike her gentleness of the two preceding days. There were little things in her manner which indicated a falling barometer, and suggested that the day might not pass serenely.

She learned from her aunt and uncle that Mr. and Miss Martell were feeling better than might have been expected, and that Hemstead was still sleeping.

"Sleep was all he wanted," said Mr. Dimmerly; "and I made it my business he should get it."

Quite early in the forenoon, Mr. Martell and his daughter felt equal to coming down to the parlor, and after dinner it was their intention to return home. A luxurious lounge was wheeled near the blazing wood fire, and on this Miss Martell was tenderly placed by her father, who, in joyful gratitude, could scarcely take his eyes from her pale face. Beyond the natural languor which would follow so terrible a strain, she seemed quite well.

Both father and daughter appreciated Mrs. Marchmont's courtesy greatly; and Miss Martell's effort to be cordial, even to Addie, was quite pathetic, when it is remembered that she felt that her supposed rival would harm her more than could the cold river.

Lottie made frequent errands to her room, and lingered in the hall as much as she could without attracting notice, in the hope of seeing Hemstead a moment alone. The impulsive girl's warm heart was so full of admiration for what he had done that she longed to show him her appreciation without the chilling restraint of observant eyes and critical ears. But he was so blind to his interests as to blunder into the parlor when she was there and every one else also.

Though it cost her great effort, Alice Martell rose instantly, and greeted him so cordially as to bring the deepest crimson into his pale face. Mr. Martell also pressed to his side, speaking words which only a grateful father could utter.

When, for any cause, Hemstead was the object of general attention, the occasion became the very hour and opportunity for his awkward diffidence to assert itself, and now he stood in the centre of the floor, the most angular and helpless of mortals.

De Forrest looked at him with disdain, and thought, "I would like to show him how a *gentleman* ought to act under the circumstances."

De Forrest would have been equal to receiving all the praise, and as it was, in view of his readiness to have saved Miss Martell if he "had only known," could have accepted, with graceful complacency, a gratitude that quite overwhelmed the man of deeds.

Hemstead's confusion was so great as even to embarrass Miss Martell for a moment, and her face, from reminding one of a lily, suddenly suggested an exquisite pink rose. But before he was aware she had ensconced him in an easy chair at her side, and with a tact peculiarly her own had rallied his panic-stricken faculties into such order that he could again take command of them.

But as Lottie saw them grasping each other's hands and blushing, her dream recurred to her with the force of an ominous prophecy. Hemstead, in his severe attack of diffidence, had not greeted any one on his entrance, but had fallen helplessly into Miss Martell's hands, and had been led to his chair like a lamb to the slaughter. But Lottie took it as much to heart as if he had purposely neglected to speak to her. And when, a little later, Mr. Dimmerly commenced a formal eulogy, Hemstead with an expression of intense annoyance raised his hand deprecatingly, and pleaded that no one would speak again of what he had done, she feared that all the glowing words she meant to say would be unwelcome after all.

Everything had turned out so differently from what she had anticipated that she was disappointed above measure, and before he could collect his scattered wits she left the room.

"And so it all ends," she thought bitterly, as she chafed up and down the hall. "I sent him out last night as my own 'true knight,' wearing my colors, and he rescues another woman. When I see him again he brushes past me to speak to the one who, owing him so much, of course will be grateful. With eyes for her alone, he wears my colors in his face, and she raises the same blood-red signal. I was looking forward to the pleasure of giving him a welcome that he might value on his return, and he has not even spoken to me. After our parting last night could anything have turned out more flat and prosaic?"

Just at this moment Harcourt, who was another victim of circumstances, entered, and Lottie, too annoyed to meet any one, fled to her own room.

He had already called early in the morning, to inquire after the invalids; but Miss Martell did not know this, and his coming now seemed a little dilatory, considering all they had passed through. Deep in her heart there was disappointment that he had not come to her rescue instead of Hemstead. Was he one to stand safely on the shore while others took risks from which true manhood would not have shrunk? Could he have dreamed that she was in peril, and still have let Hemstead go without him to her aid? These were thoughts that had distressed her during part of a sleepless night and all the morning.

Moreover, when he entered, Addie had pounced upon him in her usual style, as if she had in him certain rights of possession.

Addie's manner, together with her own thoughts, gave an involuntary tinge of coldness to Miss Martell's greeting, which he was quick to recognize, while her cordiality to Hemstead suggested to him, as to Lottie, that she might be very grateful.

Mr. Martell was more than slightly distant: he was stiff and formal. As circumstances then appeared to him, he thought that Harcourt had acted a very unworthy part. Mr. Martell naturally supposed that both Harcourt and De Forrest were at Mrs. Marchmont's, but that only Hemstead had been willing to venture to their assistance. To De Forrest he gave scarcely a thought, having accurately estimated that superficial youth's light weight. But that Harcourt, the son of his old and dear friend, should have so failed in manly duty, was a bitter trial. As he saw him and Addie together, he thought contemptuously, "They are well mated, after all. How strange that my peerless daughter can have such a regard for him!"

He had become aware of his daughter's preference, though, out of delicate regard for her feelings, he had feigned blindness.

Even had Harcourt known how greatly they misjudged him, in his sensitive pride he would have made no explanations; and he was the last one in the world to tell them, as would De Forrest, how he meant to go to their aid, etc.

His manner puzzled Alice. She could not help noting with a secret satisfaction that, while polite, he was annoyed at Addie's demonstrativeness; and at times she thought his eyes sought her face almost as if in appeal. But her own and her father's manner had evidently chilled him, and he soon took his leave. His face, in which pride and dejection contended for mastery, haunted her like a reproach.

"If Mr. Harcourt had only arrived a little earlier last evening, Miss Martell," said De Forrest, complacently, "you would have had three to thank instead of one. I'm sure if I had known that you and your father—"

"How is that?" asked Mr. Martell, quickly. "Was not Mr. Harcourt spending the evening here?"

"Oh, no. It was from him we first learned of your peril. He came tearing over like mad, a few moments after the coachman and Mr. Hemstead had gone; then he dashed off to the shore, where I soon joined him. I thought at one time," continued De Forrest, glad to say anything that would dim the glory of Hemstead's achievements, "that he would start out into the river with no better support than a plank, so eager was he to go to your aid. If we could only have found another boat we would have both gone. As it was, it was well I was there to restrain him, for he seemed beside himself."

The rich color mounted to Miss Martell's face as she gave her father a swift glance of glad intelligence, and he drew a long breath of relief, as if some heavy burden had been lifted.

"Yes," said Mrs. Marchmont, quietly, but at the same time fixing an observant eye on the young lady, "I never saw Mr. Harcourt so moved before."

Conscious of Mrs. Marchmont's object, Alice mastered herself at once, and with equal quietness answered: "It would be strange if it were otherwise. We have been acquainted from childhood."

Nevertheless, the experienced matron surmised danger to the match which she would gladly bring about between her daughter and Harcourt; and instead of fearing, as was the case with the latter and Lottie, she hoped that Miss Martell would be *very* grateful to Hemstead.

And so she appeared to be, for she talked to him so enchantingly, and for a time absorbed him so completely, that Lottie entered unobserved, and remained so a few moments. Then his eyes, that from the moment he gained composure had seemed in quest of something, lighted on her as she sat a little back of him, apparently absorbed in her fancy-work. He wanted to speak to her, and yet what could he say before them all?

The tell-tale color was again in his face, and his wretched diffidence returned. Neither courtesy nor his heart would permit him to ignore her and continue his conversation with Miss Martell. And yet it had seemed easier to go in a boat out among the ice than to think of any proper way to recognize the presence of one in whose eyes he had a morbid anxiety to appear well.

Lottie saw his dilemma, and, while she too began to blush absurdly, would not help him, and her head bent lower than ever over her work.

"Serves him right," she thought. "If he had only met me in the hall, I might—well, I wouldn't have been an icicle."

At last Hemstead concluded that he could safely say "good-morning"; and he did so in a very awkward manner over his shoulder.

"Did you speak to me?" asked Lottie, as if suddenly aroused.

"Yes," he replied, under the painful necessity of repeating something that had sounded very flat in the first place, "I said good-morning."

"Oh, excuse me. As it is so *late*, I bid you good-afternoon."

Her manner as well as her words so quenched poor Hemstead that he did not venture another syllable; and thus Lottie and her "true knight" had the meeting to which, in remembrance of their parting, both had looked forward with strange thrills of expectation.

But in the light of their flaming cheeks Miss Martell caught a glimpse of their hearts; and Mrs. Marchmont was again led to fear that more was going on than should be permitted by so good a manager as herself.

The dinner bell soon brought welcome relief to all, breaking the spell of awkward constraint.

CHAPTER XXVIII

THE TRAIL OF LOVE

MISS MARTELL improved visibly, for a most depressing fear had been removed. Though Harcourt might not return her love, he had not proved himself unworthy of it, by actual cowardice, or even by unmanly regard for personal ease. It also appeared that more than general philanthropy must have spurred him on, or he could not have acted as if "beside himself."

The hungry heart will take even the crumbs of regard that fall from the hand which alone can satisfy. The thought that her old friend and playmate had been far from indifferent to her fate was like a subtile, exhilarating wine to Miss Martell.

Her rising spirits, and her wish to show appreciation of Mrs. Marchmont's courtesy, made her as brilliant as beautiful at the dinner-table, while Lottie, in contrast, was silent and depressed. The new-fledged little saint soon became conscious that for some reason she was very jealous and very envious—emotions which she seldom had even imaginary cause to cherish toward any of her sex.

Nor were Mrs. Marchmont and her daughter disposed to be very friendly and responsive to Miss Martell's genial mood; but the young lady was possessed of that strength of mind and high-bred courtesy which enabled her to ignore the weaknesses and infelicities of those around her, and to shine with her own pure light on all objects alike.

Hemstead again was charmed with her—a fact that his frankness made plainly evident. Her bright thoughts elicited corresponding ones from him, and Lottie was reluctantly compelled to admit to herself that she had never before known Mrs. Marchmont's viands to be seasoned with Attic salt of such high flavor. For the first time the proud and flattered belle felt, in the presence of another woman, a humiliating sense of her own inferiority. She clearly recognized that Miss Martell was far in advance of her. How could the student fail to be fascinated? Her mind was the equal of his in force, and as highly cultivated. They were congenial in their views and feelings, and of course *she* would be very grateful.

Lottie's manner had puzzled Hemstead greatly. He was even more disappointed than she had been over their prosaic meeting. In his honest modesty, broad eulogy from the others was exceedingly distasteful; and yet one of his chief incentives the evening before had been the hope of a welcome back from Lottie, in which her eyes, if not her tongue, would suggest the reward his heart craved. But he had said "good-morning," and she a little coldly had responded "good-afternoon." Moreover, she was strangely silent and depressed. What could it mean? and what was the cause? That it was himself never entered his mind.

Her bearing toward De Forrest, which was anything but genial, finally led him to believe that she was again deeply mortified by her lover's lack of manhood, and that she was depressed because of her relation to one who had failed so signally, the evening before, in those qualities that women most admire.

While lingering over the dessert, Mr. Martell's sleigh was announced.

"It was my purpose to send you home," exclaimed Mrs. Marchmont. "Indeed, I had ordered my horses to be at the door within half an hour."

"I appreciate your kindness," said Mr. Martell, "but after the heroic efforts of your amphibious coachman last night, I should feel guilty if we broke in upon his rest to-day."

"I'm glad you recognize his merit," said Hemstead, quickly. "You owe far more to him than to me;" and he launched out into the most hearty eulogy of the ex-sailor.

Then, for the first time, Lottie's old, mirthful laugh was heard, as she said: "Well, in one respect, Mr. Hemstead, you and the coachman are birds of a feather, and rare birds at that. He gives you all the credit of the rescue, and you insist that you had nothing to do with it, but only went along for company, as it were. But I think we all surmised the truth, when you fainted from exhaustion at Miss Martell's feet. That was a very happy chance, and so it all turned out as well as any knight of old could have desired."

This sudden speech from Lottie bewildered Hemstead more than ever. What could she mean? But Miss Martell understood her better, and gave a keen thrust in return as she smilingly answered, "With the only exception that Mr. Hemstead fainted at the feet of the wrong lady."

This unexpected retort threw both Hemstead and Lottie into disastrous confusion, which Mrs. Marchmont was not slow to observe, and which was not allayed by Mr. Dimmerly's cackling laugh, as he chuckled, "A well-flown arrow."

"Well," said Hemstead, trying to laugh it off, "all I can say in self-defence is, that in either case my faint could not be spelled with an *e*. It was the first, and I hope it will be the last time I ever do anything so melodramatic."

"Mr. Hemstead must be an ideal knight, as we learn from his phrase 'in either case,' " said Lottie. "He would have us believe that he is entirely impartial in his homage to our sex. And, now I think of it, he was more polite to old Auntie Lammer than ever he has been to me."

"Now, Miss Marsden," said Hemstead, reproachfully, "you are again indulging in orientalism."

"Certainly," chimed in De Forrest; "that sylph so filled his eye that she became his ideal, as you told us, Miss Lottie."

"I told you ?" she answered in sudden annoyance; "your memory is better than mine."

Soon after, Mr. Martell and his daughter took their departure, with many sincere and graceful acknowledgments of the kindness they had received.

Many were the words of force and wisdom that Miss Martell had read and heard, but never had any made so profound an impression upon her as the vain vaporings of De Forrest, as he insisted on claiming all the credit he could for his action the evening before.

"Did he exaggerate," she asked herself a hundred times, "when he said, 'It was well I was there; for Mr. Harcourt was beside himself, and was ready to venture out upon a plank to your aid' ? I fear he did."

Her father surmised something of her thoughts and said gently, "I fear we have done Mr. Harcourt injustice."

"Yes, father," she answered, "I think we have."

"Well," he said, after a moment, "I never had a pleasanter duty than the amends I purpose making. It cut me to the heart to think the son of my old friend had permitted a stranger to come to our rescue."

"I feel sure that Mr. Harcourt would have come also, had it been in his power," she said, with quiet emphasis.

"You always stood up for Tom," said her father, gently.

But she made no answer.

Mr. Martell then questioned his coachman somewhat.

"Indade, sir, we was all putty nigh crazy when Mr. Harcourt druv in late last night and said you were safe. He told me to come over this morning and get your orders, and to have the house ready for yez."

"Now that was considerate. I feel, my daughter, that we owe Mr. Harcourt an apology. Do you feel equal to entertaining him at supper ?"

"I will try, father."

"Drive right on up to town," said Mr. Martell, a little later, from the steps of his piazza, "and present my compliments to Mr. Harcourt, and ask him if he will favor us with his company at supper.''

Alice gave him a shy, grateful glance, and then sought her room.

As she was unwapping herself before her mirror, she noted that a pane of glass in the window near was badly cracked, and that the lace curtain above was torn partially from its fastening.

As her maid entered she asked how it happened.

The woman in evident confusion answered: ''Indeed, miss, I meant to mend the curtain this morning, but I've not had me head straight since last evening.''

''But how did it happen?'' persisted Alice. ''Who could have been so rough and careless?''

''Well,'' said the maid, hesitatingly, ''it must have been Mr. Harcourt.''

''Mr. Harcourt!''

''Well, you see, miss, he came last night to see you, for one of the girls said he asked for you, and when he found you was out on the river he just seemed beside himself. We was a-lookin' out upstairs, and we first saw the light a-coming up after the tide turned, and we screamed to him and the coachman, and Mr. Harcourt he came upstairs like a gust o' wind. Your door stood open, and in he rushed in a way that I thought he'd break everything.''

''There, that will do. I understand. You need not mend the curtain. You must be tired after all your fright, and can rest awhile this afternoon, as I shall.''

A beautiful color dawned in Alice's face. She was recovering from her languor and weakness with marvellous rapidity. It was not strange, for no elixir was ever distilled so potent as that which now infused its subtle spirit into heart and brain.

But a few hours before, the wayward but good-hearted companion of her childhood, the manly friend of the present and future—she would permit herself to think of him in no other light—had seemed lost to her forever; to have had in fact no real existence; for if Harcourt had been content to act De Forrest's part the evening before, Alice Martell would have soon shaken off even his acquaintance. But De Forrest's words had suggested that the Harcourt of her dream still existed. She had seen another trace of manly, considerate feeling in his thoughtfulness of the servants' fears, and of their comfort. And now the torn curtain and broken glass suggested the impetuous action of one who thought of her peril rather than of the trifles around him.

Twice now she had been told that Harcourt was "beside himself," and yet never had madness seemed so rational; and her eyes dwelt on the marks of his frenzy before her with unmixed satisfaction. If he had been cool then, her heart now would be cold.

She could not rest, and at last thought that the frosty air would cool the fever in her cheeks, and so wrapped herself for a walk upon the broad piazza. Moreover, she felt, as Lottie had, that she would be glad to have no eyes, not even her father's, witness their meeting. She felt that she could act more naturally and composedly if alone with him, and at the same time show the almost sisterly regard through which she hoped to win him to his better self.

As she paced up and down the piazza in the early twilight, her attention was attracted to a spot where some one, instead of going deliberately down the steps, had plunged off into the piled-up snow, and then just opposite and beyond the broad path were tracks wide apart, as if some one had bounded rather than run toward the river.

She ceased her walk, and stood as one who had discovered a treasure. Did these footprints and the torn curtain belong together? She felt that it could not be otherwise. There was, then, no cold-blooded, cowardly Harcourt, and traces of the real man grew clearer.

"But how could he reach the river in that direction without risking his neck?" and she indulged in quite a panic as she remembered the intervening steeps. She longed yet dreaded to see him, that she might ask an explanation of the traces she had found; for, having done him injustice, she generously meant to make him full amends.

But to her great disappointment the sleigh now returned without him.

"I left the message, miss," said the coachman, "but they told me that Mr. Harcourt had a sudden business call to New York."

Alice sought to draw the man out a little, and it was also her habit to speak kindly to those in her employ; so she said: "I fear, Burtis, you will be a little jealous of Mrs. Marchmont's coachman. If it had not been for him we could not have escaped, I think."

"Well, thank God, I'm not much behind him. If he stopped two funerals, I stopped one."

"Why, how is that, Burtis?"

"Faix, miss, an' do ye see thim tracks there? They go straight to the river, and it was Misther Harcourt as made them. He was jist one second on the way after he saw the light, and by rinnin' an' rollin' an' tumblin' he was at the boat-house in a wink. When I gets there, a-puffin' an' a-blowin', he's unlocked the door by breakin' it in, and is a-haulin' at the ould boat; and because I wouldn't lend a hand in gettin' out the crazy ould craft that wouldn't float a hundred foot, he swears at me in the most onchristian manner, and tries to get it out alone. But ye know, miss, how he couldn't do that, and soon he gives it up and falls to gnawin' his nails like one beside himself, an' a-mutterin' how he must either 'save *her* or drown with *her*.' Then he dashed up the bank ag'in, and he and his black hoss was off like a whirlwind. If the Naughty Tillus, or any other thing as would float was here, ye'd had no need of Mrs. Marchmont's coachman. But I thought he'd off wid me head because I wouldn't help out wid the ould boat."

Not a word or sign did Alice place in the way of the man's garrulity, but rather manifested breathless interest, as with parted lips she bent forward, encouraging him to go on.

Was he not reciting an epic poem of which she was the heroine and Harcourt the hero? The true epics of the world are generally told in the baldest prose.

"There was one thing I didn't like," continued the man, gathering up his reins, "and I've thought I ought to speak of it to ye or ye's father. All his talk was about savin' yerself, and not a whisper of the ould gentleman, who has been so kind to him all his life. It sounded kinder onnatteral like."

"Very well, Burtis; you have done your duty in speaking to me, and so need not say anything to Mr. Martell about it. I rather think you have prevented a funeral, and perhaps I owe you as many thanks as Mrs. Marchmont's coachman. At any rate you will find on Christmas that you have not been forgotten."

So the man drove to the stable with the complacent consciousness of having done his duty and warned his mistress against a "very onnatteral feelin'" in the young man.

The moment he disappeared around the corner, Alice stood undecided a moment, like a startled deer, and then sped down the path to the boat-house. The snow was tramped somewhat by the big lumbering feet of the coachman, but had it not been, Alice now had wings. The twilight was deepening, and she could not wait till the morrow before following up this trail that led to the idol of her heart.

She paused in the winding path when half-way down the bank, that she might gloat over the mad plunges by which Harcourt had crossed it, straight to the river. She followed his steps to the brink of a precipice, and saw with a thrill of mingled fear and delight where he had slid and fallen twenty feet or more.

"How cruelly I have misjudged him!" she thought. "When he was here eager to risk his life for me, my false fancy pictured him at Addie Marchmont's side. And yet

it was well I did not know the truth, for it would have
been so much harder to look death in the face so long, with
this knowledge of his friendship. How strangely he and
Addie act when together! But come, that is no affair of
mine. Let me be thankful that I have not lost the friend
of my childhood."

A little later she stood at the boat-house. The door hung
by one hinge only, and the large stone lay near with which
he had crashed it in. She entered the dusky place as if it
had been a temple. Had it not been consecrated by a service of love—by the costliest offering that can be made—
life? Here he had said he would save her or perish with
her; here he had sought to make good his words.

She picked up one of the matches he had dropped, and
struck it, that she might look into the neglected boat.
Never was the utter unseaworthiness of a craft noted with
such satisfaction before.

"While I vilely thought he would not venture to our aid
at all, he strained every nerve to launch this old shell.
Thanks to obstinate Burtis, who would not help him."

She struck another match, that she might look more
closely; then uttered a pitiful cry.

"Merciful heaven! is this blood on this rope? It surely
is. Now I think of it, he kept his right hand gloved this
morning, and offered his left to Mr. Hemstead in salutation. Father and I, in our cruel wrong, did not offer to
take his hand. And yet it would seem that he tugged with
bleeding hands at these ropes, that he might almost the
same as throw away his life for us.

"I can scarcely understand it. No brother could do
more. He was braver than Mr. Hemstead, for he had a
stanch boat, and experienced help, while my old playmate was eager to go alone in this wretched thing that
would only have floated him out to deep water where he
would drown.

"Ah, well, let the future be what it may, one cannot be
utterly unhappy who has loved such a *man*. If he is will-

ing to give his life up for me, I surely can get him to give up his evil, wayward tendencies, and then I must be content."

She now began to experience reaction from her strong excitement, and wearily made her way back to the house.

Her father met her at the door, and exclaimed, "Why, Alice, where have you been? You look ready to sink!"

"I have been to the boat-house, father," she replied, in a low, quick tone; "and I wish you would go there to-morrow, for you will there learn how cruelly we have mis-judged Mr. Harcourt."

"But, my child, I am troubled about you. You need quiet and rest after all you have passed through;" and he hastily brought her a glass of wine.

"I needed more the assurance that my old friend and playmate was not what we thought this morning," she said with drooping eyes.

"Well, my darling, we will make amends right royally. He will be here to-morrow evening, and you shall have no occasion to find fault with me. But please take care of yourself. You do not realize what you have passed through, and I fear you are yet to suffer the consequences."

But more exhilarating than the wine which her father placed to her lips was the memory of what she had seen. Hers was one of those spiritual natures that suffer more through the mind than through the body. She encountered her greatest peril in the fear of Harcourt's unworthiness.

Letters in the evening mail summoned her father to the city on the morrow, and he left her with many injunctions to be very quiet. It was evident that his heart and life were bound up in her.

But as the day grew bright and mild she again found her way to the boat-house. With greater accuracy she marked his every hasty step from the house to the shore. Harcourt little thought in his wild alarm that he was leaving such mute but eloquent advocates.

Poor fellow! he was groaning over their harsh judgment,

but vowing in his pride that he would never undeceive them. He did not remember that he had left a trail clear to dullest eyes, and conclusive as a demonstration to the unerring instinct of a loving heart.

He had gone to the city and accomplished his business in a mechanical way. He returned with the first train, though why he scarcely knew. He felt no inclination to visit at Mrs. Marchmont's any more, for since he had come more fully under Miss Martell's influence Addie had lost her slight hold upon him, and now her manner was growing unendurable. He also felt that after Mr. Martell's coldness he could not visit there again, and he doggedly purposed to give his whole time to his business till events righted him, if they ever did.

But his stoical philosophy was put to immediate rout by Mr. Martell's message, which he received on his return. Five minutes later he was urging his black horse toward the familiar place at a pace but a little more decorous than when seeking Hemstead's assistance on the memorable evening of the accident.

"Miss Martell is out," stolidly said the woman who answered his summons.

As he was turning away in deep diappointment, Burtis appeared on the scene, and with a complacent grin, remarked, "She's only down by the boat-house, a-seein' how I saved ye from drownding."

Harcourt slipped a banknote into his hand, and said, "There's for your good services now if not then," and was off for the water's edge with as much speed as he dared use before observant eyes.

"They must have found out from the old coachman that I was not the coward they deemed me," he thought. "If so, I'll see he has a merry Christmas."

He saw Alice standing with her back toward him, looking out upon the river, that now rippled and sparkled in the sunlight as if a dark, stormy night had never brooded over an icy, pitiless tide.

The soft snow muffled his steps, until at last he said, hesitatingly, "Miss Martell."

She started violently, and trembled as if shaken by the wind.

"Pardon me," he said hastily. "It was very stupid in me thus to startle you, but you seemed so intent on something upon the river that I thought you would never see me."

"I—I was not expecting you," she faltered.

"Then I have done wrong—have been mistaken in coming."

"Oh, no; I did not mean that. I thought you were in New York. We expected you this evening."

"Shall I go away then, and come back this evening?"

"Yes; come back this evening, but do not go now—that is, just yet. I have something to say to you. Please forgive my confusion. I fear my nerves have been shaken by what I have passed through."

And yet such "confusion" in one usually so composed did puzzle him, but he said hastily, feeling that it would be better to break the ice at once, "I came here not to 'forgive,' but to seek your forgiveness."

"You seeking my forgiveness!" she said in unfeigned surprise.

"Yes," he replied, humbly bowing his head. "Heaven knows that I am weak and faulty enough, but when I have wronged any one, I am willing to make acknowledgment and reparation. I cannot tell you how eager I have been to make such acknowledgment to you, whom I revere as my good angel. I acted like a fool in the chapel last Monday afternoon, and did you great injustice. You have never shone on me 'coldly and distantly like a star,' but again and again have stooped from the height of your heavenly character that you might lift me out of the mire. It's a mystery to me how you can do it. But believe me, when I am myself, I am grateful; and," he continued slowly, his square jaw growing firm and rigid, and a sombre, resolute light coming into his large dark eyes, "if you will have patience with me, I will yet do credit to the good advice, written in a school-girl's hand, which I keep treasured in my room. Weak and foolish as I have been, I should have been far worse were it not for those letters, and—and your kindness since. But I am offending you," he said sadly, as Alice averted her face. "However the future may separate us, I wanted you to know that I gratefully appreciate all the kindness of the past. I sincerely crave your forgiveness for my folly last Monday. For some reason I was not myself. I was blinded with—I said what I knew to be untrue. Though you might with justice have shone on me as 'coldly and distantly as a star,' you have treated me almost as a sister might. Please say that I am forgiven, and I will go at once."

Imagine his surprise when, as her only response, she said abruptly, "Mr. Harcourt, come with me."

His wonder increased as he saw that her eyes were moist with tears.

She took him to the bluff, behind the boat-house, where in the snow were the traces of one who had slid and fallen from a perilous height.

"What do these marks mean?" she asked.

"It didn't hurt me any," he replied with rising color.

"Did you stop to think at the time whether it would or not? Have you thought what a chain of circumstantial evidence you left against you on that dreadful night? Now come with me into the boat-house, and let me tell you in the meantime that a lace curtain in my room is sadly torn, and one of my window-panes broken."

While he yet scarcely understood her, every fibre of his being was beginning to thrill with hope and gladness; but he said deprecatingly: "Please forgive my intrusion. In my haste that night I blundered into a place where I had no right to be. No doubt I was very rough and careless, but I was thinking of the pain of cold and fear which you

were suffering. I would gladly have broken that to fragments."

"Oh, I am not complaining. The abundant proof that
you were not deliberate delights me. But come into the
boat-house, and I will convict both you and myself, and
then we shall see who is the proper one to ask forgiveness.
What is this upon these ropes, Mr. Harcourt? and how did
it come here?"

"Oh, that is nothing; I only bruised my hand a little
breaking in the door."

"Is it nothing that you tugged with bleeding hands at
these ropes, that you might go alone in this wretched shell
of a boat to our aid? Why, Mr. Harcourt, it would not
have floated you a hundred yards, and Burtis told you so.
Was it mere vaporing when you said, 'If I cannot save
them, I can at least drown with them'?"

"No," he said impetuously, the blood growing dark in
his face; "it was not vaporing. Can you believe me capable of hollow acting on the eve, as I feared, of the most
awful tragedy that ever threatened?"

"Oh, not the 'most awful'!"

"The most awful to me."

"No, I cannot. As I said before, I have too much circumstantial evidence against you. Mr. Harcourt, true justice looks at the intent of the heart. You unconsciously
left abundant proof here of what you intended, and I feel
that I owe my life to you as truly as to Mr. Hemstead.
And yet I was so cruelly unjust yesterday morning as to
treat you coldly, because I thought my old friend and play-
fellow had let strangers go to our help. With far better
reason I wish to ask your forgive—"

"No, no," said Harcourt, eagerly; "circumstances appeared against me that evening, and you only judged
naturally. You have no forgiveness to ask, for you
have made amends a thousand-fold in this your generous
acknowledgment. And yet, Miss Martell, you will never
know how hard it was that I could not go to your

rescue that night. I never came so near cursing my
destiny before.''

"I cannot understand it," said Alice, turning away her
face.

"It's all painfully plain to me," he said with a spice of
bitterness. "Miss Martell, I am as grateful to Hemstead as
you are, for when he saved you he also saved me. If you
had perished, I feel that I should have taken the counsel
of an ancient fool, who said, 'Curse God and die.' ''

She gave him a quick look of surprise, but said only,
"That would be folly indeed."

He took her hand, and earnestly, indeed almost passionately continued: "Miss Alice, I pray you teach me how to
be a true man. Have patience with me, and I will try to
be worthy of your esteem. You have made me loathe my
old, vile self. You have made true manhood seem so noble
and attractive that I am willing to make every effort, and
suffer any pain—even that of seeing you shine upon me in
the unapproachable distance of a star. Make me feel that
you do care what I become. Speak to me sometimes
as you did the other evening among the flowers. Give
me the same advice that I find in the old yellow letters
which have been my Bible, and, believe me, you will not
regret it."

Alice's hand trembled like a frightened bird as he held
it in both of his, and she faltered, "I never had a brother,
but I scarcely think I could feel toward one differently—"
and then the truthful girl stopped in painful confusion.
Her love for Harcourt was not sisterly at all, and how
could she say that it was?

But he, only too grateful, filled out the sentence for her,
and in a deep, thrilling tone answered, "And if my love for
you is warmer than a brother's—more full of the deep, absorbing passion that comes to us but once—I will try to
school it into patience, and live worthily of my love for
her who inspired it."

Again she gave him a quick look of startled surprise,

and said hastily, "You forget yourself, sir. Such language belongs to another."

"To another?"

"Yes; to Miss Marchmont."

"Miss Marchmont can claim nothing from me, save a slight cousinly regard."

"It is reported that you are engaged."

"It's false," he said passionately. "It is true, that before you returned, and while I was reckless because I believed you despised me, I trifled away more time there than I should. But Miss Marchmont, in reality, is as indifferent toward me as I toward her. I am not bound to her by even a gossamer thread."

Alice turned away her face, and was speechless.

"And did you think," he asked reproachfully, "that I could love her after knowing you?"

"Love is blind," she faltered after a moment, "and is often guilty of strange freaks. It does not weigh and estimate."

"But my love for you is all that there is good in me. My love is the most rational thing of my life."

She withdrew her hand from his, and, snatching the rope that was stained with his blood, she kissed it and said, "So is mine."

"Oh, Alice! what do you mean?" and he trembled as violently as she had done when he startled her on the beach.

She shyly lifted her blue eyes to his, and said, "Foolish Tom, surely your love is blind."

Then to Harcourt the door of heaven opened.

When Mr. Martell returned, he saw by the firelight in his dusky study that his daughter had made such ample amends that but little was left for him to do; but he did that right heartily.

Then the Christian man said, "Alice, compare this with the shadow of 'Storm King,' and the grinding ice. Let us thank God."

She gently replied, "I have, father."

"But I have more reason to thank Him than either of you," said Harcourt, brokenly, "for had you perished I should have been lost, body and soul."

"Then serve Him faithfully, my son—serve Him as my old friend your father did."

"With His help I will."

CHAPTER XXIX

HEMSTEAD'S ADVICE, AND LOTTIE'S COLORS

SOON after the departure of Mr. Martell and his daughter, Hemstead pleaded headache, and retired to his room. Lottie, to escape De Forrest, had also gone to hers, but soon after, at her brother's solicitation, had accompanied him to a neighboring pond to make sure that the ice was safe for him. But, though she yielded to Dan's teasing, her compliance was so ungracious, and her manner so short and unamiable, that with a boy's frankness he had said: "What is the matter with you, Lottie? You are not a bit like Auntie Jane to-day. I wish you could stay one thing two days together."

As may be imagined, these remarks did not conduce to Lottie's serenity. She did not understand herself; nor why she felt so miserable and out of sorts. She had fallen into the "Slough of Despond," and was experiencing that depression which usually follows overwrought emotional states, and—her knight had disappointed her.

Having learned that the ice was firm, and assisted her little brother in putting on his skates, instead of returning at once to the house, she sat down in a little screening clump of hemlocks, and gave way to her feelings in a manner not uncommon with girls of her mercurial temperament.

Now it so happened that Hemstead, gazing listlessly from his window, saw their departure, and soon afterward it occurred to him that the fresh air would do his headache more good than moping in his room. By a not unnatural coincidence, his steps tended in the same direction as theirs, and soon he found Dan sprawling about the pond in great glee over his partial success in skating; but Lottie was nowhere to be seen. A sound from the clump of evergreens soon gained his attention, and a moment later he stood at the entrance of her wintry bower, the very embodiment of sympathy, and wondering greatly at her distress.

A stick snapped under his tread, and Lottie looked up hastily, dashing the tears right and left.

"What did you come for?" she asked brusquely.

"Well, I suppose I must say in truth—I wanted to. I hope you won't send me away."

"You ought to have given me a little warning, and not caught me crying like a great baby as I am."

"I wish I were your friend," he said humbly.

"Why so?"

"Because you would then tell me your trouble, and let me try to comfort you."

"I haven't any trouble worth naming. I've just been crying like a foolish child because I was out of sorts. There, don't look at me so with your great, kind eyes, or I shall cry again, and I am ashamed of myself now."

"Something *is* troubling you, Miss Marsden, and I shall be very unhappy if you send me away without letting me help you."

"You would think me a fool if I told you," she faltered.

"No one will ever charge you with being that."

She gave him another of her quick, strange looks, like the one she fixed upon him when he first moved her to tears by weaving about her the "spell of truth." It was a look akin to that of a child who learns by an intuitive glance whom it may trust. After a moment, she said: "If you were less kind, less simple and sincere, I would indeed send you away, and not very amiably either, I fear. And yet I should like a few crumbs of comfort. I scarcely understand myself. Monday and yesterday I was so strangely happy that I seemed to have entered on a new life, and to-day I am as wicked and miserable a little sinner as ever breathed. The idea of my being a Christian!—never was further from it. I've had nothing but mean and hateful thoughts since I awoke."

"And is this not a 'trouble worth naming'? In my judgment it is a most serious one."

"Do you think so?" she said gratefully. "But then I'm provoked that I can be so changeable. Dan just said, 'I wish you could be the same two days together,' and so do I."

"Let us look into this matter," he said, sympathetically, sitting down in a companionable way on the fallen tree beside her. "Let us try to disentangle this web of complex and changing feeling. As the physician treats the disordered body, you know it is my cherished calling to minister to the disquieted mind. The first step is to discover the cause of trouble, if possible, and remove that. Can you not think of some cause of your present feelings?"

Lottie averted her face in dismay, and thought, "What *shall* I do? I can't tell *him* the cause."

"Because you see," continued Hemstead, in the most philosophical spirit, "when anything unpleasant and depressing occurs, one of your temperament is apt to take a gloomy, morbid view of everything for a time."

"I think you are right," she said faintly.

"Now, I see no proof," he continued, with reassuring heartiness, "that you are not a Christian because you are unhappy, or even because you have had 'hateful thoughts,' as you call them. You evidently do not welcome these 'hateful thoughts.' The question as to whether you are a Christian is to be settled on entirely different grounds. Have you thrown off allegiance to that most merciful and sympathetic of friends that you led me to see last Sunday as vividly as I now see you?"

Lottie shook her head, but said remorsefully, "But I have scarcely thought of Him to-day."

"Rest assured He has thought of you. I now understand how He has sympathy for the least grief of the least of His children.''

"If I am one, I am the very least one of all," she said humbly.

"I like that," he replied with a smile. "Paul said he was the 'chief of sinners,' and he meant it too. That was an excellent symptom."

A glimmer of a smile dawned on Lottie's face.

"And now," he continued hesitatingly, as if approaching a delicate subject, "I think I know the cause of your trouble and depression. Will you permit me to speak of it?"

Again she averted her face in confusion, but said faintly: "As my spiritual physician I suppose you must."

"I think you naturally felt greatly disappointed that Mr. De Forrest acted the part he did last evening."

This speech put Lottie at ease at once, and she turned to him in apparent frankness, but with something of her old insincerity, and said, "I confess that I was."

"You could not be otherwise," he said, in a low tone.

"What would you advise me to do?" she asked demurely.

It was now his turn to be embarrassed, and he found that he had got himself into a dilemma. The color deepened in his face as he hesitated how to answer. She watched him furtively but searchingly. At last he said, with sudden impetuosity, as if he could not restrain himself: "I would either make a man of him or break with him forever. It's horrible that a girl like you should be irrevocably bound to such—pardon me."

Again Lottie averted her face, while a dozen rainbows danced in her moist eyes.

But she managed to say, "Which do you think I had better do?"

He tried to catch her eye, but she would not permit him. After a moment he sprang up and said, with something of her own brusqueness, "You had better follow your own heart."

"That is what Mrs. Dlimm said," she exclaimed, struck by the coincidence. "You and Mrs. Dlimm are alike in many respects, but I fear the world would not regard either of you as the best of counsellors."

"Whenever I have taken counsel of the world, I have got into trouble, Miss Marsden."

"There, that is just what she said again. Are you two in collusion?"

"Only as all truth agrees with itself," he answered, laughing.

"Well, perhaps it would be best to follow the advice of two such sincere counsellors, who are richly gifted with the wisdom of the other world, if not of this. Your talk has done me more good than I could have believed. How is it that it always turns out so? I'm inclined to think that your pastoral visits will do more good than your sermons."

"Now have pity on me, in regard to that wretched sermon. But I know of something that will do you more good than either, in your present depression. Will you wait for me ten minutes?"

"Yes; longer than that," she said, with an emphatic little nod.

He at once started for the house with great strides.

"My 'depression' is not very great at the present moment," she chirped, and giving a spring she alighted on the fallen tree with the ease of a bird. "I had 'better follow my own heart,' had I? Was there ever more delightful doctrine than that? But, bless me, whither is it leading? I dare not think, and I won't think."

And so, to keep herself warm while waiting, she balanced up and down on the fallen tree, trilling snatches of song as a robin might twitter on its spray.

Soon she saw her ghostly adviser speeding toward her in another guise. A stout rocking-chair was on his shoulder, and skates were dangling from his hand, and she ran to meet him with anticipating delight. A little later, Dan, who had been oblivious of proceedings thus far, was startled by seeing Lottie rush by him, comfortably ensconced in a rocking-chair and propelled by Hemstead's powerful strokes. This was a great change for the better, in his estimation, and he hailed it vociferously. Hemstead good-naturedly put the boy in his sister's lap, and then sent them whirling about the pond with a rapidity that almost took away their breaths. But he carefully shielded them from accidents.

"It's strange how you can be so strong, and yet so gentle," said Lottie, gratefully looking up at him over her shoulder.

"I haven't the faintest wish to harm you," he replied, smiling.

"That I should ever have wished to harm him!" she thought, with a twinge of remorse.

After a half-hour of grand sport, the setting sun reminded them that it was time to return.

"How do you feel now?" he asked.

"My face must be your answer," she said, turning to him features glowing with exercise and happiness.

"A beautiful answer," he said impulsively. "In color and brightness it is the reflection of the sunset there."

"I admit," she answered shyly, "that its brightness has a *western* cause. But speaking of color reminds me of something;" and her eyes twinkled most mirthfully as she caught a glimpse of something around his neck. "What have you done with my 'colors,' that I gave you last night? I know you wore them figuratively in your face this morning, when Miss Martell so enchanted you; but where are they, literally? Now a knight is supposed to be very careful of a lady's colors if he accepts them."

"I have been; and Miss Martell has never seen *your* colors."

"Oh, those so manifest this morning were *hers.* I understand now. But where are mine?"

"I cannot tell you. But they are safe."

"You threw them away."

"Never."

"Why, then, can't you tell me where they are?"

"Because—because— Well—I can't; so you need not ask me."

"If you don't tell me, I'll find out for myself."

"You cannot," he said confidently.

"Mr. Hemstead, what is that queer crimson fringe rising above your collar?"

Het put his hand hastily to his neck, and felt the ribbon that his stooping posture and violent exercise had forced into a prominence that defied further concealment; then turned away laughing, and, with his face now vying with the sunset, said, "You have caught an ostrich hiding with its head in the sand."

Her merry laugh trilled like the song of a bird, as she exclaimed, "Oh, guilt, guilt! the western sky is pale compared with thy cheeks."

Then, taking his arm in a way that would have won an anchorite, she added with a dainty blending of mischief and meaning, "I, too, am an ostrich to-night—that is, in my appetite. I am ravenous for supper."

"'I, too, am an ostrich!' What did she mean by that?" and Hemstead pondered over this ornithological problem for hours after.

CHAPTER XXX

AROUND THE YULE-LOG

LOTTIE'S radiant face at supper, in contrast with her clouded one at dinner, again puzzled certain members of the household; and De Forrest, to his disgust, learned that while he slept she had again been with Hemstead. He resolved on sleepless vigilance till the prize was secured, and mentally cursed the ill-starred visit to the country over and over again.

Bel was cool and cynical outwardly, but was really perplexed as to what ought to be done. With all her faults she had a sincere affection for her friend, and was shrewd enough to perceive that this affair with Hemstead promised to be more serious than Lottie's passing *penchants* had been previously. But with her usual weakness and irresolution she hesitated and waited, Micawber-like, to see what would "turn up."

The impression grew on Mrs. Marchmont that Lottie was fascinating her nephew; and yet just how to interfere she did not see. It was rather delicate business to speak, with nothing more tangible than what she had yet seen. That Lottie herself was becoming sincerely attached to a young man of Frank's calling and prospects, could not occur to a lady of Mrs. Marchmont's ideas of propriety and the fitness of things. It was only Lottie's "inveterate disposition to flirt." As to Lottie's "moods and emotions," she smiled at them with cool indifference, as far as she noticed them at all. "Young people pass through such phases as through the measles," she was accustomed to say.

Addie was too much wrapped up in herself to think particularly about others.

Save by queer little chuckling laughs, which no one understood, Mr. Dimmerly gave no sign that he noted anything unusual going on.

Besides, Lottie was very circumspect when in the presence of others, and Hemstead unconsciously followed the suggestion of her manner. Thus even lynx-eyed Bel could seldom lay her finger on anything and say, "Here is something conclusive."

But if ever there was an earthly elysium, Hemstead and Lottie dwelt in it during the remainder of that week. Not that they were much together, or had much to say to each other by word of mouth. Scarcely another opportunity occurred for one of their momentous private talks, for De Forrest's vigilance had become sleepless indeed.

Besides, Hemstead was shut up in his room most of the time, engaged on another sermon. For Dr. Beams was ill, and the student had been asked to preach again. He gladly complied with the request, for he was most anxious to correct the dreary impression he had made on the previous Sabbath. Lottie, too, was much in her room, at work on something which no one was permitted to see. But little was thought of this, for the house was full of the mystery that always prevails just before Christmas. Every one was cherishing innocent, and often transparent, little secrets, which were soon to be proclaimed, if not on the "house-top," on the tree-top of the fragrant cedar that had already been selected and arranged in the back parlor, suggesting to all the blessedness of both giving and receiving.

Yet, while seemingly separated, what moment passed when they were not together? How vain was De Forrest's vigilance!—how futile were Mrs. Marchmont's precautions! Lottie was the muse that sat at Hemstead's side; and every time he lifted his eyes from the paper his vivid fancy saw her face glowing like the sunset, and beaming upon him. She inspired his sermon. Unconsciously, he wrote it for

her alone, letting her need and spiritual state color the line
of thought which his text naturally suggested; and a fresh,
hope-imparting Christmas sermon it promised to be—a
veritable gospel. He was unconsciously learning the price-
less advantage to a clergyman of pastoral visitation; for, in
discovering and meeting the needs of one heart, nearly all
are touched—so near a kinship exists throughout humanity.

As Lottie stitched away at an odd bit of fancy-work—
very different from anything that had ever taxed her dainty
skill before—strange gleams flitted across her face. At times
her eyes would sparkle with mirth as she lived over scenes
in which the student was ever the chief actor; and again
she would grow pale, and her breath come quick and short,
as her fancy portrayed him—when in the darkness he could
not have been seen by human eyes—far out amid the ice
upon the river. Then again her face would grow comically
pitiful, as she murmured: "I could have brought him to
quicker than uncle. I could have given him a stimulant
more potent than the forty-year-old brandy of which uncle
is so proud. I've found out my power over him."

Then her face would light up with exultation as she exclaimed, "Oh, it's grand to have such power over a strong,
richly-endowed man—to be able to move and play upon
him at your will by some mystic influence too subtile for
prying eyes to see. I can lift him into the skies by a smile.
I can cast him into the depths by a frown. If I but touch
his hand, the giant trembles. He would be a Hercules in
my service, and yet I've got him just there;" and she depressed her little thumb with the confidence of a Roman
empress desiring to show favor to some gladiatorial slave.

Then her face would change in quick and piquant transition to the expression of equally comic distress, as she
sighed, "But, alas! where am I? Right under his big
thumb, whether he knows it or not. How it all will end
I dare not think."

When her jewelled watch indicated that the time for
dinner or supper was near, she would make the most be-

witching of toilets, and laugh at herself for doing so, querying, "What is the use of conquering one over and over again who is already helpless at your feet?"

And yet the admiration of Hemstead's beauty-loving eyes was sweeter incense than all the flattery she had ever received before.

And what hours of dainty, ethereal banqueting were those prosaic meals in Mrs. Marchmont's dining-room! The corpulent colored waiter served the others, but airy-winged love attended these two, bearing from one to the other glances, tones, accents, of the divinest flavor.

De Forrest noted and chafed over this subtile interchange. Bel and Mrs. Marchmont saw it also, and Mr. Dimmerly's queer chuckling laugh was heard with increasing frequency. But what could be done? Lottie's and Hemstead's actions were propriety itself. Mrs. Marchmont could not say, "You must not look at or speak to each other." As well seek to prevent two clouds in a summer sky from exchanging their lightnings!

Hemstead was in a maze. The past and the future had lost their existence to him, and he was living in the glorified present. He no more coolly realized the situation than would one in an ecstatic trance. In one sense he verified the popular superstition, and was bewitched; and, with the charming witch ever near to weave a new spell a dozen times a day, how could he disentangle himself? He was too innocent, too unhackneyed, to understand what was going on in his own heart.

The days and the hours fled away until Saturday—the day before Christmas—came. By noon Hemstead had finished his sermon, and Lottie had completed her mysterious fancy-work; and both were ready for the festivities of Christmas eve.

Mr. Dimmerly was a great stickler for the old English customs, and always had the yule-log brought in with great ceremony. With his own hands he suspended the mistletoe from the chandelier in the hall, which he always obtained

from Dimmerly Manor in England. Lottie, without thinking, stood beneath, watching him, when, with a spryness
not in keeping with his years, he sprang down and gave her
a sounding smack in honor of the ancient custom.

"There," said he, "that pays me for all my trouble and
expense. But you will get another kiss here, that you will
like better, before I take the mistletoe down."

"Well, uncle," said Lottie, laughing and rubbing her
tingling cheek, "I hope it won't be such an explosion as
yours was, or it will alarm the household."

"Be careful, or it may attract more attention than
mine;" and he departed with his queer chuckling laugh.

Lottie looked after him with sudden intelligence, and
asked herself, "Now what does he mean by that? Does
he suspect anything?"

At the dinner-table Mr. Dimmerly indulged in a long
homily on the importance of keeping up old customs, and
ended with a sly, significant glance at Lottie, which brought
the color into her face. But during the afternoon she foiled
all the devices of De Forrest to get her under the mistletoe
bough, and yet with such grace that, however disappointed,
he could not become angry. As for Hemstead, he was far
too diffident to attempt any such strategy, much as he
would have liked to solemnize the venerable rite.

And so at last Christmas eve came; and with it a few
guests. Harcourt and Miss Martell had been specially invited; for the fact of their engagement had become known
at once, and Mrs. Marchmont hastened to assure them, by
this invitation, that she had no regrets or resentment. Not
for the world would she have Miss Martell imagine that any
maternal projects had been frustrated.

Harcourt, grateful for all the kindness he had received
at Mrs. Marchmont's, induced Alice to accept; and so their
illumined faces were added to the circle that gathered around
the yule-log in the large dining-room, that had been cleared
for games and dancing.

In spite of the incongruous elements composing that cir-

cle, it made, with the crackling fire playing on happy faces
and Christmas decorations, a pretty picture—one that might
convert a pagan into willingness to honor the chief Christian
festival.

After some old-fashioned country dances—through which
even Hemstead had been induced to blunder, to Lottie's infinite delight—they sat down to nuts, apples, and cider.
Billets of hickory were piled higher than ever against the
great yule-log; and never did the sacred flame light up
fairer and happier faces than those of Alice Martell and
Lottie Marsden. And yet they were as different as could
be. One was the lily, and the other the rose. Harcourt
and Hemstead also looked as if some angelic messenger had
brought them "tidings of great joy."

Harcourt and Alice sat together; but Lottie, with seeming perverseness, got as far away as possible. But it was
only seeming, for she sat where she could look Hemstead
full in the face, and, with her brilliant eyes, indulge in
love's mystic telegraphy without restraint.

Now was the time for Mr. Dimmerly to shine out; and
he proposed that some one should begin a story, and carry
it forward to a certain point, then stop abruptly, while some
one else took it up for a brief time, when, in like manner,
it would again be dropped that another might continue it,
so that each one who was willing might have a chance to
contribute.

"You commence, Mr. Harcourt," said Mr. Dimmerly.

After a preface of hemming, the young man said: "Once
upon a time, in a village in the south of France, it was arranged that there should be a general fête and dance on the
village green the afternoon before Christmas. Little Ninon
was a peasant's daughter, and she was only fourteen. If she
were petite, she was also piquant and pretty—"

"Very good, very good," cried a chorus of voices; and
a round of applause stimulated the narrator.

"Until this occasion, Ninon had always been kept at
home as a child; but, after interminable coaxings, she

obtained her mother's permission to go to the fête. Now her mother was a widow, and it so happened that she could not go with her daughter, and after she had given her consent had not one whom she could send with her child as a protector. But Ninon was in such glee that her mother had not the heart to take back her promise.

" 'Now, mother, tell me what shall I say when the boys, and perhaps some of the *very* young men, ask me to dance with them?'

" 'Say, I'm only a little child who have come to see. Go thy ways.'

" 'But suppose they don't go their ways,' pouted Ninon.

" 'Go thine then, and come home.'

" 'Now, mother dear, am I not almost old enough to have a lover?'

" 'Lover indeed! Silly child, but yesterday I rocked thee in the cradle there. I'm a fool to let thee go.'

"Then Ninon, in fear, kept still, lest her mother should change her mind, a thing which women sometimes do, even in France—"

"Now I protest against innuendoes," cried Lottie. "It is the French*man*, as it is *man* all over the world, who changes his mind. Adam first said he wouldn't eat the apple, and then he did!"

"Where's your authority for that?" said Harcourt.

"It's in the Bible," answered Lottie, stoutly; at which there was a great explosion.

"Miss Marsden equals modern commentators in amplifying the text," laughed Hemstead.

"Well," persisted Lottie, "if it isn't just so written, I know enough of human nature to be sure that that was just how it happened."

"On with the story!" cried Mr. Dimmerly. "Come, Miss Martell."

"The afternoon of the fête came," said Alice, "and Ninon's mother was depressed with a boding of evil.

"'Whom shall I send with thee, my child? My heart fails me in sending thee alone.'

"'Little brother Pierre shall go with me,' said Ninon. He's an odd child, and talks to the saints and angels more than to us. If he goes with me, the saints will take care of us both.'

"This seemed to strike the mother as true, and she was comforted; and the pale little boy, with large, spiritual eyes that appeared to look into the other world, took his sister's hand without even a smile flitting across his sad face; and they started for the fête.

"Now, Miss Marchmont," said Miss Martell, with a graceful inclination to Addie.

"And the pale little boy, with big, owl-like eyes," conitnued Addie, flippantly, "stalked along as if going to a funeral, while Ninon tripped and danced at his side. But soon the young girl's steps grew slower and slower, and her face thoughtful, and she began to question her mother's words—that she was too much of a child to have a lover; and by the time she reached the village green she gave her pretty head a toss as she said, 'We'll see about this. Mother doesn't know everything.'"

"Now, Bel."

"But poor little Ninon," said Bel, "soon became sadly bewildered, for there were so many people all talking at once, and they pushed against and jostled her as if she were very small and insignificant indeed, and she began to think that her mother was right, and that she was only a child; and she grew frightened and wished herself at home again. But she kept fast hold of the hand of her brother whom the saints loved, and felt that as long as he was with her she was safe. Finally they were pushed and jostled to a quiet nook on the edge of the green, under a tree, and here they sat down. Soon the dancing commenced, and Ninon amused herself by criticising the people and making remarks to her brother about their dress and manner. But he did not seem to hear her, and his eyes were fixed on the sky, as if he saw more that was wonderful there than she upon the village green.''

''Mr. De Forrest, you next.''

''But as Ninon sat there smiling and talking more to herself than to her queer little brother, who didn't listen, the young men began to notice her, and to nudge each other and ask who she was; for in truth she reminded every one of a half-blown rose. But no one knew who she was, and no one had ever seen her before. Then the handsomest young man in the village—indeed he was the one at whom all the girls were setting their caps—stepped forward and took a deliberate survey, and soon was convinced that, among all the village maidens, there was not a face as fair as Ninon's. And while he looked at her Ninon from under her long lashes as intently watched him. At last the young man made up his mind, and said to himself, 'I will be her lover for this afternoon,' and in a manner that was the very embodiment of grace, he stepped up to her and said, 'My pretty maiden, wilt dance with me ?' ''

And De Forrest bowed to Lottie to continue. It was strange how the foolish little story was gaining the breathless interest of all present—all the more because each one was unconsciously coloring his bit of the mosaic with his own individuality. Lottie's manner by no means tended to allay this interest as she began her part of the impromptu tale. She was a natural actress, and, for the moment, became little Ninon. The scene had grown actual to her vivid fancy, and by some process that cannot be explained she impressed it upon the minds of the others as real. They saw the crowded village green, the petite maiden and her weird brother sitting upon its edge, as she began.

''And Ninon shyly raised her dark eyes to the face of the handsomest young man of all the village, at whom the girls were setting their caps, and said, a trifle coldly, 'I am only a little child who has come to see. Go thy ways.'

''And the handsome young man stalked away, haughty and offended; and the youth of the village nudged each other and smiled and wondered and said, 'She must be a princess in disguise, or she would dance with him whom all the girls covet.' So no one else would venture to speak to her. But Ninon for a while was content to be left alone to watch all the funny people and their funny ways. She didn't see any one with whom she wanted to dance.

"At last she became conscious that one who seemed a stranger like herself was watching her, and she began to look curiously at him. At first she did not like his looks at all. His dress was very plain—not a bit smart and gay like that of the other young men. Besides, he was so tall and grave; and once, when some one said a rude word to him, his eyes were so fiery that Ninon was afraid of him. But a moment later, when his eyes rested on her, they became so kind and gentle that she wondered how it could be. Then she began to grow sorry for him because, like herself, he was a stranger and had no one to talk to. But he seemed in quest of some one, for he would look all around among the people; but soon his eyes would come back and rest wistfully upon her face, as if she were the one he was looking for after all. This puzzled Ninon greatly, and she asked herself, 'Now can it be that I am the one he's looking for?' At last it seemed that the stranger wished to speak to her, but hadn't the courage, and this amused Ninon vastly. Twice he advanced, faltered, and then retreated. Ninon was convulsed with laughter and whispered, 'Oh, Pierre, isn't this the funniest thing that ever was in this great world? That big man there is afraid of me —little Ninon '

"Then she saw that he thought she was laughing at him, and that he had straightened himself up stiff and haughty and had looked the other way. But he couldn't keep looking the other way very long," Lottie said, with an indescribable air that brought out a round of applause; "and when he timidly glanced toward her again she gave him such an encouraging smile that he came at once to her side and said, 'Little sister, wilt walk with me?'

"A happy thought struck Ninon. Her mother had said she was too young to have a lover, but nothing had been said against her having another brother. So, with conscience clear, she whispered, 'Sit still here till I come back'; and the little boy sat still, looking up into the sky, while Ninon let the tall stranger take her hand and lead her away. But his eyes were so gentle and true that she lost all fear and asked, 'Why do you call me sister?'

" 'Perhaps you can tell me,' he said. 'I came here an utter stranger, and I looked all around among the people, and their faces were strange, and it seemed to me that they ever would be strange; but when I saw your face you appeared to belong to me. I think we must be related.'

" 'I never saw you before,' said Ninon, shaking her head.

" 'I've seen you in my dreams all my life,' he replied, looking at her so earnestly that the color deepened on her cheek.

" 'I never heard anything so queer in all my life,' said Ninon.

" 'You have much to learn,' said the stranger.

" 'Yes,' said Ninon, humbly; 'as mother says, I'm only a little child.'

" 'You are not a little child; you are a beautiful maiden, Ninon,' said the stranger, earnestly.

" 'Nonsense!' she said, blushingly. 'I'll never be that.' But she liked to hear him say it, nevertheless," Lottie added with an accent that again brought out a round of applause.

"I'm taking too much time," Lottie said, deprecatingly.

"Go on, go on," was the unanimous cry; and her little brother Dan, who had dropped nuts and apples and was leaning open-mouthed on her knees, said, "Lottie, if you don't go on, I'll do something dreadful."

So Lottie continued: "And the tall stranger smiled down upon her and said, 'Violets are my favorite flower, and you are a modest little violet.'

" 'Now you are wrong again,' said Ninon; 'violets are a pale blue flower, and my cheeks are burning so oddly—I ne'ver had them do so before. I know I look like the peonies in the *curé's* garden.'

"'You look like the sweetest rose in the *curé's* garden.'

" 'Is that the way big brothers talk to their little sisters?'

" 'That is the way I talk to you, and I'm in earnest.'

" 'How do little sisters treat a brother as big as you are?'

" 'Well, for one thing, they kiss them.'

" 'That's queer,' said Ninon, innocently. 'I should think it would be just the other way.'

" 'Now I think of it, you are right,' and the stranger gave her a kiss that set every nerve tingling.

" 'How odd!' she exclaimed, half-frightened, half-delighted. 'Pierre sometimes kisses me, but I never felt that way before.'

" 'And big brothers take their little sisters in their arms and lift them over the rough places, as I do.'

"And he carried her over a low stone wall that separated them from a shadowy grove.

" 'Oh, how nice!' sighed Ninon, complacently; 'I've always had to get over the rough places by myself before.'

" 'You will no longer,' said the youth, as they passed under the low branches of a sheltering tree. 'Oh, Ninon, as innocent as beautiful, can you not see that I am not your brother, but your lover?' and he threw himself at her feet.

"But Ninon clasped her hands in the deepest distress, and cried, 'Oh, why did you say that? You might have been my brother as long as you chose. But mother says I can have no lover—that I am only a child;' and like a startled fawn she fled from him, and, a few moments later, panting and breathless, was sitting again beside her strange little brother, who was still looking into the sky as if he saw a vision.

"The young stranger followed sadly, thinking how he might still win her, and teach her that she was no longer a child. Ninon soon became more composed, and looked around as if she would like to see him again. As at a distance he watched her from under his bent eyebrows, a happy thought struck him, and he said, 'I'll teach her that she is a woman'; and, stepping forward, he singled out a neglected village maiden, who seemed ready for a little attention from anybody, and whirled her into the dance. Ninon, to her dismay, saw the arm of her whilom brother and lover encircling another girl, while she, apparently, was forgotten. She could scarcely believe her eyes. She looked at him fixedly, the picture of reproach, but he never seemed to look toward her. Surprise, resentment, grief, followed each other upon her fair face, like clouds passing over a sunny landscape. At last she buried her face upon little Pierre's shoulder, and sobbed, 'He may be my lover, or anything else, if he will only leave that hateful minx and come to me once more.'

"The tall stranger saw her drooping head, and quickly led his partner out of the dance and bowed himself away, leaving her bewildered—so quickly had he come and gone.

"Ninon looked up, but he was nowhere to be seen, and the 'hateful minx' stood alone. Suddenly a voice that had grown strangely familiar said at her side, 'May I be thy lover now?'

" 'Thou art false,' she said faintly.

" 'Never to thee, Ninon. My thoughts were with thee every moment since thou so cruelly left me. Do you not see why I sought another maiden? I wished to teach you that you were no longer a child, but a woman. I *am* your lover. Your heart has already claimed me, and these jealous tears prove it.'

" 'Well, then,' said Ninon, shyly smiling again, 'if my heart has gone to you, and I half believe it has, I must follow my heart;' and she put her hand in his."

Loud and long was the applause that greeted Lottie's conclusion. Dan executed a miniature breakdown as an expression of his feelings, and it seemed as if Mr. Dimmerly's chuckling laugh would never cease. De Forrest looked uneasy, and Hemstead was in a trance of bewildered delight. Alice and Harcourt exchanged significant glances, but upon the faces of Mrs. Marchmont and Bel were traces of disapproval.

"Now, uncle," cried Lottie, "it's your turn. I have given you *comedy;* we shall expect from you high tragedy."

The word "comedy," as Lottie here used it, jarred unpleasantly on Hemstead's ear, and the thought crossed Harcourt's mind, "Can she be leading Hemstead on in heartless jest, as we proposed at first? How I have changed since that day! and I was in hopes that she had, too, somewhat."

But Mr. Dimmerly had taken up the thread of the narrative where Lottie had dropped it.

"Ninon," he said, "lived a long while ago, and did not properly refer the tall stranger to her mamma. A trysting place and time were agreed upon, and the mysterious stranger in green, who was apparently a forester, said that he had a deer to kill before nightfall; and, raising her hand to his lips, departed. Ninon sat a long time, lost in a maze of thought, and then, in the twilight, roused the rapt child from his visions, and they started for their home. But villanous faces had hovered on the outskirts of the village green, and ill-omened eyes had marked the beauty of Ninon and the spiritual face of her brother. At that time there was in France a terrible monster, known as Giles de Laval, whose emissaries were ever on the alert for such victims. It was this cruel man who suggested to Perrault his world-renowned story of Barbe-bleu, the Blue-Beard that Dan there knows all about. Well, when Ninon and her little brother were passing a thicket but half-way home, two masked men sprang out upon them, and, stifling their terror-stricken cries, carried them to a distance from the highway. They then bound bandages firmly over their mouths, and lifted them on their horses and galloped away and away, till poor Ninon felt that she could never find her way home again, even if she had a chance. Soon the shadowy walls of a great castle rose before them, with a single light in a lofty tower. The feet of the iron-shod horses rang on the drawbridge, which rose after them, and then

Ninon knew they were prisoners. At first they were shut up in a dungeon that was perfectly dark, for their cruel jailer knew the overpowering effect of such rayless gloom. But strange little Pierre said that the place was brighter than the sun, and that lovely faces were smiling at him. Ninon, however, saw nothing, and it was dark indeed to her, and she sobbed bitterly, and called on her mother and lover for help. But only stony-hearted Laval and his accomplices heard her girlish voice. A bell in one of the towers slowly tolled out eleven o'clock. A little later the door of their cell opened, and light streamed in. Two men in hideous masks seized them, and carried them up and up, till Ninon, in horror, thought that they were to be thrown from the top of the tower. But worse than that awaited them; for soon they entered a large circular room, in which, on a sort of throne, sat a dreadful-looking man, clad in sable. He had human form and features, but reminded one of the more disgusting kind of wild beasts. His eyes were small, piercing, and malignant, but his face was large, sensual, devilish, and poor Ninon lost hope from the moment she saw him. She instinctively felt that to sue for mercy from such a monster would be worse than vain. She had lost hope utterly. She and her mother had been mistaken. The saints cared for neither little Pierre nor herself, and had left them to fall into the clutches of this demon. She glanced slowly around the room in the faint hope of escape, or even for the chance of throwing herself from a window, if it were needful, in order to escape from that horrible man. But the walls were thick. No light came from without, but only from a great furnace, that was strangely constructed and made her shudder. For a long time there was perfect silence in the dreadful place. The two masked men, grotesque and horrible, stood near the furnace, motionless as statues. The sable monster on his black throne watched them without moving a muscle in his great, coarse face, only his small eyes seemed like two scintillating sparks of infernal fire, as with a fiendish kind of pleasure he marked the agony of Ninon. Although the young girl instinctively gave up all hope of life, yet never had life seemed so sweet. Its homeliest details now appeared precious, and their poor little cottage, heaven, compared with this den of infamy. She had just tasted the exquisite happiness of a new and before unknown love, and now she was to die. She thought of her mother growing gray in loneliness and grief. She thought of her lover coming eagerly to their trysting-place; but when he should come on the morrow, Christmas day, what would she be?— where would she be? and in her anguish she cried aloud, and, kneeling, stretched out her hands toward the sable throne.

"Then for the first time the coarse, thick lips of the monster distorted themselves into a hideous grin, but otherwise he did not move, and the awful silence continued in that chamber of death.

"Ninon put her hands to her face, to hide his ugly visage, and then sank down in the apathy of despair.

"There was nothing in Ninon's agony that disturbed Laval. Scarcely a night passed but some victim like herself writhed under his remorseless eyes. Their mortal fear and sufferings were his recreation before the sterner business of sorcery that followed; and the more demonstrative they were in their pain, the more highly spiced was his pleasure. At first Ninon's beautiful and expressive face kept his whole attention; but after a time he began to note the strange-appearing little boy who accompanied her. There was no fear in his calm, pale face. There was no dread in his large, spiritual eyes, that seemed to look past the monster and his thick walls to some rare vision beyond.

"'What does the little wretch see?' he queried, for Laval, like his age, was very superstitious.

"But Ninon must be goaded out of her apathy, or the night would be dull; so at last the thick lips open, and the awful silence is broken by more awful words:

"'Girl, thou who art to lose body and soul, look at me.'

"Slowly Ninon lifted her eyes to his brutal face, and gazed fixedly as some poor little bird might look into the envenomed jaws of a serpent. The fascination of fear was upon her. In a thick, guttural, monotonous voice, the human beast continued: 'The devil has shown me that there is a potent charm in thy young innocent heart, that there are powerful spells in thy warm young blood, and that with them I may discover untold wealth. When the bell tolls out the hour of midnight, I shall take your bleeding heart out of your living body, and the heart of your brother out of his body, that with them I may decoct an essence in yonder furnace that will transmute the basest metal into gold. Midnight is the hour, and at midnight you shall die. Only the spell will be far more potent if you first give yourself to the foul fiend. Therefore, repeat after me: 'I give my soul and body to Satan.'

"Mechanically the terror-stricken girl began: 'I give—' but little Pierre put his hand over her mouth. 'The saints forbid,' he said quietly.

" 'Seize the child; tear out his staring eyes,' shouted the monster, savagely."

Mr. Dimmerly stopped, took off his spectacles, and coolly wiped them as he said: "I'm through, and my part of the story is true. This Giles de Laval, or, as he is better known in French history, the Marshal de Retz, destroyed hundreds of children, at ages varying from eight to eighteen, and in ways far worse than I have described. So, Lottie, have you had enough of high tragedy?"

"Oh, uncle!" she exclaimed, with a little impatient stamp of the foot, "you have told us a horrible story. It must not break off in this way, or we shan't sleep a wink to-night. Mr. Hemstead, you take up the story where uncle left off, and, if possible, complete it in a way that won't make our blood run cold."

Thus Hemstead was put upon his mettle, and soon all present were hanging with breathless interest on his rich, well-modulated tones.

"When the monster from his sable throne uttered his merciless mandate to tear out the eyes of little Pierre, the two grotesque and statue-like apparitions sprang into life, and, snatching hot irons from the furnace, rushed toward the child. Ninon gave a shriek of terror, and sought to shelter the boy in her arms, crying, 'Do what you will with me, but spare him.' Thus again, more truly than before by jealous tears, Ninon proved that she had become a woman."

At this sentence he was interrupted by a perfect storm of applause, in which Harcourt led off again and again. But Hemstead drew his inspiration from Lottie's face, and noted with a thrill of joy that tears stood in her eyes. This was a richer tribute than he received from all the others, and with deeper and more effective tones he continued: "But just then the great bell began to toll out the hour of twelve, and the demon, from his sable throne, made a restraining gesture.

" 'Naught,' he said, 'must now interfere with our high magic and solemn sorcery. At the last stroke of the bell take their hearts out of their living bodies.'

"Ninon sank on the floor, murmuring like a dying zephyr among the chords of an Æolian harp, 'Farewell, mother dear. Farewell, my lover true. I cannot meet you to-morrow at the *fallen tree*' " (here Hemstead glanced at Lottie, whose face was instantly suffused); "and she bowed her head upon her brother's shoulder, and sobbed aloud.

"Slowly and solemnly upon the silent night the iron tongue tolled out the fatal moments.

"With increasing uneasiness the monster upon his sable throne watched little Pierre, who, from first to last, had not shown a trace of fear or trouble. Among all his victims he had never seen a child like this, and his guilty heart began to fail him wofully.

" 'He surely sees something,' he muttered, as the boy's large eyes dilated with a wondrous awe, and his face grew luminous with a great joy.

"The heavy vibrations of the last stroke of the bell resounded through the silent night.

"Suddenly, with a shrill, piercing voice that went like an arrow to the guilty heart of Laval, little Pierre exclaimed, 'It is Christmas morn! Oh, Ninon, look! there is Jesu, the Christ-Child, and the Lord of all the saints. See, He is coming toward us, bearing His cross—He is here—He is placing His pierced hands upon our heads—we are saved;' and the child knelt reverently on the pavement, and his sister knelt beside him.

"The monster tumbled off his sable throne and lay grovelling and groaning upon the floor, while his terror-stricken accomplices ran clattering down the stairs.

"Far above the tower even, Ninon thought she heard a burst of heavenly song, while little Pierre in rapt ecstasy cried, 'Listen.'

"Suddenly a clarion voice that Ninon heard most plainly, and that thrilled her to the heart, rang up from the earth beneath.

"'Harm but a hair of their heads, and I will make you suffer the tortures of the damned.'

"Even at their height they could hear the sound of galloping steeds.

"A dozen brave fellows swam the moat, and a moment later the drawbridge fell heavily, and the clangor of a hundred hoofs rang upon it.

"Up the winding stair came the tramp of armed men. A thud and a groan followed when any resisted. The dethroned monster lay grovelling on the floor, not daring to move.

"Little Pierre still looked heavenward. Ninon looked toward the door. A moment later her lover rushed in with drawn sword; and Ninon, unharmed, with a cry of joy sprang to his heart.

"But the fire of a terrible anger burned in the young man's cheek, and he raised his gleaming sword against Laval, who now pleaded piteously for mercy.

" 'What mercy would you have shown these children?' thundered the youth. 'What mercy have you shown to your other innocent victims?' and he was about to run him through when Ninon caught his arm and cried, 'Stay, kill him not this Christmas morn in his terrible guilt. It was Jesu who saved us; and does He not ever say, Forgive —even our enemies?'

"Slowly she drew down the raised arm of human vengeance. She took from his reluctant hand the gleaming sword, and returned it in its sheath.

"And now Ninon has become more than a woman—she is a *Christian*."

CHAPTER XXXI

UNDER THE MISTLETOE

INSTEAD of applause, there was the truer and more appropriate tribute of silence when Hemstead finished the mosaic of a story which, by the various narratives, had been developed so differently and yet characteristically. The eyes of more than one were moist, and Lottie hastily left the room.

Mr. Dimmerly was the first to recover himself, and, after blowing his nose most vociferously, managed to say: "Well, nephew, it was hardly the thing to get a sermon off on us before Sunday, but, since it was rather well done, I don't think we will complain. I now suggest that you young people have some games that will set your blood in motion. The last hours of Christmas eve should ever be the merriest. I will send Lottie back—the tender-hearted little minx, who must take everything in earnest."

His advice was followed, and Lottie soon returned, becoming, as usual, the life of the company. A breezy sound of voices and many a ringing laugh took the place of the former hush, as games and jests followed in quick succession.

Harcourt was good-naturedly on the alert to serve Hemstead, and, in a game that required the absence of two of the company from the room a few moments, suggested the names of the student and Lottie Marsden. They, nothing loth, went out together into the empty hall.

"Do you know," said Hemstead, "I think it a little strange I have not had a chance to speak to you alone since we were at the fallen tree in the clump of hemlocks?"

"I did not know," said Lottie, laughing and blushing, "that the 'fallen tree' was a trysting-place."

"Well," said he, eagerly, "I met a young lady there once, whom I would gladly meet there or anywhere else again."

"To see whether she had taken your advice?"

"That depends. I doubt whether she can 'make a man' of a certain individual, and I fear she will not take the other alternative."

"She will probably do as Ninon did—follow her heart."

"If one could only know whither your heart would lead you!" he said, looking at her so wistfully that she, seeing through his thin disguise, had it on her tongue to tell him. But, instead, she took a few dancing steps away, and, with no such intention whatever, stood just under the mistletoe as she laughingly said, "That reminds me of what father often says: How nice it would be to speculate if one only knew every time how it would turn out!"

"Miss Marsden!" he exclaimed, hurriedly, "you are right under the mistletoe."

She tried to spring away, but he snatched her hand and detained her, while he stood hesitatingly at her side, looking at her lips as if they were the gates of Paradise.

"Well," said she, laughing and blushing, "I have nothing to do in the matter."

"But I dare not take it unless you give it."

"And I dare not give it unless you take it."

If Hemstead did not emulate Mr. Dimmerly's "explosion," the ancient rite was nevertheless honored in a way that Lottie would not soon forget. Never did a kiss mean more, express more, or impart more, upon any occasion of the observance of the ceremony by her ancestors, back to the times of the Druids.

But this moment of bliss was of short duration, for Mrs. Marchmont unexpectedly entered the hall, and threw them both into disastrous confusion by exclaiming, in unfeigned astonishment, "Well, well! what does this mean?"

Of course Lottie was the first to recover herself, and managed to falter: "You see, auntie, by some accident—I assure you it was an accident; I didn't mean to do it at all—I got under that pesky mistletoe of uncle's, and Mr. Hemstead, it would seem, had taken to heart uncle's homily on the duty of keeping up old customs. Mr. Hemstead, you know, is so conscientious, and I suppose he felt that he must, poor man; and so—and thus"—

At this moment Harcourt's expedients of delay failed, and they were loudly summoned back to the dining-room.

"I hope there will be no more such nonsense," said Mrs. Marchmont, severely.

"Oh, no, indeed, auntie; it will never happen again. Only the strongest sense of duty could have impelled Mr. Hemstead to do such a thing;" and they escaped to the dining-room only to be subjected to a fire from another quarter. Their color was so high, and they had such an air of general confusion, that Harcourt cried, laughingly, "I more than half believe that you have been under the mistletoe."

"Nonsense!" said Lottie; "with auntie in the hall? If you think Mr. Hemstead is brave enough for that, you greatly misjudge him."

But De Forrest was wofully suspicious, and had many uneasy thoughts about the "jest" which Lottie must be carrying out; for surely it could not be possible that she was becoming in earnest.

Hemstead and Lottie made wretched work in guessing the word required of them from the nature of the game; for Mr. Dimmerly's prolonged chuckling laugh, which could be heard from the parlor, did not tend to allay their confusion.

When Mrs. Machmont entered that apartment she found her brother apparently in a convulsion; but he was only vainly endeavoring to prevent his merriment from developing into an outrageous chuckle, for he too had seen Lottie under the mistletoe.

"This thing must be stopped," said Mrs. Marchmont,

most emphatically; at which her brother chuckled louder than ever, and said, "Stopped, indeed! As if it could be, or ever had been 'stopped,' since Adam and Eve first cast sheep's eyes at each other in the Garden of Eden."

His sister left the room with a gesture of annoyance.

Suddenly the little man's queer, cackling laugh ceased, and his wrinkled face grew sad and thoughtful as he sighed: "I'm the only Dimmerly who was ever 'stopped'—fool that I was. His mother, sister Celia, would marry a poor man; and her life, in spite of all her toil and privation, has been happier than mine;" and he shook his head pathetically over "what might have been."

The marble clock on the mantel chimed out the hour of twelve, and the young people came flocking in from the dining-room, their noisy mirth hushed as they remembered that the sacred hours of the Christmas Sabbath had begun.

"I have induced Miss Martell to give us a Christmas hymn before parting," said Harcourt; and he led Alice to the piano, as if there had been some preconcerted arrangement.

Lottie went to her uncle's side, and took his arm in a sort of wheedling, affectionate way. She was beginning instinctively to recognize that she had an ally and sympathizer in him. As he looked down upon her fair face in its dewy freshness and bloom, he vowed that, as far as it was in his power, she should have her own way. Time and the inevitable ills of our lot might dim that face, but it should not become withered by a lifetime of vain regret.

"What were you laughing at so, uncle?" she whispered.

"At my nephew's painful conscientiousness and stern performance of duty. What a martyr he made of himself, to be sure!"

"Now, uncle, I half believe you think I stepped under your old mistletoe on purpose. It's no such thing."

"Oh, no, my dear. The mistletoe is haunted, and has been for a thousand years or more, and viewless elves draw under it those who are to receive kisses—prophetic of many others from the same lips.''

But here he found Lottie's hand upon his lips for a second, and then she stood at Miss Martell's side, who was now playing a prelude. In some surprise, Lottie noticed that, instead of there being a printed sheet upon the piano-rack, both the words and music were written by hand. As Miss Martell sang, in a sweet but unfamiliar air, the following words, her surprise and interest deepened:

> At midnight, in Judean skies,
>> There dawned a light whose holy rays
> Not only cheered the shepherds' eyes,
>> But filled with hope all coming days.
>
> At midnight, o'er Judea's plain
>> Was heard a song unknown before;
> The echoes of that sweet refrain
>> Are reaching earth's remotest shore.
>
> 'Twas not the sun o'er Eastern hills,
>> That shed a transient radiance round;
> Nor a feeble heir of earthly ills
>> The shepherds in the manger found.
>
> Upon the darker midnight sky
>> Of human sorrow, care, and sin—
> A night that broods at noontide high;
>> A dreary gloom all hearts within—
>
> There rose a gentle, human face,
>> Whose light was love and sympathy—
> The God of heaven, yet of our race—
>> The humblest of humanity.
>
> The night of sorrow, sin, and care
>> Still shadows many hapless hearts;
> But all who will this light may share—
>> This hope which Christmas morn imparts.

Lottie's eyes were suffused with tears when the simple hymn was finished, but they did not prevent her from following Miss Martell's finger as she turned to the title-page and pointed to the inscription:

"Music by Alice Martell.
"Words by Frank Hemstead.
"Dedicated to Miss Lottie Marsden.

"We wish you more than a 'merry'—the happy Christmas, rather, of the Christian."

Her first response was an impulsive kiss to Alice. But when she looked around to thank Hemstead he had gone.

A little later, as he came stamping up the piazza out of the snow, after assisting Harcourt and Miss Martell away, the hall-door opened, and some one darted out, and took his hand in a quick, thrilling pressure. A voice that had grown as dear as familiar said, "Before we parted to-night I wanted to tell you that I think Lottie Marsden, like Ninon, has become more than a woman—a Christian."

And she vanished, but left the night so luminous about him that he could not, for a long time, enter the house.

He felt, like the shepherds who kept watch centuries ago, that an angel had brought him "tidings of great joy."

CHAPTER XXXII

THE CHRISTMAS SUNDAY

THIS Christmas Sabbath, though marked by no unusual event, was destined to be a memorable day in the lives of Frank Hemstead and Charlotte Marsden. A chain of unforeseen circumstances and experiences, and a sequence of emotions still less understood, had lifted them higher and higher, until this culminating day was scarcely one of earthly existence.

Lottie, in her previous life, had been frivolous and selfish; but her evil resulted from thoughtlessness, rather than from the deliberate purpose to do wrong. She was the type of multitudes of her fair sisters, who, with sparkling eyes, look out upon life in its morning to see only what it offers to them, and not the tasks it furnishes them for others. Only by experience—only by God's logic of events—do they find that their happiness is in these tasks; in unselfish giving and doing.

The world had been at Lottie's feet. It had offered her all that it has to give to a girl in her station; but when, withdrawn from it by a day of suffering, she had summed up her treasures, she had found that she had nothing but remorse. She had been receiving all her life, and yet had nothing. She would then gladly have remembered that she had given even one an impulse toward a truer and happier life. But she could not. Apart from natural impulses of affection toward kindred and friends, her only thought in regard to all had been—How can I make them minister to me and my pleasure? With tact and skill, enhanced by exceeding beauty, she had exacted an unstinted revenue of flattery, attention, and even love; and yet, when, in weakness and pain, she wished the solace of some consoling memory, she found only an accusing conscience.

This experience conveyed to the practical girl a startling lesson. With all her faults, she did not belong to the class that is hopeless, because so weak and shallow. Though her handsome face might often express much that was unlovely and unwomanly, it ever expressed mind.

When she, in her turn, like hosts of others, came to realize the limitations of her being, her weakness and need, she looked around, instinctively, for help and support. Human teaching presented a God from whom she shrank in fear and dislike. The Bible revealed Jesus. When she most felt her need, the Bible presented One whose eyes overflowed with sympathy, and whose hand was omnipotent. She instinctively felt, like Mary of old, that, at "His feet," there were rest and hope.

The feeling was not reached as a mathematician solves an equation, or a theologian comes to a conclusion, but more after the manner in which some women and most children will look at a person and say, "I like him; I'll trust him."

There was nothing incongruous or unnatural in the contemporary love growing up in her heart for Hemstead, though it is possible that some may so think. In some minds the ideas of love and passion seem inseparable, and they regard religion as something far removed. These are but the right wing of that sinister class who jumble their passions and religion together, and, in pious jargon and spiritual *double entendre*, half conceal and half convey the base meaning of their hearts. In others, love, or what with them goes by the name, is equally inseparable from management and match-making, *trousseaux* and settlements—concerns pertaining to earth, and very earthy, it must be admitted. No doubt many excellent, solid people would regard Lottie's spiritual condition with grave suspicion, and ask, disapprovingly, "What business have two such *different* loves to be originating in her heart at the same t*i*me?" But, in the term "different," they beg the question. Where is the antagonism? Where is even the dissimilarity? Are not these two impulses of the heart near akin, rather? and does not a truer and deeper philosophy of life teach that love for a human object may be as certainly God's will as love toward Himself? Have these solid, excellent people aught to say against the faithful devotion of a wife, or the patient tenderness of a mother, which are corner-stones of the family, as the family is the corner-stone of all true civilization? But what is the origin of the wife's devotion and the mother's tenderness? These people, surely, are as *wise* as they are solid. They would have the day without the dawn.

At any rate, it would appear that Heaven was making the match between Hemstead and Lottie—making it as the spring comes on in northern latitudes, subtilely, imperceptibly, and yet speedily. Just how or when it came about, they did not know; but when they met on that Christmas morning, the peace and gladness of an assured and reciprocal love smiled from each other's eyes. They needed no explanations. Frank Hemstead's face had ever been as easily interpreted as his honest words; and he now had taught Lottie's face to tell the truth. A blessed truth it revealed to him that Christmas day.

As he entered the pulpit that morning his face was radiant with the purest human love, as well as love to God. So far from being incongruous, the one seemed to kindle and intensify the other. Though his sermon was simplicity itself, he spoke as one inspired. His message now was a gospel, and came to his hearers as the angel's announcement (which was his text) to the shepherds.

But his closing words were searching, and sent many of his hearers home thoughtful and conscience-smitten, as well as cheered by the great hope which Christmas day should ever bring to the world.

"I would gladly correct," he said, "the impression which

I fear was made on some minds last Sabbath. Christ is the embodiment of Christianity, and His coming to the world was 'tidings of great joy'; His coming to every sinful heart should be 'tidings of great joy.' But I fear that I led some to dread His coming, as they would purgatorial fires. How did the All-powerful One come? As a little, helpless child, that he might disarm our fears and enlist our sympathy. How did He live? The humblest among the humble, that no one on earth should be too lowly to go straight to His side with his griefs. How did He act? He took little children in His arms, and blessed them. He laid His hand on the loathsome leper from whom all shrank. He looked into the glare of the demoniac's eyes: the demons fled. Then, in meekness, He would offer to enter the poor wretch's heart, and dwell in what had been the foul abode of the foulest fiends. When men wept, He, from sympathy, wept with them, though his next breath changed their mourning into joy. When man dishonored God, or wronged his fellow-men—as did the Pharisees, with their unhallowed traffic in the Temple, their robbery of the widow and fatherless, their blocking up of the way of life with their senseless ceremonies, puerile traditions—no knight in all the heroic past ever breathed out a more fiery indignation. How did He die? In such a way that even the thief might be redeemed and live eternally. He was an ideal man, as well as perfect God. He was the servant of all, as well as King of kings. Not from his throne did He stoop to us. He stood at our side, and sustained fainting humanity with His encircling arm, as a brother. Little wonder, then, that the angel called the announcement that God had thus visited His creatures 'good tidings of great joy.'

"But there is a brief word of pointed and searching significance in this message. The angel said, 'Unto *you* is born a Saviour.' Is that true of each one of us? Is this Christmas day a mockery, reminding us of a hope that is not ours—of a heaven in which we have no right or part? Does conscience tell us to-day that we have looked upon the light that shone at Bethlehem with apathetic eyes, and heard the angel's message with unbelieving hearts, so that practically no Saviour has been born unto us? Why do you keep this day as a festival, my hearer? I can tell you why you may. If you will receive it, the angel's message is to you personally; unto *you* is born a Saviour who will forgive your past sin, and shield you from its consequences —who will ennoble your future life, and sustain and comfort you under the inevitable sorrow and suffering awaiting —and who will receive you into an eternal and a happy home at the end of your brief sojourn here. May not this Christmas pass until each one has received the abiding peace and joy of the angel's message into the depths of his heart."

After the service, Miss Martell, with glistening eyes, said to Harcourt, "I am glad you heard that sermon."

"I admit," he replied, with bowed head, "that it is better than my old philosophy. I think Hemstead must have written it for me."

As the young clergyman helped Lottie into the sleigh, she whispered, "You wrote that sermon for me."

Both were right. Hemstead had preached Christ, who is God's embodied truth, meant alike for every human heart, and alike adapted to all.

CHAPTER XXXIII

THE END OF THE "JEST"

IT is a common impression that impending disasters cast their shadows before; and especially in the realm of fiction do we find that much is made of presentiments, which are usually fulfilled in a very dramatic way. But the close observer of real life, to a large degree, loses faith in these bodings of ill. He learns that sombre impressions result more often from a defective digestion and a disquieted conscience than from any other cause; and that, after the gloomiest forebodings, the days pass in unusual serenity. Not that this is always true, but it would almost seem the rule. Perhaps more distress is caused by those troubles which never come, but which are feared and worried over, than by those which do come, teaching us, often, patience and faith.

Does not experience show that disasters and trials more often visit us, like the "thief in the night," unexpectedly?

At any rate, it so occurred to Hemstead and Lottie on the dreary Monday that followed their glorified Sunday. And yet, never did a day open with fairer promise. A cloudless sky bent over a crystal earth. The mystic peace of Christmas seemed to have been breathed even into bleak December; for the air was mild and still, and the shadow of many a slender tree crept across the snow as steadily as that made by the sun-dial on the lawn.

Within doors all appeared equally serene. The fire burned cheerily upon the hearth when Hemstead came down to breakfast. What was of far more importance, the light of love glowed as brightly in Lottie's eyes, as she beamed upon him across the table; and the spell which kept him, unthinking, unfearing, in the beatified present remained unbroken.

But the darkest shadows were creeping toward both.

To any situated as they were, and in their condition of mind and heart, a mere awakening would have been a rude shock. Some one had only to show them, with the remorseless logic of this world, what all their heavenly emotions involved, in order to cause perplexity and almost consternation. They could not long dwell, like the immortal gods, on the Mount Olympus of their exalted feeling, subsisting on the nectar and ambrosia of tones and glances.

Lottie was the fashionable daughter of an ultra-fashionable mother and a worldly father, in whose eyes sins against the *beau monde* were the most irrational and unpardonable.

Hemstead was a predestined home missionary, upon whom the Christian Church proposed to inflict the slow martyrdom of five or six hundred a year. Mrs. Marchmont but reflected the judgment of the world when she thought that for two young people, thus situated, to fall in love with each other, would be the greatest possible misfortune. Therefore, with the sincerest sense of duty, and the very best intentions, she set about preventing it, after all the mischief had been done.

Like a prudent lady, as she was, she first sought to get sufficient information to justify her in speaking plainly to both nephew and niece. For this purpose she drew Addie out on Sunday afternoon, asking her if she had noticed anything peculiar in the manner of Hemstead and Lottie toward each other. Then, for the first time, and with just indignation, to her credit be it said, she learned of the practical joke of which her nephew was to have been the victim. She skilfully drew from her daughter all the details of its inception and the mode in which it had been carried out; for, to Addie's superficial observation, Lottie was only indulging in one of her old flirtations. She neither saw, nor was she able to understand, the change in Lottie's feelings and character. She also wronged Lottie by giving the impression that she herself had had nothing to do with the plot, with the exception that she had promised not to interfere.

Mrs. Marchmont could scarcely believe what she heard, but Addie referred her to Bel, who confirmed her words and admitted that from the first she had "known it was very wrong, but had not believed that anything would come of it, until it seemed too late."

"Besides," she said, "Lottie told me that if I said a word, or interfered in any way, she would from that time treat me as a stranger, and she said it in a way that proved she meant it. Therefore, whatever you do, please let it appear that I have no part in it."

"You surprise and shock me greatly," said Mrs. Marchmont. "With all Lottie's wild nonsense and fondness for flirting, I would not have thought that she could be guilty of such deliberate and persistent effort to trifle with one so sincere and good as Frank. The most heartless coquette would scarcely call him fair game. She puzzles me too, for she does not seem like one who is acting, but more like one in earnest. Besides, look at the interest she is beginning to take in religion. She surely could not employ such sacred things for the purposes of mere flirtation."

But Bel soon converted Mrs. Marchmont to her way of thinking. Lottie had found Hemstead more interesting than she had expected, and had foolishly and recklessly permitted a mere sentiment for him to develop, which, in her case, would end with the visit, and soon be forgotten in the mad whirl of New York gayety. "But with Mr. Hemstead," concluded Bel, "it will be a very different affair. He is one of the kind that will brood over such a disappointment and wrong to the end of life."

So it was settled that Mrs. Marchmont should "speak plainly" to her nephew, and warn him against "Lottie's wiles," as soon as possible.

But no opportunity occurred before Monday morning, and then not until Hemstead had received some of the most blissful experiences that he had yet enjoyed. For, immediately after breakfast, all had flocked into the back parlor, where the laden Christmas tree revealed the secrets that had filled the air with mystery during the preceding days.

All had been remembered, and Mr. Martell's munificence toward the gallant coachman quite took away his breath.

But Hemstead was overwhelmed and troubled at first, when he opened an envelope, and found a check for a thousand dollars, with the words:

"We send you this, not in any sense as compensation—for we know enough of your character to recognize that you would have taken equal risks in behalf of the penniless—but because we wish to be remembered by you, whom we can never forget. And we only request that you invest this sum toward your library, so that, in coming years, the thoughts of your favorite authors may remind you of those whose best wishes, sincerest gratitude, and highest esteem will ever be yours.

"(Signed) HERBERT MARTELL, ALICE MARTELL."

"Now, Frank, what is the use of putting on such airs?" said Addie. "You surely expected a handsome present from Mr. Martell."

"I assure you, I expected nothing of the kind," he replied, a trifle indignantly. "Why should I? As it is, I am doubtful whether I ought to accept it."

"Why should I?" Lottie echoed with a merry laugh. "That's like you. But, unless you wish to hurt and wrong sincere friends very much, I advise you to keep it and do as they say. You are so exceedingly proud or humble—which shall I call it?—that I fear you neither expect, nor will take anything from me."

"Here is a queer-looking parcel for Frank Hemstead," said Mr. Dimmerly, with his chuckling laugh.

With intense delight Lottie saw the student hesitate, and his hand tremble as he slowly began to open it.

"It's not a torpedo, or an infernal machine, that you

need be in such trepidation," she whispered. "It won't go off."

"Is it from you?"

"Look and see."

It was a sermon holder, of rich, plain morocco without, but within, most elaborately embroidered. Most prominent among the rare and dainty devices was a single oar.

The expression of his face repaid her, as he examined it with a comical blending of reverence and affection, such as a devout Catholic would manifest toward a relic. In the blade of the oar were worked, with the most exquisite fineness, the words, "A True Knight." Within an inner pocket, where they could not be readily seen, were the words,

"With the thanks of Lottie Marsden."

But his quick scrutiny soon discovered them, and he turned and said, with an emphasis that did her good, "I value this more than the check."

"What folly!" she said, blushing with pleasure; "it isn't worth five dollars."

"I can prove that it is worth more than the check," he said, in a low tone.

"How?"

"We value that gift most which we receive from the friend we value most. There; it is proved in a sentence; but I can prove it over again."

"What delightful lessons in logic! But you surely cannot prove it again."

"Yes. If the gift from the friend we value most contains evidence that thought and time have been expended upon it, that gift, however slight its market value, has a worth to us beyond price, because showing that the friend we love supremely thinks of us in our absence."

"I did put a great deal of time and thought in that little gift, but you have repaid me," Lottie answered.

Their brief but significant tête-à-tête was now interrupted by De Forrest, who came forward to thank Lottie for her costly gift to him—a gift bought on Broadway. He had uneasily marked the fact that she had given something to Hemstead, but when he saw that it was only a sermon-cover, he was quite relieved.

"Come here, Frank, and show me your present," said Mr. Dimmerly, a little later.

Hemstead good-naturedly complied, and the old gentleman looked at the single embroidered oar, with a comical twinkle in his eye, and called again, "Lottie, come here."

She approached rather shyly and reluctantly, not knowing what to expect.

"Now, Lottie," said her uncle, reproachfully, pointing to the oar, "I did not expect that from so sensible a girl as you are. What is a man going to do with *one* oar, unless he is to take a lonely scull through life as I have? Did you mean to suggest that to Mr. Hemstead?"

"Mr. Hemstead found out another meaning than that," she said, laughing, "and I'm not going to stay here to be teased by you;" and she ran out of the room, the picture of blushing happiness.

When Hemstead again saw her it was with a great dread in his heart, and his tones were grave and almost stern.

"O—h—h, you found out another meaning, did you?" said Mr. Dimmerly, looking both kindly and quizzically over his spectacles at his nephew.

"Well, uncle, to tell you the truth I hardly understand myself. My visit here is a great contrast to my quiet seminary life, and I have been getting deeper and deeper into a maze of happy bewilderment every day. So much has happened, and I am so changed, that, like many in tales of enchantment, I scarcely know whether I am myself."

"I have seen the spell working," said Mr. Dimmerly, dryly, "and am thankful that the transformation has not been of the nature that Shakespeare portrayed in his Midsummer Night Fantasy. Your head might have become turned by the wrong girl, and you have reached the period when it is bound to be turned by some one."

"Uncle," he said, fervently, "she is the noblest and most beautiful being in existence."

"Frank, I wish to see you," said his aunt, quietly; and he followed her to her own private sitting-room.

Mr. Dimmerly indulged in his chuckling laugh as he looked after them.

"Now she's going to 'stop' it, he—he— In the meantime I'll go out and stop the brook from running down hill."

"The time has come," said Mrs. Marchmont to her perplexed nephew, with the complacent superiority with which the wise of this world enlighten those whose "heads are often in the clouds"—"the time has come when I must speak plainly to you of a matter as important as it is delicate. You are my own sister's child, and I cannot see you wronged or going blindly into trouble without warning you. Are you not permitting yourself to become interested in Miss Marsden to a degree that is not wise?"

"Why not wise?" he answered with burning cheeks.

"Have you not realized that she is one of the most fashionable young ladies in New York, and belongs to one of the wealthiest and most fashionable families? If you could but once see her mother you would understand me."

"But she herself has changed," he urged, eagerly.

Mrs. Marchmont smiled incredulously and pityingly. "How little you know the world!" she said. "In what do you expect all your sentiment to end? Only sentiment? You say you purpose being a home missionary. Can you imagine for a moment that one situated as she is would contemplate such a life? Her parents would as soon bury her."

Hemstead groaned under his aunt's remorseless words, but said in a sort of blind desperation: "Her parents! Is this Hindostan, that parents can treat their daughters as merchandise? A girl of Miss Marsden's force and nobility of character—"

"Oh, Frank, hush! It absolutely makes me sick to see

one so easily deceived. 'Nobility of character,' indeed! Well, I didn't wish to speak of it. I could not believe it even of Lottie, but nothing less than the whole truth will convince you;" and she told him of the plot in which Lottie purposed to make him the ridiculous subject of a practical joke, and intimated that all her action since had been but the carrying out of that plot.

At first Hemstead grew deathly pale, and his aunt, thinking he was going to faint, began fumbling for her salts. But a moment later the blood suffused even his neck and brow, and he said passionately, "I don't believe a word of this; Miss Marsden is not capable of such falsehood."

"Whether in your unreasoning passion you will believe it or not makes no difference," said Mrs. Marchmont, quietly. "It is true, as I can prove by Addie and Miss Parton."

He took a few hasty strides up and down the room and muttered, "I will take her word against all the world. She shall answer for herself"; and he rang the bell.

When the servant appeared he said, "Please ask Miss Marsden to come here at once."

Mrs. Marchmont regretted Hemstead's action very much, but it was too firm and decided to be prevented. She had planned that after his "eyes had been opened to his folly," and Lottie's frivolity, to say the least, her nephew would, with quiet dignity, cease his attentions, and perhaps shorten his visit. She had a horror of scenes, but feared that one was coming now.

Hemstead admitted Lottie with a silent bow and gave her a chair.

When she saw his grave, pale face, her heart misgave her strangely, and she trembled so that even he noticed it, and also another fact—she did not meet his eyes. He fastened his upon her, as if he would read her soul, for he now felt that more than life was at stake.

"Miss Marsden," he said, in a low, deep tone, "my aunt has made a strange charge against you, but I said to her,

and I now say to you, that I will take your word against all
the world. She asserts, and she gives the names of her witnesses, that your action—your kindness toward me from the
first—has been but the carrying out of a deliberate and
heartless jest. Is it true?"

Lottie's wonted quickness failed her. She had been so
happy, she had seemed to have got so far beyond her old,
false self, and so established in his affection, that such a
reverse did not appear possible. But the evil that at one
time she had feared had now come in a form so unexpected
and serious that, for a moment, she was stunned and bewildered, and fell into helpless confusion. The nature of the
case aggravated her distress. How could she explain?
What could she say? In response to his question she only
trembled more violently and buried her burning face in her
hands.

He saw in this action confirmation of fears that he at first
would scarcely entertain, and regarded her a moment with a
strange expression upon his face—anger and pity blended—
and then silently left the room.

The sleigh stood at the door, and the coachman was just
starting on an errand to Newburgh.

Mr. Dimmerly looked with surprise at his nephew's pale
face—a surprise that was greatly increased as the young
man seized his hat and coat, and said in a husky tone, "I
am going to New York for some days," and sprang into the
sleigh and was driven away.

"Well," said the old man, testily, "if she 'stopped' him
as easily as that, he deserves to lose her."

And Mrs. Marchmont, seeing Hemstead depart so silently, congratulated herself that she had escaped a scene
after all, and complacently thought, "These things can be
'stopped' if taken in time, notwithstanding brother's sentimental nonsense."

As poor Lottie's mind emerged from its chaos into connected thought, she speedily came to the conclusion to tell
Hemstead the whole truth, to condemn herself more

severely than even he could in his anger, and to ask his for-giveness.

But when she raised her tearful face to speak, he was gone.

She heard the sound of bells. A sudden fear chilled her, and she sprang to the window and saw a vanishing form that she dreaded might be his. Without a word to Mrs. Marchmont, she rushed down to the lower hall, where she found Mr. Dimmerly fuming about.

"Where is Mr. Hemstead?" she asked, eagerly.

"What the deuce is the matter? What have you and sister been saying that Frank should come down here white as a sheet?"

"But where is he?" she asked again, in a tone that her uncle had never heard her use before.

"Gone to New York for several days," he said.

Lottie tottered a moment as if she had received a blow. With one hand she steadied herself on the balustrade of the stairs, while she passed the other across her brow, then turned and wearily climbed to her room.

CHAPTER XXXIV

LOYAL

BEL was startled at the pallor of Lottie's face as she entered the room, and rose hastily to offer assistance, but Lottie motioned her away. Without a word she threw herself upon the bed and signified her grief and despair by an act as old as the oldest records of humanity —she "turned her face to the wall."

Bel knew that Mrs. Marchmont had "spoken plainly," and she had seen Hemstead drive away. She expected Lottie to come to her room in a towering passion, and was prepared to weather the storm in cynical endurance, assured that her friend would eventually thank her for having had a hand in breaking up the "whole absurd thing."

But when Lottie entered, with the expression of one who had received a mortal wound—when in silence and despair she had turned her face from all the world as if there were nothing left in it for which she cared—the nervous young lady began to fear that this affair might not pass away like an ordinary "mood."

She reasoned and remonstrated, but Lottie did not heed, and scarcely neard her. Then she went to Mrs. Marchmont, and disturbed even that lady's complacency by her account of Lottie's appearance and manner. But with approving consciences they both said, "It was time something was done."

The dinner hour came, but Lottie silently shook her head to all urging to come down. It was the same at supper. Entreaty, remonstrance, the assumption of hurt and injured tones, were alike unavailing. She lay motionless, like one stunned and under partial paralysis.

Mrs. Marchmont lost her complacency utterly, and Mr. Dimmerly proved but a Job's comforter, as he snarled, "You have stopped it with a vengeance. It's always the way when people meddle."

Nervous Bel was in a perfect tremor of anxiety, perplexity, and weak remorse; and she kept flitting in and out of the room as pale and restless as a disquieted ghost.

De Forrest thought he ought to be "chief mourner," but no one seemed to pay much attention to him.

As for Lottie, one ever-present thought seemed scorching her brain and withering heart and hope.

"He thinks me false—false in everything—false in every glance and word to him—false even when I spoke of sacred things; and he will despise me forever."

Little wonder that she was so drearily apathetic to all that could be said or done to rouse her. The fall from the pinnacle of her religious hope and earthly happiness was too far and great to permit speedy recovery.

At last she rose, and mechanically disrobed for the night: but no sleep blessed her eyes, for, on every side, she saw, in flaming letters, the word *false*. With increasing vividness her fancy portrayed a pale, stern, averted face.

The next morning she was really ill, and her aunt, in alarm, was about sending for the physician, but Lottie prevented her by saying, somewhat coldly, "What drug has the doctor for my trouble? If you really wish me to get better, give Bel another room, and leave me to myself. I must fight this battle out alone."

"Now, Lottie, how can you take a little thing so greatly to heart?"

"Is it a little thing that the one whom I most honor and respect in all the world regards me as a false coquette?"

"You surely cannot apply such language to my nephew?"

"I do; and on the best grounds. If I am young, I am somewhat capable of judging. He is not the first man I have seen. You do not know, and have never appreciated Mr. Hemstead.''

"But, Lottie, compare your station and prospects with his.''

"There is scarcely any one with whom I would not exchange prospects. I am sick of society's artificial distinctions, in which true worth and manhood—all that Heaven cares for—count for nothing. What does Mr. Hemstead care about my wealth, name, and position in New York? He looks at *me;* and you, or, rather, my own senseless folly, have made me appear a weak, false thing, that, from the very laws of his being, he cannot help despising. But it was cruelly hard in you and Bel, when you saw that I was trying to be a different—a better girl, to show him only what I was, and give me no chance to explain. He will never trust—never even look at me again.'' And, for the first time, the unhappy girl burst into a passion of tears and sobbed so long and violently that Mrs. Marchmont had a distressing consciousness that her worldly wisdom was not equal to this case at all. She would have telegraphed Hemstead to return, if she had known where to address him. She was often tempted to write to Lottie's mother, but dreaded the reproaches of Mrs. Marsden for permitting matters to reach such a crisis before "stopping" them. And so, in anxiety and perplexity, the day dragged slowly on, until at last, Lottie, wearied out, fell into the heavy sleep of utter exhaustion, from which she did not wake till the following morning.

But the respite from that most depressing of all suffering, mental trouble, had given her a chance, and her healthful nature began to recover.

She was a girl of too much force and character to succumb long to any misfortune; and, as she said to her aunt, she meant to fight this battle out to some kind of solution.

To the surprise of every one, she appeared at the breakfast table, very pale, but quiet, and perfectly self-possessed. Her bearing, however, had a dignity and a decision which would make even Mrs. Marchmont hesitate before she "meddled" again. De Forrest was half afraid of her, and began to realize that she was not the girl he had brought to the country but a few weeks since.

After breakfast, she dismissed Bel by saying plainly that she wished to be alone, and then sat down, and, for the first time, tried to clearly understand the situation. It grew more and more evident how desperately against her were appearances. She had been false at first, and, in a certain sense, must appear false to the last, in that she had not told him the truth. Besides, just when and how she had become in earnest she could not remember. The poor girl was greatly discouraged, and again gave way to tears, as if her heart would break.

But in the midst of her sore trouble, like a flash of genial light came the thought, "If Mr. Hemstead will never look at me again, there is One who will"; and she sprang up, and, having found a Bible, turned again to its shortest text, remembering, with a quick sob, how she had first discovered it. With almost the distinctness and reality of actual presence, there rose up before her mind One who, with bowed head, wept with men for men. Every tear of sympathy appeared to fall on her bruised heart; and hope, that she believed dead, began to revive. She just clung to one simple thought: "He feels sorry for me"; and it comforted her.

Then she began to turn the leaves back and forth to find places where Jesus showed kindness and forgave, and she soon found that this was His life—His work in which He never wearied—kindness to all, forgiveness for all. Then the thought stole into her heart, like the dove bringing the "olive leaf" from across a dreary waste, "If Mr. Hemstead is like his Master he will forgive me." Hope now grew strong and steadily, and the impulsive, demonstrative girl kissed the little Book, pressed it to her heart, and caressed it as if it were a thing of life.

She got out her portfolio and wrote:

"Mr. Hemstead, I sincerely ask your forgiveness for my folly, which you cannot condemn as severely as I do. Though unworthy, indeed, of your friendship and esteem, can you believe that I am not *now* the weak, wicked creature that I was when we first met? But I have not the courage to plead my own cause. I know that both facts and appearances are against me. I can only ask you, Who told His disciples to forgive each other, 'seventy times seven?'   Yours, in sorrow and regret,

"LOTTIE MARSDEN."

"I have now done the best I can," she said. "The issue is in God's hands."

At the dinner-table she again perplexed the mystified household. They, in their narrow worldliness, had no key to such a problem as Lottie Marsden had become. She was gentleness itself. The mystic tears falling from Divine eyes had melted away all coldness and hardness, and the touch of her words and manner, if we may so speak, had in it a kindliness and a regard for others to which even the most callous respond. Patient self-forgetfulness is the most God-like and the most winning of all the graces.

After dinner, Mr. Dimmerly shuffled away by himself, with a sound between a sniffle and his old chuckle, muttering, "I don't believe it's 'stopped,' after all. Anyway, I wish she were going to be a home missionary in my home."

Lottie went with Dan again to the pond, and then to the "fallen tree"; but she found no other tryst there than memories, that, in view of what had happened, were very painful.

After her return she no longer shunned the others, but sat down and talked quietly with them, as multitudes of men and women are doing daily, giving no sign that in the meantime they are patiently watching at the sepulchre of a buried hope, which may, or may not, rise again.

As with Lottie at first, so with Hemstead, the word *false* seemed to have the malignant power to quench hope and happiness. If it is faith that saves, it would seem that it is its opposite—distrust—that most quickly destroys. In no way can we deal more fatal and ruinous blows than to deceive those who trust us.

And Hemstead felt, at first, that he had been deceived and trifled with in all that was sacred. For hours both faith and reason reeled in passion, that grew and raged in the strong man's breast like a tropical storm. He plunged into the streets, crowded with his unknowing, uncaring fellow-creatures, as he would lose himself in the depths of a lonely forest, and walked hour after hour, he knew not and cared not whither.

Two thoughts pursued him like goading phantoms—she was false—he was deceived.

At last, when the frenzy left him, weak and exhausted, he found himself near a large hotel, and he went in and slept almost as the dead sleep.

In his case also sleep proved "nature's sweet restorer." In the morning faith and reason sat together on their throne, and he recognized his duty to act the part of a man and a Christian, whatever the truth might be.

He sat down at last and calmly tried to disentangle the web. Second thoughts brought wiser judgment, for, after going over every day and hour of his acquaintance with Lottie, he could scarcely resist the conclusion that if she had begun in falsehood she was ending in truth. If she, in all her words and manner, had been only acting, he could never trust his senses again, or be able to distinguish between the hollow and the real.

Hour after hour he sat and thought. He held a solemn assize within his own breast, and marshalled all he could remember as witnesses for and against her. Much in her conduct that at first had puzzled him now grew clear in view of her purpose to victimize him, and, even as late as Christmas eve, he remembered how her use of the word "comedy" had jarred unpleasantly upon his ear. But on the other hand there seemed even more conclusive evidence that she had gradually grown sincere, and come to mean all she said and did. Could the color that came and went like light from an inner flame—could tears that seemed to come more from her heart than from her eyes—could words that

had sounded so true and womanly, and that had often dwelt
on the most sacred themes, be only simulated?

"If so," he groaned, "then there are only two in the
wide universe that I can ever trust—God and mother."

Moreover, in her trial, Lottie had an eloquent advocate
to whom even deliberate reason appeared only too ready to
lend an attentive ear—the student's heart.

Therefore she finally received a better vindication than
the Scotch verdict "not proven," and the young man began
to condemn himself bitterly for having left so hastily, and
before Lottie had time to explain and defend herself.

His first impulse was to go back at once and give her
another hearing. But, almost before he was aware, he found
a new culprit brought to the bar for judgment—himself.

If the trial, just completed, had failed to prove Lottie's
guilt, it had most conclusively shown him his love. He
saw how it had developed while he was blind to its existence. He saw that his wild agony of the preceding day
was not over falsehood and deception in the abstract, but
over the supposed falsehood of a woman whom he had come
to love as his own soul. And even now he was exulting in
the hope that she might have passed, as unconsciously as
himself, into like sweet thraldom. In the belief of her
truthfulness, how else could he interpret her glances, tones,
actions, and even plainly spoken words?

But the flame of hope, that had burned higher and
brighter, gradually sank again as he recalled his aunt's
words, "How is all this sentiment to end?—in only sentiment?"

He remembered his chosen calling. Could he ask this
child of luxury to go with him to the far West and share
his life of toilsome privation? He had long felt that the
work of a missionary was his vocation. She had never had
any such feeling. He recalled her words, spoken but yesterday, it seemed: "Do you imagine that any nice girl will
go out with you among the border ruffians?"

That is the way it appeared to her then. If such a thing

were possible, that she had become attached to him, would it not be an unfair and almost a mean thing to take advantage of her affection, and, by means of it, commit her to a life for which she was unfitted, and which might become almost a martyrdom? The change from her luxurious home to frontier-life would be too great. If she had felt called of God to such a work—if she had laid herself as a sacrifice upon the Divine Altar, that would be very different, for the Master would give no task without imparting strength and patience for its fulfilment. Besides, He had Heaven to give in return.

But Frank Hemstead's unselfish manhood told him plainly that he had no right to ask any such sacrifice.

Incidentally, Lottie had mentioned the number of her residence, and he hastily went up Fifth Avenue, and saw her palace of a home. Every stone in the stately abode seemed part of the barrier between them.

An elegant carriage with liveried coachman and footman came around to the entrance, and a lady who had Lottie's features, except that they had grown rigid with pride and age, entered it, and was driven away. As he saw her stately bearing, and the pomp and show of her life, he could almost believe his aunt—that this proud woman of the world would rather bury the daughter of whom she expected so much than marry her to an obscure home missionary.

His heart grew heavy as lead, and he groaned, "Even if she loves me I have lost her."

Then came the supreme temptation of his life. Why must he be a home missionary? Who was there to compel such a sacrifice of himself? He might come to this city, and win a place as high as hers, as many poorer and more friendless than himself had done. He might even seek some well-situated Eastern church. He might aim to be one of the great popular preachers of the day; and so be able to come to the door of that proud home and ask what it would be no condescension to grant.

Again he was out in the storm; again he was in the thick

of the battle;—passionate longings and love on one hand;
stern, steady conscience on the other.   In painful preoccu-
pation he again walked unknown distances.   His aimless
steps took him away from the mansions of the rich down
among the abodes of the poor.   As he was crossing a street
his troubled eyes rested upon a plain cross over a lowly
chapel door.   He stopped before it like a superstitious Ro-
manist—not reverencing the emblem, however, but in vivid
remembrance of Him who suffered thereon.   He recalled
His self-sacrifice and His words, "Whosoever doth not bear
his cross and come after me, cannot be my disciple."

He bowed his head a moment, then turned quietly, and
went back to his hotel.

The conflict was over—the temptation passed—and he
was *loyal.*

CHAPTER XXXV

MR. DIMMERLY CONCLUDES TO "MEDDLE"

HEMSTEAD found some solace, during the next two days, in the selection of books for his library. He did not expect to visit the East again for many years, and made all his arrangements accordingly. He wrote Mr. and Miss Martell a letter, which they regarded as a model in its expression of delicate appreciation and manly modesty.

Toward the end of the week he returned to Mrs. Marchmont's, by no means sure whether he would find Lottie there or not, and quite certain that the less he saw of her the better.

He walked from the depot, and went around by the way of the pond. His resolution almost failed him, as he looked at the "fallen tree," especially as he believed he saw evidence, from traces in the snow, that Lottie had visited the place in his absence.

Lottie looked forward with a strange blending of hope and fear to the meeting with him, and had portrayed to herself every possible way in which she imagined it could take place. But it happened, as such things usually do, after the most prosaic fashion possible. They were all sitting in the parlor, after dinner, and Hemstead opened the door and walked in.

Her face became scarlet, but his was so pale as to remind her of the time when he had carried Miss Martell into that room. It was, indeed, the pallor of one who was making a desperate moral effort. But he was successful, and spoke to her, giving his hand, in almost the same manner as to his aunt. His bearing toward even De Forrest was most courteous. He then sat down composedly, and began to talk on ordinary topics.

Lottie's heart failed her. This was entirely different from what she had expected. His manner was not in the least cold or resentful, but his words seemed to come from a great distance, and his eyes no longer sought her face, as if she only had for him the true sunlight. Their old, quick, subtile interchange of sympathy and thought appeared lost as completely as if a thick wall rose between them. The warm-hearted girl could not act his part. She was silent, and her head bent low over her work.

Mrs. Marchmont and Bel were greatly pleased, and gave Hemstead credit for being a "very sensible young man, who, having been shown his folly, could act like a gentleman and not make a fuss."

Even De Forrest looked at the student approvingly, especially as he had been to a city tailor and was clothed in taste and harmony with his manly proportions. No amount of grace and virtue could find recognition in De Forrest's eyes, unless dressed in the latest mode.

Mr. Dimmerly, from behind his newspaper, stared for a long time at Lottie and his nephew, and then snarled abruptly: "It's getting deuced cold. The brook will stop running down hill to-night, I'm a-thinking—freeze up"; and he stirred the fire as if he had a spite against it.

Lottie's head bent lower. She was beginning to understand her crotchety uncle. She, too, thought that it was getting very "cold."

After a while Hemstead quietly left them, went to his room, and did not appear again till they were all at supper. He then, with a simple, yet quiet, high-bred ease—the bearing of a natural gentleman—gave sketches of what he had seen in New York, and the latest literary gossip. His manner toward Lottie was, as nearly as possible, the same as toward Bel and his cousin. He so completely ignored

all that had happened—all that had passed between them—
that Lottie almost feared to give him the note she had
written. She could not rally, but grew more and more depressed and silent, a fact which De Forrest and her aunt
marked uneasily.

After supper he remarked that he would go over and say
good-by to Mr. and Miss Martell and Harcourt.

With what a foreboding chill Lottie heard that word
"good-by!" Would he, indeed, go away without giving
her a chance to say one word of explanation? She could
endure it no longer. In accordance with her impulsive
nature, she went straight to him, and said in a low tone,
"Mr. Hemstead, will you please read that?"

He trembled, but took the note, and said, after a moment,
"Certainly," and was gone.

An hour passed, and another; still he did not return.
Lottie's head bent lower and lower over her work. Mr.
Dimmerly never played a more wretched game of whist.
At last he quite startled them all by throwing down the
cards and saying, in the most snappish of tones, "I wish
the blockhead would come home."

"Why, brother, what is the matter?" asked Mrs. Marchmont, in a tone of surprise.

"I want to lock up," said the old gentleman, in some
confusion.

"It's not late, yet."

"Well, it ought to be. I never knew such an eternally
long evening. The clocks are all wrong, and everything is
wrong."

"There, there, you have had bad luck over your
whist."

Lottie, however, knew what was the matter, and she gave
him a shy, grateful look. But the old man was still more
incensed when he saw that there were tears in her eyes, and
he shuffled away, muttering something that sounded a little
profane.

Lottie, soon after, left the room also, but as she was

passing through the hall she met Hemstead, who had come in at a side door. He took her hand in both of his, and said, gently, "I do forgive you, fully and completely, and I have your forgiveness to ask for my hasty judgment."

"And will you be my friend again?" she asked, timidly, and in a way that taxed his resolution sorely.

"You have no truer friend," he said, after a moment.

"I think it was a little cruel, in so true a friend, to leave me all this desperately long evening."

"You are mistaken," he said, abruptly, and passed hastily up to his room. She did not see him again that night.

What could he mean? Had he recognized her love, and, not being able to return it fully, did he thus avoid her and hasten through his visit? The bare thought crimsoned her cheek. But she felt that this could not be true. She knew he had loved her, and he could not have changed so soon. It was more probable that he believed her to be totally unfit to share in his sacred work—that he feared she would be a hindrance—and, therefore, he was shunning, and seeking to escape from one who might dim the lustre of his spiritual life and work. In some respects she had grown very humble of late, and feared that he might be correct, and that she was indeed utterly unfit to share in his high calling.

"But if he only knew how hard I would try!" she said, with a touch of pathos in her tone which would have settled matters if he had heard it.

That he was sacrificing himself rather than ask her to share in his life's privation, did not occur to her.

Restless and unhappy, she wandered into the dining-room, where she found Mr. Dimmerly standing on the hearth-rug, and staring at the fire in a fit of the deepest abstraction. Lottie was so depressed as to feel that even a little comfort from him would be welcome; so she stole to his side and took his arm. He stroked her head with a gentleness quite unusual with him. Finally he said, in a voice that he meant to be very harsh and matter of fact,

"Hasn't that nephew of mine got home yet? I feel as if I could break his head."

"And I feel," said Lottie, hiding her face on his shoulder, "as if he would break my heart, and you are the only one in the house who understands me or cares."

"Well, well," said the old gentleman, after a little, "others have been meddling; I think I will meddle a little."

Lottie started up in a way that surprised him, and with eyes flashing through her tears said, "Not a word to him, as you value my love."

"Hold on," said the little man, half breathlessly. "What's the matter? You go off like a keg of powder."

"I wouldn't sue for the hand of a king," said Lottie, heroically.

"Bless you, child, he isn't a king. He's only Frank Hemstead, my nephew—bound to be a forlorn home missionary, he says."

"Well, then," she said, drawing a long breath, "if he can't see for himself, let him marry a pious Western giantess, who will go with him for the sake of the cause instead of himself."

"In the meantime," suggested Mr. Dimmerly, "we will go back to New York and have a good time as before."

This speech brought to the warm-hearted girl another revulsion of feeling, and, again hiding her face on her uncle's shoulder, she sobbed, "I would rather be his slave on a desert island than marry the richest man in New York."

"And my wise and prudent sister thought it could be 'stopped,' " chuckled Mr. Dimmerly.

"But remember, uncle, not a word of this to him, or I will refuse him though my heart break a thousand times. If he does not love me well enough to ask me of his own accord, or if he does not think I am fit to go with him, I would rather die than thrust myself upon him."

"Bless me, what a queer compound a woman is! It won't do for you to go West. You will set the prairies on fire. There, there, now don't be afraid. If you think I can say anything to my nephew—the thick-headed blunderbuss—which will prevent his getting down on his knees to ask for what he'll never deserve, you don't know the Dimmerly blood. Trust to the wisdom of my gray hairs and go to bed."

"But, uncle, I would rather you wouldn't say anything at all," persisted Lottie.

"Well, I won't, about you," said her uncle, in assumed irritability. "I can get the big ostrich to pull his head out of the sand and speak for himself, I suppose. He's my nephew, and I'm going to have a talk with him before he leaves for the West. So be off; I'm getting cross."

But Lottie gave him a kiss that stirred even his withered old heart.

"Oh, good gracious!" he groaned after she was gone, "why was I ever 'stopped'?"

The next morning Hemstead appeared at breakfast as calm, pale, and resolute as ever. His manner seemed to say plainly to Lottie, "Our old folly is at an end. I have remembered the nature of my calling, and I know only too well that you are unfitted to share in it."

She was all the more desponding as she remembered how conscientious he was.

"If he thinks it's wrong, there's no hope," she thought, drearily.

After breakfast, Mr. Dimmerly said, "Nephew, I wish you would do a little writing for me; my hand isn't as steady as it was"; and he took the student off to his private study.

After the writing was finished, Mr. Dimmerly gave a few awkward preliminary ahems, and then said, "So you go West next Monday?"

"Yes. I wish to get off on the first train."

"You seem very anxious to get away."

"I am sorry, now, I ever came," the young man said, in tones of the deepest sadness.

"Thank you."

"Oh, it's no fault of yours. You and aunt have been very kind, but—"

"But you are thinking of the 'noblest and most beautiful being in existence,' as you once said, referring to my pretty little niece. You have evidently changed your mind. Did you see some one in New York you liked better?"

"I have not changed my mind. I have only learned too well what my mind is. I wish that I had learned it sooner. There is one thing that troubles me greatly, uncle. I cannot speak of it to aunt, because— Well, I can't. Do you think that Miss Marsden cares much for me? She will surely forget me, will she not, in the excitement of her city life? I do hope she has no such feeling as I have."

Mr. Dimmerly stared at his nephew as if he thought him demented.

"Well," said he, "I think you have been 'enchanted, and are no longer yourself.' You now out-Bottom old Bottom himself. Do you mean to say that you love such a gem of a girl as Lottie, and yet hope she does not love you, and will soon forget you?"

"Certainly I do. If I had my will, she would not have another unhappy hour in her life."

"Well, if you have the faintest notion that she has any regard for you, why don't you get down on your marrow-bones and plead for a chance to make her happy? If I were in your place, and there was half a chance to win a Lottie Marsden, I would sigh like a dozen furnaces, and swear more oaths than were heard in Flanders, if it would help matters along any."

"But would you ask her to leave a home of luxury, her kindred, and every surrounding of culture and refinement, to go out on a rude frontier and to share in the sternest poverty and the most wearing of work?"

"O-h-h, that is the hitch, is it?"

"Yes. Before I was aware, I had learned to love her. I trust she will never know how deeply; for if she had half a woman's heart, she would be sad from very pity. If, unconsciously to herself, some regard for me has grown during our visit, it would be a mean and unmanly thing to take advantage of it to inveigle her into a life that would be a painful contrast to all that she had known before. It would be like a soldier asking a woman to share all the hardships and dangers of a campaign.''

Mr. Dimmerly stroked his chin thoughtfully, while he regarded his nephew with a shrewd, sidelong glance. ''Well,'' said he, suggestively, ''there is force in what you say. But is there any necessity of your being a home missionary, and living out among the 'border ruffians,' as Lottie used to call them? There are plenty of churches at the East. Dr. Beams is old and sick: there may be a vacancy here before long.''

''No, uncle,'' said Hemstead, firmly, ''I fought that fight out in New York, and it was a hard one. I have felt for years that I must be a missionary, and shall be true to my vocation. It's *duty;*'' and he brought his clinched hand down heavily on the table.

''My good gracious!'' ejaculated Mr. Dimmerly, giving a nervous hop in the air. ''Between the two, what will become of me? Yes, yes; I see. You are like your mother. If she took it into her head that anything was 'duty,' all the world couldn't change her. So, rather than give up being a missionary, you will sacrifice yourself and Lottie too?''

''I should have no hesitation in making the sacrifice myself, but it would more than double my pain if I knew she suffered. And it is this that troubles me. But I must obey my orders, whatever happens.''

''Well,'' said Mr. Dimmerly, dryly, and with a queer little twinkle in his eyes, ''I cannot give you much aid and comfort. I never meddle in such matters. A third party never can. Of course you can sacrifice yourself and your own happiness if you choose. That is your own affair. But when it comes to sacrificing another, that is very different. Lottie is a warm-hearted girl with all her faults, and *if* she ever does love, it will be no half-way business with her. So be careful what you do. Sacrificing her happiness is a very different thing from sacrificing your own."

"But do you think there is any danger of such a thing?" asked Hemstead, in a tone of the deepest distress.

"Bless me, boy! how should I know?" said his uncle, in seeming irritability. "Do you think that I am a go-between for you two? Why don't you go and ask her, like a man? How do you know but she has a vocation to be a missionary as well as yourself?"

Hemstead strode up and down the room, the picture of perplexity. "Was ever a man placed in so cruel a position?" he groaned. But after a moment he became quiet and said, "When a thing is settled, let it stay settled; my course is the only right and manly one;" and he left the room saying he would be out for a walk till dinner.

But as he entered the hall Addie cried, "Frank, you must go; we won't take no for an answer."

"Go where?"

"To West Point. It's a glorious day. We want one more sleigh-ride before we break up—one that shall exceed all the others. There is going to be a cadet hop over there this afternoon, in the dancing-hall, and a friend has sent for us to come. I've set my heart on going, and so have Bel and Lottie. Mother says that we can go, if you will go with us and drive, for the coachman is ill. You will see lots of grand scenery, and all that kind of thing, which you like so much."

"And have you set your heart on the 'cadet hop' also?" asked Hemstead of Lottie.

"I think I should appreciate scenery more at present," she said, with a quick blush.

"You'll go; say you'll go. He'll go, mother. It's all settled. Let us have some lunch, and we'll start at once;" and the spoiled little beauty already anticipated the conquest of a cadet or two as a holiday episode.

So, in a single breezy moment, it was arranged, Hemstead scarcely having a voice in the matter. As he mounted to his room, reason told him that this long drive in the society of the one whom he believed he should avoid, for her sake as well as his own, was anything but wise. But he tried to satisfy himself with the thought that at no time would he be alone with her; and his heart craved this one more day of companionship, before a lifetime of separation.

As Lottie was about to ascend the stairs, she heard, for the first time since that wretched Monday, Mr. Dimmerly's odd, chuckling laugh. She looked into the parlor, and, seeing that he was alone, went straight to him, and said, "Now! what do you mean by that queer little laugh of yours?"

"Why do you think I mean anything?" he said, staring at the ceiling.

"Because I haven't heard it since that dreadful Monday, and before I always heard it when something nice had happened between me and—and—"

"Some one told me last night to mind my own business."

"Now, uncle, you know something."

"I should hope so, at my years—enough not to meddle." And he still stared high over her head.

"There," said Lottie with tears in her eyes, "everybody in the house is against me now."

The old man's eyes dropped to her flushed, disappointed face, and his features became almost noble in their expression of tender sympathy. In a grave, gentle tone, such as she never had heard him use before, he said, "Lottie, come to my private study, before you go."

While the others were at lunch, she glided, unseen, to the little study, that she might receive some comfort to sustain her fainting heart. Her uncle's first words, however, seemed prosaic, indeed, and very different from what she had expected.

"How old are you, Lottie?"

"I was twenty-one last June," she said, a little proudly.

"So you are a June blossom, eh? Well, you look like

it." But he puzzled her by his long, searching glance into her face.

"Why do you ask?" she said.

"I want to be sure that you are old and mature enough to decide a very important question."

"Well," said Lottie, her breath coming quick, "I intend to decide all questions which relate to my own life and well-being."

"Be careful, young woman. You had better follow the advice of old and wise heads like your aunt's and mother's."

"Uncle, what do you mean?" said she, impatiently.

"Well," said Mr. Dimmerly, deliberately, looking searchingly into her face all the time, "I have sounded that thickheaded nephew of mine—there, you needn't start so: do you suppose a Dimmerly would betray a woman's secret?—and what do you think he most dreads to discover as true? —that you love him a little."

"It's something he never shall discover," said Lottie, almost harshly, springing up with flashing eyes and scarlet face. "I will not go on this ride, and he shall have no trouble in escaping my society."

"Hold on, now," expostulated Mr. Dimmerly. "Nitroglycerine doesn't go off half so quick as you of late. I haven't told you why he is afraid you love him."

"What other reason can he have save that he doesn't love me, or thinks I am unfit to be a clergyman's wife?"

"He has another reason—one that will devolve upon you the necessity of deciding some very important questions. Are you old and mature enough?"

"Oh, uncle!" exclaimed Lottie, impatiently tapping the floor with her foot. "You ought to be made Grand Inquisitor General. You have kept me upon the rack of suspense —it seems an hour."

"Hold on, little firebrand. Questions concerning a lifetime should not be decided in a moment. You had better take a few years—certainly, a few months—to think over what I am going to tell you. Frank worships the ground you tread on. He does not give you the little remnant of a heart that has been left after dozens of flirtations with other girls. You have the whole of his big, unworldly heart, and from what I know of him, or, rather, his mother, you always will; but he is so unselfish—so unlike the rest of us —that he won't ask you to exchange your life of wealth and luxury for his life of toil, poverty, and comparative exile. So, while I believe he will idolize your memory all his days, he is hoping that you won't suffer any, but will soon be able to forget him. Of course I feigned profound ignorance as to your feelings, and left him in a pitiable state of distress. But he finally concluded that, even if you did love him a little, it would be very unmanly to take advantage of your feelings to get you into the awful scrape of a home missionary's life.''

As Mr. Dimmerly proceeded in this last speech, joy came into Lottie's face like the dawn of a June morning. Tears gathered slowly in her eyes, but their source was happiness, not sorrow. By the time he concluded, she had buried her burning face in her hands.

"Well," said her uncle, after a moment, "what's to be done I hardly know. He is just like his mother. If he thinks it isn't right to speak, tortures could not wring a word out of him. I don't see but you will have to propose yourself—"

" 'Propose myself'! Never," said she, springing to her feet.

"What will you do, then?—sit and look at each other, and fade away like two dying swans?"

"No, indeed," said Lottie, dancing about the room, and brushing the tears from her face, like spray. "He shall propose to me, and very humbly, too. I have the key to the problem, now. My hand is now on the helm of this big ship of war, and you shall see how I will manage. He shall do just what I want him to, without knowing it. He shall—"

"But, hold on," said Mr. Dimmerly, breathlessly. "You

look like a rainbow run wild. Listen to reason. Oh, my good gracious! the idea of her being a home missionary!"

"That is just what I am going to be—a home missionary, in his home; and all the principalities and powers of earth shall not prevent it. And now, you dear, precious, old meddler, good-by. You shall, one day, sit in the snuggest corner of as cosey a little home in the West as was ever made in the East;" and she vanished, leaving the old gentleman chuckling to himself, "It doesn't look as if it would be 'stopped' after all. Perhaps sister will find out that I know how to meddle a trifle better than she does."

CHAPTER XXXVI

A NIGHT IN THE SNOW

"WHERE have you been?" exclaimed Addie, as Lottie came down dressed warmly, but plainly. "We are all through lunch, and ready to start."

"I will not detain you, but will wrap up some lunch and take it with me. May I sit with you?" she said to Hemstead, a little later, as she came out where he was standing on the piazza.

"You will be very much exposed to the cold on the driver's seat, Miss Marsden," he said, hesitatingly; but she saw well enough what he wished, though conscience was condemning him all the time.

"So will you," she answered.

"Yes, but I am a man."

"And I am a woman," she said, with something of her old piquant style. "I do not like your implied assertion of superiority, sir. I have as good a right to expose myself to the cold as a man."

"I was not disputing your right, Miss Marsden, but—"

"Oh, I understand. You are of those who think so poorly of women as to regard them merely as men's pets —the weaker sex, you would call us—who prefer to wait till everything is made nice and comfortable, and then languidly step forward. In your reading of history, I think you must have skipped several chapters."

"You do me injustice," said Hemstead, warmly, and falling blindly into her trap. "If I had skipped all the chapters which treat of woman's heroism, in doing and suffering, I should, indeed, know little of history. She has proved herself the equal, and at times the superior of man."

"Pardon me," said Lottie, in a hurt and injured tone; "I shall reach the unwelcome truth at last: it is not woman in general who is weak, but Lottie Marsden in particular. I am very sorry that you have so poor an opinion of me, and I shall try to change it somewhat by enduring, on this drive, all the exposure and cold that you can."

As the sleigh just then came up, she settled the question by springing in and taking her place on the driver's seat.

Hemstead was perfectly nonplussed, and Mr. Dimmerly, who had stood in the door and heard what had been said, retreated rapidly, as he broke out into the most irrepressible chuckle in which he had yet indulged.

"Now, Miss Lottie," whined De Forrest, coming out muffled to his eyes, "are you going to sit there?"

"Certainly. You have Addie and Bel to talk to. Did you suppose that Mr. Hemstead was to be treated like a coachman because he kindly consented to drive us over?"

"Let me drive, then."

"No, indeed," cried Bel and Addie in chorus; "we won't trust to your driving." So De Forrest, with very poor grace, took his seat with them, and with his back to those whom he would gladly have watched most suspiciously. He had grown desperately jealous of Hemstead, and yet his vanity would not permit him to believe it possible that Lottie Marsden, of all others, could be won to such a life as the predestined missionary would lead. Like the narrow rationalists of this world, he was ever underrating the power of that kind of truth with which Hemstead was identified. To all of his class, the apparent self-sacrifice caused by love to God, and its kindred flame, love (not a passion) for some human object, has ever appeared both stupid and irrational. He did not understand Lottie, and could only curse the wretched visit, and wish it over every moment. When she returned to her accustomed life in New York, she would, he believed, soon be her old self.

Since he could not watch Lottie and Hemstead, he tried to use his ears as far as possible, but the noisy bells drowned their voices, so that he could catch but few words. He was somewhat comforted in the fact that at first they did not appear to have very much to say to each other.

Hemstead tried to introduce various topics remote from the thoughts that were weighing upon both their hearts, but Lottie did not sustain his effort. She maintained her hurt and injured air, until at last he could no longer endure her grieved, sad face, and said, in a low tone, "And could you imagine that I regard you, of all others, as weak and unwomanly?"

"What else could I think from your words? I admit I have given you cause to think very poorly of me indeed. Still it's anything but pleasant to be so regarded by those whose esteem we value."

"But I do not think poorly of you, at all," said Hemstead, half desperately. "How little you understand me!"

"I understand you better than you do me. You are a man. You have high aims, and have chosen a noble calling. But you have virtually said that I am only a woman, and a very ordinary one at that, not capable of emulating the lives of my heroic sisters. I must be shielded from the rough wind, while you, in your superiority, can face it as a matter of course. And your later words intimate that so, figuratively, it will always be, in *my case*—weak, womanly, shrinking, and cowering, ever shielded by something or somebody. History, to be sure, records what women *may* do, but that is a very different thing from what Miss Marsden *will* do."

"You go to extremes, Miss Marsden, and infer far more than the occasion warrants," Hemstead replied, in great perplexity. "Was it unnatural that I wished you to be shielded from the cold?"

"And was it unnatural," she answered, "that since one of our party *must* be exposed to the cold I should be willing to share in the exposure? But it is to your later words that I refer, and not the trifling incident that led to them. They, with your manner, revealed, perhaps, more than you intended. You once said I was 'capable of the noblest things.' I knew that was not true *then*, and to my lasting regret, and I proved the fact to you. But I think I have changed somewhat since that time. At least, I hope I am no longer capable of the meanest things."

"Miss Marsden," he said, impetuously, "you now give me credit for knowing you better than at that time—"

"Yes; and you have evidently revised your opinion very materially. But, as I said before, I can scarcely complain, when I remember my own action. But you will never know how bitterly I have repented of my folly. When that terrible charge was made against me last Monday—it came, when I was so happy and hopeful, like a sudden thunderbolt—I thought I should lose my reason. I felt that you had gone away believing I was utterly false and had been insincere in everything from first to last. I was like one who had fallen from a great height, and I scarcely spoke or moved for two days. I was not like some girls, who imagine they can find a remedy for their troubles in wealth and luxury and attention from others. I have had these things all my life, and know how little they are worth— how little they can do for one at such times. No one will ever know what I suffered. At first, when you thought so well of me, I deserved your harshest condemnation. But it did seem cruel, hard, when I was honestly trying to be better—when, at last, my life had become real and true— to be cast aside as a false thing, that must, of necessity, be despised. I dreaded, last night, that you were going away without giving me any chance to explain and correct my folly. I did mean that Monday to tell you the truth, and should have done so, if you had given me a chance. I should have condemned myself then, and I do now, more severely than even you could, who had such just cause for anger. But, Mr. Hemstead, I *have* changed. In all sincerity I say it, I wish to become a good, Christian girl, and would do so, if I only knew how. I was not deceiving you when I said last Christmas eve that I hoped I had become a Christian. I still think I have, though for two days I was in thick darkness. At any rate, I love my Saviour, and He has helped and comforted me in this greatest trial and sorrow of my life. I was led to hope that you would forgive me, because He seemed so ready to forgive. There! I have now done what I have been most anxious to do—I have told you the truth. I have said all that I can, justly, in self-defence. If I have not raised your opinion of me very greatly, I cannot help it, for henceforth I intend to be honest, whatever happens."

Lottie had said the words she so wished to speak in a low tone, but with almost passionate earnestness, and no one could have doubted their truth a moment. The horses had been trotting briskly over the level ground at the foot of the steep mountain slope, and the noisy bells that made musical accompaniment to her words, as heard by Hemstead, disguised them from De Forrest and the others. The student received each one as if it were a pearl of great price.

But now the horses, mounting the steep ascent, had come to a walk, and the chime of the bells was not sufficient to drown his words. If he had answered as his feelings dictated, the attention of the others would have been gained in a most embarrassing way. He could only say in a very low voice, "I believe and trust you fully."

But Lottie heard and welcomed the assurance.

The light of the sun, that had been too brilliant upon the snow, was now becoming softened by an increasing haze. The air was growing milder, and the branches of bowed evergreens by the wayside suddenly lifted themselves as the hold of the fleecy burdens was loosened, and the miniature avalanches dropped away. At times they reached points from which the magnificent and broadening landscape could be seen to the best advantage, and as Hemstead stopped the horses at such places to rest, even Bel and Addie abounded in exclamations of delight. The river had become a vast, white plain, and stretched far away to the north. The scene was one that would have filled Hemstead with delight upon any other occasion, but Lottie was now well pleased to note that he gave to it hurried glances and little thought.

His face was a study, and, more clearly than he realized, betrayed the perplexity and trouble of his mind. How could he give up the lovely girl at his side, whose very imperfection and need won more upon him than any display of conscious strength and advanced spirituality? Her frankness, her humility and severe self-condemnation, appealed to every generous trait of his large, charitable nature. He now believed, as never before, that she was "capable of the noblest things," and he began to suffer from the torturing thought that his course was a mistaken one, and that he wronged her by acting upon the supposition that her old surroundings of luxury and culture were essential to her happiness. Might it not be true that, in a nature like hers, something far more profound was needed to create and sustain true serenity of heart? Had she not in effect plainly said that she had fathomed the shallow depths of luxury, wealth, and general flattering attention? Had she not unconsciously given him a severe rebuke? What right had he to assume that he was any more capable of heroic self-sacrifice than she? Only the certainty that he was sacrificing himself for her happiness enabled him to make the sacrifice at all, and now he began to think that his course might be a wretched blunder which would blight them both. The very possibility of making such a mistake was agony. To have come so near happiness, and then to miss it by as great a wrong to her as to himself, would be more than fortitude itself could endure. His uncle's words were ever present: "If Lottie loved, it would be no halfway business. He had no right to sacrifice her happiness." It was her happiness that he was thinking of, and if he could secure it best by consummating his own at the same time, it seemed to him that heaven would begin at once.

A trivial circumstance had enabled Lottie to intimate plainly to him that he had virtually asserted, "I am a man, and can do that of which only the noblest and most unselfish natures are capable. You are not only a woman, but you cannot rise to the level of many of your sisters, who have left on history's page the heroic record of their triumphs over the supposed weakness of their sex." What he had not meant, but still had appeared to hint from his language, was he not, in fact, practically acting upon as true? While he had taken his course in the spirit of the most generous self-sacrifice, might he not, at the same time, be ignoring the fact that she was as capable of self-sacrifice and noble consecration to a sacred cause as himself?

If she had been sincere in her religious experiences, and in all her words and actions in that direction, how could he help believing that she was equally sincere in the language of tone and eye, which had revealed her heart so plainly that even he, who was the last in the world to presume, had come to think that she loved him? And yet he was about to make his life, and perhaps hers also, one long regret, because he had quietly assumed that she was one of those women whose life depends on surroundings, and to whose souls *mere things* can minister more than love and the consciousness of an heroic devotion to a sacred cause. Lottie had skilfully and clearly given the impression she sought to convey; and this impression, uniting with the student's love, formed a combination whose assaults caused his supposed inflexible purpose to waver.

Lottie's quick intuition enabled her to see that she had led him far enough at present, while they were in such close proximity to jealous, observant eyes and attentive ears, and so, with equal tact, she led his thoughts to more tranquillizing topics. She was employing all the skill and *finesse* of which she had been mistress in the days of her insincerity and heartless coquetry. These gifts were still hers, as much

as ever. But now they were under the control of conscience, and would henceforth be used to secure and pro-
mote happiness, not to destroy it.

And she felt that she had need of tact and skill. The
situation was not so very peculiar. Many had passed
through just such experiences before, but have all passed
on to lives of consummated happiness? She loved the man
at her side devotedly, and was perfectly aware of his love
for her, and yet woman's silence was upon her lips. They
were soon to separate, not to meet again for many years,
if ever. She could not speak. If from any motive, even
the noblest, he did not speak, how could she meet the long,
lonely future, in which every day would make more clear
the dreary truth that she had missed her true life and happiness?—missed it through no necessity that might in the
end bring resignation, but through a mistake—the unselfish
blundering of a man who wrongly supposed she could be
happier without than with him. It was her delicate task
to show him, without abating one jot of woman's jealous
reserve, that she was capable of all the self-sacrifice to
which he looked forward, and that, as his uncle had told
him, he had no right to sacrifice her happiness.

He was one of those single-hearted, resolute fellows,
who have the greatest faculty for persistently blundering
under an honest but wrong impression. But, in this case,
his impression was natural, and he was wrong, only because
Lottie was "capable of noble things"—only because she did
belong to that class of women to whom the love of their
heart counts for infinitely more than all externals. If he
had fallen in love with a very goodish sort of girl of the
Bel Parton type, the course he had marked out would have
been the wisest and best, eventually, for both, even though
it involved, at first, a good deal of suffering.

When a wife assures her husband, by word or manner,
"You took advantage of my love and inexperience to commit me to a life and condition that are distasteful or revolting, and you have thereby inflicted an irreparable injury,"

the man, if he be fine-fibred and sensitive, can only look forward to a painful and aggravated form of martyrdom. One had better live alone as long as Methuselah than induce a small-souled woman to enter with him on a life involving continual sacrifice. With such women, some men can be tolerably happy, if they have the means to carry out the "gilded cage" principle; but woe to them both if the gilded cage is broken or lost, and they have to go out into the great world and build their nest wherever they can.

Providence had given to Lottie the chance to live the life of ideal womanhood—the life of love and devotion—and she did not mean to lose it. While her high spirit would often chafe with a little wholesome friction, it would yet grow sweeter and more patient under the trials of the hardest lot, if they could only be endured at his side to whom, by some mystic necessity of her being, she had given her heart.

Therefore, with unmingled satisfaction she saw that she was sapping the student's stern resolution not to speak. She would, by a witchery as innocent as subtile, beguile him into just the opposite of what he had proposed. As she had declared to her uncle, he should ask her, in a very humble manner, to become a home missionary, and she, under the circumstances, was more ready to comply than to become Empress of all the Russias.

But, during the remainder of the ride, she made the time pass all too quickly, as she led him to speak of his student life, his Western home, and especially of his mother; and Lottie smiled appreciatively over the enthusiasm and affection which he manifested for one concerning whom she had ever heard Mrs. Marchmont speak a little slightingly. The genuine interest which she took in all that related to Mrs. Hemstead touched the young man very closely, and his whole nature was getting under arms against what his heart was beginning to characterize as a most unnatural and stupid resolution.

De Forrest was greatly relieved as he heard Hemstead

describing his humble, farmhouse home and toiling mother; for the student softened none of the hard outlines of their comparative poverty.

"The great fool!" thought the exquisite. "Even if Lottie were inclined to care for him somewhat, he has repelled her now by revealing his common and poverty-stricken surroundings."

But as Lottie became satisfied that Hemstead would not be able to go away in silence, a new cause of trouble and perplexity claimed her attention. Not that she had not thought of it often since she had realized how irrevocably she had given her love, but other and more immediate questions had occupied her mind. How was she to reconcile her fashionable mother and worldly father to her choice? She clearly recognized that what to her seemed the most natural —indeed, the only thing in life left for her—would appear to one simply monstrous, and to the other the baldest folly.

She loved her parents sincerely, for, with all her faults, she had never been cold-hearted; and, while she proposed to be resolute, it was with the deepest anxiety and regret that she foresaw the inevitable conflict.

But when she was at a loss to think of anything that could be said to soften the blow, or make her course appear right or reasonable, as they would look at it, a circumstance occurred which led, as she then believed, to the solution of the problem.

After driving between two and three hours, they reached West Point in safety, and, as they were passing along by the officers' quarters, Lottie recognized a young lady who was one of her most intimate city friends, and who, she soon learned, was making a visit in the country, like herself. Lottie told Bel and Addie to go on to the dancing-hall, while she called on her friend, adding, "I will soon join you."

The relations between Lottie and her friend were rather confidential, and the latter soon bubbled over with her secret.

She was engaged to a cadet, who would graduate in the following June.

"But he is away down toward the end of his class, and so, of course, will have to go out upon the Plains," she said, with a little sigh.

"What will you do then?" asked Lottie, quickly, a bright thought striking her. "You surely will not exchange your elegant city home for barracks in some remote fort, where you may be scalped any night?"

"I surely will," said the vivacious young lady; "and if you ever become half as much in love as I am, it won't seem a bit strange."

"But what do your parents say to all this?"

"Oh, well, of course they would much prefer that I should marry and settle in New York. But then, you know, mother always had a great admiration for the army, and it's quite the thing, in fashionable life, to marry into the army and navy. Why, bless you, Lottie, nearly all the ladies on the post have seen the roughest times imaginable on the frontier, and they come from as good families, and very many of them have left as good homes as mine."

"But how are you going to live on a lieutenant's pay? I have known you to spend more than that on your own dress in a single year."

"What are dresses compared with Lieutenant Ransom? I can learn to economize as well as the rest of them. You can't have everything, Lottie. You know what an officer's rank is. It gives him the entrée into the best society of the land, and often opens the way for the most brilliant career. These things reconcile father and mother to it, but I look at the man himself. He's just splendid! Come, we'll go over to the hall, and I will introduce you, and let you dance with him once—only once, you incorrigible flirt, or you will steal him away from me after all. By the way, who was that handsome man who drove? I fear you bewitched him coming over the mountain, from the way his eyes followed you."

"How does he compare with your Lieutenant Ransom?" asked Lottie.

"No one can compare with him. But why do you ask? Is there anything serious?"

"Will you think so when I tell you that he enters, next summer, on the life of a home missionary on the Western frontier?"

"Oh, how dismal!" exclaimed the young lady. "No, indeed! no danger of *your* giving him serious thoughts. But you ought not to flirt with such a man, Lottie."

"I do not intend to, nor with any one else, any more. But why do you say 'How dismal'? Your lieutenant will have as rough a frontier life as Mr. Hemstead, and, surely, the calling of the ministry is second to none."

"Well, it seems very different. Nobody thinks much of a home missionary. Why, Lottie, none of our set ever married a home missionary, while several have married into the army and navy. So, for heaven's sake, don't let your head become turned by one who looks forward to such a forlorn life. But here we are, and I will make you envious in a moment."

"Miss Marsden," said Hemstead, stepping forward as they were entering, "I do not like to hasten you, but there is every appearance of a storm, and the wind is rising. I wish you could induce Addie to start soon. I will go to the Trophy room for a little while, and then will drive around."

"You may rest assured I will do my best," said Lottie. "I am ready to start now."

"Beware of that man," said her friend; "his eyes tell the same story that I see in Lieutenant Ransom's."

"You have become a little lady of one idea," said Lottie, laughing and blushing, "and all the world is in love, in your estimation."

When Hemstead drove to the door, the snowflakes were beginning to fly, and the wind had increased in force. But Bel was not ready, and Addie would not hear of their going till the hours set apart for dancing were over. Even then she permitted her cadet friends to detain her several minutes longer.

As the others were, in a certain sense, her guests, they were delicate about urging her departure. Thus it happened that the early December twilight was coming on, and the air was full of wildly-flying snow, as the last words were said, and the horses dashed off for the mountains.

But the storm increased in violence every moment, and the air was so filled with flakes that the young people could not see twenty feet before them. What caused Hemstead uneasiness was the fact that the sheltered road that led from the Point along the southern base of the mountains, for a long distance before coming to any great ascent, was already somewhat clogged with drifts. Above, on the mountain's crest, he heard a sound as if the north wind were blowing strongly.

He grew very anxious, and finally said, as they reached the point where the road began to rise rapidly, that he thought the attempt to cross that night involved much risk. But Addie would not hear of their returning. Her mother would go wild about them, and would never let her come again.

"It has not snowed very much yet, and if we wait till to-morrow it may be very deep."

"The drifts are what I fear," said Hemstead.

"There were no bad drifts this afternoon," said Addie, "and surely they cannot be deep yet."

Since the following day was Sunday, and New Year's also, it was agreed that they should push on. To return would involve much that was disagreeable to the party, and create great alarm at Mrs. Marchmont's.

"It will just result in their sending after us, this dreadful night," said Addie. "I don't see why it must storm just when one most wishes it wouldn't."

"We ought to have started sooner," said Bel. "I knew the delay was very wrong, but we were having such a good time."

De Forrest, having vainly sought to get Lottie to sit with him, had sulkily taken his seat just behind her and Hemstead, where he was the most sheltered of the party, and, not supposing there was any real danger, had muffled himself up so that he was almost past speaking or hearing. He had nearly resolved with some sullenness to let matters take their course until the "cursed visit was over." New York, and not the barbarous, dreary country, was the place where he shone; and when there once more, he would soon regain his old ascendency over Lottie, and she, of course, would forget this Western monster. He noticed, during the first mile, that Hemstead and Lottie scarcely spoke to each other; and, as the storm increased, he concluded there was no danger of their making love when, if they opened their mouths to speak, the wind would fill them with snow.

But Hemstead and Lottie scarcely needed language. The old, subtle interchange of thought and sympathy had been regained. Every moment she bravely sat with him facing the storm that wild night seemed an assurance that she was both able and willing to face every storm of life at his side.

But as the wind grew more violent, and drove the sharp crystals into their faces with stinging force, he, out of regard for her comfort, said: "Miss Marsden, it is both brave and kind of you to sit here so patiently, but really the wind is growing too severe. Even if I had had the impression which you were so mistaken as to charge me with, long before this it would have been banished forever by your words and action. If you will take the next seat, and sit with your back to the wind, you will not feel it half so much."

"Will you do the same?" she asked.

"I cannot."

"Then neither can I. I shall keep my word, Mr. Hemstead."

"You are a brave girl, Miss Marsden."

"Well, that is nothing. Why have I not as good a right to be a brave girl as you to be a brave man?"

"You also appear to have the ability."

"Oh, I don't deserve any credit. I'm not a bit afraid. Indeed, I rather enjoy it. I've plenty of warm blood, and can make as good a fight against the north wind as yourself. This isn't half as hard as facing evil and unhappy thoughts before a blazing fire, and I have had too much of that to do of late to complain of this."

"But it seems a miracle to me that one with your antecedents can regard the situation in any way save with unqualified disgust."

"Do you regard the situation with 'unqualified disgust'?"

"Well, to tell the truth, were it not for my anxiety about getting you all home safely, I was never in a situation to enjoy myself more."

"What precious fools we two must be, in the world's estimation! We both have admitted that we are enjoying ourselves under circumstances in which only Mark Tapley, I think, could be 'jolly';" and the gale bore away her mirthful laugh like a shred from a silver flag.

"Oh, dear!" whined Bel and Addie; "it's perfectly awful."

And awful, indeed, it became, a few minutes later; for, having passed over a steep but sheltered section of the road, they came to a point where the northeast wind struck them strongly. At the same moment the storm appeared to develop into tenfold intensity, and to equal those terrible tempests on the prairies in which Hemstead remembered, with a shudder, that strong men and horses had perished within a few yards of shelter. They, alas! were now a long way from any house, and in the midst of the lonely mountains. It had also become so dark that he had to leave the choice of the road mainly to the horses.

At first these sagacious animals stopped, and refused to go any further. Hemstead waited a few moments, in hope that the gust or gale would expend itself, and, in the meantime, instinctively put his arm around Lottie, to keep her from being blown off the seat.

"Miss Marsden," he said, close to her ear, "pardon me, but I fear this tempest will carry you away. The horrible thought crossed my mind that you might be caught in a sort of whirlwind and spirited off in this thick darkness where I could not find you."

"Would it trouble you very much if you could not find me?"

"Oh, don't speak of it! I would give years of my life if you were safe at home."

"Don't be so reckless with your years. I am very well content to be where I am."

"But there is danger."

"There is no more danger for me than for you."

"Are you not afraid?"

"I am just about as much afraid as you are;" and, to his amazement, he found her laughing.

"Well," he exclaimed, "if you can laugh under these circumstances, you exceed any woman I ever read or heard of. We are in twice as much danger as when I went out in the boat the other night."

"Are you now satisfied that Lottie Marsden, in particular, is not weak and cowardly, as compared with her braver sisters?"

Before he could answer, De Forrest growled, "Why don't you go on?"

Addie and Bel were cowering in the bottom of the sleigh, and supposed he was merely giving the horses a rest.

Just then there appeared a momentary lull in the gale; so he merely said: "Forgive me for even seeming to hint to the contrary," and then urged the horses forward.

The road now presented its side to the wind, and so was filled with drifts, while its lower side was a precipitous bank that shelved off into unknown depths. The horses plunged with difficulty through one drift, and the sleigh tipped dangerously. Addie and Bell screamed, and De Forrest began, in trepidation, to realize their situation.

The poor beasts were soon floundering through another drift. Suddenly there came a sharp crack, as if something had broken, and one of the horses appeared to have fallen. Worse still, the lower runner of the sleigh seemed sinking in the snow to that degree that a moment later they would be overturned into the darkness that yawned in the direction of the steep mountain slope.

Hemstead instantly sprang out on the lower side, with the purpose of preventing the accident. Lottie as quickly sprang out on the upper side, and cried: "You push, and I will hold"; and so it happened that she did quite as much as he in saving the party from disaster. Indeed, if the sleigh had gone over, it would have carried him who was on the lower side down with it.

The horses, in their wise instinct, keeping still, Hemstead first came round to where Lottie stood.

"Why, Miss Marsden!" he exclaimed, "you are up to your waist in the snow."

"Well, it won't drown me. This is a great deal better than rolling down the mountain."

"I could kneel at your feet," said the student, fervently.

"Ha, ha, ha," laughed Lottie. "You couldn't find them."

"This is no laughing matter," said De Forrest, at last aroused to their danger, and standing up for the first time.

"Then get out and do something, like Miss Marsden," said Hemstead. "Come, right up the sleigh while I look after the horses."

A little later he came back to Lottie, and said: "Miss Marsden, I scarcely dare tell you the truth. The tongue of the sleigh and some of the most important parts of the harness are broken. Besides, I have been up the road a short distance, and there are drifts that are up to the horses' necks. I fear we can go no further. O God!" he added in agony, "what can I do for you? The idea of your perishing with cold in this horrible place to-night!"

Lottie laid her hand upon his arm, and said earnestly: "Mr. Hemstead, please let there be no more such talk. It's no worse for me than for you. Besides, if we will trust God and use our wits, there is no need of any one's perishing. If we were out of the wind it would not be so very cold. Why, there is enough warmth in the big bodies of those horses to keep us from freezing, if it comes to the worst."

"There!" he exclaimed, "you have given me hope and courage, and in a sentence. The coachman was captain on my former occasion of danger, and you shall be captain now. You have the clearest and best head of the party. I am at your service."

"Will you do as I bid you?"

"Yes."

"Take care of yourself somewhat, then."

"I can best do that by taking care of you."

"You can do nothing pleasing to me that will bring harm to yourself," she said. "We must get out of the wind, and if nothing better offers, must bury ourselves in the snow beside the horses. I remember reading of such things. The sleigh robes and the warmth of their bodies would keep us from freezing; I'm not so very cold."

Addie and Bel were crying bitterly, while De Forrest was groaning and cursing from where he stood, behind the sleigh.

"Come," he shouted, "what's to be done?"

"I will go straight up the bank. I may find a ledge, or some rocks, under which we may cower," said Hemstead.

"Don't go far," said Lottie, eagerly. "I should, indeed, lose hope, if you became separated from us."

He soon returned with the joyful news that a little way up the bank was a high ledge, where they would be completely sheltered from the wind.

Soon he had them all under it, and the respite from the driving gale was welcomed by none more than by Lottie, who, in spite of her courage and sustaining excitement, was beginning to suffer greatly.

De Forrest, being a smoker, had matches; but, in his impatience to light a fire, destroyed most of them.

"Here, Julian, give them to me," said Lottie, most decisively.

Then, after all the dry material which could be collected, by groping round in the dark, was gathered in the most sheltered nook, she took from her pocket a delicate lace handkerchief, and, by means of that, lighted the sticks and leaves. Soon they were warming their numb hands and chilled bodies beside a cheerful blaze.

Hemstead watched Lottie with wondering and increasing admiration. In securing a fire, they escaped all immediate danger, and she became as cheery as if the disaster, which had threatened even a fatal termination, were only an episode, and the long, wintry bivouac, in that desolate place, but a picnic in the woods.

"You are the queerest girl I ever knew, Lottie," said Bel.

"She means by that, you are the best," Hemstead added.

"Come, this is no time for compliments, but for work," said Lottie, energetically, and she set De Forrest at it also.

The robes were brought from the sleigh, and after the snow had been trampled down and cleared away between the fire and the ledge, here they were spread. Addie and Bel were, at first, terror-stricken at the thought of spending the night in the mountains, but were made so comfortable that, at last, their tears ceased.

"Our best hope is this brandy," said De Forrest, drawing a flask from his pocket.

"Nonsense!" said Lottie. "Our best hope is keeping our senses and a good fire."

But Bel and Addie were ready enough to take the brandy, and were soon sleeping heavily from its effects, combined with their exposure to the cold wind. Lottie could not be prevailed upon to take any.

"I want the use of my senses to-night, if ever," she said. "We must take turns in keeping awake, and you shall have the first watch, Julian."

Hemstead, at this time, was down getting the horses out of the drift, that he might tie them near the fire and also under the ledge. De Forrest set to work very zealously under the stimulus of Lottie's words and the brandy combined, and gathered the brush-wood that lay near, and piled it on the fire. Everything seemed to promise well, and the wearied girl laid herself down by the side of Bel and Addie, and was soon sleeping as naturally and peacefully as if in her luxurious apartment at home.

CHAPTER XXXVII

IN EARNEST

WHEN Lottie awoke the storm had passed away. The moon, in her last quarter, was rising in pale, unclouded light over eastern mountains, and bringing into dusky outline many intervening hills.

At first, bewildered, and not knowing where she was, she rose up hastily, but after a moment the events of the preceding evening came to her, and she remembered, with gratitude, how they had found partial shelter from the storm.

With something of a child's wonder and pleasure, she looked around upon a scene more wild and strange than any she had ever seen, even in pictures of gypsy encampments. Bel and Addie were sleeping by her side as soundly as if such a nightly bivouac were an ordinary experience. In like heavy stupor De Forrest lay near the fire, though the music of his dreams was by no means sweet. He had made his watch a very brief one, and, having piled the fire high with light brush-wood that would soon be consumed, and leaving no supply on hand, he had succumbed to the combined influence of the cold and the brandy; and now, with the flames lighting up his face, he looked like a handsome bandit.

The patient horses stood motionless and shadowy, a little at one side. Above her head rose high, rocky crags, from whose crevices clung bushes and stunted trees with their crest of snow. And snow, bright and gleaming near the fire, but growing pale and ghostly, dull and leaden, in the distance, stretched away before her, as far as she could see, while from his white surface rose shrubs, evergreens, and the gaunt outline of trees, in the haphazard grouping of the wilderness. Where, before, the storm had rushed, with moan and shriek, now brooded a quiet which only the crackling of the flames and De Forrest's resonant nasal organ disturbed.

But Hemstead was nowhere to be seen. She was becoming very solicitous, fearing that he had straggled off alone, in order to bring them relief, when a sound caught her attention, and she saw him coming with a load of cordwood upon his shoulder.

She reclined again, that she might watch him a few moments unperceived. He threw his burden down, and put a stick or two of the heavy wood on the fire. Then Lottie noticed that the genial heat no longer came from the quickly consumed brush, but from solid wood, of which there was a goodly store on hand.

The student stood a few moments looking at the fire; then his eyes drooped, and he swayed back and forth as if nearly overpowered by sleep and weariness. Then he would straighten himself up in a way that made Lottie feel like laughing and crying at the same time, so great was his effort to patiently maintain his watch. At last he tried the expedient of going to the horses and petting them, but, before he knew it, he was leaning on the neck of one of them half asleep. Then Lottie saw him come directly toward her, and half closed her eyes. The student looked long and fixedly at her face, as the firelight shone upon it; then drew himself up straight as a soldier, and marched back and forth like a sentinel on duty. But after a little while his steps grew irregular, and he was evidently almost asleep, even while he walked. Then she saw him turn off abruptly and disappear in the shadowy forest.

She sprang up, and, secreting herself behind an adjacent evergreen, waited for his return. Soon she saw him staggering back under another great load of cord-wood.

He at once noticed her absence, and was wide awake instantly. He seized a heavy stick for a club, as if he would pursue an enemy who might have carried her off, when her low laugh brought him to her side.

"Don't you hit me with that," she said, advancing to the fire.

"I thank you very cordially for waking me up so thoroughly," he said, delighted at finding her so bright and well, and in such good spirits, after all her exposure. "I admit, to my shame, that I was almost asleep two or three times."

"Here is another assertion of your masculine superiority," she replied, in mock severity. "I may sleep, as a matter of course; but you, as a man, are to rise superior, even to nature herself, and remain awake as long as your imperious will dictates."

"I am much afraid," he said, ruefully, "if you had not spoken to me, my imperious will would soon have tumbled helplessly off its throne, and you would have found your watchman and protector little better than one of these logs here."

"Who has decreed that you must watch all night, while the rest of us sleep? Come, it's my turn now, and I will watch and protect you for a little while."

"Do you mean for me to sleep while you sit here alone and watch?"

"Certainly."

"I'll put my hand in the fire first, if in no other way I can keep awake."

"Didn't you call me 'captain?' You will have to obey your orders."

"I'll mutiny in this case, rest assured. Besides, I'm not sleepy any more."

"Why, what's the matter?"

"Do you think I could sleep while you were awake and willing to talk to me?"

"I slept a long time while you were awake." She pulled

out her watch, and exclaimed: "Mr. Hemstead! in ten minutes more we enter on a new year."

"How much may happen within a year, and even a few days of a year," he said, musingly. "It seems an age since I tossed my books aside, and yet it was within this month. The whole world has changed to me since that day."

"I hope for the better," said Lottie, gently.

"Yes, for the better, whatever may be the future. That Sabbath afternoon, when you led me to the One whom I was misrepresenting and wronging, cannot fail to make me, and that little bit of the world which I can reach, the better. I feel that I shall owe to you my best Christian experience and usefulness."

"And I feel that I should never have been a Christian at all if I had not met you," she said, looking gratefully up. "Whatever may be the future, as you say, I trust God will never permit me to be again the false, selfish creature that I was when I first took your hand in seeming kindness."

"I trust that God has been leading us both," said Hemstead, gravely and thoughtfully.

Lottie again took out her watch, and said, in the low tone which we use in the presence of the dying, "Mr. Hemstead, the old year is passing; there is but a moment left."

He uncovered his head, and, bowing reverently, said, "May God forgive us all the folly and evil of the past year, for the sake of His dear Son."

Lottie's head bowed as low and reverently as his own, and for several moments neither spoke.

Then he turned, and took her hand as he said: "Many have wished you a 'happy new year' before, but I can scarcely think that any one ever meant the words as I do. Miss Lottie, I would do anything, suffer anything, and give up anything, save honor and duty, to make you happy. You have often laughed at me because I carried my thoughts and feelings in my face. Therefore, you know well that I love you, with all the truth and strength of which I am capable. But I have had a great dread lest my love might eventually make you unhappy. You know what my life will be, and duty will never permit me to change."

Her answer was very different from what he expected. Almost reproachfully, she asked, "Mr. Hemstead, is earthly happiness the end and aim of your life?"

"No," he said, after a moment.

"What then?"

"Usefulness, I trust—the doing faithfully the work that God gives me."

"And must I of necessity differ from you in this respect?"

"Miss Lottie, forgive me. I am not worthy of you. But can it be possible that you are willing to share in my humble, toilsome life? I fear you have no idea of the hardships and privations involved."

"I stood by you faithfully last night in the storm, did I not?" she said, with a shy, half-mischievous glance.

"It seems too good to be true," he said, in a low tone.

"Was there ever such a diffident, modest creature!" she said, brusquely. "Mr. Hemstead, you will never *enter* Heaven. The angels will have to pull you in."

"One angel has made a heaven of this dreary place already," he answered, seeking to draw her to him.

"Wait a moment; what do you mean, sir? I have made you no promises and given you no rights."

"But I have made you no end of promises, and given you absolute right over me. My every glance has said, 'Lottie Marsden, I am yours, body and soul, so far as a man with a conscience can be.'"

"All this counts for nothing," said Lottie, with a little impatient stamp of her foot. "I promised that dear old meddler, Uncle Dimmerly, that you, in deep humility and penitence for having arrogantly assumed that you could be a missionary and I couldn't, should ask me to be a home missionary; and you have wasted lots of precious time."

He caught her quaint humor, and, taking her hand and dropping on one knee, said: "Lottie Marsden, child of luxury, the prize which the proudest covet, will you leave your elegant home—will you turn your back upon the world which is at your feet—and go with me away to the far West, that you may become a poor, forlorn home missionary?"

"Yes, Frank, in your home; but never forlorn while I have you to laugh at, and never poor while I possess your big, unworldly heart."

"Have I any rights now?" he exclaimed; and, springing up, he exercised them to a degree that almost took away her breath.

"Here, behave yourself," she said. "The idea of one who had plumed himself on his heroic self-sacrifice acting so like an ordinary mortal! You have had more kisses now than you ought in a week. If we are to be so poor, we ought to begin practicing economy at once."

"You are the most beautiful and spicy compound that nature ever fashioned," he exultingly replied, holding her off, devouring her with his eyes. "I plainly foresee that you can fill the poorest little home with light and music."

"Yes, I warn you, before it's too late, that I can never become a solemn, ghostly sort of a missionary."

"Oh, it's too late now, I assure you," he said: "my mind is made up."

"So is mine—that you shall take a long nap, while I mount guard."

"Nap, indeed!" he said, indignantly. "When the gates of pearl bang after one with their musical clangor, and shut out forever the misery of earth, will one's first impulse on the threshold of heaven be to take a nap?"

"What extravagant language! You ministers talk much too familiarly of heaven, and such things."

"No, indeed, Lottie, dear! the more familiar the thought of heaven is to us, the better. You shall have a good home there, if a very humble one here. But do you realize how much you are giving up?"

"Yes," she said, ruefully, "the worst heartache I ever had. I don't believe you felt half so badly as I did."

"But when the hard and prosaic life comes, with its daily cares and weary burdens, are you sure that you will not regret your action?—are you sure that you will not wish yourself again the queenly belle, with the world at your feet?"

"Who with right claims the higher rank," Lottie answered, her lovely face growing noble with her thought—"a queenly belle with a false, selfish heart, or a Christian woman? And what is that world which you say is at my feet? Where is it to-night? Where was it when the tempest made it doubtful whether we should ever see this new year? Here I am in the solemn midnight, and upon this desolate mountain. It is not the softness of a summer night to which we are exposed; it is midwinter. And yet I am certain that there is not a queen on the earth as happy as I am. But what part has that world to which you refer had in making me happy? I knew there was danger last night. I had read of people perishing in the snow almost at their own doors. I think I realized that death might be near, but my heart was so light and happy in the consciousness of your love and God's love, that I could look at the grim old fellow, and laugh in his face. But suppose that I had had nothing better then to think of than this vague world, about which you are making so much ado? Once before, when the world was at my feet, as you term it, I faced a sudden danger in your company. Thanks to God's mercy and your skill and strength, we were not dashed down into that ravine when the horses ran away. What did the world do for me then? Did it throw a ray of light into that black gulf of death, which yawned on every side? Oh, thank God," she said with passionate earnestness, "that I was not sent out of life that night, a shivering ghost, a homeless wanderer forever! But what could the world do to prevent it? I know all about that glittering world, Frank, to gain which so many are staking their all, and I know it's more of a phantom than a reality. It flattered me, excited and intoxicated me, but it never made me one-hundredth part as happy as I am to-night. And when I thought I had lost your respect and your love, I no more thought of turning to the world for solace and happiness, than I would look in a coal-bin for diamonds. I knew all about the world, and in the depths of my soul realized that it was a sham. How far away it is to-night, with these solemn mountains rising all around us; and yet how near seem God and heaven, and how sweet and satisfying the hopes they impart! I have thought it all out, Frank. The time is coming when illness or age, mortal pain and weakness, will shut me away, like these dark, wintry hills, even from your love—much more from the uncaring, heartless world; but something in my heart tells me that my Saviour, who wept for sympathy when no one else would weep, will be my strong, faithful friend through it all, and not for all the worlds glittering there in yonder sky, much less for my poor little gilt and tinsel world in New York, will I give up this assurance."

"I am satisfied," said Hemstead, in a tone of deep content; "God wills it."

They sat for a long time without speaking, in the unison of feeling that needed no words.

At last, in sudden transition to one of her mirthful, piquant expressions, Lottie turned to her companion and said: "Frank, you are on the mountain-top of exalted thought and sentiment. Your face is as rapt as if you saw a vision."

"Can you wonder?"

"Well, I'm going to give you an awful tumble—worse than the one you feared last night when the sleigh tipped. I'm hungry as any wolf that ever howled in these mountains."

"What a comparison!" said the student, laughing heartily. Then, his face becoming all solicitude, he queried, "What shall I do?" and he was about to rise with the impression that he ought to do something.

"Do as I bid you, of course; sit still while I tell you what I shall do. I shall patiently endure this aching void, as I trust I shall the other inevitable ills of our lot. What could be more appropriate than this prelude of hunger in one proposing to marry a home missionary ?"

With an odd blending of delight and sympathy in his face, Hemstead exclaimed: "Lottie! You have received more compliments than you could count in a year, but I am going to give you one different from any that you ever had before. There's not even a trace of morbidness in your nature."

Thus, in playful and serious talk, they passed the hours until the snow-clad mountains were sparkling in the rising sun. Hemstead placed upon Lottie's hand a plain seal-ring that had been his father's, but she covered it with her glove, not wishing the fact of her engagement to transpire until they should reach home.

At last the others awoke, and what they had passed through seemed like a grotesque, horrible dream. De Forrest looked suspiciously at Hemstead and Lottie, but could gather nothing from their quiet bearing toward each other.

Early in the day relief reached them, and by the middle of the forenoon they were doing ample justice to Mrs. Marchmont's sumptuous breakfast.

Then the telltale ring on Lottie's finger revealed the secret, and there was consternation. But poor De Forrest was so outrageously hungry that he had to eat even in this most trying emergency. And yet he had a painful sense that it was not the proper thing to do under the circumstances, and so was exceedingly awkward, for once in his life.

Mr. Dimmerly chuckled all that Sunday with "unbecoming levity," his sister said.

She, poor woman, had lost all confidence in herself as a good manager. In her bosom indignation at her nephew and Lottie contended with the dread of Mrs. Marsden's reproaches.

Bel tried to think that it was not her fault, and Addie did not much care.

The holiday visit came to an end. The months sped away. Lottie's purpose was severely tested. Every possible motive, reason, and argument was brought to bear upon the brave girl. Worse than all, she had to endure the cold, averted looks of those she fondly loved. She pleaded her own cause eloquently. She frequently quoted her friend's example, who was about to marry the army officer.

"But that is very different," they said.

Only once she lost her temper. There was a sort of family conclave of aunts and relatives, and they had beset her sorely. At last she turned upon them suddenly, and asked: "Are you Christians? Do you believe there is a God?"

"Why, certainly. Do you think we are heathen?"

"Why talk, then, like heathen, and act like infidels? If it's the thing in the fashionable world to marry a trusted servant of a human government, how much better must it be to marry a servant of the King of All! I honor my friend because she marries the man she loves, and I shall marry the one I love. I am of age—I have chosen my lot. Mark my words! you will yet be proud of the one whom you now so despise; while the one you wish me to marry will cover his own and the names of all connected with him with shame;" and she left them to recover from this bombshell of truth as best they might.

But the patient gentleness which she usually manifested at length won even their obdurate hearts. Her father was the first to relent, and was finally brought, by Lottie's irresistible witchery, quite over on her side. But, in her mother's case, there was only partial resignation to a great but inevitable misfortune. Mrs. Marsden was a sincere idolater of the world for which she lived.

In Aunt Jane, Lottie had a stanch ally, and a sympathizing and comforting helper.

But the postman, who brought, with increasing frequency, letters that were big and heavy, like the writer, was the man whom Lottie most doted on in all the city.

With the whole energy of her forceful, practical nature,

she trained herself for her work, as Hemstead was training himself for his. And when, a year later, she gave him her hand at the sacred altar, it was not a helpless hand.

Years have passed. Mr. and Mrs. Hemstead are the chief social, refining, and Christianizing influences of a growing Western town. They have the confidence and sympathy of the entire community, and are people of such force that they make themselves felt in every department of life. They are shaping and ennobling many characters, and few days pass in which Lottie does not lay up in memory some good deed, though she never stops to count her hoard. But, in gladness, she will learn in God's good time that such deeds are the riches that have no wings.

She made good her warning, and never became a "solemn, ghostly sort of a missionary." She was usually as wholesome as the sunshine, or if the occasion required, as a stiff north wind, and had a pronounced little way of her own, when things went wrong at home or in the church, of giving all concerned the benefit of some practical commonsense. But she also, in the main, kept her pledge to endure patiently, as she had borne her hunger on the mountain, and many privations and trials of their lot.

While she sustained her husband's hands and doubled his usefulness abroad, he generally found at home a sunny philosopher who laughed him out of half his troubles.

With increasing frequency he said, "Lottie, you are so wholesome; there is not a morbid, unnatural trait in you."

And she inspired him to preach such a wholesome, sunny Gospel that it won even the most prejudiced.

One evening a feeble, aged man stepped down from the train, and was borne off in triumph by Hemstead to the warmest corner of his hearth.

Lottie gave him such a welcome that the old gentleman cried out: "Hold on. My goodness gracious! haven't you sobered down yet?"

Then, while Frank stood near, with his hand upon her shoulder, looking as proud of her as a man could be, and with just such a black-eyed cherub in her arms as she must have been herself twenty odd years before, her face aglow with health, happiness, and content, she asked, "Well, uncle, what do you think of your meddling now?"

Mr. Dimmerly went off into one of his old-time chuckles, as he said, "This is one of the things which the world never can 'stop.'"

THE END